ALL I WANT
FOR CHRISTMAS

By Georgia Beers

By Maggie Cummings

Totally Worth It

Serious Potential

Definite Possibility

Perfect Partners

Against All Odds (with Kris Bryant and M. Ullrich)

Brooklyn Summer

Bulletproof

By Fiona Riley

Miss Match

Unlikely Match

Strike a Match

Room Service

Media Darling

Not Since You

Bet Against Me

ALL I WANT FOR CHRISTMAS

by

Georgia Beers, Maggie Cummings,
and Fiona Riley

2020

ALL I WANT FOR CHRISTMAS

ISBN 13: 978-1-63555-764-0

THIS TRADE PAPERBACK ORIGINAL IS PUBLISHED BY
BOLD STROKES BOOKS, INC.
P.O. BOX 249
VALLEY FALLS, NY 12185

FIRST EDITION: DECEMBER 2020

CREDITS
EDITOR: RUTH STERNGLANTZ
PRODUCTION DESIGN: STACIA SEAMAN
COVER DESIGN BY TAMMY SEIDICK

ALL I WANT FOR CHRISTMAS

TRIPLE DOG DARE

Georgia Beers

Chapter One

A re you kidding me? Now? Are you *fucking* kidding me?"
"I didn't mean right this very second—"
"Oh no. I heard you. I heard you loud and very fucking clear."

That was the conversation I heard through my apartment wall, punctuated with some tiny yips from the new puppy I hadn't seen yet but had heard *a lot*, and the slamming of what sounded like drawers, as I put on my coat and gathered my things for work. I'd actually been listening to a very pleasant internal monologue in my head about what a great year we'd had before Neighbor Number Two had gone on her tirade. Excuse me, her *fucking* tirade. Poor Neighbor Number One—whose name I was pretty sure was Kennedy. I had no idea what she said or did that caused Two to question whether or not she was *fucking* kidding, but it sounded bad. I had known for a while—for the three months that Two had been living next door with One—that I would *not* want to be on Two's fucking bad side.

I shook my head and smothered a smile as I opened my door and stepped out into the hall, thinking, This is why I'm single. As luck would have it, the next door down opened too. With a slam. I winced as I thought about the divot the doorknob had likely made in the drywall but pretended to fiddle with my keys so that I could listen a bit. Yeah, I like gossip. Sue me.

"No, you absolutely meant now. I can see it in your eyes." It was Neighbor Number Two, and she was pissed. And loud. And had a beat-up blue canvas duffel bag over one shoulder that looked full and heavy. Her blond hair was pulled back into a severe ponytail, a wide fabric headband only adding to the severity.

"Cara, just calm down for a minute…"

I cringed silently. Didn't everybody know the very last thing you told a woman in the throes of a meltdown was to calm down? I could almost feel the heat from down the hall, certain that Two was shooting flames from her eyeballs at One, but too scared to look, lest I be accidentally caught in the crossfire and obliterated into charcoal.

"Do. Not. Tell. Me. To. Calm. Down." Yup, about the response I expected. "How fucking dare you?"

I risked a glance, only because I wanted to make sure One wasn't a pile of ash on the floor, but she wasn't. In fact, she stood in the doorway, holding what looked to be a Yorkie, and rather than looking upset or like a woman trying to dig her way out of the hole she'd found herself in, she just looked bored. Maybe a little tired. And totally over Number Two. I couldn't say that I blamed her.

"Look," she said, and I caught a glimpse of her red hair and the sympathetic tilt of her head before forcing myself to return to my little key performance. "Come back in and we can talk about it—"

"There's nothing to talk about. *Clearly.* All I needed was a little help from somebody who knows me, somebody who cares—or who I *thought* cared—but apparently, that's asking too much."

"You said you needed a place to stay for a couple weeks." One's voice was calm and even, and I felt a healthy respect for her not letting Two get to her enough to make her shout back. "*We were together for over a year*, you said. *You knew me once, remember? I just need a little help. A couple weeks. That's all. Please?*" One's impression of Two was shockingly good. I unzipped my purse and began to rifle through it as if I was missing something. "Those were your exact words, and that was months ago. *Months.*" When Two didn't reply immediately, One added, "You maxed out my credit cards. All three of them." Oh, that was a big yikes.

"Listen, if I'd have known buying Christmas gifts was a crime…" The wind was slowly coming out of Two's sails. I could hear it in the way her outrage seemed to suddenly dim.

"You bought Christmas gifts for yourself."

"I bought you Yorkie!" Two pointed at the dog, who yipped as if on cue.

"You bought Yorkie for *you*. Just because I ended up being the one to feed him, walk him, and clean up every damn thing he chews into teeny, tiny bits, that doesn't make him mine. And Yorkie is not his name, it's the kind of dog he is, for God's sake!" One was starting to lose her cool, and I had to bite down on my lips to keep the laugh inside. She'd named her Yorkie *Yorkie*? Classic.

"It's whatever," Two said and waved her hand through the air in a dismissive gesture. "'Cause he's yours now. I can't exactly have a dog *living on the fucking streets* with me, now can I?" Shouldering her giant bag with a huff, she lumbered down the hall to the elevator and pushed the button. Then the three of us stood there while she waited for it to arrive. I could've gotten on it with her, but at the moment, being in a tiny, enclosed, inescapable space with her was just about the last thing on earth I wanted to do. All that bad energy. I could wait.

The ding came finally. Two looked back at One—still standing in the doorway with Yorkie—gave a little snarl, and got on the elevator. Once the doors slid shut, it was as if it was suddenly safe for us both to move. One and I both let out audible breaths, then made eye contact and grinned at each other.

"Well," I said. "That looked like fun. Friend of yours?" I tried to sound light, joking. One looked like she could use some levity.

"My ex. From about a hundred years ago. Or six months. I'm not sure which." Then she dropped her head back and let out a sound that was a combination groan and laugh. It made Yorkie's ears prick up, and he licked her chin. "I'm so sorry you had to witness that."

"I'm not," I said. "It made me feel like an exceptionally reasonable person."

One grinned, then inhaled slowly and let it out. "Man, she just sucks all the air out of the room, doesn't she?"

She stepped out more fully into the hall. I didn't know her, but she was not new to me. She'd caught my eye immediately when she'd moved in last February, and I'd seen her many times since, considering A) she lived on my floor, and B) she was a lot of fun to look at. She was extremely attractive, pretty. Her hair was a soft red, her eyes large and blue. She had a cute little cleft in her chin, a great smile.

"And all the attention, apparently," I said, "because how did I not notice your lovely dress from Colonial times?" I grinned as I took in her light gray dress with the long skirt and white apron. "Are you headed out to churn butter later?"

She looked down at her outfit and laughed outright. "Oh my God! I forgot I was wearing this. I brought it home to do a few alterations. I'm playing Mrs. Cratchit tonight, and we have a dress rehearsal this morning. For *A Christmas Carol*?"

"I'm aware of who Mrs. Cratchit is," I said but gave a wink to make sure she knew I wasn't being a dick. "You're an actress?"

"Drama teacher. Over at the college. But my Mrs. Cratchit got the flu and gave it to her understudy, so it'll be me stepping in."

"Saving Christmas," I said.

Her face grew more serious. "I don't know if my Christmas can be saved." Her gaze went to the elevator, then far away for a moment. I was afraid to interrupt her, but she literally shook herself, and that serious face mostly evaporated. "I need to find some quick cash, or nobody's getting anything from me for Christmas, including the landlord, the cable company, and Verizon." She said it lightly, with a shrug like it was no big deal, but the brightness of her eyes had dimmed enough for me to know it was serious. I felt the itch to help her. Not that I would jump right in and offer money to a stranger. It was just that her eyes… something in them made me want to wrap her up and protect her from the world. Or at the very least, from shrieking, overemotional exes. "Anyway. Sorry to have been so loud this morning. It won't happen again. I don't think we've ever officially met, which is ridiculous since we live twenty-five feet apart." She stuck out her hand. "Kennedy Davis."

"Sasha Wolfe." I put my hand in hers. Her grip was somehow both gentle and firm, her skin, soft and warm. "It's nice to finally meet you." When she let go, I lifted a hand to the dog still in her arms, who had remained surprisingly quiet during our exchange. "Hi, Yorkie." I scratched his ear. He gave me a lick, then yipped, startling me. I'd jinxed it, obviously.

"Don't be fooled by this sweet face," Kennedy said. "He's already sizing up everything you're carrying and wearing, trying to decide what to destroy first." Yorkie turned and swiped his tongue across Kennedy's face once more. She grabbed his little chin and shook it gently. "Looks like I'm stuck with you. Or you're stuck with me. Not sure which." She turned those eyes back to me, and I noticed how the deep blue irises were ringed in black. "Hey, have a great day, Sasha. And if you think of a better name for this guy, he and I are open to suggestions." With that, she retreated back into her apartment and closed the door, and I was left alone in the hallway.

Well. That was the most exciting morning I've had in a very long time.

I headed for the elevator.

❖

I own a real estate agency, in case you were wondering. Wolfe Realty. It's very successful, if I do say so myself. Last year, I was awarded small business owner of the year by my city, which was a pretty cool honor. But that success came from a ton of work and a hell of a lot of sacrifice. Just ask my exes.

In December, there are only two kinds of clients. The first one is in no hurry at all. Time doesn't matter because the holidays are coming and people are busy with other stuff and there's so much to do, so let's just wait until after the first of the year. The second one is in the biggest hurry you can possibly imagine because, unlike the other kind of client, this client wants everything done *by* the first of the year. Bank approval, inspections, papers signed. Everything. So while the first client is sitting back, feet up on the desk, and sipping eggnog, the second client is running around like a crazy person about to keel over from a stress-induced heart attack.

No happy medium, which is rough on my agents.

It had been a hell of a Tuesday. It was two and a half weeks until Christmas, and I had been going nonstop all day. Phone calls, emails, meetings, agent updates, agent questions, new clients, old clients. By the time I got a chance to sit down at my desk, my phone pinged, and the group text that included me and my two sisters was active.

Picking up the new table tonight. My older sister, Melody. *S, you still owe your part.* Damn. I'd forgotten to send her money, as the three of us had gone in on a new dining room set for our mother.

Venmoing now, I typed back, then made sure to do exactly that before I got distracted and completely forgot. Something I had a habit of doing, according to Melody.

Had lunch w Mom today. That was from Cat, my younger sister. She and Melody both still lived in the small town of Bakerton, where we'd grown up. I moved to the city of Northwood after college and had hardly looked back. I wasn't that far away—about a two-hour drive—but I'd become…let's say less than good at spending time with my mother, especially since my father had passed away a little more than a year ago.

And? Melody and I both sent the same question about half a second apart.

A little quiet, but okay. Cat sent a smiling emoji after that, and it was ridiculous how much that stupid yellow circle could make me feel better. *I think she's looking forward to Christmas this year.*

Now that was a surprise.

Really? Melody asked before I had a chance.

She would like us all there for Christmas Eve. With significant others.

Uh-oh. I didn't like where that was going.

You mean me with my husband and you with your boyfriend and Sasha with a cardboard cutout of her make-believe girlfriend? Jennifer, was it? Melody didn't disappoint with her text, even though I'd known it was coming, had seen it from a mile away. She then sent about fifty-seven laughing emoji.

She's not make believe! I typed. *I've been telling you that for six months now.*

Then bring her.

I stared at Melody's words. It was like they taunted me. Cat remained silent, choosing the path she always did: staying out of it and watching from the sidelines. Probably munching on popcorn.

I'll ask. She's likely working, but I can run it by her. I bit my bottom lip and stared at the phone, my thumb hovering over the send button for way too long. When I saw the gray dots bouncing, telling me Melody was typing, I pressed, just to beat her to the punch.

"Likely working." Shocking. The quotation marks Melody used pissed me off, I admit it.

Didn't you say she's an interior designer? Cat this time. *Why would she have to work?* I cursed my little sister, who had a memory like a steel trap and could recall exact conversations word for word. She was not a woman you wanted to get into a war of that's-not-what-I-said with. Ever. I suspected her question was innocent, not meant to provoke more from Melody, but that's exactly what it did.

Good question, Melody sent before I even had a chance to think of a response.

I said I'd ask her, I typed. It sounded childish even without any tone of voice, and I knew it.

I dare you to bring Jennifer to Christmas Eve at Mom's.

And there it was. Melody wasn't playing around.

The first thing you should know about my sister Melody: she has a thing about being right. She's like a bloodhound on a scent if she thinks she's correct about something, and you'd better tell her the truth or get the hell out of the way while she digs it up. Because she *will* dig it up. Melody had long suspected there was no girlfriend. That I had completely invented Jennifer in order to appease my mother, who wanted nothing more than for me to settle down and be happy.

I must have taken too long to respond because the next words Melody sent were the final nail in my coffin.

I TRIPLE DOG DARE YOU to bring her. Complete with caps.

Well, shit.

I stared at the phone. The three of us watched the movie *A Christmas Story* every year at our parents' house. It was tradition at this point. We had dinner, got to open one gift, then cuddled up together in the family room and watched TV as a trio. If you're not familiar with it, the triple dog dare is the queen mother of all dares. There are rules, an order to things, but just like in the film, when Schwartz dared Flick to touch his tongue to a metal pole outside in the cold, Melody had skipped over several steps and went right for the triple dog dare.

I stared at the phone some more, weighing my options…except there weren't any.

Hello? Melody texted, and I could picture her, victorious smirk on her face, knowing she had me.

Fine, I typed. *I'll bring her. I'll bring Jennifer to Mom's for Christmas. Happy now?* I snarled quietly as I hit send.

There was a pause, which gave me a quick boost of happiness, knowing that my agreement wasn't at all what Melody had been expecting. Another beat went by before her text came.

Yes.

That was it. Just that one word. I puffed my chest up in great satisfaction at having shut my big sister completely down. It didn't happen often, so when it did, it was cause for celebration. I stood up from my desk and did a little football dance around my office, only stopping when I noticed Brooke, my top sales agent, watching with an amused look on her face. I stopped. Sat back down.

My joy was short-lived, though. I'd agreed to bring my girlfriend, Jennifer, the interior designer, home to my mother's house for Christmas. It shouldn't be that big a deal, but the fact of the matter was it was going to be harder than it seemed. Not because Jennifer likely had to work.

Because Jennifer didn't exist.

I dropped my head down to my desk. Lifted it slightly. Dropped it with a thud. Lifted slightly. Dropped it with a thud.

I was so screwed.

CHAPTER TWO

Y ou did *what?*" Brooke's pretty brown eyes went so wide, it was comical.

I waved a dismissive hand at her. "I don't even want to talk to you about it. I need your girlfriend. Where is she?"

Brooke tried to smother a grin, but I saw it. "She just pulled in. She's not going to believe this."

"She'll be able to help me."

"Really? Is she a magician and she's just never mentioned it?" She didn't bother to hide the grin this time. "Can she craft human beings out of thin air?"

"You're enjoying this," I accused.

Brooke held her finger and thumb a scant few millimeters apart. "Little bit."

Before I could think of a snarky-yet-not-too-snarky retort, Brooke's girlfriend, Macy Carr, burst into the office the same way she entered anyplace. Like a gust of wind. Breathless, surprising, and grabbing all the focus. She immediately dropped her purse on the floor, spilling it all over my office. As she picked it and its contents up, she asked, "What is it? What's going on? Tell me. Brooke said you did something crazy and I'd never believe it."

"She made up a girlfriend," Brooke said before I could open my mouth. Oh yeah. Ms. Stoic and Orderly was totally enjoying it.

"She what?" Macy furrowed her brow as she looked from Brooke to me and back again.

"And not only did she make up a girlfriend, she promised to bring said made-up girlfriend *home to her mother's for Christmas.*"

Macy's mouth formed a perfect O as she dropped into a nearby chair as if her surprise made her legs turn to jelly, and she stared at me in what was very obvious disbelief.

"*I know*," I said loudly, feeling the weight of what I'd done as it settled on me fully. "It's just…my sister was being her usual always-right self and she pushed my buttons and I couldn't let her win and…"

"Why not? Are you twelve?" Brooke asked.

I dropped my head to the desk for the twenty-seventh time that evening. Thank God it was after seven and the office was empty except for us. "*I know*," I said again and lifted my head back up. "I'm going to have to tell them, and God, she's never going to let me live it down. Ever."

"Or…" Macy said, and when I turned my attention to her, I recognized that expression immediately. Creativity. Spark. Macy had an idea.

"Or?" I asked, ignoring Brooke, who was already shaking her head.

"No," Brooke said, pointing at Macy. "Don't."

Macy's grin just grew wider. It wasn't like Brooke could stop her once she was on to something, and she was definitely on to something. "Or…you bring your girlfriend home to your mother's for Christmas."

I blinked at her.

Brooke mirrored my blink before explaining, "Honey. There's no girlfriend. The girlfriend doesn't exist."

"Not yet, she doesn't." Macy looked at me, and I swear to God I'd never before seen a real, live twinkle in somebody's eyes, but there was one in Macy's as she stood up and began to pace my office. "You'd need to list everything you've told your family about her." As she spoke, she ticked off one finger at a time. "You'd have to set the parameters. Be very specific with your dates and times so you don't get stuck ill-prepared."

Brooke snorted. "Too late."

Macy whirled, a finger up. She was on a roll. I recognized the spark—it was the same one she got when she had an idea for a design. "Think about it. Think about how much crap your sister will have to eat if you actually *bring home a girlfriend*. And not just any girlfriend, the girlfriend you've been talking about for…?" She looked to me with a question in her eyes.

I clenched my teeth and made a face as I ground out, "Six months?"

Brooke's laugh was like a gunshot, blasting through the empty office and making me jump in my chair. "Six months? You've been faking a girlfriend for six months? Are you freaking kidding me?"

I dropped my head back to the desk, thinking I should just live there, really. It was a good place, suitable for banging whenever necessary. Which was always, apparently.

"No," Macy said, and her confident tone had me looking up and Brooke slowly swiveling to face her. "We can do this."

"It's we now?" Brooke asked, eyes wide.

"The hardest part will be finding somebody to play the role."

"I'm sure that won't be hard at all." Brooke punctuated that with an eye roll.

"I mean, you'd need a professional. Somebody who's getting paid." Macy was walking around the office again, thinking out loud. She turned to me. "You can pay, right?"

I nodded. She'd sucked me right into this plan. I knew it was ridiculous and highly unlikely to ever come to fruition, but I was at least going to hear her out. "I can. Sure."

"She'd have to be willing and able. Somebody who looks like your type, since we're talking about your family." Macy was almost talking to herself at this point, walking and formulating a plan while we watched her and twiddled our thumbs.

I glanced at Brooke, who shrugged, shook her head, and sat back, knowing her protests were ineffective.

"She'd need to memorize all the details she can remember. Job. Family. Likes and dislikes. Not just for her, not just the stuff you've told your family, but for you. If she's supposed to be your girlfriend, she'd obviously know things about you. I mean, it would almost be like we'd give her a script, right?" That's when she turned to face me finally, snapped her fingers, and said, "You need somebody who can act. I mean, it would help if she was gay. Or bi. But it's not absolutely necessary. Most importantly, you need someone who can act."

That's when the light bulb went on over my head. I needed somebody to play a role. Preferably somebody who needed money and had some kind of acting experience, and who did I know who ticked all those boxes?

I'm sure you can see where this is going…

❖

I want to make one thing clear. Very clear. It's important to me that you know I *did* think about it. I thought long and hard about the pros and cons, the ups and downs, the possible pitfalls, and the sheer ridiculousness of the plan I was seriously considering. I'm a very intelligent woman—something you may not see at this moment, but I promise you, I am. The other thing I am? A middle child. Are you a middle child? If you are, then you already get it, and you can skip this part of the story. If you're not, here's the thing: You never win. As the middle child, you never, ever win. The oldest gets everything first. The youngest gets all the attention. And there you are, hanging out between them, kind of taking up space.

Okay. Dramatic. I know. And I'm certainly not saying I wasn't loved. I absolutely was. But Middle Child Syndrome is a thing, and when a middle child is presented with a golden opportunity to either beat their older sibling or, better yet, prove them wrong, we'll stop at nothing to reach that goal.

So. Yeah.

It was a terrible idea. I knew that. Bound to backfire. I was pretty sure of that, too. Still. If it meant I could stick it to Melody once and for all, I was so in. Anticipating the eventual look on her face when it happened gave me more joy than I care to admit.

I spent the evening with a bottle of Sangiovese and a legal pad. I wrote up notes, a makeshift script, lists. I jotted details of my life that my girlfriend should know. I thought about creating some flash cards, but decided that might be pushing it until I knew for sure if I was going ahead with this madness. And the whole time, I kept the television and music off so I could hear the elevator. Which didn't mean it was silent because Yorkie's little yips were plentiful, and I absently wondered how long he'd been alone.

I'd done a little stalking of Kennedy Davis before I even began my lists. Creepy, yes, but necessary. She was thirty-one years old and from a suburb of Charlotte. She'd been teaching drama at the community college for more than five years, having come here from a high school on the east side of the state where she'd also taught drama right out of college. She'd appeared in way too many productions to count and had directed, assistant directed, and stage-managed a whole bunch more. She'd been an advisor to the GSA at the high school where she'd started her teaching career and was now active in a handful of local LGBTQ+ organizations.

Kennedy literally ticked every box I needed for this insane plan to work. Every. Single. One.

I was nursing the last few sips of my second glass of wine when I heard the elevator ding, and I jumped up from my seat on the couch. It was nearly midnight, but I had expected she'd be late after checking the college's website to see the start and end times of the play. I figured she'd stick around and talk to the cast, meet and greet audience members, help clean up. I honestly had no idea if those were regular after-play things that were done, but I was doing my best to make up logical stuff.

I grabbed the doorknob, took a deep breath, and opened my front door. Too quickly, judging by the way Kennedy jumped in the hallway and pressed a hand to her chest.

"Jesus, you scared me," she said, closing her eyes and puffing her cheeks as she blew out a breath.

"Sorry," I said and noticed she was no longer in costume. Now, she was in soft-looking jeans and a gray hoodie. Printed on the front was a list. *Single. Taken. Sorry, I Have Rehearsal.* Of course, the third one had a checkmark next to it. Theater humor, I surmised. "How was the show?"

Kennedy looked at me like this whole situation was odd. Because it was, of course. It was very late, I had had exactly one conversation with her the entire time we'd lived on the same floor, and I was asking her a somewhat personal question like I knew her. Which I felt like I did from all my internet stalking but knew I shouldn't let on about. A very weird and difficult line to toe.

"It went really well," she said, nodding as if to herself. This casual version of her was much prettier than I'd expected, and I tried not to stare too much. "We had a good-sized crowd and no set disasters, so I'll take it." She gave me a grin and took a step toward her apartment door.

"Hey, um…" My voice stopped her, but I hadn't really rehearsed what I wanted to say. "Could I talk to you? About something?" As she blinked at me, clearly trying to figure out why I was suddenly so friendly, I mentally told myself to chill. "I mean, I know it's late and you're probably tired…"

"And I have Yorkie," she said, jerking a thumb over her shoulder as the dog barked on cue, and she walked backward toward her door.

"Right, right. Sure. Um…tomorrow? Do you have any time? It won't take long. Twenty minutes, tops."

Kennedy narrowed her eyes just enough for me to notice, and I could almost see the battle playing out in her head—fatigue from the day versus curiosity about my words. Sliding her key into the lock, she turned to me and smiled. With that smile, I felt my whole world tip just enough to make me reach out and place a steadying hand on the wall. "Sure. I don't have to be in until noon tomorrow. Coffee?"

I hoped my immense relief wasn't as obvious to her as I thought it was, and I tried not to smile too widely. "Perfect," I said. "Thank you so much. Do you know Beans & Batter?"

"That little café down the block? I love that place. Meet you there at, say, nine thirty?"

"I'll be there."

She turned back to her door and pushed it open. Then she gave me one last look, told me good night, and went inside.

I didn't want to still be standing in the hall when she came back out with Yorkie. I had already done many stalkery things that night—I didn't need to add loitering in the halls like a creeper to the list. I stepped back inside, shut my door, and went immediately for the bottle of wine. I limited myself to half a glass more as I sat and went over my notes, and I promised myself that if this did not work out with Kennedy, if she looked at me like I was a loon—which was entirely possible, I knew, in fact, it was likely—or had any reason she needed to decline my offer, I wouldn't pursue it further. I would come clean to my sisters or at least just tell them I'd broken up with my imaginary girlfriend, and that would be the end of it.

And then came the doubt, the insecurity, the realization of just exactly how stupid this whole thing was. A pretend girlfriend? Seriously? What was I, a walking Hallmark movie? The answer to that was yes! Yes, as a matter of fact, that was exactly what I was going to be. Exactly.

"Oh, for fuck's sake," I said. "What the hell am I thinking?" I downed the last of my wine and headed to my bedroom. This was ridiculous, and I absolutely could not go through with it. It was insane. I got ready for bed, slid under the covers, and exhaled a long, frustrated breath. I would meet Kennedy for coffee and make something up, but I couldn't go through with this plan. There was no way. I plugged in my phone, turned off the lights, closed my eyes. No freaking way.

I slept soundly and woke up a little nervous, but pretty clear-headed about letting go of the fake girlfriend thing.

When I came out of the shower, I saw the text from my mother. *I can't wait to meet your new girl!* It was followed by so many hearts and smileys and every other super happy emoji there was that I just stared at it. For a full minute, I held my phone and stared at the text from my mom. She knew. And she was thrilled. My sister Melody had struck again, goddamn her. And just like that, all the competitiveness came flooding back in. I ran to the living room where I'd left my notes the night before and flipped through them again.

Oh, it was on.

CHAPTER THREE

Kennedy was dressed like a regular person—jeans, a navy blue sweater, boots—when I got to Beans & Batter the next morning. Her coppery sunset hair was in a cheerful ponytail, and she looked at the screen of her laptop through black-rimmed glasses—they were super sexy and they did things to me, and I felt myself swallow. The truth was, she was an absolute head-turner, and I suspected she was one of those girls who didn't know it. Which only made her more attractive—as the song goes, she doesn't know she's beautiful. I stayed at the door for a moment longer, just watching her, until she looked up and caught my eye. She smiled, and I moved like I'd just come in.

"Hi," she said. She had a very light sprinkling of freckles across her nose. Only across her nose. I realized this was the first time I'd actually seen her in natural light rather than the dim glow of the hallway in our building. She looked fresh. Ready for the day.

"Hey," I said as I shed my coat and draped it over the chair across from her. I gestured at her outfit. "Not making porridge or doing laundry on the washboard in the river today?"

Her smile was big, her teeth straight, her lips glossy. "Porridge is Mondays, and Friday is laundry day." We laughed and then she sat back in her chair, folded her arms, and said, "I like it here in the morning. After, like, eight, it thins right out and is a nice place to work." She took off her glasses—I pouted internally—and lowered her voice a bit, not that there was anybody within earshot. "And honestly? I kind of got used to it when I needed to get out of my apartment." She clenched her teeth and made a face, and I laughed.

"I get it. Let me grab some coffee, and I'll be right back. Need anything?"

She held up her own cup, shook her head, and thanked me. Then she slid her glasses back on and returned her focus to her computer.

My notes were in my bag that was hanging off the chair with my coat, but I pretty much knew what I was going to say. I was nervous as I waited for my peppermint mocha latte, bouncing slightly on the balls of my feet. Once back at the table, Kennedy held up one finger, silently asking me to wait. I sat, sipped, then wrapped my hands around my mug and waited until Kennedy finished what she was doing.

"And...done." She closed the laptop, slid it into her bag. To my eternal sadness, she then took off her glasses and put them away, too, folded her hands on the table, and looked at me directly. Her eyes were so blue that I quietly caught my breath. "Okay. You have my full attention."

Just like that, my carefully worded and rehearsed speech sprouted wings and flew away, and I was left simply staring at her. I managed to regain my composure before things got weird. Okay, weirder. I took a sip of my coffee. Then I inhaled deeply and began.

"I have a proposition for you."

"Okay." She drew the word out slightly, as anybody who heard that statement from a stranger likely would, but said nothing more.

"We both need something, and I think we're in the unique positions of being able to help each other out."

She nodded for me to continue.

"First, know that there is no judgment here. None at all. But from our conversation yesterday when your ex stormed out, you're in a bit of a financial bind."

Her cheeks tinted pink, she chewed the inside of her lip and stared at the table, but said nothing.

"You need money." I waited a beat. I didn't want to embarrass her, but I wanted it to sink in. "What *I* need is an actress."

She looked up at me then. Her interest was piqued. I could tell by the way one eyebrow quirked up just a bit. "An actress."

"Yes."

"What for?"

My nerves reappeared, kicked into overdrive, made me suddenly feel jittery, like they were banging against my bones. I took a moment to mentally calm myself. "Okay, remember I said no judgment?"

"Mm-hmm."

"None from you either."

Kennedy narrowed those blue eyes just a touch but gave me a nod.

"I need a girlfriend." She blinked, clearly confused, and I realized how weird that had sounded. I closed my eyes, shook my head. "No, I mean, I need somebody to *play* my girlfriend. To pretend."

She sat back again, folded her arms again, studied me. "Well. I can't say I saw that coming."

"It's weird. I know."

"Totally weird. Go on." There was a glint in her eye, a sort of mischievous sparkle, and she waited.

"Okay." I took a breath, set my palms flat on the table. "I own a business. I'm rather successful."

"Yeah? What do you do?"

"I own a real estate agency. The building our apartments are in? I own it."

That got her attention, if the widening of her baby blues was any indication. "Wait. *You're* the landlord? I had no idea."

"I don't really advertise the fact. I don't want to be a landlord, so I pay a company to manage that aspect for me."

Kennedy sort of half smiled, half grimaced and said, "I am now thinking back over every loud thing I've ever done in my apartment, wondering if I've caused any damage, how many times I've called maintenance, and I remember clearly telling you yesterday my rent would probably be late...geez." That slight blush was back, and it was super cute.

I gave her a *pfft*. "You are not a problem tenant. Trust me. No worries."

"Phew." She made a rolling gesture. "All right. Keep going."

"I don't have a ton of time for a relationship."

"I call bullshit there, but continue."

I narrowed my eyes at her, but she held my gaze and waited— something I began to understand was a method of hers. An effective one. "My mother is relentless."

"Ah," Kennedy said, as if my one sentence made everything crystal clear.

Again, I stared for a second or two before continuing. "And one day, I was talking with her on the phone, and she was poking at me about not being settled down and not even dating, and I just snapped. I'd had it. I told her I had, in fact, been dating. That I'd been seeing the same woman, Jennifer, for several months but hadn't said anything because I wanted to *see where it went* first." I made the air quotes. "And then I couldn't stop. I just kept telling her details about Jennifer. That she's an interior designer. That she loves dogs and horror movies and whiskey…" I threw my hands up.

"Wow." Kennedy had gone wide-eyed.

"That's not even the worst of it."

"It's not? How can it get worse?"

"My sisters. My sisters also think I have a girlfriend. And my oldest sister, Melody, is sure I'm lying and will not let up about it."

"You are lying. Melody's right."

"I know she's right." My voice had gotten a little loud, a couple other patrons turning their gazes my way, and I consciously dialed it back about thirty-five notches. "But she always thinks she's right and she's been so…" I searched for the right words. "*Smarmy*. She's been smarmy and mean about it and…" A shrug. I fell back in my chair and felt defeated as I studied my hands. This was stupid. It would never work.

"And for once in your life, you'd like to prove her wrong."

I looked up at Kennedy and I swear to God, there was fire in her eyes.

"Listen, I have a big sister *and* a big brother, and they are forever tromping on me. About anything and everything. They're always right. I'm always wrong. Don't misunderstand, I love them both and they love me, but contrary to what they seem to think, I *do* know stuff. You know?"

"Yes." I sat up tall again, bolstered to have somebody who got it. "I absolutely know."

"So? Break it down for me. What's your plan?"

I blinked at her several times, unable to believe what was happening. "You're sure?"

"I think we owe it to little sisters everywhere."

I pulled out my notes that up till now had remained in my bag and turned them so Kennedy could see them. I started at the beginning and went through everything that had come to mind last night, and all the while, only one clear thought rang loudly through my head.

Holy shit. We're doing this.

CHAPTER FOUR

Traffic had been heavy getting out of the city in the late morning of Christmas Eve, but once we got off the Thruway and were cruising through smaller towns, things thinned out. It was cold, but clear, which was a relief. Driving home in a snowstorm was no fun. I knew. I'd done it more than once while in college, arriving at my parents' house with cramped hands from gripping the steering wheel so tightly and eyes that stung from concentrating so hard on white.

Kennedy sat in the passenger seat in jeans, a soft-looking gray hoodie, and a black puffy coat. Yorkie was curled into a napping ball on her lap. Her suitcase was in the trunk with mine, and the back seat was filled with bags of presents for my family and an empty dog carrier. Yorkie had yipped for about fifteen solid minutes before Kennedy and I looked at each other, I nodded once, and she let him out. His barking stopped. He watched out the window for five minutes, then curled into a ball, went to sleep, and stayed that way the entire ride.

"What's my favorite wine?" I asked her as we drove. We had about half an hour to go, and I'd eased up on the quizzing for a bit but was back at it.

"You prefer pinot noir, but you'll drink a robust zinfandel in a pinch." She turned that radiant smile on me.

"Man, you're good." She hadn't missed a single question I asked her.

"I'm used to learning lines. This isn't much different."

I waited a beat, then asked, "Are you nervous?"

She seemed to ponder that, scrunching up her nose in a super-cute thinking face, then shrugged. "Maybe a little? I mean, I don't want to screw up, for your sake."

"I appreciate that," I said with a laugh. "So, a little background on my sisters. Melody is going to quiz you endlessly, so don't be afraid to stop her. Act confused by all the questions. Ask why she's asking so many. Put it on her. Embarrassment always shuts her up."

"Got it."

"Cat is nicer. She's not conniving, but she's super observant. As for my mom…" I pressed my lips together as I thought about how long it had been since I'd seen her. "My dad died fifteen months ago."

"Oh God, Sasha." Kennedy laid her warm hand on my thigh. "I'm so sorry."

"Thanks. Last Christmas was kind of a blur. We were all still in the very early stages of mourning him, and the holidays just passed us by. So this year is really going to kind of be her first Christmas without him, since she barely remembers last year."

Kennedy nodded, and I could see her working through this new information in her head.

"My sisters say she's looking forward to the holiday, which is a relief…" My voice trailed off.

"But you're worried she might not be as cheerful as she seems."

How could she read me so well? Already? I touched my forefinger to my nose. "Exactly."

"I get that. When my parents died, I went through the same thing."

"Wait," I said, holding up a hand. "Your parents are both gone?" Kennedy was only thirty-one, if her online information was correct. Very, very young to have lost both parents already.

She nodded, grimaced. "Yeah. House fire."

"Oh God, that's horrible." I couldn't even imagine dying that way.

"It was. And the first couple of holidays I completely ignored, as did my siblings. And then I would pretend to be fine, even act like I was looking forward to them, but the closer they got, the more depressed I'd get." She paused, gazed out her window, and I wondered if she wasn't going to say any more. Then she did. "I'm better now, but we all seemed to scatter. I don't know why. It's like we needed to disperse or something. I'm here, my brother is in Texas, and my sister is in Oregon. We don't see each other often."

That was so sad. So sad. I swallowed an unexpected lump and searched for something to say. "That's why you were free to come with me."

More nodding. "I usually just hang out and watch Christmas movies on Netflix."

No. That was not a picture I was okay with, Kennedy all alone watching television on Christmas Eve. "Well, then, despite the reason for us doing this, I'm glad you're here with me."

She looked down at Yorkie, gave his silver-and-black back a scratch, then looked up at me and smiled. "Me, too."

I think she meant it.

"Why Jennifer?" she asked after a few moments of quiet went by.

"Sorry?"

"Did you just pick a name out of thin air?"

I chewed on the inside of my cheek as I steered the car onto the stretch of road that would take us into Bakerton. Almost there. "Just before my mom called that night, I had been watching Jennifer Garner do her Pretend Cooking Show on Instagram." I turned to look at her and she burst out laughing.

"Well, okay then."

"Seriously, have you seen it? Hilarious."

"I have not, but I'll be sure to remedy that situation."

As if getting a telepathic message that we were just about there, Yorkie woke from his nap, yawned, stretched, and put his paws up on the dash. He really was cute. Especially when he was quiet.

"Almost there, York," I said, and when he looked at me from Kennedy's lap, I had a weird sense of…To this day, I don't know what it was. Contentment? Déjà vu? The future? I couldn't put my finger on it, but it was good. It was warm. It felt right.

I was happy to see only my mother's car in the driveway as we pulled into number nineteen Pleasant Street. At least we'd have a little time before the Inquisition arrived. I braked to a stop, put the car in park, and turned to Kennedy.

"You ready for this?"

"As I'll ever be. Are you?"

"Not even close. Let's do it."

❖

We walked in the back door, and as I called out to my mother, the first thing that hit me was the smell. Every year, my mom bakes these amazing molasses cookies, and she keeps a pot of water with cloves and cinnamon sticks simmering on the stove. There's no other way to describe it than to say exactly what Kennedy said as she shut the door behind her.

"Wow, it smells like Christmas in here."

Before I could respond, my mom burst into the room, arms out wide, a huge beaming smile on her face, and came right at me, wrapped me up, hugged me so tightly, that I was torn between squirming like a ten-year-old who's embarrassed by physical contact with her mom and sinking into the hug, staying there forever.

"Sasha, Sasha, Sasha," she said softly in my ear as she gently rocked us from left to right as moms so often do. "I'm so glad you're home."

"Me, too, Mom." It was true, which surprised me. I tried to hide the tears that had sprung up unexpectedly, but when I pulled back, I saw my mother's eyes had welled up, too.

She pulled herself together. Waved a dismissive hand as she did. Smiled widely. "And this must be your Jennifer."

Kennedy held out her hand, the leash attached to Yorkie in the other, but my mother pulled her into an embrace because my mom hugged everybody. Those blue eyes widened at me over Mom's shoulder, and I gave her an apologetic shrug. But Kennedy hugged her back, I noticed. I liked that. "It's so nice to meet you, Mrs. Wolfe," she said.

"Oh no. You call me Maggie. Mrs. Wolfe makes me sound so old."

"Maggie." Kennedy gave a nod. "I've heard so much about you."

She was not lying, as part of the script I'd written for her had lots of facts about my mom in it. Kennedy had taken it seriously, which I appreciated.

"Well, don't believe everything my Sasha tells you." Then she dropped to a squat. "And who do we have here?" Yorkie gave a couple of yips and did that thing dogs do when they're uncertain—skittered backward, then took a few steps forward, then skittered backward again, until he finally decided my mom might be worth a sniff on the hand.

"That's Yorkie," I said.

She furrowed her brow and looked up at me. In turn, I looked at Kennedy.

"Don't ask," Kennedy said, then laughed.

"We're going to be good friends, aren't we, Mr. Yorkie?" And then the dog's front paws were on my mother's knees, and he was licking her face.

Kennedy and I exchanged a look of disbelief.

With a chuckle, my mom stood. "I have you girls set up in the attic. I hope that's okay. Cat's gonna sleep in Mel's old room, and Melody will be in your old room, since Ray isn't staying over." She clenched her teeth and made a face.

I hadn't even thought about sleeping arrangements and, in that moment, realized how dumb that had been of me. The attic had been remodeled since we'd all moved out and had one queen-sized bed that my dad used to be banished to when he snored too loudly. Speaking of snoring too loudly, my brother-in-law, Ray, was a big guy, and if he was staying over, he and Melody would definitely have been in the attic. Melody's old room only had a twin. And the room I shared with Cat had bunk beds when we were kids, but our parents had changed it to a double bed once Melody headed to college, and Cat and I finally got our own rooms.

"Sure, that's fine," I said, because what else could I say?

"Why don't you girls take your things up. Then you can help me down here. The other two should get here soon." Without asking, she took the leash from Kennedy's hand. "Yorkie can stay with me. We'll get to know each other."

We trudged straight up the stairs, then up another flight into the attic. It was a wide-open space with a peaked roof and a round window in the front that looked like a ship's porthole, a couple of skylights in the roof. The bed was pushed against the wall to the left. To the right was an easy chair and matching ottoman that might have been older than me, and as I stood there, a crystal-clear picture of my father sitting in that chair and reading one of his political thrillers formed in my mind's eye.

"This is awesome," Kennedy breathed as she set down her bag.

"You like it? It was kind of my dad's hideaway in the last few years before he died. He'd come up here to read or do his crosswords." I pointed to the folded-up card table leaning against one wall. "Sometimes, he'd do a jigsaw puzzle and set it up on that. He used to say they kept his mind sharp."

I felt a warm hand on my shoulder, and Kennedy said softly from behind me, "He sounds like a cool guy. I'm honored to be staying in his man cave."

I laughed softly. "He really was." I allowed myself another moment of picturing my dad in various spots in the room. It hadn't occurred to me that I'd be sleeping in what I considered to be his room.

Or that it would be hard. With a clear of my throat, I finally shook myself free of my memories. "Ready to head down?"

Kennedy took a deep breath, shook her arms out like a boxer preparing to spar. "Let's go to work."

Downstairs, we stopped to look at the tree in the corner of the living room, the stockings hanging on the mantel, some of my mom's Christmas village spread out on the new dining table—which was a gorgeous rusty shade of oak—waiting for arrangement. I swallowed down the unexpected lump that formed in my throat.

"Hey, you okay?" Kennedy asked.

I nodded. "It's not as decorated for the holiday as it usually is, but there's a lot more out than last year."

"Your mom's making progress, huh?"

I remembered texting with my sisters, Cat saying Mom seemed to be looking forward to Christmas this year, and I felt a surge of emotion. Last year, she didn't put up anything. Not one thing. She was so sad and depressed, and Christmas was just another day that came and went without my father.

"Here you go." My mom came into the room carrying two glasses, Yorkie right on her heels. "Wine for my girl. And whiskey for my girl's girl." She handed us the glasses. "I was hoping you'd help me set up the village." She gestured to the various pieces strewn about.

"We'd love to," I told her. I took a sip of my wine, savored the subtle fruitiness of it.

"Jennifer, do you mind if I take Mr. Yorkie for a quick walk? I have some cookies to drop off down the street and thought he might like to come with me."

I blinked at her. First of all, I'd never really thought of my mom as a dog person, but my dad had been allergic, so we never had animals. Second, she was cheerful and friendly and hadn't even begun to try my patience yet. Who was this woman, and what had she done with my mother?

"After being in the car so long, I think he'd love that," Kennedy said. "He's kind of stubborn, though. I'm afraid I haven't been great about training him. He was sort of…left behind, and we've been stuck with each other for the past week or two." She made a face of shame, which my mother waved off.

"Please. He's a sweet boy. Aren't you?" Yorkie was sitting at her feet and gazing up at her with what could only be described as adoration. "We'll be back in a bit. Come on, handsome." Again, Yorkie trotted off on my mother's heels.

"What the hell is happening with that dog? You didn't tell me your mother's the dog whisperer."

I was still staring after them. "That's because I had no idea. We didn't have dogs growing up because my dad was allergic."

"God, I hope he doesn't chew up anything of hers." Kennedy said it quietly, almost to herself as she scratched the side of her neck.

I shook myself out of my trance of shock and turned to the village pieces on the table. "You don't have to help with this," I told Kennedy.

"If it means I don't have to drink this whiskey, I'm in." At my surprised look, she explained. "Gives me hives."

I clenched my teeth, made a face. "Jennifer loves whiskey."

"Yeah, I know. I did some research so I can speak to it, but I'd like to avoid drinking it, if at all possible."

I wasn't sure how that would go over, but I wasn't about to force her to drink something that made her sick. I took her glass, tossed the liquid into the floor plant in the corner. "There. What else don't you like?"

"Horror movies." She made a face.

"Jennifer loves horror."

"I'm aware."

"I mean, our Christmas Eve tradition is to open one gift, then cuddle together and watch *The Texas Chainsaw Massacre*, but maybe I can talk my family into choosing a different movie this year."

"My fingers are crossed," Kennedy said with a laugh, then picked up one of the village houses. The cobbler's house. "These are so cute."

"I'm not even sure this is all the pieces." I looked around at the boxes strewn about. "Well, maybe it is. It's, like, a whole street. With trees and sleds and people."

"Let's set it up."

Working on a project with Kennedy was surprisingly…What was the right word? Calming. It was calming. Not something I expected, given that she was pretty much a stranger. But we worked in tandem, unpacking pieces, agreeing where to put them, setting up the smaller bits until the entire street was laid out along my mother's sideboard. We stood, side by side, hands on hips, and surveyed our handiwork.

"All that's left is the snow." I handed her some puffs of cotton, and together, we laid them around, weaved them in and out and in between.

Then I grabbed the extension cord and looked at her. "Ready?" Those blue eyes were shining with the delight of a child, and I found a sudden lump in my throat that needed swallowing, ASAP. At her nod, I plugged it in, and we watched as the whole village lit up. Interiors of houses, tiny street lights, the Christmas tree in the center of town.

"Well, that's a street I would live on," Kennedy said softly. "How about you?"

"Definitely." I meant it.

Basking in that peaceful moment any longer wasn't in the cards, though, as I heard the side door open, stomping feet, yips from Yorkie, and lots of commotion. Mom was home, and at least one sister had arrived. I shot a glance at Kennedy and raised my eyebrows in a silent *Are you ready for this?* Because after this, there'd be no turning back.

She gave me a thumbs-up and a reassuring smile.

And then my sister Cat came around the corner. "Mom has a dog now?" was the first thing she said.

"Ah, he's mine," Kennedy said. "But I think he likes her better." She stuck out her hand. "You must be Cat." Flipping through my family photos had paid off.

"And you must be Jennifer. It's amazing to meet you." Cat shook Kennedy's hand heartily, then looked at me. "She's gorgeous. Did you tell us she was gorgeous?"

"Pretty sure I did," I lied, but Cat wasn't wrong. Kennedy was gorgeous. Especially with the cute little blush she sported.

"Pretty sure you didn't." Melody. She strode in from the kitchen, still in her coat, apparently unable to wait to lay eyes on my girlfriend. She, too, stuck out a hand. "Melody."

"Jennifer." Kennedy shook it, made eye contact, held it, and it was as if they were having a little stare-down. She didn't seem intimidated by my sister in the slightest. Just smiled and waited her out, which earned her huge points in the column of *Things That Impress Me*. Wow. Melody intimidated everybody.

My mother came into the room carrying Yorkie, the dog doing his best to look like a spoiled little prince. Kennedy and I exchanged another look of disbelief. Mom took a look around, and her eyes welled up. She brought her fingers to her lips and said through unshed tears, "All my girls in one place on Christmas Eve."

And then my sisters and I were suddenly all emotional and looked at each other and laughed through our tears. When I turned to Kennedy, she was smiling, and she reached out a hand and brushed a tear off my cheek with her thumb. Something in my stomach—or was it lower?—fluttered, and that damn lump was back.

This was going to be one of the most memorable Christmases I'd ever had. One way or the other. I just knew it.

CHAPTER FIVE

It was driving Melody crazy. I could tell by the way her eyes were slightly wider than normal and the way she leaned a little bit forward in her seat at the dinner table.

"Has she made you watch *Friends With Benefits* yet?" Melody asked Kennedy, in what must have been the twenty-seventh in her endless litany of questions. "It's her favorite."

"I've seen it, but it's actually not. Sasha's favorite is *No Strings Attached*." Kennedy didn't miss a beat, and I had to bite down hard on my lips to keep from grinning like the proverbial canary-eating cat. "But they have similar storylines—friends who use each other for sex and end up falling in love—so it's easy to mix them up." She shoveled a huge bite of her salad into her mouth, and I wondered if that was in an attempt not to look too pleased with herself.

If I didn't know my sister so well, I'd have missed the flash of an irritated grimace that shot across her face.

"What made you choose interior design?" Cat asked. My baby sister's face was open, attentive. She'd asked a lot of questions, too, but none that were obvious attempts to trap Kennedy.

"Well," Kennedy said, then took a sip of her wine. "I have always been very interested in theater."

"You're talking stage, not movie, right?" Cat asked.

"Exactly. And I was always very good at set design. My parents were adamant about me choosing a career that I not only loved, but that I could survive on." A chuckle. "So interior design made sense."

"You don't spend the holidays with your parents, Jennifer?" That was my mother, who had been quietly listening and smiling, chiming in here and there, but mostly just sitting and looking happy to have all her children gathered around one table.

"Oh, I used to. They passed away."

Mom looked stricken. "Oh no. Oh, sweetheart, I'm so sorry to hear that." And she was. My mother can be exhausting in a lot of ways, but she has a very kind heart and she's always the first person to offer sympathy to somebody who she feels needs it.

"Thank you." Kennedy offered nothing more, and I could tell my mom—and Melody—wanted to ask for more detail, but thankfully, their manners won out, and they left the subject alone.

As if he was trying to break the tension hanging over the dinner table, Yorkie gave a little yip. I'd honestly forgotten he was with us, and both Kennedy and I looked down to where he sat politely at my mother's feet. She slipped him a piece of chicken from her sandwich. Christmas Eve, we always had a simple dinner of subs or sandwiches and salad with lots of things to pick on throughout the night: cheese and crackers, fresh fruit, tons of cookies and cakes and pies. Christmas Day was the big turkey dinner, so Christmas Eve was more casual.

"I cannot for the life of me understand how you've gotten him to behave." Kennedy was amazed—it was clear in her voice. So was I, to be honest. "I was going to feed him before we sat down, but he was being so good, I didn't want to rev him all up."

"He hasn't chewed up anything? Yet?" I asked.

"You two should stop telling fibs about this boy." My mother looked down at him, and I swore to God I hadn't seen her look that *happy* since before my dad got sick. "He's an angel." She glanced up at Kennedy. "Have you had him long?"

"Actually no, and I didn't pick him out. He belonged to a…friend of mine who ended up not being able to keep him, and I sort of ended up with him. Like, last week."

"Oh, that poor boy." My mom reached down and gave his little head a scratch. "Who wouldn't want you? Who? Tell me. Who?"

Before any more could be said, we heard the sound of the side door opening and a booming voice called, "Ho, ho, ho!"

Ray. My brother-in-law. Melody's husband. A huge bear of a man whose voice matched his presence and who sometimes rubbed me the wrong way, but who treated my sister like a princess, and that was good enough for me.

He came into the dining room, snow dusting his salt-and-pepper doughnut of hair and the shoulders of his jacket as he slipped it off and bent to kiss my mother on the cheek. "Merry Christmas, Ma."

He looked at each face around the table, stopping on Kennedy. "You must be Sasha's girlfriend. Jenna, was it?"

"Jennifer." Kennedy stood halfway, stuck out her hand, and it disappeared in Ray's meaty one. "Nice to meet you, Ray."

"Same."

My mother told him to help himself to some food, and soon he was sitting with us, regaling us with tales from the mall, as he always shopped for my sister on Christmas Eve.

Dinner finished up without a hitch. Ray's arrival seemed to temper Melody's questions, and she eased up, at least for that moment. We told my mom to go sit in the living room while we cleaned up and got into our cozy clothes for TV watching, tradition for us on Christmas Eve, despite the fact that Melody and I were forty and over, and Cat was in her midthirties. With my father gone, it felt especially important to hold tightly to our family traditions. When we were all changed and joined her, she was snuggled in her recliner under a blanket my dad had given her for her birthday a few years earlier, Yorkie looking like a little prince in her lap.

Kennedy shook her head with a grin of disbelief, as did I. "Please don't feel like you have to entertain him," she said to my mother. "I feel bad that he's demanding all of your attention."

"Sweetie, please." Mom waved her off yet again. "Truth be told, I kind of adore this boy already and will be sad to see him go." As if he understood every word, Yorkie looked up at her with that adoring look once again, and she dropped a kiss onto his head. Then he curled back up in her lap as if he'd always done so because that was his spot.

I was amazed by Yorkie's comfort with my mom, yes, but I was even more amazed by how easily and seamlessly Kennedy fit into my family. It was like she'd been there for years, and I was both relaxed and freaked out at the same time. Which didn't seem possible, but clearly was, since I was living it.

Our family room was fairly large, and it was where all of Christmas took place, aside from meals. A big rectangle, it held the tree in one corner, which stood grandly next to the fireplace. I pointed to the flames and said to Kennedy, "My dad only changed that to gas a couple years ago. The whole time I was growing up, it was wood burning. He was a pro at building a fire." Suddenly, I could see him crouched in front of the stone hearth, stacking the wood in a teepee shape, me and Cat crumpling up newspaper for him to use with the kindling. A glance at my baby sister, curled up in the other chair, her eyes shimmering in the twinkling Christmas lights, told me she was having the same memory.

Melody was on the couch, saving space for Ray. "Cat got super good at fire building."

"I was kind of bummed when he changed to a gas insert." Cat smiled, shook her head.

"I was not," my mother chimed in, absently stroking Yorkie's head. "The wood fire was nice, but I do *not* miss the entire house smelling like wood smoke. The furniture, clothes in the closet, my hair."

"Oh my God, right?" Melody said with a laugh, and we all joined her as Ray came in from the kitchen, a glass of wine in one hand, two rocks glasses with amber liquid in the other. He handed the wine to Melody, dropped heavily onto the couch next to her. Kennedy and I had opted for the floor with our backs against the couch, and Ray leaned forward, gave one of the rocks glasses to Kennedy.

"I heard you were a whiskey drinker. Try this. It's a new one a friend of mine recommended. Super smooth."

To Kennedy's credit, she smiled and took the glass, touched it to Ray's with a musical clink, then took a sip. At least I thought she did. It was hard to tell. Then she nodded and made a pretty good sound of enjoyment. "Oh, you're right. That *is* smooth. Wow." She turned to me, lifted one shoulder in a very subtle half shrug that only I could see, and winked.

My insides went all soft.

Uh-oh…

"You should give Sasha a taste," Melody said, gesturing at me with her chin.

"Why? Sasha hates whiskey," Kennedy answered, then took another sip.

"Melody." Our mother's voice wasn't loud, but it was firm. "Enough." Apparently, she'd had it with Melody, and it took everything I had to fight the urge to stick my tongue out at my big sister, who deflated like a balloon in her seat. Under the blanket, I squeezed Kennedy's thigh…and tried not to think about how great that felt.

The rest of the evening went on without issue. In fact, it felt alarmingly normal—with the exception of my father's absence, of course—and I did my best not to dwell on how that was possible as I sat on the floor under a blanket with my pretend girlfriend. Who couldn't really get any closer to me, her shoulder pressed into me, her warm leg tossed over mine, and I had to remind myself that I was paying her, that it was an act. It didn't feel like one, and I did my best not to dwell on that. Kennedy was obviously a really good actress—that's all it was.

We opened one gift each and settled in to watch *A Christmas Story*, which ran on a loop until eight p.m. the next night. Kennedy had—much to our horrified shock—never seen it from start to finish, and she was very patient as we quoted lines and spouted off all the trivia we knew about the film, giving her an education she didn't ask for. Ray prodded her about the whiskey a couple times until she really had no choice but to finish it. It only took about twenty minutes before I noticed a couple of red spots popping up on her neck. She simply pulled her hoodie up a bit higher and snuggled closer to me. Which felt warm and natural and *so good*. Again, I had to remind myself that she was acting. This was a job for her. Nothing more.

Around midnight, Ray yawned and stood, bid us a farewell until the next day.

"He has trouble sleeping in any other bed," I said in response to Kennedy's raised eyebrows, keeping my voice low so only she could hear me. "And his snoring sounds like a freight train. The house literally rumbles. Melody likes to stay, though. He'll be back in the morning."

Those of us left took our time taking empty glasses into the kitchen, folding up blankets, fluffing throw pillows that had gotten squished. When everything was clean, I headed back into the family room where my mother still sat in her chair. She'd turned off all the lights but those on the tree. Yorkie was still curled up with her. She looked sad, resigned, tired, content—all wrapped together.

"Mom?" I kept my voice soft. I didn't want to disturb whatever it was she was feeling. "You okay?"

She nodded, blinked several times, and met my gaze. Her eyes were wet. "I think I'm going to sit here a bit longer. Look at the lights. Would you get me a glass of wine, honey?"

"Sure." I poured her a glass and brought it to her, gave Yorkie a scratch on his tiny head.

"Do you think…" She waited, seemingly uncertain what she wanted to say, and Kennedy came to stand next to me. My mom shifted her gaze to look at her. "Do you think I could keep Yorkie with me for the night?" She bit her lip, clearly understanding it was a big ask.

Kennedy surprised me, though. "Oh my God, of course," she said without missing a beat. She squatted down so she was eye to eye with Yorkie, whose ears pricked up as he lifted his head. "You'll take good care of Sasha's mom, right, tiny guy?" She gave him a pet. "And no chewing anything that's not yours. I'm not joking around here. I mean it. Don't embarrass me." Damn if the dog didn't look earnest about her words.

My mother looked both relieved and happy when she turned to me, pointed at Kennedy, and said, "I like this one, Sasha. This one's a keeper."

For the first time since we'd arrived, I felt something I hadn't thought about in all my planning. Never even took it into consideration.

Guilt.

CHAPTER SIX

Once Kennedy and I had performed our individual nighttime rituals like removing makeup and brushing teeth, and we were closed up in the attic room, just the two of us, I let go of a giant breath. Relief. I knew that's what it was. We'd pulled off the first night.

"Oh my God," I said quietly, uncertain whether either of my sisters would be straining their ears to hear. "That was amazing. You were perfect."

Kennedy smiled, but the wattage of it was a little lower than usual. "Your family's fun."

"I can't believe you drank that whiskey. Your hives seem to have eased up." I grimaced.

"They weren't that bad this time." She glanced down at her chest where the red had faded to a soft pink.

"You tired?" I asked her.

"Very." She nodded, and as she stood there in her pink-and-white striped pajama set and rubbed her eyes, I thought she might have been the cutest thing I'd ever seen. "Aren't you?"

"Exhausted." It was the truth. I'd been so tense from the moment we'd arrived, mentally policing every word spoken, every nuance, by both Kennedy and my sisters, and my brain was fried. It was then that I realized we hadn't had any discussion whatsoever about the sleeping arrangements. I grabbed a blanket out of a drawer, snagged a pillow, and headed for the chair and ottoman in the corner.

"What are you doing?" Kennedy asked as she pulled the covers down on the bed.

"I was going to sleep in the chair." I smiled and shrugged, wanted to say that sharing a bed with me wasn't part of our agreement, that I certainly didn't expect that of her, but unable to get the words out for some reason.

"Please. It's cold. It's Christmas Eve. We just spent the entire evening under the same blanket with our legs tangled together." That grin, the cleft in her chin, the sparkling blue eyes, and her soft voice. All of them combined to make me feel warm and safe. "Just get in bed, weirdo."

I didn't hesitate. Which did make me a weirdo, I figured, because it should've totally been weird to share a bed with somebody I'd only known a couple weeks. Shouldn't it? I slid under the covers, and Kennedy did the same. Before I could turn off the light, there was a quick series of rapid knocks on the door and it flew open. Melody stood there trying—and failing—to mask her disappointment.

"No, really, come on in," I said.

She glanced around the room, and I could almost hear the wheels in her brain cranking away. When her gaze landed on the blanket I'd pulled out of the drawer and left on the chair, she crossed the room and grabbed it. "I need an extra blanket. Mom keeps this place like a freezer at night." She hurried back to the door, said good night, and pulled it shut behind her.

Kennedy and I lay there silently for a full ten seconds before I pulled my pillow over my face and burst out laughing. Once I caught my breath and put the pillow back behind my head, I turned to meet Kennedy's eyes.

"She was hoping to catch us, wasn't she?" she whispered.

"She so was. This is killing her." And just like that, I was ten years old again, remembering all the times my big sister had picked on me or embarrassed me or told on me.

Kennedy held her hand up, pinkie extended. "For little sisters everywhere."

I hooked my pinkie to hers. Her hand was warm, her skin soft. We lowered our hands, but kept our fingers linked. I clicked off the lamp. I didn't know about Kennedy, but I was hyperaware of her warm, breathing, very sexy form lying next to me.

Very sexy? My brain backpedaled to that unexpected thought. Unexpected, but not untrue. Kennedy was a very attractive, very sexy woman, and I had somehow tucked that away in a corner in order to play my role in this charade. But it had crept back into the light now that we were alone and didn't have to pretend for the benefit of others.

She was the whole package, really. Funny. Smart. Kind. Crazy sexy. I'd avoided those facts all night, but now, I simply sat with them.

The moon was bright, casting the room in a blue glow, almost ethereal. Snowflakes had begun, and I could see them, fat, soft puffs falling down past the window. I have always felt a sense of peace on Christmas Eve. No matter what was happening in my life at the time, that one night of the year, tucked warmly into my parents' house, always seemed to settle me somehow. It should've been wildly different that night. There I was, sharing a bed with a virtual stranger in my parents' house, fooling everybody in my family, paying the woman lying next to me. But it wasn't. I felt wonderfully, contentedly settled.

And it wasn't even weird.

Was it weird for Kennedy? It had to be. For me, she was the stranger there. For her, everybody was a stranger. I turned my head to ask her about it, but her eyes were closed, and her breathing had gone deep, even. I watched her sleep, studied her profile. Her prominent chin, her straight nose, that cascading hair, its color washed neutral by the moonlight. She'd fit right in with my family. If I wasn't careful, I was going to get too comfortable, and if that happened, I could slip up. We just had to get through tomorrow, one more overnight, and we'd be free to head home to our lives. Our real lives. Our separate lives.

I didn't want to dwell on that either. And then I didn't want to dwell on why I didn't want to dwell on that. Instead, I shut my eyes, concentrated on slowing down my breathing like I'd learned in meditation, and willed myself to relax.

Just as I faded into slumber, it occurred to me that my pinkie was still hooked around Kennedy's.

❖

I was a morning person. Never one to sleep in, even as a kid.

That being said, my mother was even more of a morning person. No matter how early I got up, she was always already in the kitchen. Sipping tea at the kitchen table, reading the newspaper when I was younger, scrolling on her iPad now that we were both older. Sometimes making breakfast. And at six on Christmas morning, putting an enormous turkey in the oven.

"My God, Mom, are the Buffalo Bills coming over for Christmas dinner?" I made an attempt to help her with the pan that had to be heavy, but she waved me off.

"Hey, I work out," she said, making me laugh and hold up my hands in surrender. She slid the huge roasting pan into the oven with zero assistance from me. "See?"

A yip of a bark sounded, and I looked around, no sign of Yorkie. Mom draped the dish towel over her shoulder and opened the back door. Covered with a layer of snowflakes, Yorkie came into the kitchen from the fenced-in yard, shook the snow off, and—to my utter amazement— sat his cute little butt right down and gazed up at my mother.

"Good boy," she said quietly, then handed him what looked like some leftover cold cuts from the previous night's dinner. "Nice," she warned, and the dog very carefully nibbled the meat from her fingers.

"Seriously, Mom. Who is this dog, and what have you done with Yorkie the Destroyer?"

"He's right here," she said, squatting down and using a baby-talk voice. "Isn't he? Isn't this my little Yorkie? Right?" She scratched him, and he kissed her, and it was ridiculous and also completely adorable.

I'd never had the opportunity to think of my mom as a dog person, but she sure as hell was. I watched, wide-eyed, as she pointed to a pile of blankets in the corner, which was apparently a makeshift dog bed, and Yorkie pranced to it, turned in four circles, and lay down. He grabbed something with his tiny mouth, and I squinted.

"Oh, those are just some of your father's old socks. I stuffed a bunch into one and tied it. He chewed up one of my old slippers last night, so I made him something to play with. Something he's allowed to chew on."

I shook my head in disbelief.

"You and Jennifer sleep okay?" Mom asked as she gestured to the full pot of coffee.

"We did." I was speaking for myself, of course, but I assumed Kennedy had slept well and continued to, as she was dead to the world when I'd left her. "It's cold in here at night, Mom."

She shook her head. "You know, your father had the thermostat set to go way down at night, and I've never adjusted it because it's too complicated. I'm afraid I'll mess it up."

"I can do it." I strolled into the dining room. My dad had installed a new thermostat a few months before he passed away. It was electronic and programmable, and while my mom was a quick study on things like the iPad or her smartphone, things to do with the house made her nervous. She'd left all that sort of thing for my dad. He had the temperature set to go down to sixty degrees at eleven at night, and I changed it to sixty-five. Took me all of seven seconds. "There," I said as I returned to the kitchen and poured myself a cup of coffee. "Done." I doctored it up, then took a seat opposite my mom at the table.

"I like her, you know." She didn't have to tell me who she meant. "She's good for you."

Good for me, huh? "You think so?" I sipped, felt the warmth, the sweetness of the sugar, the blast of caffeine all hit my system and start the process of waking me up fully.

Mom nodded, both hands wrapped around her mug, the little tag dangling from it letting me know she was drinking Christmas Blend tea. I inhaled deeply, could smell the delicious, festive warmth of cinnamon, nutmeg, cloves. "I like the way she looks at you."

I tipped my head. The way Kennedy looked at me? What did that mean? "How does she look at me?"

"Like you matter. Like you're important to her. Like you mean something."

Well.

That was very detailed and observant and *way* unexpected. Was Kennedy *that* good?

"Plus," Mom added, and oh, good, there was more, "she's polite. She has manners." Manners were big with my mom, and I hadn't really even considered that when I hired Kennedy, but she'd obviously passed with flying colors. "And you look happy around her."

I did?

That was news.

Unsure what expression I might be making, I lifted my mug and used it in an attempt to mask my face, just in case. Things were working great. My mother wasn't tormenting me about finding a spouse, and my sister wasn't gloating about being right at my expense.

But I felt weird. Guilty. Because of course I did. It was all one great big lie.

It's okay, I told myself. It was just for the holiday. Just for today. We'd head home tomorrow and that would be it. After it was over, I could ease back, talk about Jennifer less and less until I gradually faded her out, told my family it hadn't worked for whatever reason, and then I could finally step out of the corner I'd stupidly painted myself into.

"Well, Merry Christmas," my mother said, her face lighting up as her gaze trained over my shoulder.

"Merry Christmas to you," Kennedy said, and I turned to face her. She looked adorably sleep tousled, dressed in gray leggings, an oversized green sweatshirt with a Santa face on it, and her red hair pulled into a messy ponytail. She didn't miss a beat. Didn't hesitate for a second, simply walked toward me, leaned down, and gave me a gentle kiss on my temple, lingered for a second or two. I let her, didn't move, didn't flinch or jump in surprise. It was as if I was expecting it. As if it was the most natural thing in the world. And the weirdest part was that it felt exactly like it *was* the most natural thing in the world. "Good morning. Is there coffee?"

I pointed in the direction of the pot on the counter, speechless, as she got herself some coffee, visited with Yorkie, and started a conversation about him with my mom. *She's playing a role.* I repeated it several times. Reminded myself that Kennedy was an actress and a drama teacher, and I was paying her to do exactly what she'd just done. Things were going perfectly. Just as I'd hoped. Exactly according to plan. *And I was paying her.*

So why was I so off-balance?

CHAPTER SEVEN

That feeling of being just slightly off stayed with me all morning as I watched how seamlessly Kennedy fit right into my family, like the last piece of a jigsaw puzzle finally snapped in place.

My mother wasn't kidding about liking her. It was clear in the way she looked at her when she spoke, touched Kennedy's arm in the same maternal way she'd touch me or either of my sisters.

Melody woke up armed with a renewed list of quiz questions and started right in, asking about coffee, obviously wanting to see if Kennedy knew how I liked mine. She did. By the time she asked Kennedy if I had overheated her with my flannel pajama pants and shirt and socks, my fake girlfriend was apparently ready to use the weapon we'd discussed.

Kennedy looked at Melody for a moment, squinted as if studying her. With a slight tilt of her head, she said, "Sasha doesn't wear pajamas." I had worn some last night because, hello? In bed with somebody I didn't know well. But she was right—I hated them. Melody tried to catch her own crestfallen expression, but Kennedy wasn't done. "What's going on with you?" she asked my sister. Her voice was gentle, not accusatory, but firm enough to catch the attention of both me and my mother. And Cat, who was approaching from the hallway.

"What do you mean?" Melody asked, doing that thing where the cornered person tries to busy herself, and got herself some coffee.

"I'm just wondering what's with the endless litany of questions. It feels a little bit like I'm constantly taking a test I didn't study for."

Except she did study! Ha! I wanted to shout. I managed to keep my mouth shut, thank the good Lord above.

Melody at least had the good sense to blush, and her eyes flicked in my direction, then quickly away and back to her cup as she lifted one shoulder in a half shrug. "I'm sorry. I don't mean to make you feel like I'm testing you."

Liar.

"It's okay." Kennedy. She waited until Melody looked in her direction, opened her mouth as if to say something, then closed it again, leaving my sister waiting for words that didn't come. Holy crap, she was good.

Cat came the rest of the way into the kitchen, kissed my mom on the cheek, and wished us all a Merry Christmas, and just like that, things went back to normal and the discomfort burned away like morning fog.

I looked at Kennedy, and with her back to the rest of the room's occupants, she winked.

I was probably going to have to give her a bonus.

And then that thought made me feel weird and off-balance all over again.

"I'm going to grab a shower," I said, because I suddenly needed to get away from all of them. I felt like I couldn't breathe, and my head was feeling more jumbled, and I didn't know what to do with any of it.

So I fled.

Just to the bathroom, but still. Fled. I was totally fleeing.

My parents' house wasn't new or modern or fancy. They were comfortably middle class but weren't people who splurged for the sake of splurging.

That being said, there were a few instances where only the best would do, and their bathroom was one. I can't remember a time during my high school years when something new wasn't being added to, ordered for, or built in to that room, and when it was finally finished, my father continued to periodically update things here and there. Paint colors. Light fixtures. Faucets. It was gorgeous and one of my favorite rooms in the whole house, weird as that sounded.

As a nearly middle-aged woman, I could definitely appreciate a good-quality bathtub. My parents had a big garden tub with jets, set into the corner with a window and surrounded by gorgeous sand-colored ceramic tile dotted with candles in various sizes, shapes, and scents. Next to it was a glass-enclosed shower, oversized, with a rainfall showerhead, a seat on one side, and temperature control. My dad had also added a bigger water heater so the hot water would last. Because the truth was, nobody wanted to get out of that shower once they got in.

I was no exception.

I loved my apartment, and I had sprung for a rainfall showerhead of my own, but my shower itself wasn't nearly the same. I closed the bathroom door, set my pile of clothes down on the hamper, and draped a big, thirsty chocolate brown towel over the clear glass door of the shower. I turned on the water, adjusted the temperature, and stepped inside. A soft moan worked its way up from my lungs as the hot water cascaded over my head, my body, warming me, relaxing my muscles, making me close my eyes and lean my forehead against the wall and want to stay in there until spring came. Because honestly, I was feeling some stress. I mean, how could I not be, considering the charade I was masterminding, right?

I wasn't sure how long I'd been in there when I heard a bit of a commotion out in the hallway. Before I could assess what was happening, the bathroom door flew open, and I heard Melody's voice saying, "Mom won't care, for God's sake, you're her girlfriend. Go on in."

Kennedy stumbled into the bathroom as if she'd been pushed. Which I thought she might've been. The door shut behind her, and she stood there, stack of clothes in her arms, wide-eyed and blinking at me. I mirrored her stance and blinked back at her.

We stood there.

Blinking.

Standing and blinking.

It wasn't until her eyes moved slowly downward and goose bumps broke out across my skin that I remembered how very naked I actually was. Weirder still was that I didn't move to cover myself right away. I just stood there, wondering what that was about, and I would like to point out that while I didn't hurry to cover myself, Kennedy didn't hurry to stop looking.

When I finally reached for the knob and turned the water off, then pulled the towel down and wrapped it around my body, it was like I broke the spell. As I opened the shower door and stepped out, Kennedy coughed and turned her entire body to face the other direction. Where there was a mirror, of course, so she could still see me.

She scratched roughly at her neck. "I'm sorry," she said, and her voice was hoarse, as if she needed to clear her throat. "I didn't mean to just…" She gestured at the door, moved her hand around in what I assumed was some kind of sign language for *bust through the door while you were naked and in the shower*.

I did my best to ease her discomfort because the shocking truth was that I didn't have a whole lot of it. "It's perfectly okay. My sister can be kind of pushy."

"Literally," Kennedy said, her eyes wide in the mirror's reflection. And then we both laughed softly.

"I mean, we *did* sleep together last night," I joked, keeping my voice low. "Seeing me in the shower does seem like a logical next step."

Kennedy did clear her throat this time. "Actually, I think your sister expected that we'd shower together. She kept talking about how big the shower is"—she glanced back at me and over my shoulder—"which she was not kidding about."

Ah, so if Melody couldn't catch Kennedy with her endless quiz questions, she was going to test us this way. I silently cursed my sister. And also had to give her kudos because she was a hell of a competitor, and that move was brilliant, much as I hated to admit it.

"I don't think we have a choice if we're going to convince her." Kennedy's voice was barely a whisper. "She's like a dog with a bone." When I grimaced and nodded, she laughed through her nose. "I can totally see why you wanted to prove her wrong."

"Right?" I whispered back. "You get me."

"I do." We stood there for a moment, and I swear to God, the air crackled. "So. I should…" She pointed at the shower. "Because…"

I nodded my agreement as we continued to whisper. "She may very well be waiting out there and listening." I switched places with her so that she was near the shower door and I was facing the vanity.

And the mirror.

My eyes were damn traitors. They would not stay closed. They would not look away from the reflection. No, they tracked every move Kennedy made. When she pulled the rubber band from her hair and shook it loose, my eyes took in all the various shades of red and gold. When she grasped the hem of her shirt and pulled it over her head, they raked across the creamy expanse of bare back and freckled shoulders. When she stripped off her leggings and bikinis—black, Lord help me— they roamed over her rounded ass and down her surprisingly shapely legs.

The woman I'd hired to pretend to be my girlfriend was ridiculously attractive and alarmingly my type. I liked everything about her personality. Her values and morals seemed in line with mine, at least what I'd learned of them. She was funny and kind, and now that I'd seen her naked and the physical attraction warning went from a gentle beeping to air horn levels...I stifled a groan. I wasn't sure why that possibility hadn't crossed my mind before that moment, but as Kennedy stepped into the shower and closed the glass door, the reality crashed over me like an avalanche.

I braced myself on the vanity with both hands, forced my gaze away from that gorgeously naked—and, somebody come save me, slick and wet—body and down to the sink where I had to calm my breathing and remind myself that this was a job for Kennedy. *A job.* I hadn't hired her so I could ogle her in the bathroom like some sort of creeper. But developing an actual attraction to her had caught me off-guard, and I knew it would cause problems if I didn't step carefully.

Just get through today and tonight, I told myself. *Then, tomorrow afternoon, you guys can get in the car, finally breathe, and head home.* The thought of that—of the whole charade coming to an end—eased the stress for me a little bit. And also caused new feelings of uncertainty that I was just not ready to analyze.

When I let my gaze drift back upward, the steam on the glass obscured much of my view, and that was probably a good thing, despite being a little bit disappointing. Kennedy was lathering her hair, her arms up, head back, her hands massaging the shampoo into her scalp. The suds were trailing down the middle of her back in a creamy white line to her beautiful ass, and I was jealous of them. Meanwhile, I stood there, still in my towel, and tried unsuccessfully to swallow the lump of arousal in my throat, to tear my eyes away.

This was bad. Oh, this was so bad.

I shook myself. Literally gave a full body shake while Kennedy's face was in the spray, and I was sure she wouldn't notice. Then came the mental pep talk where I told myself I was a grown-ass woman who had control of herself, not some fourteen-year-old boy who thought about sex once every five minutes. I told myself to pull it together, to act like the professional I was. Another shake. I turned my back to the shower, avoided the mirror, pulled the towel off, and focused on the pile of clothes I'd brought in.

As I stepped into my bikinis, I did glance up at the mirror once more, quickly.

Kennedy didn't meet my gaze in the reflection because she was looking right at my naked body.

CHAPTER EIGHT

Turned out we were right about Melody. She was in the hallway when Kennedy and I exited the bathroom, both of us dressed and with wet hair. Melody said she was "looking for something for Mom" in the hall linen closet, which seemed awfully convenient. When Kennedy and I exchanged a knowing glance, I felt myself warm inside. It was like we were a team, and I hadn't felt that with anybody in a very long time. And when she grabbed my hand, entwined our fingers, and led me up to the attic, I felt it even more.

We dried our hair, did our makeup, and changed from the cozy clothes we'd taken to the bathroom into nicer outfits for Christmas. Getting dressed ended up being the most interesting process yet, even more so than being in the bathroom together. We stood at opposite sides of the room, backs to each other, but every now and then, one of us would glance over a shoulder toward the other. We caught each other looking more than once, smiled, blushed, kept going. I hadn't asked Kennedy to wear anything in particular for the holiday, but when I finished dressing and turned around, she was wearing a deep, deep green dress that clung to her curves like it was sewn just for her. Three-quarter-length sleeves, a hem that fell just above her knees, and a V-neck that didn't plunge so much as casually lead my eyes gently toward the peek of cleavage there. Her hair was down, sunset-colored waves skimming just past her shoulders. She didn't wear a lot of makeup—mascara, eyeliner, lip gloss in a deep crimson—and she was easily one of the sexiest, most beautiful women I'd ever laid eyes on. Not an exaggeration. A fact.

"My God, you're stunning." It slipped out before I could catch it, and I knew Kennedy wasn't wearing blush because her cheeks blossomed with pink, and she glanced down at her feet for a second or two. When she looked back up and met my gaze, her eyes had gone dark, were slightly hooded.

"You're one to talk," she said, and her voice was so low and husky that my stomach fluttered with arousal. "You look…" She said nothing more, just shook her head. In a good way.

I was wearing a black sweater dress. It wasn't at all revealing—in fact, it had a mock turtleneck and long sleeves. But the material was ribbed, and the dress clung to me in all the right places, which is why I bought it, and I will admit that it wasn't what I'd intended to wear that day. I'd brought another, simpler outfit and tossed the dress in on a whim at the last minute—I always prefer to have too many clothes with me than not enough. But something about the atmosphere since we'd arrived, the way I'd been feeling—which was only amplified by our shared bathroom time—had me pulling the dress out and stepping into it without really thinking about what I was doing or why.

Kennedy's reaction made me glad I did.

We stood facing each other, still at opposite ends of the room, and again, the air felt charged. Crackling. Electric. We said nothing, but we didn't have to. Our gazes held, and that was enough.

"Ready to head down?" I asked, part of me wanting to stay in that attic with her, just like that, until spring.

She gave a nod, stepped to the door, and waited for me to meet her there. Her hand on the knob, she looked at me and said, very quietly, "You look beautiful, Sasha." Without waiting for a response, she pulled the door open and waved for me to go first. I swallowed hard, wet my lips, and headed down the stairs. Comments like that? When it was just the two of us? Not part of the deal. I hadn't paid for that, and it meant more because of it.

At the base of the stairs, I could hear voices and laughter. Ray had arrived, Cat was there, Yorkie gave a yip or two. Kennedy made a sound, and I followed her gaze down to our feet. One of my mother's mittens was on the floor, a sizable hole chewed at the tip of it.

"Oh no. God, I really need to keep a better eye on him." She picked up the mitten and looked stricken.

I grabbed her arm. "It's totally okay. My mom told you she wanted to watch him, so this isn't your fault." I gestured to the mitten. "Come on."

It always amuses me how a kitchen is a place of congregation, no matter how large or small a room it is. Everybody stood in my mother's right then. It was loud. It was hot. It was crowded. It smelled delicious. And the smile on my mother's face was wide and bright, which made everything else just fine.

"Oh, sweetie, don't worry about that," she said when she saw the mitten in Kennedy's hand and the worried look on her face. "I have endless mittens. And if I run out, I can knit myself some more."

"I'm so sorry," Kennedy said, her face red regardless of my mother's reassurances. "I haven't had him that long. He was my, um, roommate's. She didn't train him, and she sort of just left him, and I admittedly haven't worked with him as much as I should. My schedule's a little crazy. I wasn't paying attention, and I should've been." She held up the mitten casualty with a grimace.

Yorkie sat on the blanket pile in the corner and looked very pleased with himself, watching us with interest as if he understood every word.

"Listen to me. Do not be sorry. You have no reason to be. I told you to leave him here with me. Yes, he likes to chew things, but he's a baby still. He'll learn. And he has been wonderful company for me." Something in my mother's expression softened even more as she turned to look at the little guy. "Haven't you, Nicholas?" A glance back at Kennedy and a sheepish grin, and she said, "You'd mentioned you were open to a new name, so I'm auditioning that one. Because it's Christmas? Saint Nicholas? Get it? What do you think?"

Instead of answering her, Kennedy turned to me and said, "Okay, your mom is seriously the most adorable woman on the planet."

And those warm and mushy feelings I was starting to have around her? Yeah, they tripled. Because when somebody adores your mom, her stock skyrockets. You know?

Oh, this was so bad.

❖

It was only the second Christmas without my father, but I'm shocked to be able to say that it was a great day. My mother was happy, that was the big thing, and I knew it was in large part because she thought I was happy, which meant all her kids were. She repeated an old saying to me once, that a mother is only as happy as her saddest child, and of the three of us—at least in her eyes—the saddest child was me. For the record, I didn't really consider myself sad, but I could admit to being a little bit lonely, that I had times I wondered if that was how my life was going to go for always: running a very successful business by day and going home to an empty apartment at night. Much of the time, I was just fine with that. But the holidays could be hard.

"Jennifer, come here." It was Cat, holding her phone. "Sasha said you're a horror movie fan. Me, too! Did you see the trailer for *Blood Moon*? It's crazy. Here. Watch."

To Kennedy's credit, she stayed in character and did *not* shoot me a terrified look as she sidled up to my sister. The kitchen filled with bloodcurdling screams and highly tense music, and I watched the color drain from her face until she was white as the snow outside. I rolled my lips in and bit down on them, tried to busy myself for the two and a half minutes the trailer lasted.

"Wild, huh?" Cat asked, her eyes wide with excitement when it was over. "Opens next month."

"Totally." I saw Kennedy's throat move as she swallowed hard. "I'm so there." She came back over to me, and I bumped her with a shoulder.

"You okay?" I whispered when Cat left the room. "You looked like a woman with a tic, trying to keep your eyes open, but also wanting to close them."

"Oh, I'm fine. I mean, I'll have nightmares for the next week, but other than that, I'm absolutely fine. No worries at all." But the grimace she gave me turned into a soft smile, and I felt better. I think she did, too.

We exchanged gifts in the early afternoon just before we ate. By five o'clock, Melody and Ray had to leave to visit with Ray's family. Melody hugged us both and took a moment to squint at Kennedy, like she was sure she'd missed something, and she wasn't giving up. I won't pretend I wasn't relieved to see her go because I felt like Kennedy and I could both breathe again. Cat's boyfriend, James, stopped by to pick her up and give my mother flowers, and then they headed off to visit his parents, though Cat planned to come back later and spend the night again. She had her own place, but I knew she liked to come stay the night with our mom on occasion, and I was thankful for that.

I usually headed home after Christmas dinner and was glad I had decided Kennedy and I would stay a second night because the idea of leaving my mother alone on Christmas night—even with Cat returning later—didn't sit well with me. Not that year. I was worried she'd end up getting lost in sadness and missing my dad, and while I knew that would probably happen anyway, I didn't want her to be alone when it did.

"I'm so glad you two are here," she said later that night as we set up the Scrabble tiles at the new dining room table. And that right there was enough.

The ease with which Kennedy slid right into my family was both amazing and unnerving. I was notoriously bad at Scrabble—which was likely why Mom wanted to play it—but Kennedy gave her a run for her money. While the majority of my words consisted of three or four letters, Mom and Kennedy dueled with seven-letter and eight-letter and ten-letter words, things I had to look up.

"There is no way fizgig is a word," Kennedy said to my mother, her laughter infectious. "You made that up."

My mother shook her head, laughing as well, and gestured to me. "Nope. It's a firework. Sasha?"

I flipped through my dad's old crossword puzzle dictionary, the pages worn, the spine cracked, until I found the *F* section. "Uh-oh," I said and shot a sad face at Kennedy. "Fizgig. Noun. A type of firework that makes a loud hissing sound."

"No!" Kennedy made a humorous sound of defeat and dropped her head to the table with a clunk.

"One hundred seventeen points, thank you very much," Mom said, marking her score down as Kennedy closed her eyes and shook her head.

"I give. I give." She held her hands up. "You win. You are the official Scrabble Queen. I bow to your prowess." She dipped her head and Yorkie, er, Nicholas yipped in apparent celebration from somewhere.

When Cat came in, we were still cracking up. I met my little sister's gaze over my mother's shoulder, and I knew exactly what she was thinking. She shot me a huge grin, her eyes wet, and I knew we were both thrilled to hear our mother's laughter, something that had been missing from the house since our father got sick.

Cat wrapped her arms around our mother's shoulders from behind. Mom grasped Cat's forearms with both hands. "Hi, baby girl of mine. I'm glad you're back. Did you have fun with James?"

I wanted Cat to have time with Mom, so I pushed my chair back and began putting Scrabble tiles back in the box. "I think we're going to head up," I said, then glanced at Kennedy for confirmation.

"Good call," she said with a nod. "I am so full and so tired, and this was one of the best Christmases I've ever had." The expression on her face was genuine. Either she was an even better actress than I thought, or she was telling the truth.

"That makes me so happy," my mom said and reached out a hand to grasp Kennedy's.

The guilt really hit me then, and I swallowed hard, tried to tamp it down as I put away the game.

"I should take Nick out," Kennedy said, but I saw my mother tighten her hold on her hand.

"I can do it." Then my mother—the woman who raised three daughters, worked full-time, and survived the long and drawn-out death of her husband—made a face like a small child. Shrank back into herself and said in a soft and uncertain voice like she was asking if she could stay up past her bedtime, "Do you think he could sleep with me again tonight?"

Kennedy's face softened, and her smile was warm. "Hell, I think he should live with you. He definitely loves you more than me." She squeezed my mother's hand. "Of course he can sleep with you. I will still let him out, though, so you don't have to do that." Heading toward the kitchen, she clucked her tongue and called, "Come on, Nicholas. Outside." The clicking of little doggy nails on the hardwood under the table near my mother's feet went right into the kitchen to the back door as we all looked at each other. "Has he been there the whole time? I figured he was on the blankets."

"Nope. Right here." Mom grinned. "With his chin on my foot." It was obvious the dog felt like he was home.

Kennedy just shook her head, her face a sketch of happiness, and went to let him out. As soon as the door clicked shut, Mom turned to look at me.

"That girl," she said, Cat's arms still wrapped around her. "Will you please, please keep her?"

I didn't answer, mostly because I wasn't sure how.

"The way she looks at you." Cat shrugged as she stood up straight and let out what could only be described as a dreamy sigh.

"Right?" my mom chimed in. "And the way you look at her. You two are almost too perfect for each other." She nodded, clearly thrilled that her stubbornly busy middle daughter had finally found somebody worthwhile.

I tried to ignore the wave of guilt that hit again, but when I did that, I had to focus on what they'd said. Did I look at Kennedy a certain way? Did she look at me like that? I mean, her look was one thing, since I was paying her for it. But did *I* look at *her* that way?

"Ready?" Kennedy interrupted my train of thought. Which was a good thing, since it was about to chugga-chugga-chug itself right off a bridge.

"I am." We said our good nights. I kissed my mother, hugged her, and she whispered that she loved me in my ear.

Kennedy held out her hand, and I didn't even hesitate before taking it, feeling its warmth, its solidity. I turned back to look over my shoulder. Cat sat at the table. Nicholas the Yorkie was perched on my mom's lap like he'd never sat anywhere else. My mother's smile lit up the whole room.

My heart was full.

I followed Kennedy upstairs.

CHAPTER NINE

We were both quiet as we got ready for bed. I was exhausted, and when Kennedy took her turn down in the bathroom, I sat on the bed and tried to examine why.

I mean, there was the obvious, that I was playing a role, in a sense. Not the way Kennedy was—and not as well, frankly—but I was pretending. Wasn't I? When I'd started this whole charade, it seemed like a great idea. And I could admit to finding immense satisfaction in Melody's disappointment at not being right. Yeah, yeah, I know she actually *was* right, but *she* didn't know that, and I took the time I could to bask in one of my very few sisterly victories over her. But as I sat there and tried to calm my racing thoughts, I also had to admit that I was fighting a much wider array of emotions than I expected.

I sat with that for a moment. Took a deep breath.

Be honest with yourself. Truly honest. The thought echoed through my head, and I closed my eyes and did my best to let the truth come through.

I liked Kennedy. A lot.

It's not that I hadn't expected to. She was, as I've already said, a nice person, kind, funny. But I *liked her* liked her, and it wasn't until that exact moment that I actually let myself hear that, feel it, roll it around. In any other circumstances, I'd be interested. I might ask her on a date. Take her to dinner and a movie. Or something else. Something fun and unusual because I thought she was the kind of person who would like fun and unusual.

The door opened, startling me. I must have jumped because Kennedy made a face of apology. "Sorry, didn't mean to scare you."

I waved her off. "Oh no, that was me. Daydreaming over here."

Kennedy dropped her stuff on her bag. "Is it daydreaming if it's nighttime?" She pulled the covers down and got into bed, and it shocked me how easily and nonchalantly she did it. Like we'd been sharing a bed for years.

I smiled softly. "I guess not." I exhaled and got in bed next to her, tried not to notice the warmth coming off her body.

"Wanna talk about it?"

I thought about it. I really did. Instead, I just smiled and turned my head to meet her gaze. Her blue eyes were soft, inviting. I felt like I'd be safe in them. "It's okay."

She studied me for a moment. "Can I say something?"

"Sure."

"And you promise not to get mad?"

Interesting. And not something I'd ever promise, let's be realistic. "I will do my best."

Turning her gaze to the ceiling, she blew out a long, slow breath. "I hate that we're lying to your mom."

"I know. I do, too." It was the first time I'd actually admitted it out loud, and it was the truth.

"She's so nice. I love how sweet she is with York—I mean Nicholas. She loves you and your sisters so much, and she just misses your dad." She looked at me again. "I don't think she meant to bug you about dating. She doesn't want you to be lonely, that's all. Because she is, and she doesn't want that for you."

I blinked at her for a couple seconds. "And how do you know all of this?"

A shrug. "I talked to her. I had lots of little chats today."

I thought back through the day and realized there were several times I'd left the two of them alone. Setting the table, taking care of opened gifts, dishing out dessert. And the other strange thing? I hadn't been worried about it. Not once. It never occurred to me that I shouldn't leave them alone together. I was that comfortable with Kennedy.

"Does that bother you?"

Her question pulled me back to the present. I must've stayed quiet too long. I shook my head. "No. Not at all."

"I just feel a little weird is all." We were quiet for a beat, and then I felt her hand on my arm. "I'd never tell, though. Don't worry about that. We have an agreement, and I promised. That's not what I'm saying. It just…feels a little weird."

"It feels weird to me, too." What didn't feel weird? Was lying there next to her in my T-shirt and bikinis, her warm hand still on my arm…

Now, I am not a person who normally throws caution to the wind. I'm practical. I am a logical woman. And aside from paying somebody to be my fake girlfriend for two nights and three days, I didn't do a lot of crazy things. I don't know if it was the exhaustion and my near nonexistent coping skills or if it was the wine I'd had earlier or if it was the warmth of the very attractive woman next to me in bed, but I threw the caution. Oh, did I throw it.

"You know what's weird to me?" I asked her, ignoring the voice in my head screaming, *Don't say it! Do not say it!* "That it doesn't feel weird being here. With you. Like this."

While it felt to me like an hour and a half ticked by, I'm sure it was only a couple seconds. And then that smile lit up Kennedy's face, her blue eyes widened a bit, and she let a quiet laugh escape. "Oh my God, right?" She put a hand to her forehead, shook her head back and forth on the pillow. "I have been thinking that since we got in the car to come here. That it should be all weird and uncomfortable." Those blue eyes found mine, held them. "But it's not."

"It's not." My voice was a whisper this time because I knew what was coming. I couldn't have stopped it if I'd wanted to, and I most certainly did not want to. I rolled to my side, pushed myself up on an elbow, and took a beat to look down at Kennedy's beautiful face. The dark lashes that framed her eyes, making the blue pop. The fullness of her lips. They way her breath hitched, quietly and like it surprised her.

I stroked my fingertips across her forehead, tucked a lock of hair behind her ear, then cupped her face and brought my lips down to meet hers.

I took my time, gauging her reaction, giving her a chance to pull back, but she didn't. I felt her hand move up the back of my neck, her fingers slide into my hair, and she pulled me in more firmly, parted her lips, touched my tongue with the tip of hers.

Oh God.

The kiss deepened. I'd like to say it was my doing, but I think it was both of us, because Kennedy gave as good as she got, and for the first time since the thought had entered my head, it was clear that she'd been feeling the same way I had. At least close to it. Because I was unsure about a lot of things, but one thing that was super clear was that Kennedy was *not* acting.

We may have kissed for a long time. It might have been hours. It was hard to tell. At some point, one of us turned off the light, and it was just the two of us in the dark, limbs entwined, mouths fused together, just kissing. When we were finally both in need of air, we slowly ended the kiss, our faces still very close, breathing the same air.

Kennedy tried to speak and had to clear her throat, which was seriously cute. "Wow," she said, her voice husky. "I had a feeling we'd kiss well together, but that was…"

I waited to see if she'd come up with a description, and when she didn't, I gave her mine. "Beyond?"

"Yes. Beyond. That's the perfect word."

I nodded because she was absolutely right. Kissing Kennedy was…I tried to come up with the right description. Sensual? Erotic? Perfect? Unexpected? Sexy as hell? All of the above and then some was the correct answer.

We lay quietly for a moment, facing each other in the dark, our faces only inches apart. I played with a lock of Kennedy's hair, twirled it around and around my finger. I don't think we were lost in our own thoughts so much as simply basking in the closeness of each other. At least, that's what I was doing, because I suddenly understood that being close to Kennedy gave me that wonderful, mushy, fluttery feeling in my stomach, and I wanted to hold on to it if I could.

"This wasn't part of the deal, you know," I whispered. "It wasn't expected of you."

"It wasn't expected, period." Kennedy smiled softly at me.

"Sleepy?" I asked her as I watched her eyelids grow heavy.

She nodded. Smiled.

"Me, too." I rolled onto my back and lifted my arm. We didn't have to say anything. Kennedy scooted closer and tucked herself against me, her head on my shoulder, her arm draped across my middle. We agreed without words that it was too soon for sex, though my body was hot and buzzing, and I wouldn't have put up much of a protest if she'd made any kind of moves. I got the impression she was in the same boat, so I squeezed her tightly to me.

"I really wasn't expecting this," she whispered again after a few quiet moments. "When you approached me about it. I mean, I was super attracted to you, but—"

"You were?" I interrupted. That was news.

Kennedy lifted her head and looked me in the eye. Hers were wide—I could tell even in the moonlight. "Oh my God, yes. Have you seen you?"

I felt the heat in my cheeks, the warmth in my gut. "Well." I cleared my throat. "I wasn't expecting it either. And the feeling was mutual."

She continued to study me for a beat before she settled back down on my shoulder. "Huh."

"Yeah."

A gust of wind kicked up outside, and the snow blown at the windows pelted the glass in tiny clicks. Kennedy snuggled in closer. I pressed a kiss to her forehead even as I felt sleep coming for me. "Merry Christmas," I whispered.

It was like the kiss had knocked down barriers or something. The first night at my mom's, Kennedy and I had somehow—consciously or unconsciously—kept an acceptable amount of space between us as we'd slept. We'd woken up safely on our own sides of the bed, far from touching each other.

The second night, though? Not even close.

I woke up in the role of Big Spoon, curled up against Kennedy's back. My nose was in her hair, my arm draped over her side, hers covering mine, my leg between her legs. She was warm and soft and smelled *so* good, and I was pretty sure I didn't have to move for the rest of my life.

It was early, the sky just sliding from deep purple toward pink. The snow had stopped, and I could see the tree in the front yard, bare brown branches topped with clean white snow. Beautiful. I loved winter. I loved fresh snowfall. It was like everything got a new start. Clean and blank. I felt like that, too, my life slightly different this morning than it had been yesterday.

I had lain awake for a little while after Kennedy had fallen asleep the night before and rolled things around in my head. Nothing had been resolved, of course, because there was too damn much going on. This morning, the rolling started right up again, my brain whirring, examining. Because it had been a very long, whirlwind, crazy-ass less-than-forty-eight-hours for me, including making my mother ridiculously happy, outwitting my sister finally, and starting to fall for the woman I was paying to be my girlfriend. Needless to say, there was a lot to think about. *A lot.*

Kennedy's breathing changed and signaled me that she was waking up. I knew the moment she was fully awake and remembering last night because she pushed her ass back into me and tightened her arm over mine. "Morning," she mumbled and squeezed my hand.

"Morning. Sleep okay?" I nuzzled into her hair.

"I did. You?"

A nod. "I actually slept better last night all wrapped up in you than I did the night before."

"Me, too. I think because I wasn't hyperaware of trying not to touch you." Her shoulders moved as she laughed quietly.

"I'm sure." I let a beat or two tick by before I broached the thing I'd been thinking about. "Listen. I know we were going to head out late morning, early afternoon today, but…" I cleared my throat. "How do you feel about sticking around for a few extra hours?"

Kennedy turned in my arms and her just-woke-up face was adorable, all blinky eyes and tousled hair. "Totally fine. I'm on break at work, so I don't have to rush back."

"Great. I want to take you someplace."

"Where?"

"It's a surprise."

"Ooh. A surprise? Can I get a hint?"

"Nope." I kissed the tip of her nose, then got out of bed. "We'll take our time, have coffee, breakfast, shower and dress, then go. Sound good?"

She shrugged and nodded her assent. "You're the boss."

"I like that you realize this." I pulled on leggings and dodged the pillow she tossed at me. We both laughed, and when our eyes met across the room, we just held it. A connection of some sort—a sizzle, a crackle, a zap, whatever you want to call it was definitely there, and again, I thought about how kissing Kennedy had knocked down so many walls that had been erected for safety. Walls I hadn't even realized we'd put up until we kissed, and they crumbled into piles of rubble around us. "Meet you downstairs." She watched me leave from her place in bed, and I felt that familiar flutter in my stomach at *knowing* she was watching me. I shook my head as I headed down the stairs.

How had things changed so quickly?

CHAPTER TEN

Y ou're kidding me." Kennedy's blue eyes were almost childlike in how wide they went. She turned to me from the passenger seat, her face bright. Excited. "You're *kidding* me."

"I'm not. You up for it?"

"For roller skating? Please. I am so in. I mean, I had Rollerblades when I was about ten, and that's the extent of my roller skating experience, but I am *so* in."

We were in the parking lot of All Skate, which had altered its name to All Skate Fun and Games in recent years. Nostalgia washed over me immediately, like a warm blanket being laid on my shoulders.

"You look all…remembery," Kennedy said, smiling at me.

"Remembery?"

"Yeah. Like you're remembering something." She unbuckled her seat belt and turned in her seat so she was facing me. "Tell me?"

Something about those two words. What was it? The tone of them? The openness of Kennedy's face? The curiosity in her eyes? Whatever it was, it wrapped around me, made me feel safe. Which was weird and unexpected and weirdly unexpected.

"This was my hangout as a kid. Bakerton's a small town, and we really didn't know that roller rinks had pretty much gone out with the eighties. My sisters and I used to come here almost every Saturday. We'd hang out all afternoon, stuffing our faces with junk food and whispering in the corner about boys while the boys stood in the other corner and whispered about us." I couldn't help but smile, that innocence flooding back into my brain. "And then Melody became a freshman and didn't want Cat and me hanging near her and embarrassing her around her friends, so it was just the two of us. And then I hit high school and did the same thing to poor Cat."

Kennedy laughed through her nose. "The sibling cycle, right?"

"Exactly." I grabbed my purse. "It's cold out here. Let's go in."

All Skate wasn't busy, but it was busier than I'd expected. It was the day after Christmas, and it seemed some people had been looking for things to do. I pegged the addition of the Fun and Games part right away. The arcade portion had been doubled in size. There were several pool tables, Skee-Ball, and air hockey. It was a little bit old-school and a little bit new age blended nicely into one big hangout. I was impressed.

"It smells the same," I commented.

"Like hot dogs and cotton candy and Teen Spirit?" Kennedy asked.

I burst out laughing. "Exactly like that."

We approached the counter, which was manned by Cody, according to his name tag—and I use the term *manned* loosely because he looked to be about thirteen. As we gave him our sizes, and I paid for the skate rental, I thought about what we were doing there, why I had decided to bring Kennedy to a place that meant so much to me as a teenager. And while an exact explanation wasn't within my grasp at that very moment, the brightness of her face, the sparkle of joy in her blue eyes, made me very happy we'd come.

"After we skate," she said as we sat on a bench to put wheels on our feet, "can we play a couple video games?"

"We don't leave here until we see if they still have *Frogger* in there."

"*Frogger*? How old *are* you?"

I gasped. "How dare you? *Frogger* was my very favorite game ever, and I was good at it."

"We'll see." Kennedy winked at me.

We shoved our things under the bench and gingerly made our way toward the rink's entrance. The music so far had been an interesting mix of pretty much anything with a beat, from the eighties on up to present day, the Go-Go's to Ariana Grande.

"So," I said, holding tightly to the side, "I just remembered that I am, in fact, not sixteen."

"Yeah? Well, good, because I just remembered that I was terrible on my Rollerblades."

We held one another's gaze and burst out laughing.

"Falling's gonna hurt a lot more today than it did back then," I pointed out.

"God, you're so right. We're gonna be giant black-and-blue marks."

I took a deep breath, straightened my posture. "Okay. Like riding a bike." I held my hand out to Kennedy. "Ready?"

"Don't let me fall," she said, and something in the tone of her voice slid in and wrapped itself around my heart.

"I won't let you fall," I said quietly. And I meant it.

It was surprising to me how quickly I picked skating back up again. It really *was* like riding a bike. I was *not* going to fall. We took a slow lap, Kennedy staying close enough to the wall to reach out for balance if she needed to, me staying close to Kennedy. The younger kids kept more toward the center, so that was helpful. I also noticed a few teenagers and, surprisingly, several people who seemed to be our age. It was a very eclectic mix, and my gaze traveled from Kennedy to the other skaters, and back to Kennedy. After the second lap, I was able to turn so I was skating backward and facing her. I held out my hands.

"Come on. Let go of the wall."

"Listen, the wall is keeping me from ending up on my ass."

"*I* will keep you from ending up on your ass."

She looked up at me, eyes a little wider than normal. "Promise?"

"I promise," I said.

The music shifted from a recent song by The Weeknd back to the greatest hits of the eighties. The lights dimmed and Foreigner began singing "I Want to Know What Love Is." Kennedy held tightly to my hands, doing that thing where she bent forward, then stood up, then bent forward again, trying to steady her feet, doing more stepping than skating.

"It's all about rhythm," I said to her. "One foot, then the other— one foot, then the other. Nice and slow, nice and steady."

Kennedy was stepping like she was trying to walk in her skates, and it made me smile. "Stop laughing at me," she said, adding a pout for good measure, but I could tell by that sparkle that still hung out in her eyes she was kidding.

"Listen to me," I said and matched my strides to my voice slowly. "One." Left foot stride. "Two." Right foot stride. "Match me. One. Two."

Kennedy kept her eyes on our feet, and when her tongue peeked out at the corner of her mouth, apparently to help her concentration, I felt my smile widen. I kept counting, and the mellow music definitely helped. By the end of the song, Kennedy had just about matched me and had stopped bending forward. Two songs later, she was able to let go of my hands. Which I had mixed emotions about.

"Did you have a place you hung out when you were in high school?" I asked her when we took a break and got hot dogs and Cokes.

"I was a big theater geek," she said and took a bite of her dog. "Even as a teenager."

"So it's always been your thing."

She nodded, gazed off at the rink, and I studied her face. It seemed to me that every time I looked at her, I found myself more attracted to her. More curious about her. I wanted to know everything. Enlightening. That's what it was. Because I suddenly knew what it meant.

"It has always fascinated me. My aunt took me to see *The Phantom of the Opera* when I was twelve, and that was it for me. I was hooked." She got a dreamy, sort of faraway look on her face, but in a good way. In a way that made it obvious she was talking about something she loved. "I went to theater camp. I was involved in all the plays the school put on. Summer stock. Everything I could be involved in, I was."

"You found your passion so early. That's amazing. Some people don't find it until they're middle-aged. Some don't ever find it."

"It's true." She sipped her Coke. "What about you? Is real estate a passion for you?"

I thought about that, chewed a bite of hot dog. "You know, it really is. Not the business itself, but the people. The clients. Helping people find exactly what they want. My favorite is the first-time homebuyer."

"Yeah? How come?"

I put my forearms on the table and leaned forward. "It's the light in their eyes. The excitement. I love to watch them as they picture themselves in a house I'm showing. I love their faces and their voices when their offer is accepted. And while I didn't really do much more than find and show them something they liked, it's an amazing feeling to be a part of such an important moment in somebody's life." I blinked a few times, realized I'd gotten a little lost in what I called Real Estate Mode. "Sorry about that." I waved a hand, felt myself blush a bit. "I can get a little excited."

"Why would you apologize?" Kennedy asked, then reached across the table and grasped my hand. "I love that you love what you do."

We sat quietly as we finished our lunch. Something hung in the air between us. We both knew it. I could feel it myself, and I was sure I could almost feel Kennedy's awareness. I wanted to think of it like a cloud following us, hanging over us, except it wasn't ominous. It wasn't gloom and doom. It was lighter. Brighter.

It was possibility.

Not something I had expected from these three days. Not in a million years.

"I think it's time for video games." Kennedy grinned at me, and I was grateful for the interruption to my thoughts. "Ready to play *Frogger*?"

"If you're asking if I'm ready to *school* you in *Frogger*, then the answer is absolutely. You'd better gear up."

❖

I swear to God, I could not remember ever having a better time than I did that day with Kennedy. We actually got looks from the kids in the place because we were laughing and joking and screaming at the machines like we were fifteen. When we both noticed a couple of boys looking at us, their voices hushed, Kennedy said, rather loudly, "Hey, you *wish* you were as good at this game as she is." And after a few rounds, when I found my groove and had my frog hopping safely across highways in record time, I even ended up with a few kids standing behind us, watching.

"I feel like I'm in a John Hughes movie," I said to Kennedy, and when she laughed, I added, "Thank God. I was afraid you were going to ask me who John Hughes was."

I got a playful punch in the arm for that one.

When I saw that it was after three, I shot a glance at Kennedy.

"Time to go, huh?" she asked.

"We probably should." I didn't want to. Ever. It sounded silly, but it didn't feel silly to want to stay in an arcade playing old video games with this woman I really wanted to keep in my life.

Yeah. There it was. That was the thing.

I'd been feeling it for a while now, but it was in that moment, that very second, that it whacked me over the head.

We sat in my car in the parking lot of All Skate, heat on full blast, defrosters blowing, but I didn't drive. I sat. Thought. Tried to capture the things spinning through my head like wicker patio furniture in a tornado. I'm not sure exactly how long I sat there silently before Kennedy touched my arm.

"Are you okay?" she asked.

"Would you go out with me?" I blurted.

She blinked in surprise, and her mouth formed a perfect O. A second blink. A third. And then the most amazing thing happened. That

O collapsed, shifted, and was replaced by a very wide take-a-look-at-my-pearly-whites smile. "God, yes," came her response. Quickly, though, she held up a finger. "You mean really, right? Like, a real date? Not a pretend-you're-my-girlfriend-I'll-pay-you one?"

I felt my entire body relax, which was funny since I hadn't realized I was tense. But I must've been because my shoulders dropped, my thighs melted into the driver's seat, and my neck suddenly felt loose and comfortable, rather than made out of a concrete pillar.

"A real date," I said and held her gaze. "I just..." I threw up my hands. "It's so weird, isn't it?" I was assuming she felt the same way, which I knew was a dangerous assumption on my part. I felt my smile dim as I looked at her. "I'm paying you to act like you're into me. I'm paying you..." I wasn't sure how to say what I was trying to say.

Kennedy picked up my hand and sandwiched it in both of hers. "I *am* into you. Job or not. Acting or not. Money or not. *I am very into you.*"

"Yeah?" My relief was so intense, my eyes welled up.

"I have been trying to figure out if it would be a bad idea to ask you on a date. A real date. I was going to wait until this was over, and we were back home." And then her cheeks got pink, and her gaze slid away from mine. "I really like you, Sasha. I didn't expect to." Her grasp tightened, and she hurried to add, "I mean, like that. I didn't expect to like you like that. Is what I meant. Not that I didn't expect to like you at all. Because I do. You're super nice. But I meant..." She blew out a breath and her shoulders dropped. "Yeah, I'm going to stop talking now."

"Why?" I asked, teasing her. "You're adorable when you're flustered."

She gave me a playful shove. "Shut up."

"Hey, I'm not the one babbling away."

We both laughed. Then we both got quiet. We looked at each other.

"Listen," I said, and I waited until she let go of her embarrassment and met my eyes. "I brought you here to..." I searched the car's ceiling for the right thing to say. "It was kind of a test."

Kennedy's light red eyebrows rose. "What kind of a test?"

I nibble on the inside of my cheek when I'm nervous, so at that point, I fully expected to chew a full-blown hole right through it. I toyed with several different explanations but decided it was okay to be completely honest with Kennedy. It's the only thing I wanted with her, no matter what happened in the next five minutes. Complete honesty.

"I wanted to see how we'd be together. Out. Together. Just the two of us with no pressure or roles to play."

She nodded, didn't seem at all put off. In fact, she didn't even seem surprised. She held my gaze for a beat or two before asking, very quietly, "How'd I do?"

That question. That question alone. It warmed me up from the inside. It set my heart to beating faster. It made my stomach flutter. "Flying colors," I told her.

Her smile was big, genuine. "Well, that's a relief."

"Yeah?"

"Yeah."

"I like you, Kennedy," I whispered. "I like you a lot."

"Well, that's a happy coincidence, 'cause I like you, too. A lot." She leaned in until I could see the black that outlined the blue of her eyes, until I could see the tiny mole at the edge of her left eyebrow and the small divot at the top of her nose that got deeper when she was thinking hard. I could smell the coconut of her shampoo and the musk of her body spray.

And then she kissed me. Slowly. Tenderly. It wasn't tentative at all. It was more…familiar. Like we had been kissing for months. Years, maybe.

She kissed me like she knew me.

I kissed her back, leaning in to her—no, pushing myself in to her. I wanted more, so much more of her. I wanted all of her, if I was going to be honest with myself. But I knew it was way too soon for that, that slower steps were the way to go, but my God, I'd never been that drawn to somebody like that in my life. The proverbial moth to flame, magnet to steel. All I knew was that the possibility there, the idea of what could be, what could actually be? Was major. It was surprising and unexpected. And I'd be a fool if I didn't at least try to grab it.

Don't ask me how I knew all that stuff. I just did. It was like I woke up with that knowledge, like somebody had uploaded it to my brain while I slept. It was weird and scary and absolutely true.

When we finally extricated ourselves from each other, the windows of my car were fogged up. I looked around the interior. "Well." I swiped at the driver's side window with my sleeve. "This brings back memories."

Kennedy laughed. "Did a lot of making out in the roller rink parking lot, did you?"

"Hey, you don't know me," I teased.

"Not yet. But I will." Her voice was low and sexy as hell.

"I would really, really like that."

"Good."

We sat quietly again, just looking at each other, and I learned that day that when you're comfortable enough with somebody to hold eye contact like that, when it doesn't feel weird, and you don't have to struggle to not look away, that's a person worth holding on to.

I took a breath, because there was one more thing we needed to discuss, and I wasn't sure how it would go over. I glanced down at my hands, wet my lips. "I think, if we're going to do this, if we're going to try this, there's one more thing we need to take care of."

And she was right there with me. I could see it on her face as she nodded, not needing me to elaborate. "I agree a hundred percent."

"Good."

We buckled our seat belts, and I put the car in gear. We were quiet for the entire drive back to my mom's house, but Kennedy kept her hand on my thigh, and that made everything absolutely right in my world. We pulled into the driveway behind both Cat's and Melody's cars. I inhaled deeply, let it out slowly, butterflies churning in my gut. But when I turned to look at Kennedy, she had a big smile on her face. She patted my thigh.

"Let's do this."

I nodded once, turned the car off, and we headed around to the back door. I could see through the window that they were all in the kitchen: Cat, Melody, my mom sitting with York—er, Nicholas in her lap. She smiled when she met my eyes through the glass, and I scratched at my head, took another big breath.

Kennedy held out her hand. I grasped it. She looked at me, and I have never gained strength from another person the way I did from her in that moment. Without waiting another second, we pushed through the door.

"Well, hello there, you two," my mother said as Nicholas yipped excitedly from her lap. "Did you have fun?"

"We did." I cleared my throat.

"It was awesome. I loved it there. We're definitely going back." This from Kennedy, her enthusiasm perfect in the moment. And super genuine. I realized I could read her facial expressions pretty well, actress or not, and that one was real.

"So," I said as we stood there holding hands, still in our winter garb. "Mom. Cat. Melody." I looked to each of them as I spoke their names. I tugged on the hand in mine, then held it up a bit as I finally said the words. "I'd like you to meet Kennedy Davis. Kennedy, this is my family."

"*I knew it!*" Melody cried.

EPILOGUE

That Christmas will go down in history as the year I hired my own girlfriend…and kept her. It's been almost a year now—we had Thanksgiving at my mom's a week ago and Christmas is just around the corner again—and things have only gotten better. Which seems impossibly perfect, and some of our friends joke about hating us, but it's true. It *is* perfect.

"What do you think?" I ask Kennedy from where I'm sitting on the couch in my apartment. It's almost eleven at night and she has just come home from the last show of the college semester. She dropped her stuff on the floor, kissed me on the lips, went straight into the kitchen to pour herself a glass of Riesling, and now she flops onto the couch next to me. We both stare at the gaping hole in the wall that now leads from my apartment into hers.

She nods, stares, sips, nods some more. "Well, *that* is a hole in the wall." She leans her head onto my shoulder.

"It really is."

We're exhausted. In addition to both our very busy work schedules, we've spent the past month planning the merging of our apartments into one very big one, which will include redesigning the entire layout and building a gorgeous master bedroom and en suite. A perk of being the owner is that you can sledgehammer walls if you want to. I did that today. I took the first swing. Kennedy took the second. Then we turned it over to the professionals and went about our days. When I got home about an hour ago, everything was neat and tidy, the floor swept, all the debris gone. And I could sit on my couch and look right into Kennedy's living room.

"It's pretty cool, actually," she says, her head still on my shoulder.

I love having her this close to me. She's always warm, and she smells amazing, like peaches today.

"Agreed."

"Can we get a tree this weekend?"

I nod. "Absolutely." It's not quite our first Christmas together, but it'll definitely be our first tree together, and that makes me smile.

We sit quietly. We can do that, sit in silence, and it doesn't feel weird, and there's no urge to fill it with words. We're very content to be quiet together. We can sit on the couch at opposite ends, our feet in each other's laps, and just read. Maybe we'll have some instrumental music playing softly in the background. More likely, show tunes. It shocks me how many Broadway soundtracks Kennedy knows every single word to. She'll hum along or sing quietly while she's reading or working or whatever, and I'm so at peace then. So content. Being content is a new thing for me but feels completely normal when I'm with her, like it was always supposed to be this way.

"Mel called today." Kennedy lifts her head, sips her wine. Her blue eyes are sparkling when she turns them to me, and her dimples make an appearance. "She says she's got some new trivia game online that she wants to play over Christmas."

"You'd better brush up," I say, and Kennedy makes a snorting sound that's equal to a dismissive *please.*

My sister and Kennedy have become BFFs, which was really weird for a while but something I got used to, and now, I find it endearing. Apparently, it just took me finding somebody awesome to temper my sister. She's still competitive as hell, though, as evidenced by the fact that she wants to play trivia when we're all home. I'm very good at trivia, but Kennedy is *amazing.* I don't know where in her brain she's made room to keep all the useless information she knows, but she knows a lot. This oughta be interesting.

"Your mom also texted me."

That's when I laugh because my girlfriend has more contact with my family than I do. And I'm totally okay with it.

"She said Nicholas passed his training class with flying colors." She pulls out her phone and scrolls, then shows me a photo of my mother, looking ridiculously proud of the Yorkie in her arms.

"Oh my God, he's wearing a little graduation cap."

"Right? She went on and on about all the tricks he can do. She can't wait to show us."

Leaving Nicholas with my mother was one of the best decisions we've ever made. It tugged at Kennedy's heart a little bit, but it was her idea. Between the two of us, our schedules are kind of nuts, but it wasn't even that. It was seeing how happy that little terrier made my mom and how happy he seemed to be when he was around her. It didn't matter that he'd chewed up two shoes, four mittens, one Christmas ornament, and a decorative pine cone while we were there—all things my mother tried to hide from us. What mattered was that he adored my mom, and my mom adored him. And I felt better that she wasn't alone in that big house.

"Honestly, it's like we gave her a grandchild." We both laugh and then get quiet.

"Maybe one day, we'll give her a human one," Kennedy says.

"I think we will."

Yep. I'm gonna have babies with this woman. I'm going to marry her, and I'm going to become a parent with her, and she's going to grow old with me. And it only took a month or two before we both knew it.

She rests her head back on my shoulder. "I love you," she says, and it's one of the things I love most about her—she's not afraid to say it. After the first time we each said those three words, it was like a dam opened up, and now she says it all the time. Every day. Several times a day. Often for no reason. Sometimes, she'll just randomly say she loves me, and it catches me off guard. I get all, *Why? Why are you saying that right now? What happened?* Kennedy just shakes her head at me. *Just because* is her standard response.

It's a good answer. I'm getting used to it.

A few beats pass, and Kennedy points at a package next to the door. "What's that?"

"Our Christmas Eve wardrobe," I say.

She lifts her head. "The dogs ones?" And she's up and rifling through the box and pulls out one set of pajamas. They're flannel, bottoms and a button-down top, red with various breeds of dogs printed all over them, every pooch wearing a Santa hat.

Yes, my girlfriend and I are going to dress in matching pajamas on Christmas Eve. I'm that girl now. I grin because I can't help it. And because I love it.

"These are so cute." And she grasps the shirt in her fists and buries her face in it like a kid. "I can't wait to put 'em on and cuddle up and watch *A Christmas Story* with your sisters." She picks up the box. "I'll wash them first, so they're soft and smell nice." She stops, holds out a hand to me. "Coming to bed?"

I nod, push myself to a standing position, and take her hand, then let her lead me to the bedroom.

And as I have every single night since last Christmas, I thank the Universe for making me accept the best triple dog dare *ever*.

Hustle & Bustle

Maggie Cummings

CHAPTER ONE

"D eeper. You need to go deeper."

"You think?"

Hannah Monroe tilted her phone to reexamine the image. Picture and angle aside, she was proud of her efforts. The display was on point, if she did say so herself. Sixty square feet wasn't much to work with, but she'd maximized every inch. Little white lights framed the edges of the product display tables. Twinkling holly garlands bordered the booth and hung from the ceiling. Even if it was corny, the presentation filled her with holiday spirit and pride. The booth showcasing Gaia's Glow was going to look amazing when the sun set.

"The lights are a nice touch." Priya Sundjaren, her best friend and business partner, stood next to her and nodded approval.

"Thank you." Hannah tilted her head to the side. Something wasn't right. She stepped forward and pulled a short, stout decorative Nutcracker in front of a grand princely one in the back. "Ah, much better."

Priya waved her hand in a circle. "Did you bring all of your decorations from home?"

"Not quite," she said, but she'd hardly skimped either.

Even though it was still early November, Hannah had gone full boat with the holiday decor. Christmas came around once a year, and as far as the Central Park Holiday Market was concerned, that season started on the heels of Halloween. Some folks found that off-putting, but Hannah played right into the logic, dressing her pop-up shop to the hilt. Gaia's Glow was her baby, and like any proud parent she wanted her pride and joy to shine.

"I just think we need to take advantage of this opportunity. Really try to draw people in, you know?"

She'd posed the question sort of rhetorically, but Hannah believed in her own rationale. With no real store to speak of, their natural skincare company survived through online sales and the investment of a few small retailers they'd been able to seduce along the way. This tiny booth in New York City's open-air holiday market was the closest Gaia's Glow had ever come to having a storefront, and Hannah wasn't about to let the opportunity slip by.

To that end she adorned it with pine boughs and greenery all around. She'd even crafted custom sachets full of product samples and tied them with berry-festooned ribbons. For the perfect finishing note, she'd adorned the booth with various nutcrackers of all sizes from her personal collection. There was no tie-in, just a nod to her favorite ballet and a touch of home to make her feel comfortable.

"It looks fantastic." Her uber-pragmatic business partner leaned over her shoulder to examine the photo again. "But you were too close for the picture. Back up and try again."

"I thought I was in charge of setup and social media," Hannah teased.

"Partnership through and through." Priya waved her backward. "The same way you hung around the lab until we found the right aroma profile for the new moisturizing line. I'm here to do my part to ensure our presence at this holiday market is leveraged to the fullest." Priya adjusted her headscarf. "That includes having an opinion on our Instagram presence."

"So bossy." Hannah stuck out her tongue just to make sure her BFF knew she was kidding.

"There. That should be far enough," Priya said, moving out of the frame.

Hannah assessed the image before taking the picture. One more step would really be better.

"Ow!" she said, as she bumped right into something behind her.

"Oh my gosh, are you okay?"

It was a person. A cop, to be precise. The impact was so solid Hannah hadn't expected it to come from another human.

Hannah could feel herself stumbling as she tried to find her footing, and she was keenly aware of the cop's strong grip keeping her from completely wiping out. She fixed her gaze on the silver shield and nameplate at her eye level and grounded herself as she focused on the uniformity of the letters in Officer Beckett's name.

"Hey. Are you all right?" The officer was still holding her arm, and it took her a minute, but Hannah finally snapped out of her daze.

"I'm okay." She was more embarrassed than anything but shook it off with a smile. "Sorry about that."

"I thought we were both going to bite it there for a second," the cop said with a laugh.

"It was my fault," Hannah admitted. "I wasn't paying attention to what I was doing."

"No worries." The officer patted her arm. "You sure you're good?"

"Yes." Hannah blinked slowly using the extra second to find her composure. "I'm fine. Are you?"

"Good as gold," she said with a radiant smile. The cop was tall and female, which threw Hannah even though she knew the thought was ridiculously closed-minded. Hannah forgave her instinctual bias on the spot, blaming the sturdiness of the officer's stature. Quite frankly it had felt like she'd backed into a brick wall. But in contrast to her formidable build, the officer's voice was soft and even, and her eyes had a kindness to them that was almost enchanting. "Do you want me to take a picture of you and your friend?" She nodded toward Priya, standing in front of their storefront.

"No. Um, no," Hannah stammered out. "I just need a shot of the booth. Thank you anyway," she said, finding her manners.

"Okay. If you change your mind, feel free to grab one of us. I'm Officer Beckett," she said pointing to her own chest. "But you can snag any one of us if you need something." She ticked her head toward a gaggle of officers close by. "We're here to help any way we can."

"Sure," Hannah said with a wave as she backed the few steps to her booth, very nearly knocking into Priya setting out some giveaways.

"An officer of the law?" Priya's nod said she was surprised but supportive. "Not what I expected. But I have to say, I'm into it."

"Shut up."

"Mm, I don't know," she crooned. "You looked awfully good together. The way you almost fell on your butt, and she caught you with ease and steadied you as you gazed in each other's eyes. You had that beauty and brawn thing going on." Priya nodded at her romanticized description. "I dig it."

Hannah laughed outright. It cracked her up that her bestie was always trying to marry her off. Whether it was a newly single worker in their small factory or their divorced local honey supplier, no one was off-limits, and Hannah imagined Priya would have her coupled up with a myriad of other vendors and patrons over the next eight weeks.

"You have an overactive imagination," she said, just to keep her friend in check.

"And you, my dear friend, have an underserved libido. It's the holidays. Live. It. Up."

"I love that your advice is always so carpe diem, when you got married at the ripe old age of twenty-five."

"I can't help that I found the love of my life in college. I wasn't expecting it either, but I seized that moment because I was not about to let Dev slip away. Nuh-uh. Sue me for wanting the same kind of happiness for you." Priya whacked her with a product brochure. "Anyway, let me see how the picture came out."

Dammit. The picture. In the chaos of her near spill and the aftermath, she'd forgotten to take the picture. Hannah winced, mortified that she had to admit it.

"I…um…about that," she said with a finger raised high in the air. "It seems I may have actually neglected to take the picture."

"Hannah!" But Priya wasn't mad. On the contrary, Hannah recognized signature excitement in her voice, her eyes growing wider by the second. "I knew it."

"Relax, Priya. It's not what you're thinking."

"If you say so." Priya stared at the circle of officers crowding the novelty doughnut booth across the way. "She's looking over here," she said.

Hannah resisted turning around. "Who?"

"Don't you *who* me. Your future wife, that's who."

Hannah rolled her eyes, but she couldn't keep the smile from emerging. "You're ridiculous—you know that, right?"

"Protest all you want, but I'm not the one who practically forgot my name after locking eyes with a sexy cop."

"Gross."

"What's gross?" Priya's tone called her right onto the carpet. "Is it her strapping physique or her sweet smile that turns you off?" She held a finger up, even though Hannah hadn't even tried to interrupt. "Wait. Wait. I know." Priya nodded in agreement with herself. "It was her chivalry." Priya's eyes widened as if to underscore her disapproval. "I, for one, would not have minded a pic together. For the record." Her shrug was playful, and Hannah couldn't help but laugh.

"Her smile is lovely," she said almost under her breath as she recalled Officer Beckett's face. She was attractive in an unusual way. Square jawed with full lips and short hair hidden under the police hat. She had a smooth complexion, and her eyes were a soft, dark brown. Rich and expressive, even at a glance. What was she doing? A cute cop was still a cop and, ugh, no thanks. "How come the entire NYPD has to congregate right across from our space?" she said, switching gears.

"Well, Hannah"—Priya surveyed the corridor of booths that made up their section of the market—"I'm going to go with the obvious. The cops are interested in that fancy doughnut stand and the custom coffee booth right next to it." She straightened a row of age defying serum so that the boxes lined up perfectly. "The cute girls in Santa hats flirting with them are probably just an added perk."

"Exactly my point."

"Which is?"

"They're barely here to protect and serve. More like hook up and party with the vendors. Most of whom are from out of town, all of whom are here for business."

"You couldn't sound more uptight if you tried." Priya dropped a look on her. "You should get over there and get in on the action."

"Excuse me?"

"It's the first day of the market. There's no one interested in buying yet. Probably because it's all locals, and it's too early in the season for them to commit." Priya braced her shoulders in support. "You're not interested in the cop? Fine, have it your way. Talk to the doughnut vendors. Maybe you'll find a love connection there."

"What if I'm not looking for a love connection?"

"I refuse to entertain such malarkey," Priya said with an exaggerated sigh. "But if that's the line you're going with, it wouldn't kill you to make friends. At least some folks to maybe grab a drink with after work when I'm back in Queens making nice with my relatives."

"I hate that you can't stay at my dad's with me." Hannah pouted.

"I suppose I could. But my aunt and uncle would be so offended. It's not worth hurting their feelings."

Hannah tipped her head back in exasperation. She had no idea how she was going to entertain herself night after night in the city. "I know our participation here will be good for the company." At least that was the gamble on this venture. "But the price may be my sanity."

"Which is precisely why you should offset work with some fun extracurriculars." Priya licked her lips and added an over the top wink.

"And your top contender for me is a cop? Get real." Hannah stared at Priya's belly. "I think pregnancy is messing with your brain. It's like you don't even know me."

"Your hang-ups will leave you a spinster. I think this could be the perfect holiday romance. The city cop, the country girl." Priya hugged herself and spun in a small contained circle. "Think of the possibilities."

"First of all, I'm not from the country. I was born in Manhattan, in case you forgot, and the town of Hudson is hardly rural." Hannah stole a glance across the way in spite of her objections. "Secondly, you read too many romance novels."

"Pshh. I read too many medical and chemistry texts. Not enough romance novels."

"Well, if you think I'm going to settle down with a cop, you've lost your mind."

"Who said anything about settling down? I swear, Hannah, you're your own worst enemy sometimes."

Hannah made a big show of looking around so her BFF would know she was lost. "So you didn't just suggest I find love with one of New York's Finest?"

"I was merely suggesting you make nice with a rather attractive police officer. Where it goes, it goes." Hannah shook her head to signify utter disbelief at the suggestion, but Priya was still talking. "Just think of it. A Christmas rendezvous characterized by holiday windows, hot chocolate, and mistletoe. Long winter walks with carols playing in the background."

"Let me get this straight," Hannah said with a laugh. "You want me to have the montage section of a Hallmark holiday movie?"

"Yes!" Priya was all excitement as she grabbed her hands. "That is exactly what I want."

Hannah was a sucker for how much her bestie always championed romance. But then, she imagined it was easy when you'd already found your person. For a fraction of a second she let Priya's enthusiasm rub off on her because, honestly, it didn't sound terrible, and the cop was adorable. But when she cast another look back at the doughnut stand, the police officers had already dispersed.

"I hate all that stuff anyway."

"You hate Christmas and romance?" Priya was aptly horrified. "Since when?"

"Not Christmas," Hannah corrected. "I love Christmas. But the crowds and the city." She shuddered just thinking about the weeks ahead. "So not my thing. Especially this time of year. It's all mayhem."

"Where's your sense of adventure? The spirit of the season?"

"I do love your energy, Priya." She rubbed her friend's forearm, knowing that in spite of her outlandish proposal, Priya's heart was in the right place. "Anyway, I'm content focusing on growing our exposure and making mad cash." She crossed her fingers in anticipation.

"Doesn't mean you can't have fun." Priya smiled. "Single lady and all…"

"Eternally, it seems."

"Only yourself to blame for that."

"I'm actually not assigning blame at all," she said as she made slight eye contact with a patron perusing the wares of a crystal harvester set up diagonally from them. "I don't even think it's a bad thing," she added. Even though it was the truth, she did get lonely sometimes. And while she'd outwardly pooh-poohed Priya's idea of a fling, she'd be lying if she didn't admit allowing herself some fantasizing in anticipation of her time in the city. She was only human.

Hannah could see it now: a nice meet-cute with a gorgeous, arty millennial. Perhaps they'd converge over the latest provocative MOMA exhibit, which would naturally lead to talking politics and culture over espresso, subtly touching and laughing as they discussed their favorite guilty pleasure movies and books. Subway travel would find them tossing spare change and small bills into the hat of a street musician mellowing out "Auld Lang Syne" on the sax. They'd hold hands on the sidewalk and kiss under the shadow of a red and green illuminated Empire State Building.

Okay, so maybe she'd thought about it a little.

"I can see the wheels turning. You're considering it. Maybe not the cop, but something."

She almost hated how well Priya could read her. Through the years they'd endured highs and lows, seen each other through girlfriends and boyfriends, family drama and heartache, tackled the trials and challenges of starting and maintaining a business together. There wasn't anyone in the world who knew her better, and she was about to say exactly that, but she was distracted by the sight of two cops escorting someone down the aisle in handcuffs. They were just steps from her booth, and Hannah could tell it was the officer from before. The one with the nice eyes. Beckett.

"Nice and easy." Officer Beckett's calm, even voice preceded her. "We're just going to walk straight toward the exit," she instructed.

But the person didn't listen. In fact, he did the exact opposite and tried to make a run for it.

Both officers caught up easily, but not before they all bumped into Gaia's main display table, knocking the exfoliating masks clear onto the makeshift wooden floor.

"Sorry." Officer Beckett's whole expression echoed the apology, and it almost seemed she wanted to say more, but she turned back to her charge and guided him back on course.

"See," Hannah said as she bent down to pick up the scattered products. She pointed at a parade of officers holding traffic so they could cross the street. "That is exactly why I've no interest in dating a brute cop."

"Oh, please. You don't even know what happened. For all we know, that guy is a homicidal maniac."

"Sure, Priya. I bet all the murderers come hide out at a sparsely attended holiday fair on the first day it's open. Yeah, right."

"You're right. It was probably a shoplifter." Priya tossed a coy smile. "You should probably thank Officer Hotness personally when she returns. You know, for protecting our business and for keeping the market from being vulnerable."

"Or I could charge her." Hannah held up a crushed box of organic eye cream. "This is toast. Ooh, maybe I can even use the opportunity to educate her on racial profiling," she said with an arched brow. "I'm sure you saw the kid they carted off was a person of color. All the officers—white as snow."

"Hard not to notice." Priya seemed contemplative for a second. "Believe me, as a brown-skinned person, that dichotomy is not lost on me. Dev and I talk about these issues all the time." Priya took the dented eye revitalizer and tried to salvage it. "And here's an opportunity to go right to the source. I say use it."

"What does that even mean?" Hannah asked.

"It means…" Priya spoke with a devilish lilt in her tone as she smoothed the box against her palm. "We don't know what went down." Her eyes glinted in challenge. "But you, dearie-pie, have a direct line to the inside. Find that woman in uniform. Get the facts. Use the occasion to educate and enlighten. And, in the name of all that is good and mighty, find some time to flirt while you're at it. Because there is nothing sexier than a woman advocating for a just cause."

"You are incorrigible." Hannah folded her arms and shook her head at Priya's twisted fantasy, even though it sounded pretty good.

"Hannah, it's the holidays. You're in the best city in the world. At the greatest time of the year. All I'm suggesting is that you open your mind to the possibility of having just a teensy bit of fun." Priya cradled her stomach dramatically. "If not for me, do it for the baby."

Hannah laughed at her dramatic flair. "I'm making no promises." She was still out on the idea of befriending a police officer, but there was a whole marketplace full of prospects and a city bubbling with potential beyond those borders. Priya had a point. "It's possible I could be open to the idea of…something." She batted her eyes for effect. "We shall see."

"Sheesh. Was that so hard?"

Chapter Two

S arge." Toby Beckett raced to catch up to the sergeant en route to the afternoon muster. "Hey, Sarge," she called out again.

"What is it, Beckett? I'd rather not be late for my own roll call."

"I know. Me either." Toby was winded from booking it the entire block from the precinct. "I just wanted to let you know I ended up vacating that arrest from this morning." She knew Sergeant Ng didn't share her sympathy for teens on the precipice, but from a stats perspective the boss needed to know the outcome of every collar, and Toby owed it to her old friend to deliver the news firsthand. "Obviously Lieutenant Rodgers did the actual void out. But you know what I mean."

"Saint Toby strikes again," Sgt. Ng said with a shift of her shoulders. "What sob story did Jerrell lay on you this time, might I ask?" She checked her watch. "Or do I even want to know?"

"He's a punk. Not a criminal mastermind."

"Well, I'd like to remind you that the New York City Police Department is not a catch-and-release program."

"He lifted one wallet from the display. One." Toby put up a single finger to support her decision. The reality was Aaron Jerrell was a kid with a good heart but not a lot of means. The universe had dealt him a tough hand, and lately he'd been struggling with temptation. That much she knew from patrolling this neighborhood. She also knew the system was unbalanced, and a single arrest could damage a person's entire future. Jerrell just needed to find his path. He definitely didn't need the repercussions of a petit larceny arrest following him around for the rest of his life. "If it's any consolation, the vendor was even waffling over pressing charges," she said. "I honestly think showing some discretion will have a more substantial impact."

"I know you do."

Toby simply didn't see the point of gambling with Jerrell's future over a shoplifting charge. Whatever his motives for the theft, one mistake shouldn't hold that amount of sway. But she knew Ng wasn't going to entertain her thoughts on the failures of the criminal justice system. At least not right now, anyway.

"Come on, Monica." Sgt. Ng stopped in her tracks and her glare told Toby to get in line. "I'm sorry, *Sarge*," Toby said, remembering the perks of rank. "Where's your heart?" she asked, taking an entirely different tack. "It's the holidays."

"Look, Toby." Ng folded her arms across her chest. "I'm thrilled to have you on the team for this assignment. Honestly." Toby loved working the Christmas market and she'd volunteered immediately once word filtered out the detail was short staffed. "It helps that you know the neighborhood, and the guys look up to you," Ng said.

"They look up to you too, Mon—" Toby caught herself this time. "Sergeant. Give them time. It's day one."

"Exactly." Ng's eyes showed her anxiety. "And you're out here setting the neighborhood riffraff free."

She didn't agree with Ng's take but opted for the path of least resistance. "I get what you're saying."

"I don't think you do. I know the squad will look to me to make decisions, tough calls, all that. But out here, in the street, they watch you. And they will absolutely follow your lead. I need you to be someone in the field I can rely on."

"Yes, Boss."

"I mean it. You can't help everyone."

"You do hear how ridiculous that sounds, right?" Toby knew she was pushing it, but she could hold her tongue for only so long. "Monica," she said, dropping the formality to appeal to her boss's humanity. "We're cops. It's literally our job to help people."

"You know what I mean." Ng's voice softened but she still looked hella stressed. "Just don't bail on me out here. I need to know I can count on you."

"Ten-four, Sarge." Toby made sure her expression stayed serious for the moment. She understood their mission was to keep the marketplace safe for the vendors and patrons, and she would do her part to achieve that goal. But she also wanted Ng to lighten up and enjoy the season. She smiled big and lobbed a fake jab at the sergeant's uniform chevrons before she started backpedaling toward the rendezvous location. "Come on, slowpoke, let's get to roll call."

Toby was stoked that the open space next to the doughnut booth had become the location of the daily muster. She didn't care about the doughnuts really, but the coffee booth next to it had an incredible selection. Plus the location was directly across from the pretty vendor she'd met earlier in the day.

She still owed the woman a real apology for careening right into her booth during Jerrell's arrest. She hoped nothing had been damaged.

Toby tried to remember the details while paying attention to the global terrorism update. Ng gave out tour assignments, and she was only slightly dismayed that for the remainder of the shift she was stationed on the exterior of the market at the opposite end of the horseshoe.

"You know the drill." Ng sounded like she was wrapping up. "Keep an eye out for unattended bags, backpacks, totes. Be vigilant. Like we tell everyone else, if you see something, say something. Stay sharp. One more thing," Ng said. "Remember, it's the holidays. We want the retailers and shoppers to feel safe and to know that we're here to ensure a good experience for everyone. That means communicate, collaborate, get to know the vendors, assist the tourists. Be a community." Ng looked right at her, and even though it was a little on the nose, Toby responded with a righteous nod of support at her sentiment.

Donning her uniform hat, she checked her gear as she hoofed it over to settle into position on the other end of the market. This was going to be fun.

❖

"You probably don't remember me, but we met on the first day."

Toby's opener had sounded much smoother when she'd practiced it in her head, but with four days to rehearse, the greeting came out as flat as overworked dough.

"I remember you. Beckett," the woman said matter-of-factly. She barely looked up from the display she was rearranging. "Can I help you with something? Are you in the market for skincare products?"

"No. Not at all." Why was she so nervous? It was her job to talk to people. She reminded herself to stay on task. "I actually just came by to apologize."

Her overture got some attention, and the woman looked up with a question in her eyes. Make that her fucking amazing eyes. They were a mix of brown and green with a hint of amber near the pupils, and Toby stared deep into them, transfixed by the sheer beauty.

"Apologize for what?"

"Oh, right," she said, finding her voice. "The other day. I made an arrest, and the kid tried to hightail it." For a split second she wondered how Jerrell was faring. She hadn't seen him since the incident and hoped that was a good sign. "Anyway, I think we crashed right into your stuff. I just wanted to say I'm sorry for any damage we might have caused."

"It's fine. Water under the bridge," she said with a terse smile.

"I wanted to come by sooner, but I had a few days off and then I was in court," Toby said, hoping her amends might still be accepted despite the lateness.

"What happened with the perp? Isn't that the terminology?" she asked as she tidied the area around the register.

"I guess." Toby laughed in earnest. "Although Aaron Jerrell is more of a bored teen than a perpetrator in my opinion."

"But you took him to court anyway?"

"No. I was in court on a previous arrest. Sometimes the system can take forever." Toby didn't know where to take the conversation, but she wanted to steer clear of the details of Jerrell's release. The vendors needed to feel safe in the space and confident that their businesses were being protected. She looked around for a distraction and picked up a bar wrapped in thick paper labeled *Charcoal Loaf*. Instinctively she turned it over to see the price. "Holy crap," she said, before she could filter.

"Our products are all natural and made with locally sourced ingredients. They are gentle on the skin but very effective. Being toxin-free does drive up the price, I'm afraid." She seemed a touch defensive. "We do have coupons, though." She reached under a makeshift counter.

"That's not necessary," Toby said. "I was just intrigued by the label. Charcoal?"

"It's soap. Charcoal is good for oily skin. Acne especially. It also reduces pore size and provides a host of other benefits." She scrunched her nose a bit. "It would be wasted on you. Your skin is perfect."

Toby felt her pulse race at the compliment even though this was probably just part of a well-practiced sales pitch.

"I could show you some other stuff, though, if you're interested."

Toby was interested in staying and talking to the lovely proprietor. The beauty products she could take or leave.

"I should probably get back to work," Toby said, channeling professionalism. On cue, her portable radio crackled with activity.

"Duty calls," she said, even though the message was just a general transmission of sector activity that required no response whatsoever. But Sgt. Ng would be making her rounds soon, and she was way off post. She took off her hat and tried to fix the hat head that was surely on display. "Anyway, it was nice to meet you…"

"Thank you," the woman blurted out instead of inserting her name. "I didn't thank you."

"For?"

"Sorry." She looked just the slightest bit flustered as she continued, "For catching me the other day." She fingered her long brown curls, and Toby wondered if they were as soft and silky as they looked. "When I bumped into you, I would have fallen if you hadn't saved me."

"Yeah, no problem." Toby could feel herself blushing. She blocked it out. "I'm Toby," she said.

"Well hello, Toby." The voice came from behind her, and it honestly almost made her jump. Not a good first impression for a cop. "I'm Priya, Hannah's partner. Her *business* partner," she said with added emphasis.

"Hi." Toby spun around so fast she almost knocked over another display. "Whoa," she said as she kept a bottle of serum from spilling. "I'm a liability to your shop," she said, hoping it played as comical and not annoying.

"Nonsense." Priya touched her shoulder delicately. "You are welcome here anytime. Isn't that right, Hannah?"

Hannah seemed to shake her head and roll her eyes at her colleague, but a warm smile came out just the same.

"You're not leaving, are you?" Priya asked.

"I should get back to work."

"Did Hannah give you any free samples at least?" Without waiting for an answer, she started loading up a small paper bag with tiny bottles and tubes. "Here's a cleanser. This is for your T-zone," she said, describing the product. Priya assessed her quickly. "Fair to light. Excellent skin, no lines. Eh, I'll throw in the youth concentrate anyway."

"Hold on." Toby put up both hands. "I can't take this stuff."

"You can. It's fine," Hannah said. Her voice was kind and lyrical. It seemed like giving away her merchandise made her happy, and Toby hated to kill the vibe.

"No, no. I couldn't."

Both vendors looked dumbfounded, and Toby knew she needed

to explain. "I appreciate your generosity. Honest. You're both so nice to offer me stuff, even if I have no idea how to use...a coconut clay detoxifying mask," she said as she examined a small square package.

"Hannah could show you." Priya's tone left zero room as to her implication, and even though she was flattered, and maybe interested, Toby had no idea how to respond.

"It's actually pretty self-explanatory." Hannah let her off the hook. She seemed both amused and somewhat mortified at Priya's overt attempts at matchmaking, and her cheeks flashed with a hint of pink. It was divine.

"Either way. If I take that stuff, it wouldn't look right," Toby said. "Not to mention the department has strict policy about accepting gifts."

"Of course. We totally understand." Priya rested her hand on her forearm, and Toby couldn't help but wish it was Hannah touching her.

"I should get back to my post." She didn't really want to leave, but the last thing she needed was to overstay her welcome. She put her hat back on and looked at Hannah from under the brim. Toby didn't know what she expected, and on the surface the exchange was fine. Normal, even. But when their eyes locked, something physiological and primal occurred. Under the fabric of her navy blue uniform shirt, beneath the thin impermeable shield of the ballistic vest, her heart pounded like crazy.

CHAPTER THREE

Toby hid behind a sixteen-ounce gourmet coffee, pacing back and forth as she waited for the morning roll call to start. She was easily fifteen minutes early, which, truthfully, was her norm, but inside she knew she had an ulterior motive. It had been three full days since she visited Hannah's stand, and even though she'd spent at least a few minutes catching up with the vendors she remembered from years past and getting to know the market newbies, she'd yet to manage anything more than a wave when she passed by Gaia's Glow.

It was all nerves.

Which made absolutely no sense. Not that Toby didn't get the jitters when she talked to someone she was interested in, but there was no way she was going to pursue anything with a woman who was literally here for a few weeks.

She knew it happened. Every year, she heard the stories of her colleagues hitting it off with one shopkeeper or another. There'd be flirting during the market hours followed by evening adventures into a city dripping with Christmas spirit. The hookups reminiscent of the whirlwind romances that were celebrated in every romantic holiday movie.

It didn't sound terrible, to be honest. The problem was longevity. Where others might be fine with fleeting passion, Toby wasn't built that way. She didn't do anything halfway. When she let herself go, she fell hard and fast. And she'd rather not willingly set herself up in a match that would inevitably dissolve at the apex of the holidays. Who needed that kind of heartbreak at Christmas?

Yet despite her own conventional wisdom, she thought about Hannah. More than she should. She replayed their two brief exchanges over and over in her head and pictured Hannah's alluring eyes without even trying. Only when Toby fantasized, her mind went beyond their small marketplace interaction. In her daydreams, she and Hannah were walking along the city streets together, holding hands as they strolled the high-end windows decked out for Christmas, cuddling on Fifth Avenue as they braced against the biting cold watching Saks's holiday light show on loop. They skated by the tree, then kissed in front of the seventy-foot Norway spruce adorned with thousands of colorful lights in the epicenter of the world, in the virtual beating heart of Christmas.

Jesus H. Christ, she needed to get a grip. Toby hadn't even found the courage to stop by and chat this week, yet she was envisioning their Christmas courtship.

"Okay, folks, listen up." Sgt. Ng called the group of officers to attention and not a moment too soon. Another minute and she'd really be off in la-la land. Head in the game, focus on the job, she reminded herself. She hooked her thumbs on her duty rig and listened to the details and assignments, very nearly doing a fist pump when she scored the foot post across from Hannah's booth.

The view was perfect.

She gave Hannah and Priya a chin nod of a greeting as she set herself up on post. She went through her standard routine of assessing her surroundings and doing a visual inventory of bystanders, tourists, and locals. One set of directions to the crosstown shuttle later, and she was ready to roll.

Toby drummed up a couple of different greetings in the short walk over to Gaia's Glow, but just as she got there, a customer arrived and stole Hannah to ask a thousand questions about vegan body butter. She was about to retreat, but Priya stopped her.

"Officer Toby, you're finally stationed near us," she said.

"Yes, I am." Toby crossed her arms and looked down the corridor of booths. "How's business so far?"

"So far, so good," Priya said with enthusiasm. "And it's not even peak season. I imagine it's much more crowded once December arrives."

It seemed to be a question, and Toby used all her might to resist focusing on Hannah as she relayed details of the rush of tourists and locals who would descend on the city between Thanksgiving and Christmas.

"It's kind of madness, but the good kind," she said, hoping she wasn't overselling it.

"Sounds hectic," Hannah said, joining the conversation. "Hi, Toby."

Hannah remembered her name. Toby felt her spirit soar ridiculously at the detail. "After all that, no sale?" she asked, attempting to play it cool as she watched the customer drift empty-handed toward a candlemaker a few kiosks away.

"Win some, lose some I suppose." Hannah shrugged amiably. "What about you? No arrests today?"

"Mostly just giving out directions," she said with a smile.

Priya looked between them. "Hannah, if you're okay here, I'm going to grab some food. Me and the peanut need to eat."

"I'm good, Priya. Take your time."

"Do either of you want anything? Snacks, drinks?"

"No, thank you," Toby said. She was appreciative of the offer but even more grateful for the one-on-one time with Hannah. Not that she needed to be alone, but it felt easier to be herself without an audience. "What did she mean by *the peanut*?" Toby asked as Priya strode down the market corridor.

"Priya's pregnant. She refuses to use gender-specific pronouns, so she usually just refers to the baby as the peanut or the munchkin. Occasionally the alien, but that's only when she's not feeling well."

"I didn't even notice," Toby said honestly. "And she's holding off on finding out the sex? Interesting." In today's instant gratification world, it seemed everyone wanted all the information immediately.

"Actually I think they might know the assigned gender by now." Hannah seemed to be mulling the possibility in her head or maybe she was doing gestational math, it was hard to tell. "Priya's husband is trans," she said. "I think it's more of a conscious choice to be non-gender specific."

"Oh. That's cool."

"It is. They're a great couple. Dev handles a lot of the business for Gaia's. In fact, he's holding down the fort in Hudson so we can be here."

"Nice. That must take some of the pressure off. Do you have a store up there?" Toby had done a few minutes of research on her phone, but the website was vague on that particular detail, and she couldn't contain her curiosity.

"We don't have a store per se." Hannah bobbled her head side to side like there was more to that story. "We have a small factory where we create and manufacture our products. We run our business from that location."

Toby had about a million questions as to how it all worked, but she forced herself to remember this was their first real conversation. She didn't want to be overwhelming or off-putting. She tried to keep it simple. "Do you live up that way, as well?" So much for being cool.

"Yes." Hannah nodded and smiled. "My apartment is right on Warren Street. Are you familiar with Hudson?"

"Eh, not really." The truth was Toby was mildly familiar with the area because it was home to Wayfinder, a pretrial intervention program she'd researched to the hilt. She was always on the lookout for alternative solutions to formal processing, and Wayfinder stood out for its high success rate working with at-risk youth. But the last thing she wanted to do was to bore Hannah with a lecture on social justice reform. Instead she racked her brain to come up with other tidbits she knew of Hudson, New York. "It's like an artist's community. Is that right?"

"Not exactly, but kind of." Hannah smiled at her contradictory explanation. "There are a fair amount of galleries and antique stores. But it's more than that. It's kind of a whole vibe. A bit hipster, but easygoing. Chill. The architecture is lovely."

"Sounds amazing." Toby made a mental note to do a deeper dive, just so she could see what generated the wistful look in Hannah's gorgeous eyes. "Are you commuting back and forth daily?" Toby asked, wondering what the travel time on that journey was.

"No. Thank goodness." She covered her chest with one hand. "That would kill me," Hannah said with a laugh. "It's a two-hour train ride. Each way." Hannah widened her eyes in horror. "I'm staying at my dad's apartment here in the city."

"Oh, that works." Toby kept one eye on some touristy shoppers across the way just to keep from staring. "Did you grow up in the city?"

"We lived in Manhattan until I was four," she said. "But my mom moved up to Hudson when she got divorced. So I've lived up there basically my whole life."

"If your expression is anything to go by, it seems you love it."

"I do." Her smile was nostalgic. It was sweet. "I'm sort of missing it while I'm here."

"I'm sure." Toby couldn't imagine being away from the comforts of her home for more than a few days. Even when she went to visit her parents in North Carolina, her restlessness kicked in after forty-eight hours. "Are you at least enjoying some of the city while you're here?" She fidgeted with the handcuff case on her gun belt. "I guess it's hard to get out since you have to be here for most of the day," she said answering her own question. "But there's cool stuff happening at all hours. The city that never sleeps, as they say." She raised her eyebrows and hoped she didn't sound like a total cheeseball.

"We're just settling in with all this." Hannah looked around her small makeshift shop. "But maybe one of these days."

"Officer Toby, you're still here. How nice." Priya's tone hid nothing. She obviously approved of her presence. That had to be a good sign, right? "You two are getting to know each other, I hope."

Toby smiled at how forward she was. She wished she could harness some of her chutzpah right now. "I was actually just asking Hannah if you two have been able to see any of New York City while you're here. I didn't realize there's so little downtime, though."

"I'm afraid I'm tied up with my relatives most nights, but Hannah's free." Priya peeled back the foil on her falafel. "If only she wasn't so timid about doing things by herself."

"It can be hard to do stuff alone," Toby said in defense, even as she wondered if that was a missed cue to invite Hannah out. Dammit.

"I keep telling her to go out, make friends. At least go see a show."

"I'm going to see a show," Toby blurted out. "Tomorrow night." Way to bumble the offer. She felt her cheeks get red on the spot. "What I meant is…I'm going to see a show tomorrow night, if either of you is interested. But I should be clear—it's not a Broadway show like you're probably thinking."

"What is it?" Hannah seemed intrigued, but it was probably only because of her bizarre explanation and awkward delivery.

"My cousin puts on these shows." She tried to come up with a way to describe it that sounded halfway normal. "He takes a classic story and modernizes it. Tries to make it contemporary, political. Satirical, sometimes." She cringed slightly, remembering last year's wild take on *Annie*, but at the same time she thought about the clever spin he'd put on *The Crucible* a few years back. "Anyway, the productions are staged in a black box theater on the West Side."

"Is your cousin an actor?" Hannah asked.

"Actually, he's a banker." Toby chuckled, knowing how random that sounded. "Theater is his passion, though." She was proud of Ned even if some of the performances were kind of out there. "He and his husband spend all their spare time coming up with these ideas and then developing them into stage productions."

"That actually sounds amazing," Hannah said.

"Are you…I mean…do you want to come?"

"I think I do," she said with spirited hesitation.

"Fair warning, the plays Ned produces…they can be kind of avant-garde."

Hannah nodded agreeably. "I'm totally down for that."

"Really?" Toby could not keep the smile off her face. "Wait, do you want to know what the show is before you decide?" she asked, reaching for her phone to do a quick search.

"Nope. I want to be completely surprised."

"Gotta love that blind faith," she said, texting Ned. "What about you, Priya? Can I count you in for a low-rent, possibly racy, definitely unforgettable night of amateur theater?"

"Sounds exciting," she said, doing a little cheer from her stool in the corner. "I have to pass, though." She patted her belly. "Me and the little one need our beauty sleep."

"What time is the show?" Hannah asked.

"Eight o'clock," she said as she confirmed two tickets with Ned. Crap, the market stayed open until eight every night. "I just realized that could be an issue. Sorry."

"It's fine," Priya piped up. "I can close up on my own. She'll be there."

Toby wanted to check in with Hannah, though. "You sure?" she asked. "Otherwise we can sneak in late and grab seats in the back."

"You heard the woman." Hannah lifted her shoulders in submission to the schedule being made for her. "I'll be there."

"Perfect." Toby was sure she was beaming. She didn't even care. "I should get back to my post," she said with a nod toward the west entrance of the market. "See you later?"

"Wait." Hannah reached over and grabbed a glossy business card. "That's my cell phone on the bottom. Text me the address."

"You got it."

CHAPTER FOUR

Hannah opted to walk to the theater from her dad's apartment. The Citymapper app said it was just over a mile, and she could use a distraction from her nervous energy. Business had been slow all afternoon, so she'd cut out early to take some time to properly primp. She spent the extra time straightening her hair, but the evening wind was having a field day with it anyway. It would probably be a wreck by the time she got there. Not that it mattered. This wasn't a date, no matter how much Priya teased her that it was. This was simply a native New Yorker showing kindness to an out-of-towner.

Toby had made it clear the first time they'd literally bumped into each other—she and her fellow officers were available to offer support in all sorts of ways. She imagined that included acting as ambassadors to the city. In fact, she witnessed it daily as Toby made her rounds to so many of the vendors, smiling and laughing and chatting away. Truth be told, Hannah had been kind of bummed she hadn't been on the circuit before today. She didn't buy Priya's theory that Toby's avoidance was a side effect of their unacknowledged mutual attraction, but the thought made her heart skip a beat anyway.

What was she even thinking?

She was here for a strictly limited time. She was not going to fall for anyone, let alone a cop. Even one who went to amateur theater on a Wednesday night or who happened to have the sweetest brown eyes she'd ever seen. Nope. She shook her shoulders out as though the latent desire she felt might fall away with the small action. She needed to get her head on straight. Smoothing her hair down, she turned the corner onto Fifty-Second Street, ready to take control of her wayward hormones and prepare herself for a night of innocent companionship.

"You made it."

It wasn't the words that made her swoon. It was the way Toby said them, as though she was both elated to see her and mildly concerned she was going to ghost.

"Did you think I wasn't going to show?" She smiled big, so Toby would know she was excited to be here.

Toby stuffed her hands in the front pockets of her jeans and looked a little bashful. "I guess I was a little nervous."

OMG. How freaking cute was she? "I will admit I almost didn't recognize you out of uniform."

Dressed in dark jeans and a corduroy trucker jacket, Toby looked completely different than just a few hours ago. It made no sense, but she seemed taller and slimmer. Or maybe she just appeared less bulky since she was devoid of all police gear. But holy hell, what threw her the most was Toby's hair. Tapered up on the sides, the top was all short lustrous waves perfectly styled and begging for her touch. The rich dark brown locks precisely matched Toby's eyes, and Hannah had to stop herself from reaching up to run her hands through it.

"Are you ready for this?" Toby asked.

Not by a long shot, she thought, even though she knew Toby was asking about the play. "Tell me," she said. "What adventure are we in for tonight?"

"I think it might be kind of fun," Toby said. "It's a riff on *It's a Wonderful Life*. Ned put a queer spin on it. Now it's *Fabulous*," she said with added drama.

"Is that a joke, or is that actually what it's called?"

"That's the title." Toby held the door to the theater open. "After you," she said. "Even though I'm not really sure what we're in for, let's get good seats."

In fairness, Hannah had low expectations, but everything about the show absolutely blew her away. It was witty and charming even while it made a statement about big banking that was surprisingly poignant. It was also loaded with the sentiment of the old film, and when the final curtain dropped, Hannah was full of holiday happiness.

"That put me in the best mood," she said as they hit the cool sidewalk air.

"Awesome." Toby seemed legitimately pleased and possibly a touch relieved. "I know some parts were off the wall, but it still somehow captured the heart of the original."

"Yes!" Hannah said as they walked past a restaurant whose front window was fully adorned in festive lights. "It really got me feeling Christmassy," she said as she turned to take another look at the pretty window.

"Do you want to go in?" Toby asked.

If it was a coffee shop or a bar she would have said yes in a second. But the place was a straight up restaurant, and she wasn't feeling food. "I'm not really hungry," she said with a glance at her watch. "It just looked so cozy with the lights and decorations."

"I know. It's nice, isn't it?" Toby said, but it seemed like she was expressing agreement rather than asking a question. "If you're not itching to get home, there's a cute little wine and espresso bar a few blocks up. They usually do a nice job with holiday decorations. Although they may still be decked out for Thanksgiving, now that I think about it."

Hannah was most definitely not ready to call it a night. "Only one way to find out," she said, letting Toby lead the way.

❖

"Do you go to all of your cousin's shows?" Hannah sipped her Chianti as she took in the subtle and charming Christmas decor. Turned out Sergio's was just what she'd been hoping for—quiet and chic with lovely decorations and soft holiday music playing in the background.

"I try to support Ned as much as possible." Toby toyed with the handle of her fancy cappuccino mug. "Partly because he's family. But honestly, I enjoy his vision. Even when a show goes off the rails, it keeps me thinking. I like that."

"I can see that." Hannah thought about the production they'd just sat through. It was nothing if not provocative.

"He only puts on one or two a year, though, so I have to find other outlets too. I'm going to an art show next week," she said with a casual shrug.

"You are?" Hannah couldn't keep the surprise out of her tone. "Is it like a gallery opening?"

"It's at a gallery on the Lower East Side. But not an *opening*, I wouldn't say. I think it's just a showcase of some local artists. No one famous or anything. My sister's friend has a few pieces being shown."

"That's exciting."

"It is. My sister is an artist as well, but she moved to North Carolina.

So I'm kind of representing to support her friend. Also I think it'll be cool. The theme is winter around the world, whatever that means."

"This is fascinating to me."

"Really?"

"Yes," she said even though she was as intrigued by Toby's interest in the arts as much as anything else.

"You could come if you're interested."

"Heck, yeah, I'm interested," she said, not taking any time to talk herself out of it. She took a long decadent sip of her wine and made no secret of looking Toby up and down. "Who are you, Toby Beckett?"

Toby's laugh was a deep hearty chuckle. "What does that mean?"

Hannah fanned over her aura. "I don't know." She narrowed her eyes suspiciously. "You're a cop…who likes the arts?"

"I guess I am," Toby said with an adorable grin. She tilted her head to the side. "Does that surprise you?"

Hannah didn't want to admit her inherent prejudice. In her defense, the news was constantly highlighting stories of police brutality and excessive force. Such behavior seemed so contradictory to everything about Toby's persona.

Toby read her silence. "Oh my God, it does. You think we're all the same." She hung her head and covered her heart as if mortally wounded.

"I don't. I don't," Hannah protested through a wince. "I'm sorry," she said, adding an apology for the presumptions her expression all but admitted. "You are changing my mind, though."

At least Toby didn't look mad. In fact she looked downright gorgeous. Her smile was soft, and her dark eyes sparkled in the dim light of the café. "Look, I'm not naive. I know there's tons of problems in policing. In the whole criminal justice system, to be honest." Toby stirred her drink with the tiny silver spoon. "But I also believe the majority of people who choose this profession have a fundamental desire to do good. To help people."

Christ almighty. If this was a line, it was a good one. But then, Toby seemed so sincere, Hannah believed that she was being genuine.

"Did you always want to be a cop?" she asked.

"No." Toby let out a weird little laugh before adding, "Not at all."

"Okay." Hannah emphasized both syllables in dramatic fashion. She took a deep breath before encompassing Toby's essence with a few small finger circles. "See, the look on your face and that sinister laugh would suggest you're not into your job." She took a sip of her wine just to stop herself from laying it on too thick. "You forget, though. I see you every day. You act like you love it. You're practically the mayor of Christmas Village."

"I can't fight you on that." Toby's smile made her eyes crinkle, and Hannah felt herself melt the tiniest bit. "Working the holiday market is my favorite," Toby said. "I really love talking to people."

"That's a great quality." Hannah leaned forward, itching for more details. "Is that what drew you to the field?"

"In a way, yeah." Toby took a small sip of her drink. "When my original plan didn't pan out, I felt kind of a pull toward policing."

"What was your original plan?" she asked, pretty much dying for the details.

"Well, I always knew I wanted to work with people. I have a hard time sitting still. Which you probably noticed during the show." Hannah liked the way Toby seemed shy but not embarrassed at the admission. "I just knew I couldn't be trapped behind a desk all day. I'd go crazy."

"I get that."

"So I started out in social work, figuring I could get right in the mix and, you know, hopefully make an impact. Help people."

"Hold up." Hannah put the brakes on with two hands in the air. "You were a social worker?"

"I was," Toby said with a definitive nod and a wistful smile. "I got my MSW from Fordham and went right from my graduate school program to working for a city agency for two years."

"But, like, what happened?" Hannah's head was spinning at this unexpected origin story. "Did you not like it?"

"I think it was more that it wasn't a good fit for me." She shrugged and smiled. "I loved the ideology and the people. Oh, *the people.*" She covered her heart with one hand and looked nostalgic. "But the bureaucracy frustrated the bejesus out of me. Everything was hurry up and wait. Red tape on top of red tape. It felt like I was going in circles a lot of the time. And really not making a difference at all."

"So you joined the police department?" There was no masking her surprise. But going from social work to policing? It seemed like a one eighty.

"I know it seems random," Toby said with an adorable chuckle. "But hear me out."

Hannah was all ears. The cop with the sweet brown eyes was suddenly a social worker too. Why did that turn her on?

"The thing with police work is that it inherently embodies a lot of the qualities I know I need in a job." Toby tapped out a tiny beat with one finger on the tabletop. "Constant stimuli, human connection, the opportunity to foster change." Toby juggled the air as though she might still be weighing the odds of her decision. "I thought, I don't know, if I could adapt some of the concepts I learned in school and in the field to this job, I might actually be able to do some good."

"I am sure you do." It was probably too much, but Toby had an earnest quality that made her believe it was true.

"Maybe. Some days it feels like there's hope. Sometimes this line of work is just as frustrating as anything else. Maybe even more so. The system seems rigged in a way."

God, if that wasn't the truth. "But hey, at least they have someone like you who cares about the issues," Hannah offered.

"I guess." Toby stared into her cappuccino mug. "Not to sound too self-absorbed, but I'm still convinced there's a better fit for me out there. I always have my eyes open for new opportunities. You never know, right?"

"Absolutely," she said, still kind of enchanted by Toby's journey, her outlook, her philosophy. She seemed open and free and so opposite the one-note, conservative law enforcement officer Hannah initially had her pegged as.

"Anyway, I have completely dominated the conversation. What about you? Was it always your dream to run a business?"

"Yes." Hannah laughed at the certainty of her own response.

"Awesome," Toby said with unfiltered enthusiasm. "Tell me everything."

Even though it wasn't in her nature to drop everything on day one, Toby made her feel relaxed and comfortable, so she went all the way back and walked Toby through her friendship with Priya. How they'd met in college studying science and medicine, and how they'd used that foundation to build on their joint desire to create holistic skincare products. One hefty investment from her dad later, and voilà, Gaia's Glow was born.

"But you don't have a store, you said earlier. Did I understand that right?"

"Right." Toby had paid attention. Did that mean she was interested? "We're very heavily based in online sales," Hannah said, forcing herself to stay on track. "But we're kind of lucky. We have a secret weapon," she said.

"Oh? What's that?"

"Well, my mom and my aunt own a day spa up in Hudson. It was a hair salon when I was growing up." Hannah tried to sum up her life without boring Toby. "Mom and Aunt Lindsay are hair stylists. And then a few years back, my younger sister and my cousin, who's practically my sister also, they both trained to be massage therapists. So Mom and Aunt Lindsay made over the salon and turned it into a spa and wellness center where they use all Gaia's Glow products for hair, massages, everything."

"That's amazing."

"We're really very lucky." Hannah never took her good fortune for granted. Her family was amazing on so many levels. The fact that they all helped push sales on a daily basis was only a small part it.

"Hudson gets some good tourist business too, right?"

"It does actually. There's nice restaurants and shops. Cute inns. It's very quaint, but there's also fun stuff to do. Plus, there's lovely views of the mountains and the river." Hannah knew she was beaming. She always had trouble reining in her affection for her hometown.

"I really like how much you love it. It's nice."

"I know I'm a dork," she said, owning her enthusiasm. "There's just so much culture and history. I bet you'd love it."

"I'm sure I would."

For the briefest second, Hannah pictured Toby there. The image surfaced without any forethought whatsoever. But in her mind she and Toby were walking Warren Street. Holding hands? She stuttered at the thought, and felt her words catch in her throat before reaching her lips.

"You okay?" Toby asked. "You looked like you saw a ghost for a second."

It was a premonition for sure, but not one that had any chance of coming to fruition. It wasn't even something she really wanted. Was it? No. That was just a blip. The result of being single too long and having one nice evening with a new friend. She shook her head quickly. "I'm fine. Sorry. I just zoned for a sec."

Toby looked at their empty drinks. "We should probably get going. Work in the morning and all."

"Good point," she said.

"Where is your dad's place?" Toby asked.

"Seventy-Third and Central Park West."

"Ooh la la la. An apartment on the Park. Fancy Delancey."

Hannah couldn't help but laugh at Toby's silly, accurate description.

"It's nice to have money, I guess." Not that she would really know. Gaia's Glow was paying the bills, but only that.

"I'm just teasing. How is it staying with your dad? Do you two get along?"

"We do." Hannah put her hands in her coat pockets to shield them from the wind. "He's actually out of town, though," she admitted. "I saw him for a few days before he and his wife went to Europe." It had been a nice brief visit, and Hannah only felt slightly guilty that she'd been relieved not to have to make conversation with them every day for almost two months. "They're off on a business trip and then spending holidays with Mai Ling's family in the Philippines."

"Is that a bummer?"

"Hardly. I love them, but it's nice having the place to myself." They were walking north on Eighth Avenue, and Hannah wondered if Toby needed to grab a subway. "Where do you live?" she asked.

Toby thumbed behind them. "I'm down on Forty-Seventh Street," she said.

"Wait." Hannah stopped in her tracks. "You're walking in the opposite direction."

"I was going to walk you home, if that's okay." Toby seemed shy all of a sudden, like she might be overstepping. It was positively irresistible.

"You do not have to walk me home. I'm fine."

"I'm not trying to imply that you need an escort." Toby looked around at the brightly lit street where traffic flowed steadily. "Obviously it's completely safe out here. I'm just having a nice time talking to you."

"I feel bad dragging you so far out of your way. It seems crazy," she said, even though she liked the company.

"I don't mind, if you don't," Toby offered.

Hannah didn't mind one bit. She was actually enjoying herself more than she thought possible. So rather than fight it or even try to make sense of the unlikely emotion she felt after such a brief connection, she fully gave in to the moment and indulged in Toby's presence as they strolled uptown and talked about the city, the play, the other vendors, and the market itself. It was a glorious night, brisk and full of energy she couldn't quite make sense of. But rather than even try, she chose instead to relish every second of it right up to the front door of her dad's place, where Toby bid her a perfectly mannered good night.

Chapter Five

How was your date?" Priya passed Hannah a napkin as she bit into her breakfast sandwich. "I want all the details."

"It was not a date." Hannah wiped the excess cream cheese from her sesame seed bagel as she replayed the night in her head. A show, a drink, a lovely walk home. It was going to be hard to be honest and not have Priya challenge her.

"Tell me about the play." At least Priya started small.

"It was good. Wild, in a way. But really good." Hannah pictured the way Toby sat on the edge of her seat paying attention to every detail throughout the performance and the fun they'd had dissecting it on the way home. "It was a takeoff on *It's a Wonderful Life*. Toby's cousin Ned did an amazing job with it."

"Did you meet him?"

"Yes. After the show Toby introduced me to Ned and his husband Javi. They were very nice."

"Meeting the family is important, you know." Priya smirked.

"Stop it." Hannah threw her napkin right at her. "You're ridiculous."

"Am I, though?" Priya was clearly playing, but Hannah was distracted by the cops congregating near the doughnut stand the same way they did every day right about this time. She gave in to the urge to break eye contact with Priya so she could see if Toby was there. "Oh my God, you're looking for her."

Priya whipped her head around just in time for Toby to catch them both staring. Hannah was embarrassed at their joint lack of subtlety, but Toby waved and, God damn it, it gave her butterflies. Instinctively, Hannah ran her tongue along her teeth and wiped her mouth in case there was any breakfast residue visible.

"She's not a superhero. There is no way she can see crumbs on your face from that distance," Priya teased. "But, please, keep telling me how you're not interested."

"I honestly don't know what I am, Priya." It was all the defense she could really manage. She was too distracted by Toby standing across the way to think about anything else, and she was already overanalyzing the small wave she'd just given as a morning hello. It roughly mirrored their thoroughly tame good-bye from last night.

At the end of their walk Hannah had secretly held out hope for a hug, and she supposed she could have initiated, but she worried about the signal it might send. Even more than that, she worried that the message would be sent but not reciprocated. That the buzz she felt between them was all wishful thinking.

"She's coming over."

"What?" Hannah was so caught up in her head that she'd lost all focus on the present.

"Good morning." Toby gave them each a charming smile, but Hannah thought they locked eyes for an extra second. Was she going off the deep end?

"Hannah loved your cousin's show," Priya said as she cleared away her trash.

"The production was a trip, that's for sure." Toby's laugh was smooth and measured. "It was a really nice night, though."

"It was," Hannah echoed.

"Which reminds me," Toby said, turning to face her directly, "I never gave you the details for the gallery event next weekend. I know it's over a week away, but do you have a preference for Friday or Saturday?"

Behind Toby, Priya opened her mouth and eyes wide. Hannah tried to hold it together. "Whatever you want. I'm easy," she said regretting her word choice on the spot. Toby didn't react, but in the background Priya mimed a hip thrust and Hannah almost lost it.

"Let's plan on next Friday. Anything changes, let me know." Toby fiddled with her gear. "I should get to it," she said with a nod at the market around them. "I'll swing by again later if that's okay."

"Definitely."

Hannah let her eyes follow Toby the whole length of the market. She didn't even try to hide it. Something about Toby made her feel tingly in all the right ways. She couldn't explain it. Heck, she didn't even understand it. On paper Toby Beckett was all wrong for her. A police officer who lived in hectic New York City. It was basically strikes one and two, back to back. But she found herself looking for her nonstop and thinking about her even more. It made absolutely no sense. There was no point in overthinking it or analyzing it to death. Not now anyway. So she quashed her feelings, and when she turned around and saw Priya poised with about a thousand questions, she smiled, booped her friend's nose, and shut her down with a smile and an overly perky "Nope."

The weekend flew by thanks mostly to almost nonstop customers. Sales continued into Monday and Tuesday, and Hannah was thrilled for the steady business, not to mention each day that passed was a step closer to the Friday art show with Toby. The only downside to so much business was that Priya had to make an emergency midweek run up to Hudson to restock their supply, leaving her alone in the booth on this rainy Wednesday afternoon.

"Hey there."

Since the night of the play Toby's pop-ins had become a regular occurrence. One that she looked forward to way more than she should. But this visit was an extra-special surprise because Toby had already come by an hour earlier.

"Hi," Hannah said, unable to keep the enthusiasm out of her voice as she came out from behind the register. "What's all this?" She nodded at the thin cardboard tray and two cups Toby was balancing.

"I come bearing gifts," she said with a grin. "Afternoon sustenance." Toby wiped off some moisture that had pooled on her uniform jacket and set the box down on the edge of a display table. "I figured with Priya heading upstate, you might not be able to get out to grab something to eat."

"Toby." Hannah tried to keep the emotion out of her tone but she was genuinely touched. "That is so sweet. What'd ya get?" she asked peering close to have a look.

"Bavarian pretzels from the German food vendor around the way." Toby handed her a giant pretzel wrapped in wax paper. "And on my way here, I grabbed hot cocoa from the fancy chocolatier."

"Wow." Hannah assessed the size of the pretzel. "You're going to have to help me eat this," she said.

Toby answered by holding aloft a pretzel of her own. She smiled big. "I didn't realize how huge they were until after I ordered."

"Oh, well," Hannah said. "We'll just have to do our best." She reached for the spare stool from the corner and brought it out for Toby to sit. "Can you stay and eat with me?" she asked.

"I'm on my meal break, so I actually can. The only thing is I'm not allowed to sit."

"Wait, really?"

"True story." Toby took a bite of her pretzel. "The department has all sorts of rules about things you can and can't do in uniform."

"Sitting is against policy?"

"Not formally." She smiled her adorable smile. "But Sgt. Ng is a stickler for looking professional, and me chilling out under the cover of a tent in the rain, eh, might look a little cozy." The comfort of it was the very thing that appealed to Hannah. "But this"—Toby gestured between them—"me and you talking and breaking bread, that's just community interaction."

"I'll take what I can get," Hannah said.

"You can sit." Toby pulled the stool closer so they could share the table.

Normally she would refuse. A lot of the same logic applied to business. A seated salesperson gave off an air of indifference. But the weather was putting a dent in pedestrian traffic, and she liked the convenience of having a place to set her food so readily. The fact that she was so near Toby in the small quarters was just a bonus. "I think I will, if you don't mind."

"Not at all." Toby took the lid off the hot chocolate, and steam wafted through the damp air toward her perfect mouth. "This smells outrageous. Have you tried it yet? Before today, I mean."

"Between sales and inventory I haven't visited too many of the other booths," Hannah admitted as she took the first sip. It was rich and velvety and just the right temperature to warm her up without burning her tongue. "Wow." She rubbed her biceps against the chill in the air. "This is the perfect day for it."

"Are you cold?"

Her thick cardigan had been enough when she left the apartment that morning, but the temperature had dropped substantially in the last few hours.

"A little. It's fine."

"Here, take this." Toby unzipped her heavy uniform jacket. "I just have to remove my shield and stuff." She pulled one side away from her body and peered inside, seeming to assess the best way to accomplish the task.

Hannah was truly moved, but she didn't want Toby to get in trouble. Without thinking about it, she reached up and stilled her hand. "If you're not allowed to sit down in my shop, there is no way it's okay for me to wear your uniform. I feel confident that's a definite no-no."

"Sometimes rules are made to be broken. Amirite?"

Toby's eyes were lively and loaded with invitation. Were they... flirting? It seemed unlikely yet obvious. And they were still touching. Very nearly holding hands, to be honest. Hannah's whole body sizzled with excitement, and the look on Toby's face said that she felt it too.

Maybe.

Hannah truly had no idea. There was only one way to find out.

She was going to have to say something overtly flirty. Or at least try. Cutesy dialogue and playful banter were not her strong suit. But everything about this scenario was way out of her comfort zone, including the object of her affection. She took a deep breath, ready to go for it, just as a loud crash from across the way stole her moment.

Twenty feet away a commotion was brewing over at Kustom Kandles. From the distance it was hard to tell what was going on, but already a small crowd formed at the entrance. Hannah turned to check in with Toby and get her take on what might have happened, but it was too late. She was already on the move.

Cradling her cocoa with both hands, Hannah stared as Toby expertly took command of the chaos by issuing calm orders for space and distance. As the onlookers dispersed, Hannah saw Toby on her knees on the ground next to the middle-aged proprietor of the candle shop where she stayed, rendering aid and comfort, until an ambulance crew arrived and took over.

A sea of NYPD blue had clustered around the booth, and she watched Toby giving a verbal report to the female sergeant she recognized as the leader during daily meetings that took place next to the coffee stand. Toby talked and nodded, and as though she knew she was the center of Hannah's attention, she turned her head and gave her the most discreet smile. It was a sweet, random moment, and Hannah couldn't help but feel oddly connected to her. Or maybe it was just the way her dark eyes stood out against the backdrop of a dreary gray New York City day that made her gush inside.

Why she was romanticizing any of this, she had no idea. But even as she internally scolded herself, she couldn't tear her eyes away, and when Toby walked away from the market, presumably headed back to the station house, Hannah felt her spirit sink. But it was for the best, she reminded herself. The fake romance she imagined blossoming with Toby was only that. A one-sided fiction to entertain her mind and, okay, her fantasies. It was a distraction. A completely pleasant one, and all alone on a rainy afternoon with potential for profits slim, she let herself indulge over and over.

Toby had full lips and strong hands, and Hannah imagined her kiss would be firm and sensitive, her embrace sturdy but gentle. Her whole energy was full of strong tenderness that seemed contradictory and yet utterly enticing. Hannah could not stop thinking about waking up in Toby's arms, a night of decadent passion behind them as the sounds of Christmas and the city sleepily welcomed them into a brand new day.

"Sorry about the disappearing act." Toby's voice caught her off guard, and she jumped like someone who'd been caught with her mind in the gutter. "Didn't mean to sneak up on you there," she said, clearly witnessing her surprise.

"I was just daydreaming for a second."

"About something good, I hope."

Ugh. So good, Hannah thought as she swallowed past the lump in her throat and found her voice. "What happened over there?" she asked as she looked in the direction of the candle shop. She prayed a change in conversation would keep any sign of lust from being written all over her face. "Is the shopkeeper okay?"

"I don't know really. The guy who runs the business had a seizure. He seemed as stunned by it as everyone else. I'm sorry I bolted without saying anything."

"It's your job, Toby. I totally understand."

"After that I had to take care of some paperwork back at the precinct. I was able to grab this for you while I was there." Toby held out a thick NYPD hoodie.

"Oh my God, are you serious?" Hannah felt her heart speed up at the gesture—not to mention the sweatshirt was warm and soft and smelled entirely of Toby.

"Of course. It should help you keep warm for a bit."

"Thank you so much," she said slipping it over her head and hugging into it for warmth. "This is amazing. You're amazing."

It was out before she could really stop it, and she saw Toby register her words. Their eyes met, and Toby's smile was a hint shy. God, had she said too much? What if she was imagining the connection between them?

Toby licked her perfect lips, and for a second it looked like she was going to say something, but her radio chirped between them, destroying whatever the moment might have been. "Work," she said with a sigh. "I should probably get back to work."

Toby took a few baby steps backward as though it was a struggle to leave, and Hannah felt the sentiment deep in her bones. Despite all rational thought, she wanted Toby to stay. To talk and laugh and flirt. To ask her a thousand questions and answer just as many. She was desperate to take the budding energy of this sweet afternoon and coast right into the evening.

If only she had the nerve to suggest hanging out after the market closed for the night, but she was terrible at this kind of stuff. At least she had the art show to look forward to in two days. She was practically counting the hours. Toby backed away, and Hannah went for it as best she could. She wagged her fingers and put on her best pout, hoping it did a proper job of representing just how bummed she felt at seeing her go.

❖

"What are you going to wear?"

"What are you talking about?" Hannah focused on the budget to see where the week's sales had gone. She knew what Priya was asking. The art show had been front and center of her mind for days, truthfully since Toby invited her, but now with only hours to kill before she went home to get ready, she was one hundred percent sure Priya was fishing for details.

"Don't play coy with me. I know you too well." Priya stood at the edge of the booth ready to entice shoppers in. "Is the gallery event tonight fancy or casual? I've never been to a showing before," she said.

"Me either." For all her interest in the arts, she'd never been to a legit showing of any kind. "I guess I'm not really sure."

"So what are you thinking?"

"I have a dress that I can accessorize up or down," she said, not looking up from her spreadsheet.

"Color?"

"Black."

"Length?"

"Short."

"Heels?"

"Duh."

"I love that you're pretending to be all blasé about this, but you're going with an LBD and heels. Keep telling yourself this is friendship."

"What's an LBD?" she asked.

"Little black dress," Priya answered. "And heels, don't forget that."

"The dress I'm wearing needs heels. That's just fashion. Don't hate." Hannah forced a laugh not to sound defensive. "And it is friendship. For now," she added.

"I knew it."

"Don't get all crazy," Hannah warned. "Toby's just...she's not what I expected, that's all."

"You always did have a tendency to put people in boxes."

"That's not true."

"It's a little true," Priya said as she handed a product pamphlet to a passerby. "I'm not criticizing you, Hannah. I'm merely pointing out that you're human. And I'm glad you're opening your mind to the idea of Toby."

"She was a social worker." Hannah was still wrapping her head around that sexy detail. "Did I tell you that?"

"You did tell me. It's very interesting. Almost as interesting as you falling for her."

"No one is falling for anyone," she said, despite the fact that her heart beat uncontrollably every time she thought about Toby. "I'm just making the most of my time here, that's all." She wondered if she sounded remotely convincing.

"Well, since this is your third date"—Priya wiggled her eyebrows suggestively—"make sure you're prepared."

"It's only the second. Outing," Hannah corrected with a wince.

"The theater, the pretzel date, the gallery. That's three by my count."

"I don't think eating lunch together qualifies as a date," she said, even though she wore Toby's hoodie nonstop when she was alone at her dad's place just so she could constantly smell her musky cologne. Thank God Priya wasn't in on that detail.

"The fact you don't count your rainy romantic hot chocolate rendezvous as a date only shows how out of touch you truly are." Priya walked over to her. "Look, Hannah. I'm not trying to get all up in your business." She touched her arm softly. "As your best friend it's my job to be here for you. To advise you on the signs you might be missing due to your self-imposed celibacy."

Hannah knew this was all part of Priya's silly setup, but she couldn't resist anyway. "And what pressing advice do you have for me, O wise one?" she asked, waiting for the punch line.

"I think it's great that you're going to wear a little black dress. Sets the tone." Priya smiled devilishly as she waved a finger up and down Hannah's torso. "Do yourself a favor and put a little thought into what goes underneath it."

CHAPTER SIX

In front of her closet Toby debated between her two favorite button-down shirts.

If this was a real date, she'd go black micropattern all the way. It was a nice look without being too formal, and she'd gotten some compliments when she'd worn it in the past. Eh, why not, she thought shaking off her momentary hesitation. She reached for the shirt, ready to at least play it up. Whatever was—or more accurately wasn't—going on with Hannah, there was no harm in looking the part.

Every day she talked herself out of truly pursuing Hannah. She knew it was the smart choice. Her logic always boiled down to the same point—there was no joy in gearing up for what could only be a short high. Even if their energy seemed bonded. But maybe that was all in her head. And even if it wasn't, she reminded herself that connection didn't necessarily mean anything more than friendship.

But, nah. There were sparks. She would swear it.

At the very least there had been a moment the other day when she gifted Hannah her spare hoodie. Hannah had clutched it like it was a prized possession. And the look between them, forget it. She'd almost gone for it right there. But then she'd chickened out of asking her on a real date, and now here she was, pretending they were going on one anyway. What was she even doing?

"Shit."

In her slight stumble down the rabbit hole that was Hannah Monroe, Toby had neglected to keep an eye on the time. Working some product through her hair, she threw on a jacket and raced out of her apartment.

"Sorry I'm late," she said, practically jumping out of the back seat of the cab she'd hailed just to get across town in a hurry.

"You're not." Hannah's smile was gorgeous and forgiving as she stood on the sidewalk in front of the art space. "In fact, the gallery just opened," she said.

"I get weird about being late for things," Toby admitted. Sometimes being a nerd was the worst. "I hope you weren't waiting too long."

"Not at all. I just got here a minute ago."

She saw Hannah's gaze drift down the front of her body like she was checking her out. It was small, but the quick overview and the way Hannah seemed to subconsciously lick her lips gave her the assurance she needed. There was something happening here.

"I guess we can go ahead in." Toby held the door and tried not to gawk as Hannah entered. Her artist friend waved to her from the center of the room, and not a moment too soon because Toby was definitely staring. In the perfect lighting of the gallery, Hannah's beautiful eyes stood out even more than usual and the sexy black dress she had on... whoa. "Come on," Toby said over the catch in her throat. "I'll introduce you to one of the artists."

For the next hour Toby resisted reaching for Hannah's hand as they perused lovely paintings of winter wonderlands near and far. When they finally exited into the brisk night air, Toby was slightly buzzed off two glasses of complimentary champagne.

"Did you love it?" Toby asked as they hit the street. Her enthusiasm was too much, but she didn't even care. She was high on a night filled with great conversation, beautiful art, an amazing woman.

"I did." Hannah looked at her, and her expression mirrored the way Toby felt inside. Happy, smitten, perhaps the slightest bit woozy. "Your friend's paintings were amazing. There was one—you could almost hear the quiet coming through the forest scenery. It reminded me of being on the trails near my house."

"That sounds lovely."

Hannah brushed against her shoulder, and Toby hoped it was by design. "I swear you would love Hudson."

"I don't doubt it."

"You should come see it."

Toby wondered if she really meant it or if the invitation was simply part of casual conversation.

Hannah seemed to read her. "I'm serious. It's crazy that Hudson is so close and has so many things you'd be into, and you've never even done a day trip." Hannah hooked her elbow, and she felt her pulse race. "When the market's done, come up and visit me."

She stopped herself from overthinking and spoke right from her gut. "I would honestly love that."

"Good." Their eyes locked and Hannah said, "I would too."

They were walking up Third Avenue to nowhere in particular, and one thing was for sure: Toby didn't want the night to end.

"Do you feel like going for a drink?" She didn't care that it sounded like she was asking Hannah out because...maybe she was. As a matter of fact, even though it went against her daily internal monologue, she wanted it to be clear to Hannah that she was interested. In what, she wasn't sure exactly. But she felt confident those details would figure themselves out in time. Or they wouldn't. Either way, this was what she wanted right now.

"That would be nice." Toby felt Hannah squeeze her arm gently. "There's one thing, though." She paused and Toby's heart dropped into her stomach. Maybe she had misread the cues, and this was the moment when Hannah was going to make sure everything remained platonic. Toby felt a wave of nausea, and the backs of her knees started to sweat despite the cold air all around them. She willed herself to hold it together no matter what Hannah said.

"What's up?" she asked, annoyed at the uber high pitch that came out to cover the preemptive disappointment already coursing through her body.

"I know it's Friday night, but do you think we could find somewhere that's not too crowded?" Hannah looked nervous to even ask. "I'm sorry if that's annoying, but wall-to-wall people"—she shivered—"even the thought of it makes me kind of anxious."

For a solid second Toby froze, waiting for the other shoe to drop, until she realized that was it. Crowds were the caveat. No secret boyfriend or girlfriend waiting back home, no friendship disclaimer.

"Right this way." Toby grabbed her hand and guided them down the street, hoping the fact that she was leading the charge was a passable excuse for gratuitous hand-holding.

Ten minutes later they were seated at a kitschy corner booth in Tennessee Tubbs Cereal Sit Down—a wacky offbeat spot that served up booze and breakfast cereal. There was always good music and a chill vibe, and because it was more of a diner than anything else, at this weekend hour ripe for partying, the clientele was sparse.

"This is honestly perfect," Hannah said as she took in the colorful space.

"I am so glad you like it." Toby tapped her laminated menu on the edge of the table. "I didn't know about your aversion to crowds," she said, realizing in the moment there was so much she'd yet to learn about Hannah. "How do you deal at the market every day?"

"It can be stressful at times," Hannah said. "Even though it gets busy, it feels different because it never reaches that intense level where everyone is basically shoulder to shoulder up against each other. That's what triggers my anxiety, if that makes sense."

"It does."

"It helps that I have my own space there. Gives me a sense of control. Plus, I have Priya for support. And you," she added with a sweet smile. "You both make me feel grounded. In very different ways."

Toby's heart was beating like crazy. This was it. The window she'd been waiting for. But damn if they weren't seated in a booth with three feet of table between them. At least she could use the opportunity to set up their next outing, but armed with this new intel, she needed to amend her initial idea.

"Do you have plans on Wednesday night?" She was so nervous she didn't wait for Hannah's answer before continuing, "The thing is, I was originally going to see if you wanted to go to the tree lighting at Rockefeller Center together. My buddy is in charge of the security detail, and, well, he could hook us up with a good spot." She waved her hands to signal that offer was off the table. "Now that I know how you feel about crowds...suffice it to say, that is a nightmare scenario."

"It's sweet that you thought of me, though."

"I think about you a lot," she admitted. "The tree lighting is iconic," she said dialing it back as she shifted gears. "We shouldn't miss it entirely." She saw Hannah squint as though she was trying to figure out what she was angling at. "I have a gigantic television. I'm thinking you, me, and a pizza. It'll be just like we're there, minus the masses."

"I love this plan," Hannah said.

Hannah's hand was just inches from hers, and she touched their pinkies together just to drive it home. "So...it's a date, then?"

It was worth every second of fear it took to say it when Hannah smiled and said, "Most definitely."

❖

Toby checked the clock for about the millionth time. She knew Hannah was staying to close up the booth, and since she didn't live too far from the market, she expected her any second now. She was as excited as a kid on Christmas morning, and she about hit the ceiling when her apartment buzzer sounded.

"Hi," Toby said as she opened the door to her fifth-floor walkup. "Come in."

Hannah lifted a bottle of wine. "I brought red—I hope that's okay."

"It's perfect." Toby had done a quick pop in to the liquor store after her shift. She only had beer and seltzer in her fridge and she knew Hannah was partial to wine. She wanted her to feel at home. Was that weird? She blocked it out. "The pizza beat you here by a few minutes. I was trying to time it just right, but I failed." Toby frowned. "I can heat it up in the oven, though."

"I'm sure it's fine," Hannah said. "New York pizza is the best. It might even be better at room temperature." She seemed to be pondering the thought as she took off her coat.

Toby took it and hung it up on a spare hook just for an excuse to walk away and not stare at Hannah. In fitted jeans and an oversized sweater, she looked casual but still so freaking sexy. It was odd—she saw Hannah nearly every day, but tonight she looked different. But maybe it was simply that everything felt different. All the anticipation of what she hoped would happen ratcheted everything up to the next level, whatever that might be.

"Ooh, it's already started," Hannah said as she glanced at the tree lighting ceremony on-screen behind them. "Did I miss it?" she asked.

"Not at all." Toby reached for the remote and unmuted the volume. "They do a whole big lead-up before they flip the switch. We still have time."

Toby hooked them up with wine and pizza, and they sat side by side at the island watching the show and talking about everything under the sun.

It was a clear, dry night, and they toasted the courageous souls packed like sardines as they stood outside waiting for the big event. They praised celebrity performances of holiday carols updated and remastered for the hundredth time, cringing together as puffs of oxygen emerged when they sang their hearts out in the bitter cold. When the camera spanned the hordes of spectators waiting for the magic moment, Hannah visibly gulped.

"I would be an absolute wreck there," she said. "I hope you're not disappointed. For me, this is one thousand times better." Hannah touched her knee. "Thank you for inviting me over."

"This is perfect," Toby echoed. It very nearly was. They were about to light the tree, and as soon as they did, she was going to make her move. They listened to the hosts give a small countdown before the giant tree burst into a colorful array of lights. Toby turned to Hannah, and there was no mistaking it, their eyes locked. She licked her lips and started to lean in, but a loud chime from Hannah's phone on the counter broke the moment. Toby was all for ignoring it, but when it dinged several more times in a row, she couldn't help but laugh at the interruption. "You are in high demand," she said with a laugh.

"I'm sorry." Hannah glanced at her phone. "It's my mom," she said with a dismissive eye roll.

"You should check it," Toby encouraged. "It could be important."

"I highly doubt it," Hannah said under her breath, but she was already opening the message. "Yep. Matter of life or death," she said with a silly laugh as she tilted the screen to show Toby a series of photos of women drinking and celebrating together.

"Tell me who's who," Toby said, leaning close enough to smell Hannah's lovely light perfume.

Toby could feel Hannah press into her a bit, the heat from her body sending a surge right through her entire being.

"That's my mom and Aunt Lindsay," she said, pointing to two older women. With two fingers she zoomed in on the group shot. "This is my sister Aubrey, and that's my cousin Sadie."

"Everyone looks like they're having fun."

"We do have a good time together. It's so cliché and so true."

"Do you miss them?"

"Of course. Aubrey and Sadie are super tight. It's almost like they're sisters sometimes. I'm closer with Priya in a way." She seemed more matter-of-fact than broken up over that fact, and before Toby could press further Hannah turned to her.

"What about you? What's your family like?"

"They're great. I don't see them as much as I'd like, but we're close anyway."

"Do they live nearby?" Hannah asked.

"Not anymore." Toby briefly reminisced to when her parents lived a few blocks south in Chelsea. "My parents retired about three years ago. Well, my dad retired, I should say. They moved to North Carolina after that."

"Is that a bummer?"

"Eh, I guess in a way." She missed the emotional security of knowing she had family nearby, but it was also nice having a place to visit outside New York. "I see them a bunch throughout the year."

"Do they come here or do you go there?"

"Mostly I go there," Toby admitted. "New York City is great but expensive, as you obviously know." She finished her wine. "That's actually why they moved. With my dad retired, I think they get more bang for their buck outside New York. My sister and her husband had already moved there a few years back. Mom and Dad missed being around the grandkids."

"Was your dad a cop too?"

Hannah's expression was so earnest, Toby couldn't even tease her for stereotyping. Instead she moved to the other side of the kitchen to grab the wine and refill their glasses.

"Actually my dad was an art teacher. He worked in the public school system. My mom is a psychologist. She still practices part-time."

Hannah dropped her head into her hand dramatically and looked out from under her gorgeous dark hair. "Do I always just say the wrong thing?"

"Not at all." Toby smiled and rubbed her forearm softly. "It's kind of cute that you have me typecast. I hope I'm not letting you down."

"Um, far from it." Hannah blinked long and slow, and Toby wondered what she was really thinking. "You're not at all what I expected."

"That's good, though, right?" she asked, even though she was pretty sure she knew the answer.

"It's…" Hannah brought both hands to her head and mimed being mind-blown. "I just, I don't know, I get nervous and say things I don't even really mean."

"Don't be nervous." Fueled entirely by red wine and Christmas spirit, Toby reached across the island and traced an invisible infinity symbol along the top of Hannah's hand. "Let's just be ourselves and enjoy whatever this is." She shrugged at her own lack of eloquence, but there didn't seem to be a way to describe what was happening between them. And even though she was bummed over their thwarted kiss, she was positive the opportunity would come back around. For now she was content just to be in Hannah's presence.

Even though time was most definitely not on their side, Toby didn't want to rush this part. She wanted to savor every moment, so she sipped her wine and asked a zillion questions. Hannah must've been equally curious because over the course of the next two hours it felt like she asked nearly as many. They laughed out loud when they discovered they were both mildly obsessed with the same true crime podcast, and they went into detail about favorite episodes, pinkie swearing to listen together at some point down the line. The plan evolved so naturally that Toby didn't spoil it by highlighting the fact that in under a month Hannah would be back in Hudson, which put a serious wrench in the prospect of future dates. Instead, she chose to ignore that minute detail and give all her attention to the perfect night she was having right now.

CHAPTER SEVEN

Hannah's cheeks hurt from smiling. Toby was funny and sweet and made her laugh without even trying. She liked hearing her stories of growing up in the city and was ridiculously elated to discover they liked so many of the same TV shows and music.

There was only one problem. They had yet to kiss, and Hannah was dying over it. Every pulse point throbbed, her heart was going a mile a minute, and her hands shook amidst a series of almosts. First her mom had hijacked the moment with a text as the tree was lit. Then Toby got a pile of group messages that required her attention. And a minute ago, Toby's boss called just in time to interrupt another near-perfect buildup.

"I'm sorry about having to deal with all this." Toby jotted something down on a notepad at her kitchen counter. "Two guys called out sick for the early tour tomorrow, and the sergeant wants to make sure everything is covered."

"Does that mean you have to go in early?" Hannah asked.

"Yep." Toby's optimistic energy was adorable. "It's no big deal, though. I don't mind the extra hours."

"I should probably get going." Hannah checked the time and was shocked to realize it was almost eleven. Now that Toby had an early shift, she didn't want to overstay her welcome. "I didn't realize how late it was," she said, standing up and hugging herself in consolation for the slight disappointment she felt.

"Can I at least walk you home?" Toby asked.

Her dad's apartment was almost thirty blocks north, and it was near freezing out. Hannah had thoroughly intended to order a ride share. But extra time with Toby wasn't something she wanted to pass up.

"Are you sure?" she asked. Now that the offer was out there, she didn't want Toby to rescind, but she also didn't want to take advantage of her kindness. "It's seems crazy to make you leave your warm apartment."

"Nah." Toby waved her off and grabbed their jackets. "If you're not in a rush to get home, I kind of want to show you something." She looked impish and shy, like she had something up her sleeve.

"I am in no rush to get home." It was an invitation, and Hannah hoped her tone indicated just how deeply she felt it. "But where are we going?" she asked playfully.

Toby stepped into her space and whispered, "Do you trust me?"

Hannah didn't even have to think about her response. "Ridiculously," she said, gazing into Toby's brown eyes.

"Good." Toby's smile hitched up on one side as she leaned forward. The kiss she placed was delicate and deliberate and oh so divine. Hannah felt like she'd waited an eternity for this moment, but the payoff made every second worth it. Toby's lips were like a perfect pillow. Plush and soft, warm and welcoming. She could get lost in them for a very long time.

Hannah felt a genuine shiver down her spine when Toby caressed her neck as her kiss lingered, and when their tongues finally touched, she legit went weak in the knees. Who even knew that was a real thing that happened? But my God, did it ever. Toby was strong and sweet, and in this perfect moment, as they stood making out in the hallway of her apartment, she was everything Hannah never knew she wanted. A smart, sensitive cop who talked about art and social justice and just happened to kiss like a freaking movie star. What in the actual fuck?

A little breathless, Toby stepped away, leaving her longing for more as she dropped a soft kiss on her lips. "Come," she said. And if she hadn't led her by the hand down into the street, Hannah just might have.

❖

Hannah had no idea where they were headed as they walked at a decent clip up Toby's block toward Eighth Avenue. The truth was she hardly cared. Right now, in that moment, she probably would have let Toby lead her straight into a mob as long as she never let go of her hand.

Just as they passed Radio City Music Hall and turned up a brightly lit Forty-Ninth Street, Hannah got an inkling of what might be in store.

But what she was picturing didn't hold a candle to the glimmer in Toby's eyes when she squeezed her hand and pulled her close.

"There is absolutely no reason you shouldn't get to experience this." Toby guided them right up to the railing that overlooked Rockefeller Center's skating rink situated at the foot of the world-famous tree. The view was perfect, and Hannah was in awe of how the tree seemed both larger and smaller than it did on television. The long branches swayed in the light breeze, the lights twinkled. She felt ooey and gooey inside, full of holiday spirit and legitimate emotion. It was crazy and stupid, and she didn't care that she was probably off her rocker.

"How is there no one here?" she asked. It was wild to think that just hours ago thousands of people were vying for the very spot where she stood, and now she had her choice of vantage points.

"The lights go off at around midnight," Toby said. "We still have a few minutes." She leaned back from the railing and ushered Hannah in front of her. Through the thickness of her coat, Hannah felt Toby hug her from behind. "All those people we saw on TV had probably been queued up for hours. These folks here"—she gestured to the few onlookers scattered about—"they're probably locals. Like us." Toby nestled into her shoulder and held her. "This is literally the best time to see the tree."

"And definitely the best way to see the tree," Hannah said, turning to find Toby's lips again. Toby smiled her sexy smile and kissed her in a way she'd truly never been kissed before. It was safe and public but so full of desire Hannah thought she might burst on the spot.

In the center of New York City, under a giant tree sparkling with Christmas spirit, they kissed and cuddled and laughed at themselves as they took a dozen selfies. And as the clock struck midnight and the lights went out, Hannah let any lingering inhibitions fade out with them.

There were no two ways about it: she was an absolute goner.

❖

At ten a.m. the next morning, Hannah was still smiling when she stacked the new hair product that Dev had sent in the latest restock. It was a honey-based pomade that gave good texture without being too sticky. It would be perfect for Toby. Ugh, Toby. Her heart skipped just thinking about last night. She'd barely slept, her mind racing through one spicy scenario after another.

"Morning, ladies." Toby's voice caught her off guard, even though Hannah had been keeping an eye out for her since she opened up shop.

"Hi," Hannah said, letting the word spill out of her mouth. She was almost embarrassed at the lilt in her tone because she knew it revealed just how much she was swooning inside. But it hardly mattered. Toby's shy grin said the feeling was mutual.

"I have to get to the shift change roll call," Toby said with a nod of her chin toward the daily meetup spot. She wagged a finger between her and Priya. "Afterward, can I bring back coffees for you both?"

"Ooh." Priya's face practically lit up. "Light and sweet for me. Thank you, Officer Toby." Priya batted her eyes, and Toby laughed. She looked so cute. Hannah wanted to kiss her right now, and she bit her lip just thinking about it.

"Hannah?" Toby said, pulling her mind from a perfectly divine, imaginary make-out sesh. "Coffee?"

"Sure." She shrugged. The travel mug she'd brought from home was still half-full of tea, but who was she to turn down bonus Toby time? "Light and sweet for me too." Toby nodded and winked and sauntered away. Hannah didn't even pretend not to ogle.

"So…" Priya brushed off a tiny fallen leaf from the front display. "How was your date?" She straightened a row of hand lotion so the boxes aligned. "I know, I know. It wasn't a date," she said, clearly gearing up to go straight into mockery mode.

"Oh no." Hannah swallowed her grin as she stared at Toby's behind as she stood at ease in a semicircle of cops. "It was definitely a date."

Priya nearly knocked over the sea-salt scrub. "Do. Tell."

"I went to her place, we talked, we laughed." Hannah didn't know how to adequately describe the night really. On the surface, it was a regular first date. They ate pizza, they drank wine, they chatted. But when she was in Toby's presence, she felt different inside. "She is…I don't know. She's something." She couldn't really explain it, so rather than doing it a disservice with a lackluster description, she didn't even try.

"Oh no. No. No. No." Priya walked right over to her. "I do not accept that. I need details."

"I don't know what to say, Priya. I like her. A lot." She knew it sounded ridiculous—she barely knew Toby. But there was a connection between them. She could feel it, even if she couldn't put it into words.

"Did you kiss?"

"Yes." Hannah covered her heart with both hands. "It was…ugh." She exhaled dramatically. "Un. Real," she said as she remembered the softness of Toby's lips, the strong, tender way she held her when they stood under the tree.

"Oh my God, did you…?" Priya used her hands to mime scissoring.

Hannah reached over and whacked her. "No!" She swatted away the crude gesture before she scared potential customers away. "I can't believe you just did that," she said, covering half her face. Hannah knew she was blushing. Fact was she'd spent the entire night and half the morning fantasizing about Toby.

"Spare me the virgin routine," Priya teased. "Anyway," she said with an eye roll, "give me all the particulars about last night. Please." She added a cheesy smile. "But hurry." She cast a glance at the briefing still underway. "Those meetups break up quick."

Hannah told Priya about their easy conversation and watching the coverage of the tree lighting before their late night surprise visit to Rockefeller Center. But even though she heard herself swooning, she knew she wasn't really doing it justice. There were simply no words to describe the feeling of actually clicking with someone. God, she wondered if she was just going crazy. Was it possible Toby felt the same way?

"Two coffees, light and sweet." Toby balanced the drinks stacked one on top of the other. "Someone better grab these before I spill them everywhere. I do not have a great track record in your booth."

"You're fine," Hannah said. She took the coffees and placed a hand on Toby's forearm in thanks. Okay, so she wanted to touch her. She was only human. "What do I owe you for these?" she asked.

"As if I'm going to charge you for coffee I offered to buy. Tsk-tsk." Toby squeezed her hand discreetly. "Nice try."

"Thank you," Hannah mouthed silently. She looked over her shoulder and was grateful Priya was pretending to be busy with inventory. "I know you came in early. Are you tired?" It was almost one thirty when they shared their final good-bye kiss outside her dad's apartment, and she knew Toby was expected at work bright and early this morning.

"I'm okay. This is keeping me going." She raised her cup. "And seeing you. That's a pick-me-up, for sure."

It wasn't the words, although hearing the compliment didn't hurt any. It was the look in Toby's eyes that got her. Toby was genuine. She could just tell. It was suddenly obvious that Toby had been waiting to see her today. To check in, to say good morning, to buy her coffee. The realization made her want to rush into her arms, to kiss her perfect full lips, to run her hand down the front of her uniform and get to the softness underneath.

"What are you doing tonight?" Hannah asked.

"Whatever you want," Toby said.

But that was the problem. She didn't have anything lined up or planned out. Before Toby, she'd expected to spend her entire time in NYC catching up on her Netflix and Hulu accounts.

Toby read her face. "What's wrong?"

"Nothing." She shook her head at herself. "We're in this huge city, and I can't think of anything to do."

"Leave that part to me." Toby smiled her gorgeous, crooked smile. "I'll come up with something." For a split second Hannah thought Toby was going to kiss her, but then she blinked and shook her head, laughing as though she'd just remembered where she was. "I have to get to work." Toby bladed her body with purpose and found her hand. With the gentlest touch she pressed their fingers together. "See you in a bit."

Hannah's heart raced. Her pulse throbbed. It was barely ten thirty in the morning, and she was wet and ready. There was absolutely nothing she could do to conceal it.

"You better jump on that," Priya said from her mindless task in the corner. "And I do mean literally."

Of course she did. Hannah rolled her eyes at her bestie, but for the rest of the day Hannah's mind raced with possibilities about where they'd end up tonight and if it would involve either of their beds. She should probably slow down. Maybe Toby didn't even want to take it to that level. But then, for the love of baby Jesus, she should not be able to kiss like that.

Forcing herself to get a grip, she focused on what they might do tonight. She felt slightly bad at dropping the ball on coming up with an actual plan, and she texted Toby as much, but Toby didn't seem to mind. Instead she responded by asking sporadic questions throughout the afternoon about everything from favorite foods to movies to whether or not Hannah knew how to ice skate.

It was nearing dusk, the market's busiest hour owing to the convergence of commuters and tourists and the post-work, pre-dinner crowds. Sales had been great all day, and Hannah was almost wishing customer flow would wane so she could text flirt with Toby more. Her heart rate sped up when she spotted Toby headed her way. But instead of stopping at the booth, Toby rushed past, clearly on a mission.

A few yards away Hannah saw Toby join a fellow officer who was already in the middle of a heated conversation with a shopper. She watched intently, ignoring the twinge in the pit of her stomach. Hannah reminded herself that Toby was smart and rational and probably just what the situation needed to resolve it without incident. But then everything went haywire.

Voices rose. Arms flailed. Toby was right in the middle of it all, very obviously trying to keep the peace until she was pushed aside and fell to the ground. Hannah's instinct was to run to her, but Priya clutched her forearm and held her back. It hardly mattered—a swarm of officers were suddenly there, whisking everyone out of sight.

Chapter Eight

A re you sure you're okay?"

"I promise I'm fine." Toby used the cover of the table to massage her bruised knee. Turned out Hannah had seen the whole ugly scene unfold in the market, and while it was thoughtful when she offered to cancel their date this evening, Toby had been looking forward to seeing her all day. She wasn't about to let one botched assignment usurp their night. Even if her minor injury had forced her to go with plan B. "The food here is amazing," she said, hoping to keep the conversation from getting too heavy.

"This place is lovely." Hannah looked around the quaint Spanish restaurant Toby had selected mainly for its ambiance. "The menu looks amazing," Hannah said, but her voice harbored hesitation.

Toby felt herself starting to panic. Maybe this was all too much. The romantic dinner, the quiet setting. But no. The last few weeks had always been building up to last night. Their connection was so easy, their chemistry off the charts. And there'd been no weirdness today. In fact, their messages had gotten exponentially flirtier as the day wore on. Until the market debacle. Fuck. It hit her like a heavy weight.

"You want to talk about today, don't you?"

"Could we?" Hannah placed her menu to the side and looked so intense, Toby wondered how it had taken her so long to realize all Hannah wanted was real conversation. God, she was such an overthinker sometimes. She'd been so busy trying to keep things from getting too serious that she'd gone and made it awkward.

"Of course."

Hannah drew a lazy circle on the tablecloth. "I'd be lying if I said it wasn't on my mind. And it's not like we need to spend the whole night deconstructing everything. It's just...I saw you get involved in something—I'm not even sure what, really—and then you got hurt. And I feel like I know you well enough to know you must be processing it all. Why won't you talk to me about it?"

"You were the first person I thought about when it happened." Toby blurted out the truth without filtering. She hadn't stopped thinking about it for a minute. Something about the way it all went down encapsulated the very things she hated about her job. The overt profiling, the massive egos, the quick escalation to aggression. "But this is a date. I didn't want to be a mood killer."

"Maybe I'm the crazy one." Hannah covered her heart, looking completely vulnerable. "But it feels like there could be something real here. Between us." She shrugged like there was no fighting it. "Let's just be ourselves. You be you. I'll be me." She took a sip of sangria, a signal it was decided. "In my opinion, that means we talk about things. We can start with easy stuff. How's your knee? I know it's bothering you."

"It's honestly fine."

"Toby, you were limping the whole way from the subway stop."

"I was not." Toby dropped her mouth open pretending to be offended, but Hannah's look called her bluff. "Okay, okay," she said, giving in. "But only a little. Funny thing is, all day I was gearing up to take you ice skating tonight."

"Aw." Hannah smiled sweetly, and Toby couldn't help but be marginally disappointed in having to shelve the skating plans. But that setback was completely outweighed by the realization that it wasn't all in her head. There was a real connection between them. She knew she felt it, but it gave her a thrill to know Hannah did too. It was amazing and perfect, even if it went against all her self-imposed regulations about falling too hard and too fast.

"So, when I was tossing around ideas of what to do tonight…Well, there's a French film that got great reviews playing at the Angelika Film Center."

"Ooh," Hannah responded with wide eyes.

"I know," she echoed, hoping she hadn't picked wrong. "It sounded cool. But sitting in a movie would mean I wouldn't get to talk to you for almost two hours." Toby frowned. "I wasn't willing to give up that kind of quality time just yet."

"Good call." Hannah reached for her hand in obvious support of the decision.

"And then I thought…Wollman Rink inside Central Park is nice and close to the market and it stays open until ten every night. Maybe even later, this time of year," she said, voicing her uncertainty of the specifics. "It's less intense there than the skating rink at Rockefeller Center. Doesn't get nearly as crowded."

"You're sweet." Hannah dropped her chin in her hand and laced their fingers together on top of the table. "Thank you for considering that."

"But then, when I fell down"—Toby winced, remembering the impact of the solid ground—"I did hurt my knee." She rubbed it out of reflex. "It's nothing serious. It's just banged up a bit. But I thought skating might not be the best move tonight."

"I think that's wise." Hannah squeezed her hand supportively. "So tell me what happened today? What was that all about?"

Toby wasn't even sure where to begin. "These types of open-air Christmas markets are targets. For terrorism. All over the world and here." She took a deep breath, hoping this wasn't too much. "The Counterterrorism Division is constantly analyzing intelligence. When there's a credible threat, security gets ramped up."

"And there was danger today?" Hannah asked.

"I mean…somewhere." Toby didn't even really know the details. "I don't think it was specific to the Central Park Holiday Market, necessarily. It could be there was chatter about holiday fairs in general. They don't always tell us." She took a small sip of her wine. "This is why we have signs posted all over the market that all bags are subject to random inspection."

"And that guy today had a massive backpack."

"Exactly." Toby shifted in her seat, revisiting how it had all unraveled. "The thing is it did not have to go down like that."

"What do you mean? Explain it to me."

"The other cop. Steve Walton. He's a hothead. And even from my post, I could tell by his body language he was going on the offensive. See, when you stop people, they don't always want to open their bags." She was trying to explain it in a way that represented both parties' interests and emotions. "I get it. It's invasive, and honestly, sometimes people have contraband or personal items they don't want you to see. But in this scenario, compliance is pretty much required." Toby felt her blood pressure going up again. "But there is a way to achieve that end without any kind of confrontation. It involves clear communication and mutual respect." She gritted her teeth. "Walton doesn't share that philosophy."

"So you stepped in to help."

"I was too late." Toby hated to admit it. "You saw what happened."

"You tried, though. That's what matters."

Maybe, but she wasn't convinced it was enough. "I need to do more." Toby was mostly thinking out loud, but the way Hannah looked at her as she listened felt like support, and it was exactly what she needed. "Unnecessarily escalated situations like this can have devastating outcomes. Serious ripple effects beyond what we even see." She shook her head, knowing that the world was unbalanced in that way. "I just believe there's a way to ensure safety and effect change without ruining people's futures."

"It sounds like there's something brewing in there." Hannah leaned forward and kissed her temple. "Tell me."

"There's programs that have been successful, using a blend of alternative solutions, to intercede with people in the crosshairs of the system. Like, intervening before things get to a crisis point."

"You want to work for one of those programs?"

"Or build one."

"Wow." Hannah's smile was full of pride. "Really, wow."

"Don't get me wrong. I'd be happy to work for one. Ecstatic, actually. But I've been researching, and believe it or not, I haven't found anything locally that matches the methodology of some of the more progressive and successful programs out there. I guess I've just been thinking about ways that my social work and law enforcement backgrounds combined might prove useful."

"I think it's genius. And I love your passion." Hannah licked her gorgeous lips. "Your drive, or maybe it's just this conversation, reminds me of Parker." She held up one finger to indicate she was going to explain after a sip of her drink, but the pause was long enough for Toby to chime in.

"Who's Parker?" Toby squeezed her eyes closed in playful drama as she mouthed, "Please do not say your ex. I can't take any more trauma today."

"Ha. Hardly." Hannah leaned in close. "Here's a little secret," she whispered in Toby's ear. "You're in a different league than anyone I've ever dated." She added the most demure little shrug, and Toby was positive that was a good thing. "But before we dissect that little tidbit, let me just tell you about Parker."

Inches from Hannah's face, lost in her beautiful hazel eyes, Toby wasn't even sure she cared. "Parker, right," she managed.

"Parker is my friend Susan's brother. Sue and I went to high school together, which is beside the point. Parker works at some Outward Bound–style program up in Hudson. I don't know really what it is, but it sounds sort of similar to what you're talking about. It's called, like, Way-something. Wayward? Wayfair? I don't remember."

"Wayfinder?" Toby couldn't keep the absolute shock out of her voice.

"Yes. Wayfinder. That's it. You've heard of it?"

"I've more than heard of it. I've studied it. It's literally one of the most successful programs in the country. I can't believe you know someone who works there."

"I think he's like a director, even. I'll put you two in touch. Parker is super nice. You can pick his brain, ask for ideas, whatever you want."

"You would do that?"

"Um, yeah." Hannah leaned forward and kissed her. "The world needs people like you in all fields. Like you said, you just need to find your fit. Maybe Parker can help." Her shrug seemed supportive. "If I can facilitate that connection, I'm happy to do it. Until then, I'm here to bounce ideas off of and brainstorm, if nothing else."

"Thank you." Toby was choked up at the gesture.

"But before we save the world, we need to order. Because I'm starving."

Goddamn, Hannah was something. But why did she have to leave in three weeks? At least it was only to Hudson, which suddenly didn't seem so far. Toby decided not to dwell on the future, choosing instead to relish their time together. For the rest of the night, they talked about life and their families, the French film they'd go see next week. They gushed over the homemade churros they split for dessert, and Hannah even made a racy innuendo involving the chocolate sauce that was served alongside them.

They kissed on the corner of West Fourth and Charles Street as they waited for their Lyft, and when they pulled up outside her apartment, Toby leaned over and whispered, "Do you want to come in?"

"So much," Hannah answered. "But I'm not going to." Hannah asked the driver if he'd mind taking her up to Seventy-Third Street, and when he agreed, she walked Toby to the front door of her apartment building. "You're exhausted." She dropped a decadent kiss on her lips. "It was a long, harrowing day for you." Hannah let another kiss linger. "I want you to ice your knee and get a good night's sleep. Tomorrow night, after the market, we'll stay in and watch *The Holiday* at my place. Rest up." Hannah bit her lower lip with purpose. "I'm going to need you to be fully functional."

Toby's heart pounded, and she felt her entire body blaze in excited anticipation. "Yes, ma'am."

Chapter Nine

Twenty-four hours later and Toby's heart rate was still through the roof. The day seemed to drag on, but she knew it was all because of what lay ahead. The prospect of a night in with Hannah sent her mind to all sorts of amazing places.

But what if that wasn't what Hannah was looking for? What if she was just looking for someone—anyone—to have a light fling with? No way. Everything about Hannah's energy said she wanted more. And she'd admitted as much last night. Hadn't she? Or was that just wishful thinking on her part? Toby would swear their connection went beyond lust. It had all transpired in a short time, but with Hannah she felt a bond deep and true and utterly indescribable.

It just felt…well, real.

Be cool. Be cool. Toby talked herself down as she glided through Hannah's father's impressive lobby and pressed the button for the fourteenth floor. The problem was that she wasn't cool. At all. Instead of being easy-breezy, she was full of jitters and jangles over what she hoped this potential relationship might hold. If there was an opposite of chill energy, she was it.

"Hey you." Hannah met her at the door with a sweet, sultry kiss that somehow quelled all her manic anxiety.

"Hi," Toby said, still slightly breathless.

"Why does it feel like I haven't seen you in forever, when it's only been a few hours?" Hannah's giggle was adorable, and the way she smiled against her mouth was intoxicating.

"Because we haven't done this in a whole day."

Toby held Hannah's face and kissed her long and deep and slow. She heard Hannah whimper lightly against her body when she broke them apart. "It was torture being so close and not being able to kiss you," she said.

"We have to hold back no longer," Hannah said with a smile. "Come in. I'll get you a drink." Hannah held her hand and guided her into the pristine kitchen. "I ordered some noshies in case you were hungry." She fanned at a plate of antipasti and vegetables with hummus.

"Maybe in a bit," Toby said. She was way too nervous to eat just yet.

"Red? White? Beer? Seltzer?" Hannah glided a hand down her back. "What are you feeling?"

"I don't know. What are you having?"

"I'm thinking white," Hannah said as she bopped around reaching for glasses.

"That sounds good," Toby said. She almost offered to open the wine, but Hannah produced a fancy gadget to uncork the bottle. She seemed so comfortable in the space that Toby wondered if she was being given a glimpse into her relaxed homebody persona. She pictured Hannah upstate, in an apartment she couldn't envision, and it made her immeasurably sad. At the thought, she felt a sting in her throat, a sucker punch she didn't see coming. She spun around and took in the enormity of Hannah's dad's expansive apartment just to have something to focus on.

The open-plan living room and kitchen area was four times the size of her whole place.

"Welcome to the mini-palace of Marc Monroe," Hannah said, reading her awestruck face.

"I don't know what I expected." Toby let out a chuckle. "Definitely not this. It's unbelievable." In her downtime Toby had researched Gaia's Glow online. Once she realized it was affiliated with Hannah's mom's salon, she'd browsed that website too, and then the entire city of Hudson. It was all very…granola. She knew that knowledge had influenced her expectations of Hannah's current digs, ridiculous as that thought process might be. "I think I expected it to be sort of…I don't know. Like, hipster, maybe."

"That would be more my mom than my dad. If she lived here… forget it," she said with a wave of her hand. "Also, she would never live here," Hannah added with a laugh. "I wonder if she and my dad would have stayed together if he was hipster." She seemed to be pondering the theory. "My dad's a total modern yuppie. He manages a bunch of hedge funds and dabbles in venture capitalism."

"I don't know what any of those words mean," Toby said with a laugh.

"It means he's fantastic with money." Hannah laughed at her own joke and padded into the main living area, hooking her pinkie and bringing her along. "But he's super generous. He gave me and Priya start-up money for Gaia's Glow. And he helped my mom finance her salon too."

"That's nice. Do they get along, your parents?"

"They do." Hannah smiled and rolled her eyes. "They're, like, really good friends. My mom is even tight with Mai Ling. That's my dad's wife."

"That's awesome." She enjoyed hearing about Hannah's family. "Did your mom get remarried too?"

"No. She dates, though. Actually, she just broke up with her girlfriend of three years. Tania. So she's really on the prowl these days." Hannah shook her head good-naturedly but Toby was still trying to catch up. "She's fluid, my mom."

"Cool." It was interesting and seemed so opposite her parents' traditional marriage. "Are you?" she asked. "Fluid, I mean."

Hannah placed her wine on the expensive-looking antiqued coffee table and brought the snacks over too. "Aren't we all?" She popped an olive and twisted her mouth as she chewed. "All of my serious relationships have been with women, though. I have a definite preference." Hannah capped her statement off with a sip of wine. "What about you?"

Toby laughed. She hadn't even looked at a boy since junior high. "I don't disagree with you. I think there's a spectrum. I happen to be at the very far end of it," she said with a grin.

"Lucky for me." Hannah leaned forward and kissed her. It was hot and heavy but only for a minute before Hannah pulled back. "We should put the movie on," she whispered.

"Sure," Toby said.

Cuddled on the massive couch, they kissed and held hands and talked through the bulk of *The Holiday*. Listening to Hannah divulge details of her life made Toby feel close and connected in a way she couldn't really put her finger on, and when the movie ended, Toby's spirits sank because she knew leaving was inevitable.

Hannah huddled close and kissed her neck. "What time do you have to be in to work tomorrow?"

Toby held her close and found her lips. "I'm off tomorrow," she said.

"Really?"

"Yes." She narrowed her eyes at Hannah's excited voice.

"That means you don't have to race home." She shrugged and pouted. "Kinda not ready for you to leave."

"Good to know." Toby inched forward, fully ready to make a move just as Hannah jumped up.

"I have something for you," she said. "I keep forgetting." She bent down and placed a kiss on her lips. "Hold that thought."

She was only gone a second, and when she came back, she held a bevy of Gaia's Glow products in both hands. Hannah waved a small box. "This is our new hair pomade." She handed it over. "I thought you might like it. My mom says her clients rave about it."

Toby opened the box and took out the tub inside. It was beautifully labeled like all of Gaia's creations. She unscrewed the cap, and it smelled awesome. Earthy and light without being floral. She approved. "Thank you so much. I can't wait to try it."

"If you hate it, it's fine. I know that people are particular about what works for their hair." Hannah reached up and ran a hand through her thick waves. "Whatever you're doing here needs absolutely zero improvement."

"I'm sure I'll love it," Toby said. They were so close, and the way Hannah was stroking her hair, Toby simply could not resist. She leaned all the way back into the cushions and brought Hannah with her. The kiss that followed was deep and leading, and it was all she could do to keep her hands to herself.

Hannah was into it. The way she moaned and moved on top of her said as much. But when Toby opened her eyes, she saw that despite the heavy make-out session underway, Hannah was still holding on to a tube of product in her other hand.

"What is that?"

"Mmm." Hannah nuzzled into her neck and piled the baby kisses on before making a big deal of having to tear herself away. "This"—she held up the tube—"is for your knee."

Toby had a thousand questions, but all she could muster was a very confused, "What is it?"

Hannah sat upright and patted Toby's abdomen. "Sit up for a second," she said. She flipped over the tube and seemed to be evaluating the ingredients. "This is a healing balm," she said, continuing to read the label. "It's derived largely from arnica, which is a kind of natural pain reliever. It helps with bruising and soreness." Hannah rubbed her knee gently. "How is it today?"

"A little banged up," Toby admitted. "Not too bad, though." The fact that Hannah thought about her comfort was almost as much of a turn-on as anything else.

"Let me see," Hannah said.

Toby swallowed hard, and she looked down at her knee before meeting Hannah's eyes. "Um, that would require…" She waved over her jeans. "I mean, I'd have to take these off."

Hannah's expression was sexy and mischievous when she shrugged. "I'm okay with it if you are."

"Okay," Toby said. She unbuckled her belt and unzipped her jeans, stripping down like it was no big deal. She sent out a mini-message of gratitude to the universe that she'd worn her best boxer briefs as she sat back down on the couch.

Toby's knee was puffy and just starting to bruise. Hannah touched it gingerly. "Does that hurt?"

"Not really."

Hannah squeezed some of the balm on her hands and massaged it around her knee with the lightest touch possible. Toby couldn't help but laugh.

"Why are you laughing?"

"Because it tickles. And it's cute that you care about my knee." Toby leaned forward and kissed her. "And I'm in my underwear," she whispered.

"Oh, I'm aware." Hannah kissed her, and Toby felt a finger trace along her thigh and slip under the fabric of her boxers.

It was on.

Toby leaned forward and kissed Hannah's face and neck and chest. She found her mouth and kissed her soft and slow until she lost her willpower and gave in to the hard, hungry desire coursing through her body. Hannah's fingernails grazed the skin of her stomach and then lower until her palm rested atop the crotch of her boxers. It drove her crazy in the best way. Without even thinking about it, she maneuvered Hannah into a straddle on top of her and lifted her shirt over her head.

She ran her lips along the curve of her breasts and felt Hannah's hands tug her hair and pull her closer as she moaned in approval.

"Hannah." Toby looked up at the gorgeous semi-clothed woman on top of her and paused before unhooking her bra. In a way it was a formality, but in her mind it also signaled a threshold that, once crossed, meant they were really going for it. Toby needed to check in. "Are you sure you want to do this?"

Hannah's breathless expression was an answer in and of itself, but she nodded anyway. "Yes." She found Toby's lips and kissed her over and over. "But perhaps not on the couch." With that single disclaimer, Hannah stood and held Toby's hand as she led the way down the hall.

They were in Hannah's bedroom, or maybe it was the guest room—Toby had no idea really. It didn't matter. All she was aware of was Hannah's perfect mouth on hers as they discarded what remained of each other's clothes. Hannah slipped under the covers and guided Toby with her. Naked, she could feel Hannah's nipples against her body, and she lowered her head to appreciate them fully.

"Your lips are amazing," Hannah whispered.

Toby smiled against Hannah's smooth skin, placing a baby kiss on a beauty mark just below her breast. She felt Hannah's legs spread wide as she moved against her. Toby wanted to go slow. God, she wanted to. But her body throbbed like crazy, and the way Hannah was writhing beneath her said the time for waiting was over.

She caressed the inside of Hannah's thigh all the way up to her center, and Jesus Christ, she shuddered at how wet she was. Toby slipped inside with ease, and her mouth dropped open when Hannah tightened around her fingers. She moved with purpose, her own breathing keeping time with Hannah's short, staccato gasps. When she couldn't resist any longer, she gave in to what she'd wanted all night, all season, and kissed her way down Hannah's beautiful body.

CHAPTER TEN

Was this what ecstasy felt like?

Hannah tossed her head from side to side, trying to hold off her impending orgasm. It was going to be epic, she was sure of it, but she wasn't ready for this part to end. Where Toby might have kissed like a dream, in bed she was a freaking deity.

Toby's hands were soft and strong, generous with perfect touches and divine pressure. Hannah wanted her touch everywhere, all at once, impossibly at the same time. She needed it in a way she hadn't even been aware of. And her mouth. My God, her mouth. Warm, inviting, lush, and lavish. There was no way to adequately describe the mastery of feelings Toby was able to evoke.

Hannah stopped edging and let herself go entirely. She was probably writhing and moaning, possibly pulling hair, maybe leaving scratch marks. She honestly had no idea. When her orgasm hit, it was like an out-of-body experience. She felt like she was hovering over the bed, drifting on a cloud of euphoria, the mortal world a foreign universe beneath her, ignorant to the blissful realm she temporarily inhabited.

Toby kissed her way up her body and snuggled against her. Hannah felt her lips on her neck and shoulder but she directed Toby's face to hers, kissing her soundly.

"That was…You are…" Hannah blinked slow and let her words hang because she knew there was nothing she could say to do the moment justice. Toby kissed her eyelids, and she melted even more. "How do you do that?"

"What?" Toby said as though she had no idea the skill level she possessed. Her obliviousness was sexy as hell.

She tugged Toby's wild hair. "What am I going to do with you?" she said mostly to herself.

"Pretty much whatever you want." Toby smirked. "And if you don't want, that's cool." Toby settled into the pillows, holding her close as she dropped a peck on her shoulder. "No pressure."

"Babe." Hannah kissed her chest. "Please don't tell me this is off-limits." She waved over Toby's body. "I have pretty much been fantasizing about you since I bumped into you on day one." She found Toby's lips. "I just need a minute. My body is rebooting as we speak."

"Did it shut down?" Toby's tone was slightly smug, and Hannah kind of loved it.

Hannah closed her eyes and pursed her lips. "Whatever you did to me...pretty much activated the kill switch."

Toby laughed, and it was a glorious sound. Lively and sexy and fun, full of happiness and thick with emotion.

It was absolutely perfect, and it set the tone for the entire night.

Under the covers, in her dad's spare bedroom, they kissed and cuddled and talked about everything. Dreams of families, hopes for the future, fantasy vacations. But it wasn't all wine and roses. Even their fears and anxieties went on the table. Hannah learned that Toby stressed she'd never find her true calling, and in turn, she revealed that she constantly worried her company would go under.

Hannah would never remember the exact words Toby said to make it all okay, but in Toby's presence, she felt like she could accomplish anything. It was like Toby's enthusiasm and sheer faith gave her confidence. When she brushed her fingers through Toby's hair, she encouraged Toby not to give up hope, as she reminded herself to get Parker's contact info. Toby smiled in response and her soft expression said she took the words to heart.

What was happening between them? And why did it have to end with the holidays?

At one a.m., wrapped in Mai Ling's super high thread count bedsheets, she sat on Toby's lap in the kitchen feeding them carrots and hummus and Gouda with rice crackers.

"What will you do for Christmas?" Hannah asked.

"Good question." Toby seemed to consider her options. "I have the week off, so I could go see my parents, I guess. Or I could just go over to my Aunt Joan's for the day and pick up overtime shifts the rest of the week. I haven't decided yet."

"Spend Christmas with me." Hannah didn't allow herself to overthink it, or think about it at all really. She knew if she did, she'd chicken out. "Come to Hudson." She hitched her shoulders up like the invite was the most normal thing in the world. "We'll go to my mom's for dinner. You'll meet my aunt and my sister and my cousin. Priya and Dev will be there. All the people who are important to me." She kissed Toby's temple. "I know it's crazy, but you're on that list. I think about you, like, constantly."

"Okay." Toby's smile said the feeling was mutual, and Hannah hugged her like a giddy teenager.

"Really?"

"This...you..." Toby licked her lips like she was at a loss. "I didn't expect any of it." She shrugged. "But there's no doubt there's something here."

Hannah wasn't a hundred percent sure what they were even talking about. She knew what she felt. Ludicrous as it was. And even though neither of them used any specific words, it seemed whatever they were in, they were in it together.

"Come on, let's go back to bed," she said, getting up to put their leftovers away in the fridge.

"You don't want me to go home?" Toby asked. It was sweet that Toby offered in case she wasn't ready for an overnighter, but Hannah most definitely did not want her to leave.

"I want you to stay." She shut the refrigerator door, panicked that she'd come off bossy. "Only if you want, though."

"Heck, yeah, I want to." Toby looked adorably bedraggled and a touch sleepy. "I just didn't want to assume a sleepover. I'm a little worried about coming on too strong and scaring you away."

Her nervous laugh didn't undermine the seriousness of her statement. But Hannah knew that was the furthest thing from happening. It was fast, for sure, but she'd never felt this kind of connection with anyone, and she wasn't ready to let it slip away.

"The way I see it"—she reached for Toby's hand and guided them toward the bedroom—"time is of the essence. I vote sleepovers from here on out." She punctuated her decree with a definitive nod, loving that Toby cuddled her from behind as they shuffled down the hall.

"No argument here," Toby said.

"One thing, though," she added.

"Anything." Toby was kissing her neck, and it drove her crazy.

"I'm oddly not tired anymore." She turned to face Toby. "Can you think of anything to tucker me out?" She giggled at her own silly lure, but it was okay because there was heat in Toby's sweet brown eyes.

"Say no more," Toby said.

She couldn't if she tried.

❖

When her alarm went off at eight thirty, Hannah groaned. She'd reset it dozens of times over the course of the early morning hours when she and Toby went round after round, talking and touching. She kept adjusting the wake-up call to allow for as much sleep as possible. But as much as she cared about being rested, she also didn't. In the moment the only thing that mattered was Toby.

"How do you feel?" Toby spooned her from behind.

"Exhausted. Amazing," she answered, hugging her close. "Four hours of sleep isn't terrible." Hannah wondered if she was trying to pep talk herself. "I am going to hop in the shower, though." She rolled over and kissed Toby's forehead. "I'll be right back."

When she returned, she was both pleased and disappointed that Toby was up and dressed. If Toby hadn't moved, she'd definitely have crawled back into bed, and while that would be a great start to the day, she still needed to get to the market. So she dressed super-fast and felt a ridiculous amount of emotion when she saw that Toby had made the bed, which was maybe the cutest thing ever.

"You are adorable," she said when she found Toby playing on her phone in the kitchen. She peppered her face with baby kisses. "You made the bed."

Toby shrugged. "It's the least I could do." She felt Toby's arms wrap around her as she pulled her in tight and kissed her for real. "You have to go to work. I get to go nap the day away."

"Tease," Hannah whacked her chest playfully.

"Come with me." Toby's hands roamed. "Blow off work and come to my apartment."

"I wish. Priya would kill me."

"Nah. She's been shipping us since the beginning."

Hannah laughed out loud. "Not subtle, that one." She reached for her keys and her phone and put them in her bag. "Walk me to work?" she said with a light plea in her tone. Hannah didn't want to sound pushy, but she wanted to capitalize on every minute together.

"Already planning on it," Toby said as she took her hand.

They walked the short distance, talking and holding hands the whole way. When they got to the market entrance, Hannah wasn't sure what to expect with Toby's coworkers scattered about. But her concern was for naught. The kiss good-bye Toby dropped on her was nothing short of decadent. Hannah practically floated on a cloud into the booth.

"Well, well, well," Priya started, clearly witness to the entire display. "It seems someone's gotten her battery charged."

"Is that even a euphemism?" she asked with a laugh.

"It is now."

Priya rested her chin in her hand obviously waiting for details, and Hannah was generous with them, right up to and including how deeply she felt about Toby. True to form, her bestie was all encouragement with no judgment, channeling her lifelong mantra that when the right person came along, it was something felt in the soul. Timelines simply didn't come into play. It might happen over the course of a year or in one conversation. When you knew, you knew.

Hannah listened intently, considering long-distance for the first time. Two hours was not a backbreaking distance. Honestly, she knew people who did the commute from Hudson to NYC daily, and while the city wasn't her favorite place in the world, Toby made it feel special and not overwhelming. Or maybe it was just that everything with Toby was better.

It was cheesy and corny and a reality Toby proved day and night.

In the evenings that led up to Christmas, Toby led her all over the city. But instead of the hustle and bustle that she always imagined was New York City this time of year, Toby had a way of finding the quiet joy she so desperately craved.

Hand in hand they strolled the holiday windows of Fifth Avenue at an off-peak hour when there was no crowd. Toby took her to see the lights of Dyker Heights in Brooklyn, where they walked the neighborhood streets, gaping and smiling at the homes that went above and beyond with decorations. Through it all they kissed and canoodled, making goo-goo eyes at each other during the market hours and following through on those promises every single night.

Two days before Christmas Eve, Toby strolled up to the booth at ten a.m. sharp.

"You're here early," Hannah said as she began her morning shop routine.

"I switched tours with one of the early morning guys," Toby said. She seemed antsy as she looked around.

"What's wrong, babe?" Hannah winced in apology for her use of the familiar term while they were at work. "You seem frazzled."

"I'm fine. I was actually hoping to catch Priya."

"Um…something you want to tell me?" she teased.

"Ha-ha." Toby fidgeted with snaps on her belt that kept her gear in place. "I was hoping you could sneak out early tonight. I know it's nearing the end of the market, but it's pretty important."

She wanted to say yes. To unequivocally agree on the spot. But Gaia's Glow was a partnership, and with only two full days left of the market, she didn't want to abandon Priya. "How early?" she asked.

Toby ticked her head back and forth like she was trying to figure it out without revealing whatever surprise she was concocting. "Seven thirty would be the absolute latest we should leave here and make it in time." Her brow creased adorably.

"For the record, it is taking all my willpower not to beg you to tell me what's in store."

Toby's grin was wicked and gorgeous. "I think you'll like it." She held up both hands, fingers crossed.

It could be almost anything in the world. If Toby was with her, Hannah was a thousand percent sure she would love it.

CHAPTER ELEVEN

W e'll be there in two minutes—stop trying to figure it out."
Toby's order was all in jest as they strolled west along Sixty-Fifth Street. She figured Hannah might be on to her anyway because when they met up at seven fifteen at the edge of the Central Park Holiday Market, Hannah had changed into a completely different outfit.

Either way, she was about to find out for sure as Lincoln Center came into view. The arches of the Metropolitan Opera House were illuminated a bright gold against the dark night sky. A beautifully decked tree was visible behind the iconic fountain.

Hannah stopped dead as they reached Columbus Avenue. "We're not...Are we going to..."

"I got us tickets to *The Nutcracker*." Toby finished Hannah's sentence. She was still a little nervous it might not fly. She knew *The Nutcracker Suite* was one of Hannah's faves, but she also knew the ballet—this ballet, three days before Christmas—would be mobbed. "I know it's going to be packed. We don't have to go in if you don't want."

"Toby." Hannah's eyes watered. "Of course I want to go." She wiped at her tears as they crossed into the square. "But how did you know?" Her voice faded as though she was in utter disbelief. "More importantly, how did you get tickets? This must have cost a fortune."

"You have all these decorative nutcrackers in your booth. And there's even one in the bedroom at your dad's. Plus you get this gorgeous faraway look in your eye every time the 'Dance of the Sugar Plum Fairy' plays. Which is like nonstop this time of year."

Hannah squeezed her hand and leaned up to kiss her cheek. "How did you land tickets, though?" They were stopped between the fountain and the theater entrance, and Hannah seemed to be taking it all in. "Do you know, this was the only thing I even considered doing when I knew I was going to be stuck in New York City for nearly two months."

"Really?"

"Yes." Hannah's eyes widened. "Then I saw the price tag and almost fainted."

Toby held her hands and looked into her beautiful eyes. "Merry Christmas," she said.

Hannah hugged her and kissed her. She was completely crying, but Toby knew they were tears of joy. "I just…" She shook her head. "I cannot believe you did this for me."

Toby swayed Hannah in her arms, and everything she was feeling rushed to the surface. "The thing is, Hannah—and I know this is crazy." She laughed and shrugged, not the least bit nervous over what she was about to say. "I'm in love with you." She kept talking, so Hannah felt no pressure to say it back. "I didn't expect it. I wasn't looking for it. But these past few weeks have been amazing. You're sweet and funny, and I don't know, you just get me. I can't explain it." She touched their foreheads together. "I don't know how you feel, not really, but I'm hoping if it's at least a percentage of what I do, you'll consider trying to figure out a way to make this work, even after Christmas—"

Hannah silenced her with a finger over her lips. "I love you too." She followed her confession with a perfect kiss. "For a second there I wasn't sure you were going to let me say it." She laughed through her tears. "I love your giant heart and the way you want to help people. God, I love how happy I feel when I'm with you. I don't want it to end."

"So we're doing this?"

"We definitely are." Hannah kissed her again. "Let's go see this amazing show. We have all night to figure out the details."

Two nights later, they packed up the booth before heading up to Hudson. They arrived late on Christmas Eve. It was almost midnight, but they popped by Hannah's mom's for a quick visit anyway. After weeks apart, Hannah was itching to see her fam, and witnessing the reunion firsthand melted Toby. Hannah's mom brought her in for a group hug, and it was clear she was up to speed already. It touched her in a way she didn't quite expect.

On Christmas morning they slept in, cuddling and lounging in Hannah's cozy second-floor apartment on Hudson's main drag. She sipped coffee in front of the window and smiled as she watched the townsfolk on the street greet each other. When Hannah snuggled her from behind and kissed her shoulder, she felt her heart beat with joy. No fooling, less than twenty-four hours in, and Toby could get used to this. She laughed at her own all-in approach to relationships, but everything with Hannah just felt right. The way they could talk about anything, how comfortable she felt to be herself right from the start. There was no explaining it, but this was the real deal.

Midafternoon, they headed back through the adorable town to Hannah's mom's house. Toby felt like a dolt that she didn't have a single gift for anyone, but Hannah told her not to sweat it—her family wasn't big on gifts anyway. Whether they toned it down for her or not, she would never really know. What was clear beyond any doubt was that this was a family that loved being with each other, and that love seemed to extend to her already.

"Hannah says you're the best police officer in the NYPD," Marisa Monroe said over her eggnog.

Toby sent a devilish look to Hannah, who simply shrugged in response.

"How is your knee, by the way?" her sister Aubrey chimed in. "Did the balm help at all?"

"It's much better, thank you." She was curious just how much the gang knew, but Hannah answered with a kiss to the cheek.

"I was worried about you. Aubrey studied physiology." Hannah draped an arm across her shoulder and rubbed her abdomen in a way that had become familiar. "Please don't be mad at me for seeking input."

"I'm not mad at all," Toby said. "Far from it." She dropped a kiss on Hannah's temple, so grateful to have such a thoughtful girlfriend.

"My family loves you," Hannah whispered when they had a moment alone by the tree.

Toby cradled her from behind. "They're amazing. Just like you." They were almost kissing but a loud affectionate sigh made them both turn.

"I love *love*." Aunt Lindsay clutched her chest before waving them over. "Come on, cuties," she said. "Marisa and I cooked up a feast. Let's eat."

Christmas in Hudson went beyond Toby's expectations in every way. The day was magical, the week amazing.

Toby was loving life. It seemed every day was easier than the day before, but harder also. Her weekend trip expanded to three days, then to four. Hannah begged her to stay until she absolutely had to leave, and she complied willingly. She didn't want to go.

They hiked and talked the days away, then made the most of the nights together. Over the half dozen walks they took on the lost days between Christmas and New Year's, they settled on something of a schedule for the future that revolved around Toby's shift work. Hannah had offered to come down to the city twice a week, but Toby knew she wasn't totally comfortable there, so she volunteered to spend her days off up in Hudson.

The stark truth was she loved it here.

It was all Hannah. She would have traveled to the end of the earth to be with this person she had so perfectly, so unexpectedly fallen for.

But Hudson itself was appealing too. It wasn't rural in the way she expected. The town fostered an urban, artsy feel that she could truly get down with. There were bars and restaurants, boutique hotels. It was a chic little city. Gritty and hippie and bursting with ambiance.

On her final afternoon, they were walking out of Marisa's salon headed to Hannah's favorite brunch spot. They'd eaten there several times already that week, but Toby lobbied hard for it anyway. She was going to miss the signature quiche and homemade pumpernickel rye when she returned to the city tomorrow.

"Babe." Hannah stopped dead. "Did you pick up my phone by any chance?" She searched her purse quickly. "I'll be right back," Hannah said, racing back inside before she could even answer.

Toby stayed outside and basked in the glorious sun shining over the vista as she tried not to eavesdrop on a dude who paused to finish up a phone call. Her attention was drawn to his longish hair and full beard, and she wondered if he'd come to the salon for a haircut.

"Thanks, Mom," Hannah called out before the door closed behind her. "Oh my God, Parker!"

"Hey, Hannah," the guy said, ending his call and climbing the stairs to give her a hug. "Merry Christmas and all that."

"Do you have an appointment with my mom today?" she asked. "I didn't see your name on the schedule."

"Nah." He rubbed his cheeks. "I was actually stopping by to pick up some of the beard tonic you sell. Stuff's awesome."

"Parker, this is Toby." Hannah reached for her hand and held it. "The person I spoke to you about. My girlfriend." Hannah was beaming, and Toby was too smitten to be embarrassed she'd sort of dropped the ball on reaching out to him.

"No way. Toby." He extended his hand. "Hannah said a bunch of awesome stuff about you. You have an MSW and you're a cop, right?"

"Yeah."

"Wanna come work for me?" He laughed at his own joke, but honestly it sounded fucking great. Toby opened the salon door and they all headed back inside. Parker turned to talk to her while Hannah rang up his product. "Hannah mentioned you're interested in programs like Wayfinder. Come see what we do." His invitation felt off-the-cuff and genuine at the same time. He grabbed his beard oil. "Hannah has my number. Hit me up." He backed toward the door with something of a grin. "I know I made light of it, but I was halfway serious. If you decide to move to Hudson, definitely let me know. We could use someone with your skill set at Wayfinder."

Well, holy fuck.

❖

Toby woke up early. She'd stayed in Hudson a full week, something neither she nor Hannah planned, but it seemed so right. Unfortunately, New Year's Eve meant a mandatory night tour in the middle of thousands of people in Times Square.

"I don't want you to leave." Hannah cuddled in close against her.

Toby kissed her bare shoulder. "I didn't know you were awake."

"Can't you call out sick?"

When Hannah turned and pouted, Toby was almost tempted. Instead she kissed Hannah's cheeks, her forehead, her chin, her nose. "I could." She found her mouth and kissed her long and slow. "But that would be irresponsible." Hannah looked so sad it made her chest feel hollow. "I'm sorry, babe. I really am. I don't want to leave."

"You'll be so cold tonight."

"There'll be places to warm up. Honest." Toby lay back and hugged Hannah close, loving the feel of their naked bodies touching everywhere. She was going to miss this togetherness for the next few days.

"Promise me you'll be careful." Hannah kissed her soundly, and Toby felt it everywhere.

"I'm always careful."

"I'll be thinking of you at midnight."

"I know. Me too." She throbbed when Hannah shifted and straddled her.

"Do not kiss any drunk girls," Hannah ordered playfully.

"Are you crazy?" Toby responded. She knew Hannah was teasing, but there was only one person she wanted to kiss at midnight, and she wanted her to know it.

"About you? Yes." Hannah's tone dripped promise and emotion.

"I'll call you as soon as the ball drops," Toby said between kisses as she tried to keep her emotions in check. "And I'll be back in a few days."

"Toby."

"Yeah," she breathed out.

"I love you."

"I know." It was exactly what she wanted and needed to hear. Honestly it would never get old. "But Hannah?"

"Yes?" Hannah's response was faint as she writhed on top.

Toby sat upright to kiss her beautiful face. "I loved you first."

"Yeah…I don't know about that," Hannah said through a measured giggle.

"I do."

Toby absolutely loved to see Hannah smile. Her laugh was gorgeous and infectious, and she needed to store it up to last the days they were apart. She flipped them so she was in position to kiss her all over. She started slow, finding Hannah's lips, her perfect mouth, her face, her neck, and beyond, so ready to take her time proving the depth of her love.

With any luck it would take forever.

Epilogue

One year later

"Five minutes, babe."

Toby knew she was cutting it close, but she wanted everything to be perfect. "One second," she called from the kitchen as she reached in the fridge and took out the champagne she'd hidden behind the oat milk. She grabbed two flutes from the top shelf of the cabinet and twisted the wire fastener that held the cork in place.

"Everything okay in there?" Hannah sounded not quite stressed, but not chill either, and Toby knew she was worried about missing the key moment.

"Yep," she said. Just one more nudge, and with a teensy pop the cork released and the sparkling wine bubbled over. Toby managed to get most of it into their glasses and wiped the excess off the floor with a dish towel. Squaring her shoulders, she paraded into the living room, presenting their drinks to mark the occasion.

"Here we go," she said as she handed Hannah a glass. She saw Hannah's eyes light up and fill with affection and love at the gesture.

"You got us champagne," Hannah said.

There was a certain amount of unbridled sentiment in her voice, and even though Toby couldn't quite name it, she felt it flood through her entire being. "I did," she said, trying to keep her emotions in check. "It's probably ridiculous, and I know we joke about it, but I will always think of this entire season as our anniversary." She shrugged and smiled. "Tonight seemed like a fitting time to celebrate."

"You're so right." Hannah covered her heart.

They often joked about whether the timeline of their romance began the night of Ned's play or the tree lighting or even the first time they bumped into one another. But it hardly mattered. Christmas, New Year's Eve, the entire holiday season would forever be their time. In her heart she knew it, and she suspected Hannah did too.

"I love that you're such a romantic," Hannah said.

"You bring it out in me." Toby dropped a kiss on her cheek, knowing it was the truth. She draped her arm along the back of the couch, so Hannah would snuggle into her the way she loved. She glanced at the countdown on the TV showing just under two minutes as the camera panned the hordes of people in New York City waiting for the ball to drop in Times Square. Toby shivered as she remembered years of being cold and alone among the masses as she lined the street to keep order in the chaos.

"Do you miss it?" Hannah asked.

Toby looked at her like she was crazy just so Hannah would know how much she appreciated being exactly where she was. Inside, in their apartment, warm and toasty and in love with her absolute soul mate.

"Not even a little," she said, just in case there was any lingering doubt in Hannah's mind.

Once Toby left the NYPD, she never looked back. It all happened so seamlessly that it was as though this was meant to be her path all along.

Six months into a truly easy long-distance romance, she and Hannah had been going strong. On the rare occasion she hadn't been able to make it upstate on her days off, Hannah came to the city and spent the night. But more often than not, Toby chose to maximize her time in Hudson, because Hannah had been right. She loved it. The town, the hills, the hikes, the culture, the vibe. Hannah. It was heaven.

Wayfinder had been her destiny. Parker welcomed her on board as though she belonged. Because she did. She owed some of the credit for the transition to Hannah, but she brought enough to the table in her own right. She had great contacts in the city, and she was happy to share them. The career change was hardly even an adjustment. This was what she was born to do, and she knew it the minute she stepped foot in the door. It was the perfect fit.

"Well, I, for one, am glad that you are here with me," Hannah said. "I like you safe and close and bringing goodness to the world right near me."

"Good to know," Toby said.

"As if you didn't know that already," Hannah teased.

It was true, but Toby would never tire of hearing Hannah flirt. "I think we should do this every year," she said, turning the light moment slightly serious with the proposition of a tradition. "Celebrate our anniversary on New Year's Eve."

"Me and you and champagne." Hannah nodded agreement at the perfect simplicity of the suggestion. "I can't think of anything more perfect."

"You sure?" Toby asked feeling her adrenaline spike in anticipation of the leap of faith she was about to take.

"I love you so much, Toby." Hannah leaned forward to kiss her even though it wasn't quite midnight.

Toby smiled against Hannah's mouth, and her heart raced as she checked a look at the countdown timer. They were down to the final ten seconds, and she reached into her pocket as she slipped onto one knee, just as the television crowd chanted single digits in unison. She saw Hannah cover her mouth with both hands, obviously clued in to what she was doing.

Three. Two. One.

"Will you marry me?" Toby asked.

Hannah shook her head first, clearly stunned at the proposal before changing course and nodding over and over. "Yes. Yes. Yes." Hannah dropped to her knees on the floor and kissed her. "Of course I will marry you."

Toby held her tight and touched their foreheads together, breathing out a sigh that was both exhilaration and relief.

"Babe, were you nervous?" Hannah said through a string of kisses to her face.

"Yes, no, I don't know." Toby laughed. "Maybe a little, I guess." She found Hannah's lips. "I just love you so much. I guess sometimes I think it's too good to be true."

"It's all true." Hannah kissed her, and she let herself truly sink into it, knowing this was only the beginning of their journey together. Against a background of cheers and a chorus of "Auld Lang Syne" in the distance, they held on to each other, knowing so many memories were yet to be made.

"Happy New Year," Toby said, when she finally found her voice.

Hannah draped her arms across her shoulders and shook her head, a fake frown on display. "Happy *life*," she corrected.

Toby beamed ear to ear as she leaned in for one more kiss.

Happy life, indeed.

A Christmas Miracle

Fiona Riley

CHAPTER ONE

Mira Donahue looked out at the bar before her and smiled when she noticed the framed article from the *Improper Bostonian* awarding her bar, The Mirage, the title of Best Bar in Boston. Opening this place had been a labor of love and hard work for fifteen years. But it was finally everything she had ever wanted and dreamed of. And the last year and a half of endless nights and weekends slinging drinks and managing her hand-picked group of bartenders had totally paid off—she officially had the hottest bar on the block. And business was booming, which was great. What wasn't great was that her events coordinator, Kelly Shannon, was going out on maternity leave earlier than expected and leaving her high and dry during her busiest and most dreaded event season: Christmas. She hated Christmas.

"You're gonna do fine," Kelly said as she rubbed Mira's shoulder. "And I'm always just a call away."

"I'm not going to call you while you're in labor, Kelly. And we both know I'm going to need you the most when you're in labor, and unavailable, because that's how these things pan out." Mira tried not to pout. Aside from missing Kelly's unmatched ability to handle all needy and demanding event clients, she was also her most reliable and popular senior bartender. And her best friend. She was going to miss having her around and being able to count on her to pick up the slack if things got out of hand. Which they almost always seemed to do.

"You're pouting." Kelly poked her in the ribs.

"I'm not. But I want to be," Mira said, giving in to the pout.

"It's going to work out, I promise." Kelly pulled out the file folder and placed it on the bar in front of them. They still had an hour before opening, so the place was spotless and ready to go, but quiet. Like the calm before a storm. Mira was glad for the quiet, so she and Kelly could work out the details.

Mira thumbed through the file and laughed. "Damn, this is organized."

"Well, I wasn't going to leave you unprepared." Kelly pointed to the barrage of colored flags and highlights on the papers in front of them. "Each event for the holiday season has a title, a contact person, a theme, and all the necessary details you'll need to know about, listed here and here. The colored flags will help you navigate the clients and any important details. Like this one"—she pointed to one of a few red flags—"this one means pay attention to the allergy list of the attendees and double-check the caterer order. That's all."

"That's all, huh?" Mira stared at the overflowing file folder, and her vision blurred with all the technicolor directions. "Piece of cake."

"Exactly." Kelly patted her hand. "Just look them over tonight, and let me know if you have any questions. I'll sort out whatever you need, or simplify it if you need me to, but you're a smart lady. You'll be fine."

"I can't believe you're leaving me." Mira frowned.

"I'm having a baby, not leaving you," Kelly corrected.

"Yet," Mira supplied.

"We'll see." Kelly squeezed her hand. "I'm in no rush to give up this bar or you—I'm just going to be focusing on Baby Shannon for a while."

"If it's a girl, will you name her Shannon Shannon? Because that would be hilarious," Mira teased.

"Shannon Squared has a nice ring to it," Kelly joked. "I'll run it by Sarah, but I feel like she might squash it."

"Fine, fine," Mira acquiesced. "I'm sure you'll pick something not cringeworthy."

"Thanks for the vote of confidence," Kelly said as she placed a hand on her significant baby bump. "Oof, she's kicking up a storm today."

"Wait, I thought you weren't going to find out the sex?" Mira asked excitedly. She'd been hoping it was a girl.

"We aren't. I just…I don't know—I've been having a lot of dreams lately that she's a girl, so I'm just going with it up until the big day." Kelly shrugged.

"Which is when?" Mira asked, consulting the events calendar Kelly had stapled to the inside of the file folder. Kelly had circled the date with hearts and stars, and Mira remembered why she had mentally blocked it out.

"Christmas Day," Kelly said, and Mira groaned.

"Poor kid."

"Listen, Grinch. Not everyone hates Christmas. Most people love it."

"Most people aren't born on Christmas. Ask little Shannon Squared if she loves it when she has to share her birthday with a fat man in a red suit. She'll forever be eclipsed by a fictional burglar who brings you ugly Christmas sweaters and more unwanted socks."

"Or maybe she'll be lucky enough to share a Christmas birthday with her Auntie Mira." Kelly squeezed her hand. "Because you were born on Christmas, and I think you're pretty awesome. I know that she will, too."

"You're just saying that because I agreed to your strong-armed request for sixteen weeks' paid leave," Mira said, though secretly she was hoping that Baby Shannon would share the day with her, since it had long lost its luster. She could use a reason to learn to love the season again. And a new baby would definitely help with that.

"You love me," Kelly said, and Mira did. They'd been friends for over a decade, and she was over the moon that Kelly and her wife were starting a family. They were good people, and she was sure whatever child they brought into the world would continue that legacy. "Okay, I'm going to be late for my OB appointment if I don't get out of here before you open for the night. You're going to do great. I promise. You won't even miss me."

"Not likely," Mira said as she met her friend and gave her a hug. Shannon Squared kicked her in the gut during the embrace. "Man, she's got a boot."

"Don't I know it," Kelly said as she rubbed the spot and winced.

"Just because you're leaving me doesn't mean you don't still have to update me about every appointment and exciting development," Mira reminded her.

"Yes, Mom," Kelly said as she struggled to pull on her jacket.

"I'm not old enough to be your mom," Mira called out as Kelly pushed open the door, letting the cold wind sweep into the space.

"Noted, Mom." Kelly waved as the door closed, leaving Mira alone with her thoughts and the massive folder full of events she had no idea how to manage in Kelly's absence.

"I'm so screwed."

Chapter Two

Courtney Rivers loved Christmas. She loved all holidays, but especially Christmas. She loved the good cheer and generosity of the season. And warm hot cocoa by the fire with your girlfriend, and sure, she didn't have a fireplace or a girlfriend to have hot cocoa with, but that didn't matter. Because the Christmas season was full of promise and gratitude and presents and Christmas carols. And who didn't like Christmas carols?

She was especially excited about this Christmas because she'd managed the impossible feat of booking The Mirage for her company's Christmas party this year. It was promising to be the event of the season. She just knew it. And since there was now an open position in the Event Planning and Marketing division at their sister company, she wanted more than anything to prove her worth and secure that transfer. She was done running errands and making copies as an administrative assistant to the executives at Buxby Partners. She'd dreamed of being a party planner for as long as she could remember, and scoring a comfortable, deep-pocketed corporate gig was the launching point she needed to branch off and start her own business. Eventually, that was. But she knew that this party being a success would go a long way.

And after she killed it on the planning front, she had her much-anticipated trip with her family to her grandfather's ski cabin in Colorado to look forward to. They would decorate the massive twenty-foot tree in the grand room while overlooking the mountain view below, and they'd make popcorn garlands like her grandmother used to. It was all going to be epic.

"What's up, Rivers? How's the planning going?" her boss, Chet Buxby, asked, trying and failing to sound young, despite his graying temples. He'd inherited this firm and its success from his now retired parents. He was nice enough, but Courtney didn't like working directly for him. He had a wandering eye and gave her the creeps when they were alone, which thankfully, wasn't often. She worked for a few of the higher-ups, not just Chet, but he was the one standing between her and that dream job.

What was unique about Buxby Partners, and what had drawn Courtney to them originally, was their connection to philanthropic work. In her heyday, Chet's mother had started Buxby Philanthropic, an offshoot of the business, as a way to give back to the community. They operated as a separate company, but under the umbrella of the Buxby name. Aside from their incredible community impact, their events and fundraisers were some of the best attended and most lauded in the city. Everyone in the planning business wanted to work with Buxby Philanthropic. But that meant that few positions in the Event Planning division ever opened up. Until now. Courtney had hoped that applying in-house would give her the edge, but Chet seemed to be dragging his feet on pushing her application. Until he needed her, that was.

In the past, both parts of Buxby celebrated their holiday parties together, planned by Philanthropic, but this year, things were different. Chet and his colleagues decided to have a smaller, more intimate event just for their branch, with the plan to join the big company-wide soiree after the New Year. The problem was that almost every place was booked already, and Events were up to their eyeballs planning fundraisers. That was the opening Courtney needed, and she volunteered immediately. She could plan this party. She was made for this. If she could impress Chet, that Events transfer was as good as hers. Courtney knew she had the favor of most of the partners, but Chet was the keystone. So when The Mirage had a last-minute cancellation, and her doggedness put her first in line to take the slot, she was all in.

"Great. It's going great." She forced a smile, mentally reminding herself that she needed to stay on Chet's good side.

"I'm counting on you. Remember our agreement. You do an awesome job, and I'll put in a good word with my mother's people," Chet tried to sound less entitled than he was, but he failed. Still, Courtney appreciated that he was willing to hold up his end of the bargain.

"You've given me a healthy budget. I'll make it the party of the century," she replied.

"Aces." He gave her a thumbs-up and a wink before heading back to his corner office.

She sighed. He was such a tool.

She settled into her desk chair and put in her headphones as she scanned her inbox. She hummed along to the Christmas station on Pandora that was playing in her ears when an email from Kelly Shannon made her squeal. This was it—this was the final communication before the big day, three weeks from now, and she just knew it was going to be everything they had planned and more. She was so excited about this party she could scream.

And scream she almost did, because the email from Kelly was to inform her that she was going out on maternity leave and wouldn't be handling the party planning moving forward.

Wait, what?

She'd been working closely with her for months. When did she mention she was having a baby?

Courtney scratched her head and thought back to their last in-person conversation. She felt like she would have noticed if Kelly was pregnant. She scanned through her inbox and looked at the email exchange and frowned. Huh. Had it really been that long since she'd seen Kelly in person? It occurred to her that most of their planning had been via email or phone calls. And try as she might, at no point could Courtney recall her mentioning she was pregnant or would be unavailable for the biggest event of Courtney's professional life.

She sighed and counted to ten. No biggie. This was no big deal. They'd already worked out the details of the party—all she had to do was confirm the final head count and the catered foods and approve the holiday themed cocktails she'd personally requested be added to the buyout package. And then things would be fine. Nothing to worry about.

She scanned the email again and found the name of the new person she would be dealing with. Someone named Mira Donahue would be reaching out to her via email or phone over the next few days to finalize the party information. Perfect. Mira was a perfectly nice and friendly sounding name. This should be no problem. All she had to do was wait, and everything would be as magical as a White Christmas, which was her favorite kind of Christmas and also the song playing on her headphones at that exact moment. Speaking of which, maybe she could convince her new best friend Mira to let her bring fake snow to put on the bar and tables. She picked up the phone to reach out to Mira, because as patient as she was, she also knew that good things came to those who hustled and made the holiday cheer phone calls.

❖

"Yes, Mom," Courtney said into the receiver as her mother prattled on and on about the upcoming family party. Of course Courtney was beyond thrilled to see her baby brother, stepbrothers, and her cousins, but that also meant she'd be seeing her parents and their significant others, which was always a crapshoot.

Her parents had divorced when she was nine, but they'd made it a point to always spend Christmas Day together, even if at times, it was tense. As the years went on, though, her mother and father remarried, and their Christmas celebration grew as the extended family did. But once her grandmother died, and her grandfather moved in with her mother, the holiday traditions changed a bit.

People started to get older, and the faces around the tree on Christmas Day began to change. Cousins began bringing girlfriends and boyfriends, and dinner was moved up to accommodate her grandfather's medication needs. And the friendliness her parents had had in her youth had dissolved with new marriages. Her father's new wife, his third now, hated her mother. And her mother hated her right back. So the last few holidays had been a strain, but this year the family vowed to get along and head to Colorado like old times, once more for Grandpa. He was getting older, and there were no guarantees in life, so they decided to put aside their differences this year to celebrate him and all the wonderful lives that had been brought together during his time as the patriarch of the family. It was promising to be a sweet and memorable event, and Courtney was looking forward to escaping her day job and forgetting about life for a while. Plus, it was Christmas. And everyone knew how magical Christmas could be.

"Anyway, your father is bringing that woman again," her mother said.

"His wife," Courtney corrected.

"Right," her mom agreed, the distaste in her voice deafening. "She'll be there with the twins, so make sure you pack Tylenol and ear plugs."

"Will do." Courtney nodded and made a note. Her father's latest marriage had brought twin boys to her life. Two eight-year-old balls of energy and fury who exhausted you before you spent five minutes with them. She still couldn't wrap her head around how her conservative, stiff, and sometimes short-tempered father managed those rambunctious whirlwinds, but she bet it had something to do with his twentysomething-year younger wife, Oksana. She and Courtney weren't that far apart in age, though they had almost nothing in common. Which was fine, since she only saw her a few times a year. She was pleasant enough as long as Courtney's mother wasn't around to draw her ire. Then it was a different story entirely.

After a pause, her mother asked, "Are you bringing anyone with you this year?"

That was a loaded question. Courtney had to give her mother credit—clearly she had practiced her delivery because it almost didn't convey the pity Courtney knew existed on her face on the other end of the line.

"No, Mom. Just me." Courtney didn't need to be reminded that she would be spending her favorite holiday alone again. It hadn't always been that way—she'd been in a long-term relationship with her college girlfriend Jess up until two years ago. Since then she'd casually dated, but she hadn't found anyone to catch her interest yet. Her mother blamed that on what she called the *unrealistic romantic expectations* of the holiday movies Courtney obsessively watched this time of year. Maybe she was right.

"You'll find someone." This time the pity was front and center in her mother's reply.

"I know." Courtney really believed that. And there was something about the holidays that felt so lovely. Like a miracle was waiting around every corner. That's why she loved Christmas so much, because it felt like anything could happen at any minute. Just like in those movies her mother hated that she watched.

"Oh, your brother is calling on the other line. I'll call you back tomorrow," her mother said, her tone instantly changing now that Greg was on the line.

"'Night, Mom."

"Bye, dear."

Courtney dropped her cell phone next to her and stretched. Relationship woes aside, work had been increasingly busy as they neared the end of the quarter. They'd had conferences and teleconferences, and deadlines, and meetings, and everyone seemed to be rushing to reach their end of year goals. Which was fine, except Courtney didn't have any end of year goals to look forward to. The fact was Courtney was only excited about the Mirage party and not much else. Well, besides the Colorado trip. Because sometime in the last few years she'd lost some of her passion for work. Or rather, she never had it to begin with. Which was why she wanted this transfer so badly. She needed a change, and she needed to find her fire again.

She stood and walked toward her kitchen, ruminating about that as she prepared some leftovers for dinner. When she'd graduated college and dreamed her big dreams, not one of them ended up with her working as a shared administrative assistant to a group of financiers in a stiff, corporate culture that limited her creativity. She'd dreamed of doing something creative, but she'd found herself jobless after graduation, and suddenly a paycheck was more important than fulfilling her dreams. So when the Buxby position became available, she'd jumped in with both feet. And she'd stuck with it because a part of her had hoped that being an employee of the company would open doors for her within Buxby Philanthropic. But now, five years later and in essentially the same position, she couldn't help but wonder—if she had held out longer—if she had looked a little harder—would she have found what she was looking for?

The microwave beeped, jarring her from her thoughts. She gathered her dinner and grabbed her favorite blanket off the back of the couch, and she settled in for the night.

"You have a good life, Court," she said to herself. "You don't need to have everything figured out overnight."

She looked up at her modest but glittering Christmas tree and at the holiday ornaments she and her brother had made when she was little. She didn't have to have life figured out. She didn't have to have the perfect job or the perfect solution. Or even the perfect girlfriend, although she wouldn't hate that. No, she only needed to find the beauty and charm of the season and hold on to it. Because Christmas only came once a year, and she wasn't about to let the moody blues chase that away.

She reached for the TV remote and inhaled the smell of her favorite chicken soup from the deli down the street. A Christmas movie would certainly cheer her up. Well, that and her favorite soup. And as the opening scene from *It's a Wonderful Life* filled her screen, she started to feel better already.

Chapter Three

Mira wasn't sure how long she had been resting her head on her hand, but she was sure that if it continued for much longer, she'd certainly fall asleep like that.

She shook her head in an attempt to perk up and looked around her office with a sigh. This place was a mess. Her mother would be horrified if she saw the unorganized piles of papers and discarded clothes that she'd forgotten to take home over the past few weeks after busier and busier shifts. It looked like a frat house in here, and Mira couldn't concentrate because of it.

These last few weeks had been busier than usual. And though she was sure some of that was because of the *Improper Bostonian* article, she also knew that The Mirage had developed a hearty—and thirsty—base patron group. She had the best regulars, and they were being crowded by the curious newcomers the article brought in. Which was awesome, except they'd been understaffed by not one, but two bartenders. Kelly was home safe on maternity leave waiting for the baby's arrival, but Taj's weekend ski accident and resultant broken leg took him off the schedule entirely. Which meant Mira was doing triple duty: owner, bartender to cover the missed shifts, and events coordinator. And she'd already screwed that last part up twice now.

Somehow, even though she'd read Kelly's notes a dozen times, she'd managed to contact the wrong person for the first party. And that had been fine, except she'd called the person for the second party and accidentally mixed up their catering orders, so each party ended up with the wrong food. Which was mostly fine, except the person who booked the second party was deathly allergic to shellfish, and the raw bar she'd ordered for the first party—that never showed up—showed up at the second party instead. Because she'd mixed up the dates, and the contact people. And long story short, she ended up comping most of both events in apology, and the bar buyouts had been nearly a wash. Gratefully, both parties ended early enough for her to recoup some of the costs from her regulars, but still, Kelly was going to be mortified when she found out.

Her desk phone rang, and she nearly fell out of her chair in surprise.

"Yes?" She juggled the receiver like it was a hot potato.

"Your mom's here. Can I send her back?" Teagan, her second most reliable bartender after Kelly, asked.

"Uh, give me a sec," she said as she looked out at the mess before her. "You know what? On second thought, I'll come get her in a minute. She likes a wine spritzer with a strawberry. Buy me some time, will ya?"

"On it, Boss."

She disconnected the call and stood from her desk, deciding to tackle the leather and brass buttoned couch first. This couch was one of her oldest and dearest possessions. It had traveled with her through all the bars before this one and had even served as her bed on more than a few occasions when she was between apartments or saving money to make opening her own bar a reality. She'd lost count of the times she'd thanked past-Mira for splurging on the pullout-bed option when she bought it a dozen or so years ago. And though she didn't need to crash on it like she had in the early days, especially since she now had a house of her own to call home, she still couldn't part with it. There was so much history with that couch. But as of right now, it was serving as a mock laundry counter that she knew her mother would die over.

"Shit," she said as she cleared the discarded shirts covered in cocktail stains and organized the extra pairs of shoes she kept on the floor in front of the couch.

She moved to the wall calendar and whiteboard she used to monitor stock and order needs, erasing the curse words she'd scrawled there out of annoyance after a vendor call yesterday.

Next was the desk, which looked like an entire paper mill had been dumped on it and a tornado had blown through. Shit. She started with the bills and tucked them neatly into the top drawer, to be paid later. Then she moved the events folder to the center of her desk since she had some confirmation phone calls to make later. That left the unopened mail, advertisement flyers, time-off requests, and miscellaneous stuff in a pile to the right. She shuffled it to make it look like it had some semblance of order. That would have to do.

She looked down at her handiwork. "Perfect."

A knock at her office door told her she'd finished just in time.

"Mira," her mother's voice sounded from the other side. "Can I come in?"

"Yeah, Ma." Mira met her at the door with a smile. "I was going to meet you out there."

"I couldn't wait." Her mother pulled her into a tight hug, and Mira savored the feeling. Her mother gave the best hugs. And if she was being honest, she'd been needing a hug lately.

"Hey, Ma. It's nice to see you." She snuggled into the embrace and swayed with her side to side a bit.

"What's wrong?" Her mother pulled back, touching her face, and looking her over with the scrutiny that only her mother seemed capable of. "Something's wrong."

"It's not. Nothing's wrong." Mira swatted away at her mother's hands as she poked and worried over her appearance.

"Don't lie to me—I'm your mother. I'm immune to lies." Her mother fussed with her hair until Mira stilled her hands with her own.

"I'm a grown woman, Ma. I don't need you fixing my hair for me."

"You sure about that? It looks like you haven't slept in days. And this office, Mira. It's a mess." Her mother chastised her as she pointed to the clothes on the edge of the couch.

Mira frowned. "I'll have you know I folded those just moments ago. It looked far worse before that."

Her mother sighed. "You work too much."

Mira sat against the front of her desk, careful not to disrupt the piles of papers she'd made, as she braced herself for the impending lecture.

"I know you want to be successful, and you already are, love. But you don't have to kill yourself in the process. And when are you ever going to find someone to make sure you come home at night and launder your clothes? You are too wonderful to keep all to yourself, Mira." Her mother's kind brown eyes surveyed her with sadness, and Mira wanted to die on the spot. She felt like she was five years old again. Her mother had a way of doing that to her.

"I can take the tidiness jabs but not the relationship ones, okay?" Mira wasn't in the mood to be reminded that she was going to be alone on the holidays—on her birthday—again.

"I'm sorry." Her mother worried her bottom lip. She seemed nervous. Why was she nervous? Mira felt her hackles go up.

"Something's wrong," she said, turning the tables on her mother. "What's wrong?"

Her mother sighed and looked down. "You know that contest at Auntie Celeste's work that she entered a few months back?"

"The all-expense-paid Caribbean adventure in the VIP suite on the famed *Majestic Princess* cruise ship that includes excursions at every stop on the trip and a private dining experience with the ship's hot female captain? Um, yeah. How could I forget?" Mira had often dreamed of jumping on a plane and traveling someplace warm this time of year, but she didn't have anyone to run the bar or, more importantly, anyone to go with. And as independent as she was, she wanted someone to share fruity cocktails and long, passionate nights under the bright Caribbean moon with. Maybe someday she'd find that person and take that adventure.

"Right, well, Celeste won."

"That's awesome!" Her mother looked up and her brown eyes did not reflect the excitement Mira immediately felt for her aunt. "Wait, why aren't you excited? Is she taking someone else? Because she promised you that second spot. And if she picked that woman from her bridge club, I'll kill her."

Her mother laughed. "Relax. She's taking me. No need to commit homicide yet."

"Yet? And why aren't you over the moon? This is going to be so much fun, Ma." Her mother and her aunt were best friends. Which was something that Mira knew her mother regretted not having given Mira—a best-friend sibling. But it just wasn't in the cards for them, and Mira was okay with that. She had a tight family unit—her mom and her aunt were enough for her, and they always had been. They had supported her through every endeavor she had ever undertaken and sacrificed plenty through the years to make sure she was successful. They both deserved a chance to experience luxury and relaxation. It was their time to live their best lives now. She just wished she had been the one to provide that for them.

Her mother looked anything but excited. In fact, she looked devastated.

"Ma. What's wrong?" Mira was getting worried.

"The cruise leaves in three weeks." She sniffled.

"All the better," Mira supplied. "That's right about when the weather will be at its worst around here. Sunny skies and warm weather sound like the perfect antidote to a New England winter. You might miss Shannon Squared's arrival, but I'll take lots of pics. I promise."

Now her mother was full-on crying. Were her photography skills that subpar? Mira would have been offended if her mother wasn't so distraught.

"Ma?"

"Your birthday, Mira. I've never once missed your birthday, but this is a Christmas cruise, and if I go, I won't be here to celebrate with you."

"Oh." The weight of her mother's statement sat on her like a stone. With her mother and her aunt gone on Christmas, she'd have no one. Even Kelly wouldn't be available for her to tag along with. She'd be truly alone. That realization stunned her.

"I know. That's why I came to tell you that I'm not going and ask you to encourage your aunt to find someone else to go with. She'll need a pep talk, I think." Her mother wiped at her tears as she started to pace. "We'll have to be really convincing, but I think between the two of us, we can do it."

Mira felt like she was underwater. On one hand, she was glad to know her mother would skip the cruise to be with her, but on the other hand, she felt guilty because she knew this was the trip of a lifetime for them both. And it was one they were so looking forward to. Christmas and her birthday were just one day in a calendar year—granted, the same day—but just one day. A blip. What did it matter if she saw her mother on that day or not? She'd survive, right? She would work late and go to bed right when she got home, and then it would all be over, and she wouldn't even realize she'd been alone. She could do it. She could certainly do it for her mom and her aunt, the two people who had given her everything.

"No," Mira said as she reached out and stopped her mother's pacing. "You're going with her, and you're buying me all the unnecessary tchotchkes that you find along the way. We'll celebrate when you get back."

"Mira." Her mother looked offended. "No. I'm not missing your birthday. It's Christmas, Mira."

"I'm aware." Mira tried to hide the disappointment in her response. "But there will be other birthdays. And we can't escape Christmas, see?" She pointed to the remaining holiday decorations for the bar in the box by her desk. "There's so much holiday yet to celebrate. Plus, you know I leave the decorations up until New Year's. We'll celebrate when you get back."

"Mira, you never decorate. You have one little ceramic tree."

"But it's a cute tree," Mira countered.

Her mother didn't look convinced.

"Ma, just think about it, okay? I'll be fine." Mira repeated this more for her own needs than her mother's. She'd be fine. She would. *She hoped.*

"I don't know," her mother said as she shook her head. "I'm not comfortable with—"

"Just think about it." Mira pulled her mother into a hug. "I have a few meetings with different holiday buyout clients starting soon, but I'm off tonight. I'll stop by with dinner later. We can chat more then."

"Okay." Her mother's muffled reply into her shoulder made her heart sad. She could tell how disappointed she was.

"I'll bring that chocolate cake you like." Mira tried to bribe her into any semblance of happiness.

"With the ice cream?" Her mother looked up, the sadness fading from her eyes.

"Obviously."

"I love you," her mother said.

"I love you, too," Mira replied. "Now, go. I have to find the file for my meeting. I think it's over there somewhere." She motioned toward her desk, which from this side of the room looked a lot less tidy than she'd hoped.

The look her mother gave her told her that she was being judged about it. She needed to work on her tidy game.

"I know, I know. I'm a mess." She kissed her mother's cheek. "I'll see you later."

Her mother took the folded dirty clothes off the couch and put them under her arm. "I'll just take these with me and make sure they get washed. Someone has to do it."

"You're the best," Mira said as she ushered her mom through her office door. "I'll see you later."

She closed the door after her mom left and collapsed into her office chair. She knew sending her mother and her aunt on that cruise was the right thing, but selfishly she was more than a little sad about it. But it was the right thing to do. And she'd make damn sure they both knew she was on board with them boarding that ship.

She let out a heavy sigh before leaning forward to grab the phone receiver. She'd order that cake, and then she'd call her aunt. They would have to work as a team to convince her mother to go, but she was sure they could do it. They would just have to strategize a little first.

As she hung up with the bakery, Teagan knocked at her office door.

"Come in."

"Your first appointment is here. That guy from the tax place," Teagan said with that crooked grin of hers. "He's waiting at the bar."

"Thanks." Mira dialed her aunt's number. "I have to make a quick call. I'll be right out."

"Sounds good." Teagan disappeared, and Mira was alone in the quiet once more.

"I can be alone on December twenty-fifth. It's just a day on the calendar." She hoped that if she kept saying that, it would feel that way to her lonely heart.

Chapter Four

Courtney loved what they'd done to the place. Tiny, white fairy lights glittered along the exposed wooden beams of the tall ceiling, and multiple strands hung down with intentional elegance, giving a breathtaking quality to the room.

Lush, deep green flora and bright red berries speckled the mirrored glass shelves behind the bar in a tasteful way. And Courtney was pretty sure there was mistletoe braided into some of the lit garland that ran between the hanging pendant lights over the tall bar top tables. That same lit garland, sans mistletoe, was draped around the enormous black window frames, showcasing the New England winter outside the bar and giving an extra warmth to the interior. The holiday setup at Mirage was unparalleled, in Courtney's opinion. And she was thrilled about it.

She deposited her coat at the coat check and walked toward the black marble topped bar that stretched well over forty feet along the far wall. The wall behind the bar was filled with every mixer and spirit she could imagine, and the gentle underlighting on the shelves gave each bottle its own spotlight moment. The attention to detail in the design here was amazing.

Though not a beer drinker, Courtney noted the multiple beer and cocktail stations spaced out along the gleaming countertop. She knew the partners at the firm would want easy and convenient distribution of drinks and guest spacing at the party. Mirage had that in spades. There was more than enough room to keep everyone happy. Courtney was convinced this was the most perfect bar in the city.

The bar wasn't busy at the moment, but she figured that was because it was midday during a workweek. And even though it wasn't bustling as it had been when she toured the bar to pick the company party location, there were still plenty of people around. Which was why she thought it was okay to stare at the gorgeous brunette at the small L-shaped end of the bar while she waited for her meeting with Mira, since she was early anyway. There was no reason to pass up an opportunity to appreciate a beautiful woman, right? Because this woman was stunning.

"Can I interest you in a drink?" a short-haired, androgynous-looking bartender asked her.

"I probably shouldn't," Courtney said as she gave the bartender a bashful look. She knew she'd been caught staring.

"We have mocktails for those working nine-to-fivers who still want to feel like it's a forever weekend, even if it's only a lunchbreak." This person was charming.

"Mocktail me," Courtney said with a smile.

"Are you into fruity and sweet things, or a dryer cocktail?"

"Fruity and sweet." Courtney extended her hand across the bar toward her new friend. "I'm Courtney."

"Teagan," she replied with a firm handshake. "Nice to meet you."

Teagan started mixing something that looked wonderful, but Courtney found herself distracted by the woman at the end of the bar again. She was on the phone, talking to someone about something that sounded important. Or maybe it wasn't important, and Courtney was just being lulled by the sexy tone of her voice, which sounded authoritative but somehow also friendly. She found herself wanting to hear that voice directed toward her, so she could pinpoint what about it made her so hot and bothered. But it wasn't just the voice that drew her in—it was the relaxed casual beauty the woman absolutely owned. Her long dark hair fell in calculated waves beyond her shoulders. The few times she smiled while speaking, Courtney got a glimpse of a gleaming white set of perfect teeth that were framed with light pink lips that Courtney thought looked delicious.

The woman was wearing all black, and her tight-fitting dress shirt was rolled at the forearms, though the right cuff slipped out of place over and over. After ending the call, she stood from her seat and stretched, exposing a tiny sliver of her stomach. She rolled her shoulders and closed her eyes while she stretched her neck. Courtney looked at the long column of visible flesh over her pulse point, and she found herself wanting to kiss the skin there.

God, she thought, she really needed to get laid.

"Fruity and sweet." Teagan said as she placed the mocktail in front of her, startling her in the process.

"Oh, great. Thanks." Courtney clumsily reached for the drink, nearly knocking it over.

She looked up to find Teagan looking amused.

Courtney sipped her drink. "This is incredible."

"Thank you." Teagan flashed her a crooked grin as she hand-dried a glass.

Though she'd successfully focused on something else since Teagan had busted her for staring, the mystery woman laughed, and the sound drew her attention again. She heard Teagan snicker at her in response.

She gave her a playful death stare.

"If you're into fruity and sweet, she's probably not your type." Teagan nodded toward the end of the bar, and Courtney didn't bother following her gaze. She could hear Lady McHot Lips on the phone again, and she'd already embarrassed herself enough.

She sighed. "Okay, I'll bite. Why's that? Is she not fruity enough?"

"If by fruity you mean gay, then she's totally fruity enough." That piqued Courtney's interest. "But I wouldn't call her sweet."

"Who's not sweet?" The mysterious dark-haired stranger joined Teagan behind the bar, and Courtney almost choked mid-swallow. She was even more attractive up close. Damn.

"You," Teagan replied.

"You wound me." Lady McHot Lips held a hand over her heart and feigned being hurt.

"I mean, you have your moments, but…" Teagan teased before leaving to help another patron.

"I'm not exactly a Hallmark heroine."

Courtney looked back at McHot Lips to find a pair of warm, honey-brown eyes appraising her. McHot Lips was talking to her.

"You say that like you expect me to be a sappy Hallmark holiday movie watching sad sack," Courtney said as she sipped her drink just to occupy her hands.

McHot Lips raised her hands in defense. "You totally seem like the Hallmark holiday movie watching type, but sorry if I pigeonholed you."

"You aren't wrong." Courtney was only offended because she totally *was* that person. "What gave it away?"

"Frosty." McHot Lips pointed to the little snowman ring on her right hand that her grandmother had given her when she was thirteen.

"A snowperson, really?" Courtney was skeptical.

"Nah, it's the Hallmark movie schedule you have open on your cell phone screen, and the fact that you were singing 'Santa Baby' when you walked in earlier. But I figured noticing the cute little snowperson ring would feel less like I was blowing up your spot." McHot Lips shrugged.

"Damn." Courtney looked down and saw that she was right. She had been skimming over the Hallmark schedule as she waited. And had she been singing when she came in? She must have been. But McHot Lips would have only known that if she'd noticed her when she'd walked in, which was a promising development.

As Teagan walked past, McHot Lips asked, "Hey, can you make a cranberry vodka martini for the woman by the window?"

"Sure." Teagan grabbed a glass and started reaching for a bottle when she paused to add, "Oh, by the way, this is Courtney. And she thinks you're cute."

McHot Lips arched a perfectly sculpted eyebrow in Courtney's direction, and she wanted to sink under the bar from embarrassment.

"I thought bartenders were supposed to be great secret keepers," Courtney muttered as she toyed with the napkin under her drink.

"That's probably a stereotype that is unfairly applied to most of us. Teagan can't keep a secret to save her life." McHot Lips flashed an award-winning smile, and Courtney was reconsidering her nickname for her. "But I can."

"Good to know who and who not to share my innermost secrets with, then," Courtney said, finding it hard not to be mesmerized by the woman in front of her.

"You can tell me anything." This woman was beyond charming.

"Something tells me you say that to all the girls," Courtney replied, wary but also intrigued. McHot Lips was flirting with her.

"Only the ones who think I'm cute."

Courtney dropped her head into her hands, mortified.

"If it makes you feel any better, the feeling is mutual." The soft, flirty reply emboldened Courtney to peek between her fingers just to confirm what she thought she heard.

She had McHot Lips' full attention. So much so, that she was leaning her forearms on the bar, closer to her than she had been moments before. Almost dangerously close, in Courtney's opinion.

"Oh, well, thanks." Courtney sat up straighter, trying not to blush.

"Thank you for thinking I'm cute," she said.

"To be fair, *cute* didn't really cross my mind. I was thinking more along the lines of sex—" Courtney put her hand over her mouth to stop herself. What did Teagan put into this drink?

This garnered her another arched eyebrow, this time accompanied with a licked lower lip. Courtney was a goner.

"Can I get you another?" Her voice was like velvet. Courtney was sure she'd take anything this woman would offer her.

"Another what?" She was staring at the full lips in front of her. What had come over her?

"Drink." She motioned toward the glass Courtney hadn't realized she'd drained.

"I probably shouldn't. I'm meeting someone soon." Courtney was only vaguely aware of her reason for being here today. Because if flirting with this woman wasn't the true reason she was here, then the day seemed wasted.

McHot Lips checked the receipt in the empty glass Teagan had left at the inner edge of the bar. "Looks like you were having a mocktail. Let me make you another, on the house, just so you don't get thirsty before whatever it is you have planned."

"Okay," Courtney agreed, largely because McHot Lips had already taken her glass and replaced it with a fresh one.

"Any requests?" McHot Lips asked as her hands hovered over bottle tops just below the bar's surface.

"Something festive," Courtney replied, though something told her anything this woman made her would be delightful.

"I've got just the thing." She winked, and Courtney felt herself swoon.

Courtney watched as she expertly moved behind the bar and around Teagan, who seemed engrossed in her own cocktail making endeavor.

After a few moments, McHot Lips placed an elegant looking cocktail in front of her. Seeds of some sort floated on the carbonated bubbles of a deep red drink, and Courtney felt herself squeal internally with delight. It was beautiful.

"What is it?" she asked.

"A virgin version of our Pomegranate Royal. Which normally contains pomegranate liqueur, champagne, and pomegranate seeds to add some texture to the drink. It's very popular." McHot Lips was leaning on the bar top again. The cuff of her right sleeve appeared to have rolled down from making Courtney's drink.

"It looks wonderful, thank you." Courtney gave in to her desire to fix the wayward sleeve and touch the gorgeous, charming bartender. She carefully rolled the end of the shirtsleeve and tucked the fabric into itself, securing it like the other side.

"Try it." McHot Lips placed her hand on the one Courtney still had on her forearm. She gave it a gentle squeeze, and Courtney let her hand linger there for a moment before returning to her glass.

Courtney sipped the drink but held the bartender's gaze. This was fantastic. And very festive. Exactly the type of thing she would like to have at her company's party. Shit. The meeting.

"You don't like it?" Those warm eyes looked concerned.

"No, yes. I do. It's incredible. I just—" Courtney shook her head to clear the lust fog she was in. "I seem to keep forgetting about the meeting I'm supposed to be having. I blame you."

"Sorry, not sorry." The wicked grin that accompanied the reply did little to dissipate Courtney's newfound infatuation with this woman.

After a pause, the woman asked, "Is the meeting for work or pleasure?"

"Work." Though the only thing on Courtney's mind at the moment was pleasure.

"Work can wait," she replied in that same sexy tone from earlier. "I have to admit I'm glad it isn't a pleasure meeting."

"Why's that?" Courtney traced the rim of her glass, and McHot Lips' eyes followed the movements of her fingers.

"I'm not ready to have to fight anyone off for your attention." Those pink lips parted, and Courtney wanted to taste them.

"Oh? And do you think you have my full attention now?" Courtney realized she was leaning in as she spoke. She felt pulled to this woman.

"I know I do. And I like it that way." McHot Lips was killing her.

"You know, it occurs to me that I don't know your name yet. But you know mine, thanks to that traitor, Teagan. And though I'm happy to keep using the one I've made up in my mind, I'd like to know your actual name."

"So you can scream it later?"

Courtney felt her jaw drop and her sex clench.

McHot Lips reached across the bar and took Courtney's free hand. "I'm kidding."

Courtney shifted in her seat. "Too bad."

McHot Lips surveyed her curiously while still holding her hand. "What's the name you've been calling me in your head?"

"The formal or the informal name?" Courtney turned her hand over and stifled a shudder when McHot Lips traced lazy circles on her palm.

"Let's start with informal." The circles continued.

"McHot Lips." Courtney would have been embarrassed by her admission, but she was too entranced by this woman's touch to care.

She laughed that sexy laugh from before. "And the formal name?"

"Lady McHot Lips."

She stopped her ministrations to briefly squeeze Courtney's hand before pulling back. "I hope my lips are worthy of such a regal title."

"They appear to be." Courtney made no attempt to look anywhere other than the full pink lips before her.

"Maybe we should do a test just to confirm your assumptions." She leaned forward infinitesimally, and Courtney wondered how quickly she could vault over this bar.

"First, a name. Please." Courtney bit her bottom lip to keep herself in her seat.

"Are you sure? Kissing a stranger seems like something really sexy, right now." She leaned closer still.

Courtney squeezed her thighs together. This woman's confidence and swagger were impressive. And Courtney certainly wanted to kiss her, among other things.

"And if we do, and it's as good as I imagine it will be, what will I moan into your ear when I ask for more?" she asked, fishing for a name again.

"*Please* would probably do the trick," McHot Lips answered. Courtney laughed because she'd walked right into that one.

"I have excellent manners," Courtney said. "I might even say thank you afterward."

"After what, exactly?"

Courtney had meant kissing, but the conversation seemed to be taking a different tone, and she didn't hate it.

"Whatever," she said with a playful shrug.

She was rewarded with a broad smile. "This is getting better and better."

"So"—she motioned across the bar to her—"you are…?"

"Mira," she replied as she took Courtney's hand again. "And it's very, very nice to meet you."

Mira. That was a beautiful name fit for the gorgeous woman

who was looking at her like there was no one else in this entire room, and Courtney was all for it. Mira. Mira. Wait. Why did that sound so familiar?

"Oh." It dawned on her, and she pulled her hand back out of reflex. "Shit. You're *Mira*, as in Mira Donahue. That Mira."

Mira leaned back and crossed her arms over her chest. "Are you going to serve me with a subpoena or something?"

"What? No." Courtney shook her head. "I'm just supposed to be meeting with you right now."

"We *were* kind of in a meeting, don't you think?" Mira teased, and she momentarily forgot why she was freaked out.

Because of course the most beautiful woman in the room, who was flirting with her, would be the point person for her very important work event. This was cruel.

Courtney huffed. "I hate my life."

Mira gave her a confused look.

"I'm Courtney," she tried.

"I'd gathered that," Mira replied, not picking up on what she was trying to get across.

"Courtney Rivers. Your three o'clock meeting. For the Buxby Partners holiday buyout party."

Mira's face dropped. "Oh God. I am so, so sorry. That was entirely unprofessional, and I can't believe I just—" She palmed her forehead. "Okay. Let's just…Let's start over." She stood up and spun around, straightening her shirt before facing Courtney again with a welcoming but much less sexually fueled smile. She extended her hand in Courtney's direction. "I'm Mira Donahue—it's nice to meet you."

Courtney sighed—she already missed the banter. "Courtney. Nice to meet you, too."

"So," Mira said as she let out an exhale. "About that event your company booked—"

"Hey, Mira." Teagan walked up. "Your next appointment is here."

Courtney checked her phone and groaned. How had she managed to miss her appointment time while talking to the person she was supposed to be meeting with? She was due back at the office, and she'd managed to accomplish nothing but get turned on, only to get her hopes dashed. Fuck this day.

Mira frowned. "Wait, give me a second." She grabbed a piece of paper from behind the bar and scribbled something down. "This is my personal number. I owe you a meeting, whenever is convenient for you, whatever day or time. I promise. I'm sorry—I got caught up talking to you and forgot anything else was on my agenda."

Mira looked apologetic, and Courtney hoped that the silver lining to this bust of a meeting was that Mira had gotten caught up talking to her because she liked her.

"Was this all a well-crafted plan to give me your number?" Courtney accepted the paper and the promise it held for another chance to spend time with Mira. Which didn't sound bad at all.

"I wish I were that smooth," Mira said as she ran her hand through that luscious looking dark hair. "But I won't say I mind that this is where things ended up."

"Me neither," Courtney admitted.

"I look forward to hearing from you."

"You bought my first and second rounds. Make sure you tip Teagan well," Courtney said as she pushed her empty glass toward the back of the bar.

"Will do," Mira said as she collected the cup.

"Bye, Mira Donahue," Courtney said as she slid off the barstool and headed toward the coat check.

"Don't forget to call me," Mira called out.

She hazarded a glance back at the bar and her heartbeat picked up at the sight of Mira watching her walk away. She added a little extra hip sway for good measure as she resumed humming "Santa Baby." Suddenly this holiday season seemed a little sexier than usual, and that kind of holiday enchantment was very welcome.

CHAPTER FIVE

Mira knew she'd dodged a bullet tonight. She wasn't sure how, or what forces were at work, but she knew she'd caught some cosmic break. And she was grateful for it.

She'd successfully managed to navigate her final buyout meeting, but it was a bit of a blur. Truthfully, everything after Courtney walked through her bar's door was a blur.

She'd been inside the coat closet, checking some of the spillover storage they kept there, when Courtney came in, quietly singing "Santa Baby." She'd heard her before she'd seen her, but looking up at her from her place on the floor at the back of the closet, Courtney looked like a haloed, blond angel in that white jacket with the fluffy, gold-trimmed, faux-fur hood. She'd handed her coat to Kevin and smiled at him brightly, and her blue eyes shone with an innocence that Mira hadn't seen in a long time.

Mira had lost track of her when she'd left the closet to answer the vendor call, but she'd spotted her talking to Teagan at the bar, and admittedly, she was a little jealous.

Teagan had a way with the ladies, and Mira wasn't exactly looking for trouble or a girlfriend—which usually came in the same package in her experience as of late—but there was just something about the way this woman spoke and held her glass that drew Mira in. And when she'd noticed her watching her, well, all bets were off.

She hadn't gone over to Courtney with the intention to flirt, though it happened more easily than she'd expected it to. And up close, Courtney glowed. The loose curls of her blond hair were swept up into a clip, and the red of her silk shirt made her cheeks look pink and slightly flushed. And that snowman ring was adorable, as was her bashfulness over the Hallmark movie list. But the more time Mira spent with her, the more she saw what else Courtney had to offer—she was sarcastic and funny behind those bright, seemingly innocent blue eyes. And that innocence transformed to sexy as hell when she was flirting back. Mira had been captivated by her.

Mira couldn't remember the last time a patron had come into her bar and struck her in such a way. But this wasn't just any patron. And that's where Mira knew she'd caught a break tonight because Courtney could have absolutely freaked when she'd made the connection that Mira had missed. She'd been completely in the wrong in her attempt to seduce one of her buyout representatives. And had she known, she never would have crossed the line. But she hadn't known. And Courtney was so alluring sitting across from her, licking her lips and asking what name she should moan in Mira's ear…

But this was a business, and Mira knew better than to mix business and pleasure. And the Buxby Partners buyout was the largest one of the season. They were pulling out all the stops, from what Kelly's notes had said, and Mira knew that this could be a long-term client relationship if things went well. And as much as she hated the holidays and the endless holiday parties, they made up a huge chunk of her winter business when the sometimes treacherous New England weather kept her regulars at home, and not at their favorite stools.

Courtney not being offended by her flirting was a major win. And so was the opportunity to see her again. Which Mira hoped would be sooner rather than later.

"Mira," her aunt said. "Did you hear anything I just said?"

"Hmm?" Mira blinked and looked across at the woman who looked so much like her mother.

"You were totally somewhere else just then," Celeste said with a knowing shake of her head. "It's a pretty girl, isn't it?"

Mira laughed. "I was thinking about work."

"I bet a pretty girl was at work, and you're holding out on your old aunt." Celeste gave her a disappointed frown.

"Auntie, there are more things in life than attractive blond snow bunnies and getting laid," Mira said.

"Who said anything about blondes and getting laid?"

"I didn't, you just—" Mira scrunched her nose once she'd realized she'd fallen for her aunt's baiting. "Damn."

Celeste clapped. "I knew you were daydreaming about a pretty lady. Now I know she's a blond snow bunny. Spill."

"I have no knowledge as to the snow thing, but I will say she had an impressively warm looking ski jacket." Mira had never kept secrets, especially not from her gay aunt. She knew she was lucky to have one of her only two family members also share a love for women. It had made her own coming out to her mother a nonissue. She could, however, do without the relationship coaching her lifelong bachelorette aunt never stopped giving her.

"You know, if you want to get her to like you—" Celeste started, and Mira held her hand up to stop her.

"I've got it under control, Auntie. I assure you."

"Oh yeah, has she called you yet?" Celeste pressed.

Mira frowned. "It's been, like, three hours."

"That's three hours of lost sexting opportunities!" Celeste said disapprovingly.

Mira rolled her eyes. "Listen, we only have a few minutes before Ma gets back. Let's brainstorm."

"I won't be mad if you tell us to stay home, Mira. You know that, right?" Celeste asked, and Mira knew that was true. But she couldn't live with herself if she was the reason they didn't go.

"I know. And I'll tell Mom the same thing I told you—I'm going to be working around the clock, with Kelly and Taj out during the holiday party season. You two can spoil me rotten when you get home, and maybe we can do a mini-Caribbean vacation as a group when things quiet down at work. Then you can regale me with all the stories and stops you did together and act like townies as you show me around."

Celeste watched her for a moment without saying anything. The intensity made Mira uncomfortable.

"Missing your birthday is going to kill us both."

"I know. And I also know that it's one day out of three hundred and sixty-five," Mira said to her aunt. "I'll be fine. Now, let's shelve that concern of yours and figure out a way to get Mom on that ship with you."

Her aunt hesitated but eventually nodded. "What's the plan?"

"Research."

Celeste frowned. "That sounds like a terrible plan."

Mira laughed. "Research regarding the trip and all the excursions and the stops you'll make along the way. We need to sell this to her like the trip of a lifetime. We Donahues have charm for days—it's time we used it for good, not evil."

"Not just for getting laid, you mean," Celeste said as she winked.

"Yes, fine. That, too."

"Okay, what's my assignment?" Celeste grabbed the shopping list next to her and flipped it over.

"First, get me a copy of your itinerary, and I'll handle the heavy lifting." Mira had this all planned out. She just needed to know the highlights.

"Oh, that's all?" Celeste pulled out her phone, and Mira's pinged a moment later. "Done."

"Great." Mira looked over her shoulder as her mother's footsteps sounded on the basement stairs behind her. "Your second assignment is to assuage Mom's worries that I can't handle myself for ten days without you two."

"Ten days during which time your birthday and Christmas fall, you mean," Celeste pointed out.

"Same day, Auntie. Same. Damn. Day." Mira shook her head. She was never not annoyed that her birthday fell on the day that everyone in the world had a party and presents. She'd always envied those kids with summer birthdays who had pool birthday parties and jumpy houses in their backyards. That was a hard thing to pull off in the dead of winter on a day everything was closed and everyone else had plans. She had never once had a birthday party on her actual birthday that included anyone other than her mother and her aunt. Not ever.

"What are you two conspiring about?" her mother asked as she placed Mira's freshly laundered clothes on the table beside her.

"Nothing," Mira said as she stood to kiss her mother on the cheek. "Thanks for always cleaning up after me."

"It doesn't matter how old you get—you're still my baby."

"Mira met a cute girl at work named Courtney, and she's in love," Celeste blurted out, and Mira shot her a look.

"Oh?" Her mother sat in Mira's empty seat and looked up at her expectantly.

"How did you know her name was Courtney?" Mira asked her aunt, not bothering to correct her. If her mother thought she had a dating prospect, maybe that would help her agree to that trip. She knew her mother didn't want her to be alone.

"Because she just texted you, Romeo." Celeste's grin was comical.

Mira lunged for her phone, and her aunt put it just out of her reach.

"This one really made an impression on you," her mother commented, and Mira felt herself blush.

"It's a work thing—don't listen to your sister."

Mira snatched her phone from her aunt and tried to suppress a smile at the text that was waiting for her: *Hey it's Courtney. Are you free anytime Friday? I get out of work at 5. We can redo our meeting then if you aren't busy. Let me know.*

"That's a big grin for a work thing," her mother said, and clearly Mira had been unsuccessful in her attempts to hide her delight about receiving the text.

"I'm leaving now," Mira said as she gave them both a look. "Please refrain from gossiping about my personal life until after I've left the premises."

"See? This is a personal matter, not a work one. Told you," Celeste said to her mother, and they high-fived.

"I love you. I'm leaving. Enjoy the rest of the cake."

She kissed them both on the cheeks and was headed toward the front door with her clean clothes when her aunt yelled out, "Should we save a piece for Courtney?"

Mira would have flipped her off if she was anyone else, but she blew her a kiss instead. She had the best family.

❖

"Working late, Rivers?" Chet asked as he poked his head out of his office door.

"Just finishing up some things around here," Courtney replied. It was nearly six, and the last-minute project Chet had dropped on her lap just before noon was taking every waking minute to complete. She'd skipped lunch in an attempt to end her day on time, but it had been for naught. She was still here and not at Mirage, like she'd planned to be. And she was not happy about it.

Mira had texted her back the other night almost immediately. Her reply was professional, but she added a few friendly emojis. So Courtney thought that maybe there was hope for future flirtation, which she was totally on board with. Plus, she'd gotten an immediate reply. So there was that.

Courtney had been thinking about Mira a lot since their nonmeeting. Mostly she'd been thinking about how much she'd wished she'd kissed her when she had the chance. She couldn't remember another time when she'd felt such an immediate attraction and chemistry with someone. It was exciting.

Her stomach grumbled as she reached for her phone to text Mira an update. She'd sent her two apology messages as the clock approached five and it was obvious that she wouldn't be done in time. She'd have to eat something at some point because the Tic Tacs from the back of her top drawer were not cutting it.

She texted: *I'm so sorry I'm late. Let me bring you dinner.*

A few bubbles filled the screen before disappearing, and Courtney thought that maybe it was too late. Mira did run a bar, after all—her night was probably just starting.

"Oh, I didn't expect to run into you here," said Stephanie from Accounting, sounding as surprised as she looked.

"I work here." Courtney didn't much like Stephanie, especially since she'd heard through her HR contact that Stephanie had also applied for the same position she was aiming for.

"I know that, silly. It's just, you know, late." Stephanie looked uncomfortable.

"I could say the same thing to you," Courtney replied, knowing full well that Stephanie was hoping the floor would be empty because the rumor around the office was that she and Chet were carrying on some extracurricular activities.

"Oh, wow. Look at you two overachievers, working late on a Friday." Chet walked out of his office, his feigned surprise fooling no one.

"I'm just finishing the project you gave me before lunch." Courtney didn't care if her tone was sharp.

"And, I, um, was just finishing some work," Stephanie said weakly.

"On the wrong floor?" Courtney couldn't help herself.

"Yeah, good point." Stephanie looked down at her feet.

"Well, I'll walk out with you," Chet said as he strolled up next to her, "since I'm headed that way anyway."

"The buddy system," Courtney said. "That's smart."

"Teamwork makes the dream work, right, ladies?" Chet was such a cretin.

"Yup." Courtney gave them a wave so she could get back to the more important fact that Mira had just texted her back.

I could eat. What did you have in mind?

You. Courtney typed but then thought better of it. She went with *Pizza, Thai, Sushi?*

Mira wrote back immediately, *This feels like a test. Are you testing me?*

Maybe.

Sushi. Wasabi on the side. I like salmon and tuna, but I'm not picky.

Courtney cheered. Sushi was what she really wanted, but she knew that wasn't for everyone. So far, Mira was checking off all the necessary boxes. For what, she wasn't sure, but this was a solid check in the pro column.

I'll be there in twenty.

Sounds good.

Courtney tossed the remainder of Chet's bullshit project aside, to worry about on Monday. Tonight was about perfecting the party that was going to clinch her promotion. And she might or might not also be having a dinner date with the hot bar owner with the dreamy smile and unforgettable lips. Score.

CHAPTER SIX

The bar was busy, but thankfully Teagan had agreed to pick up an extra shift tonight to cover the bar with Shaun since Mira had to meet with Courtney again. Something she was more than grateful for, when an unexpected large group showed up in the hopes of having an impromptu holiday celebration. Teagan was solid when it came to high-stress patron volumes and demanding customers. She wasn't as fast a drink slinger as Kelly, but she could deescalate a drunk patron better than anyone. Well, with the exception of Mira. But that was part of the job, right? The ability to navigate tricky situations was vital for career longevity in this line of work.

Tonight's meeting with Courtney in a packed bar, with a rowdy group of finance types hoping to shuffle enough tall tables together to make a holiday party in the back corner, presented discrete challenges that when lumped together could be disastrous. Mira was hoping that wouldn't be the case.

She slipped into her office to take Kelly's call.

"I got the goods," Kelly said on the line.

Mira laughed. "When you say it like that, it sounds dirty."

"I have very little excitement in my life these days. I'm bored. This assignment has been my only source of entertainment outside of my endless HGTV-watching zombie time. But I'll warn you, I definitely have to go on a Caribbean vacation when this baby pops out. I might be obsessed now."

"That's why I asked for your help. I can't be distracted by perfect clear-water beaches and tropical drinks brought to me by women in bikinis. I have a bar to run in your absence," Mira said as she leaned back in her office chair.

"I'd do anything for your mom," Kelly said, and Mira knew that. She had good friends and a great family. Her circle wasn't big, but it was solid.

"So, what are we looking at here? What did you find?" Mira wanted to catch up with her friend, but she did have company coming. Sure, it wasn't a woman in a bikini bringing her a frozen drink, and they didn't have a tropical locale, but it was sushi with a smart, funny, and captivating woman who she happened to be wildly attracted to.

"I organized a PowerPoint presentation with fully functional video links of all the amazing things Mama Donahue and Celeste can do on their trip. I also paired each chapter of the presentation with a cocktail or food from the islands they will be visiting, to give a taste of what they can expect," Kelly said nonchalantly.

"You did *what*? A PowerPoint presentation? Food pairings? This thing has chapters?"

"Mira, your mom is as practical as they come. She's not into anything flashy or over the top. This is the trip of a lifetime for her because she would never take it without us forcing her to. She needs to see all the pros out in list format with a piña colada in front of her and a spicy conch taco with mango salsa. If we're doing this, we're doing it right." Kelly was telling her, not asking her. And Mira loved her friend a little more for loving her mother as much as she did.

"Okay. Send it along. I'll get Celeste on the food aspect, and I'll gather the cocktail ingredients. We'll make a show of it."

"Record your mom's reaction to slide eleven in chapter three for me," Kelly said, her tone more mischievous than before.

"Do I even want to ask?"

"Probably not. It's for your mom, not you. Just film her, and report back. This was so much fun, Mira. Thanks for the homework."

"You're the best. I gotta fly, but I'll catch up with you later." Mira ended the call and checked her text messages. Courtney was a few minutes away.

She headed back out to the bar and was glad to see things had quieted down a bit. The group in the back was still laughing and cheering, and every seat at the bar was filled, but she recognized most of those faces. The more regulars on a night like tonight, the better. If there needed to be bartender shuffling or a few extra minutes between rounds, the regulars would be understanding. Plus, she just liked seeing all the friendly faces. They were the ones who made this job fun.

"You're smiling. Is that because I brought food?" Courtney's voice sounded from across the bar.

"Food is fine, but I'm more interested in the company," Mira said as she took a minute to appreciate Courtney's pencil skirt and nearly sheer blouse. She was stunning.

"Good." Courtney smiled, and Mira was glad she decided to flirt again. She knew she had to remain professional, but there was no need to deny her attraction to Courtney. Especially since Courtney checked her out in return. There was clearly something brewing between them. No reason to stifle that.

"Thanks for meeting with me again," Courtney said as she brushed a piece of hair behind her ear, and Mira found herself wondering if it felt as soft as it looked.

"Of course. I owe you at least that." Mira motioned for her to meet her at the end of the bar. "There's a couch and low table in the back that I reserved for us, if that's okay?"

"Sure." Courtney met her at the end of the bar and offered her a hand as she ducked under the bar top. Mira accepted the brief contact because it was Courtney, and it was sweet. She certainly didn't need the help, but any excuse to touch Courtney was fine by her.

Courtney settled on the sofa and placed the take-out bag on the table before them as Mira sat next to her. She was careful to make sure she had a full view of the bar, in case Teagan and Shaun needed help. They were far enough from the rest of the room for privacy, but close enough to the large group of business guys to help if necessary.

"They seem cheerful." Courtney motioned toward the somewhat boisterous group.

"Some of them I recognize, but most of them I don't. This is their attempt at a mini-holiday party, I think." Mira opened the container Courtney gave her and picked up the chopsticks on the table.

"What gave it away, the Santa hat they keep passing?" Courtney teased as she ate a piece of maki.

"That was a good indication," Mira said between bites of her own plate. "This is amazing. Where did you go?"

"Someplace by my work. They're fast and reliable—I've never had a bad roll there," Courtney replied.

"It's great, thanks. I completely blanked on a meal plan for the night, so you're a lifesaver," Mira replied.

Courtney scrunched her nose. "I might be trying to butter you up."

"Oh, why's that?" Mira didn't think she'd need much buttering when it came to Courtney.

"I have some requests about the party. And I want you to be open-minded to them."

Mira paused. "How open-minded?"

"How good is the sushi?" Courtney challenged.

"Very good," Mira admitted.

"So about that amount of open-minded, then." Courtney gave her a mischievous look.

"I'm listening."

"Well, I read the contract, and Kelly was pretty firm about some of the things in there, but I wanted to know if there was any wiggle room on an issue or two."

"Such as?" Mira had another bite.

"Signature cocktail options," Courtney replied. "I'd like to propose a few drink additions to the usual offering on the contract."

Mira paused as she thought about the holiday party package she'd mapped out with Kelly. The idea was for it to be as fun as possible, with everyone ending up happy. That meant that Mira had to limit some of the more extravagant requests in order to protect her bottom line. They kept the bar open to everyone the entire time but usually limited signature cocktails to one or two, since they required extra ingredients and some training for the bartenders and waitstaff she often had to supplement for these events. "What did you have in mind?"

Courtney reached into her purse and produced a list. A list that appeared to be pretty long from Mira's vantage point.

"Is that for me?" Mira asked, holding her hand out for the paper.

Courtney began to hand it to her but pulled it back at the last minute. "Are you being open-minded?"

"Trying," Mira said as she flashed her most flirtatious smile. "Can I?"

"Fine." Courtney sighed. "But remember how good that tuna is."

Mira popped a piece of tuna into her mouth with her free hand. "Scrumptious," she mumbled as she chewed.

Courtney gave her a look. She was adorable.

Mira looked over the extensive list as she swallowed. "There are eight drinks on here."

"Nine," Courtney corrected as she turned the paper over in Mira's hand to reveal another one on the back.

"Okay. There are nine drinks here," Mira repeated. "What are you proposing?"

"Well, the guys at my office like whiskey, scotch, and beer. But the women mostly like cocktails and wine. So I think it might be cool to have a few of these as offerings, as well, to make it all a bit more festive."

Mira looked over the list again. Courtney had included the name of each cocktail and the list of ingredients with the proportions, all mapped out, like a detailed recipe.

"Where did you find these?" Mira asked as she laughed at some of the names. "Drunk Jack Frosties? Jingle Juice?"

"The internet mostly, although the Jingle Juice name was all me," Courtney replied.

Mira looked over the ingredients and did a mental tally of her current inventory. She had just about everything that was necessary. She'd have to increase her shredded coconut order, and blue curaçao was out of season for her typical delivery, but she could work with this. "How many do you want?"

"How many can I get?" Courtney was facing her on the couch. Her hands were resting on her knees as she leaned forward, waiting for Mira's reply. She was close enough to touch.

Mira surveyed her, weighing her options. They already had the deposit for the party, and the package Courtney had chosen included an open bar. Buxby Partners would be on the hook for any opened container, the cost of the caterer, and the rented space, but that was it. She could work with Courtney if she made a few amendments.

"Okay, let's do this—all top shelf alcohol is available, on the opened container clause that Buxby already agreed to."

"Yes, and…?" Courtney was practically vibrating with anticipation.

"I'll have a white and a red wine option available but have to limit the variety of wines in order to accommodate the expansion of your requested signature drink list."

"And?" Courtney had scooted closer on the couch, seemingly hanging on her every word.

"I can do any four of these, with the exception of the Drunk Jack Frosties because I'm not sure I can get the amount of blue curaçao we'd need, and if your colleagues don't drink it all, I'll be stuck with it until it expires."

"Yes!" Courtney cheered. "I can work with four."

"Good," Mira said, glad to have come to an agreement.

"Now, how do you feel about fake snow?" Courtney dived right into another negotiation.

"How much fake snow?" Mira asked.

"How much can I have?" Courtney countered.

Mira grinned. She liked this woman—she was tenacious. "Do you have a plan for this fake snow proposal à la this encyclopedia?" She motioned toward the drink list in her hand. "Or are you just going to walk around with a fake snow cannon and light this place up?"

Courtney seemed to consider this.

"No snow cannons. I was kidding," Mira added.

"Grinch," Courtney said.

"That wouldn't be the first time I was called that," Mira mused. She heard that a lot this time of year.

"I was thinking a little bit of snow on the tabletops and around the food trays, maybe with some white garland here or there to edge the serving table would be nice," Courtney suggested.

Mira wasn't so sure about the white garland. "You're going to make my bar look tacky."

"No, I won't. It will be tasteful and festive, I promise."

"White garland is not tasteful," Mira said.

"That's a matter of opinion." Courtney shrugged. "I happen to think it can be really pretty when done sparingly."

Mira wasn't convinced.

"So yes to the snow?" Courtney pressed.

"Some. But I have final say the night of if it looks like it's getting out of hand," Mira said.

"And the garland?" Courtney gave her a slow, flirty blink.

"Don't push it," Mira replied.

"Fine," Courtney said, her tone playful. "You'll be here the night of the party, huh?" She looked intrigued by this information.

Mira nodded. "Kelly is out of commission, and our other senior bartender has a broken leg. So I'll be helping out and playing boss that night."

The tune for "A Holly Jolly Christmas" rang out from Courtney's purse, and she fumbled to answer it. Each ring got louder and louder until it drew the attention of the frat boy bankers nearby. Soon the entire back of the bar was singing along to the tune, overjoyed and terribly off-key. Courtney held the phone but let the ringtone play out until the lively and obviously inebriated group lost the chorus and cheered anyway.

Mira rolled her eyes.

"What? Not a Johnny Marks fan?" Courtney sent the call to voice mail.

"Johnny Marks?" Mira asked.

"Sure, he wrote most of the holiday standards, just for other people. I'm a fan of Burl Ives's take on that song, but Michael Bublé does an amazing job, too." Courtney's blue eyes were so alive when she spoke. Mira was captivated once again.

"I've never heard of Johnny Marks in my life," she admitted.

"He wrote 'Rudolph, the Red-Nosed Reindeer' and 'Rockin' Around the Christmas Tree,' too," Courtney supplied. "All the catchy ones were Johnny's."

"You seem to know a lot about Christmas music." Mira was impressed, even if that wasn't her thing.

"I love Christmas. It's the best time of the year." Courtney's expression was almost angelic. "Who doesn't love Christmas?"

"Me." Mira hadn't meant to be so candid. That sort of slipped out.

Courtney looked mortified. "You, what?"

Mira shrugged. "It's not my thing."

Courtney shook her head. "Wait a second, you have the most coveted holiday entertaining space in all of Boston, and you don't like Christmas?"

Mira didn't mention she *hated* Christmas—that seemed dramatic. "You ask that like I have to."

Courtney just blinked at her, her mouth slightly open for a moment before she replied, "I've never met anyone that didn't like Christmas. Like, ever."

"Well, I suppose there's a first time for everything." Mira didn't know what to say to her.

Courtney watched her for a moment, her expression curious. "Are you afraid of elves?"

"Elves?" Mira laughed.

"Allergic to holiday cheer?" Courtney asked.

Mira fake sneezed.

"Oh!" Courtney slapped her knee. "Aha. I know, your grandmother got run over by a reindeer. That's the secret to your distaste to all things holly jolly—an aversion to accidental trampling. Am I close?"

"You guessed it. My poor MeeMaw didn't stand a chance against that hoofed ambush," Mira replied.

"I knew it," Courtney replied with a nod. "It's always the reindeer."

"Never the big guy in a red suit who breaks into your house and eats your food while leaving sooty footprints all over your carpet?" Mira played along.

Courtney examined her appearance. Mira looked down at herself to make sure she looked okay.

"What are you looking at?" Mira asked.

"Anything out of place. But I see nothing. So on top of the reindeer fear, you are also a neat freak. I'm making mental notes." Courtney pretended to jot something down.

"Oh? And why's that?" Mira asked, intrigued.

"So I know what to get you for Christmas, silly," Courtney answered, as if that was obvious.

"Oh no, no, no, no, no." Mira put her hands up. "No, thank you."

Courtney looked offended. "Do you doubt my gift-giving prowess?"

"I don't do Christmas gifts," Mira said.

"Who doesn't do Christmas gifts?" Courtney asked, exasperated.

"Someone who doesn't like Christmas," Mira supplied with a small smile. "But I appreciate the thoughtfulness."

Courtney looked dumbfounded. "I don't know what to do with this information. It's like I hardly know you."

"You do hardly know me," Mira pointed out.

"I know, but wow. Okay." Courtney looked so disappointed that Mira almost apologized for letting her down. "Is it a religious thing? I'm such a moron. It is, isn't it? I'm sorry, that was so insensitive of me."

Mira reached out to settle Courtney's jumping knee. "It's not a religious thing. I just don't like Christmas, okay? It's not that big a deal."

Courtney gaped at her. "That's like saying you don't believe in angels getting their wings when a bell rings, or that yuletide cheer isn't the best kind of cheer there is."

"You're like some kind of Christmas cheerleader, aren't you?" Mira teased.

"This is not a laughing matter. This is serious business." Courtney pouted.

Mira squeezed Courtney's thigh before moving her hand away. "Okay, I'm sorry. I didn't mean to squash your festive fun. I promise not to judge your holiday enthusiasm if you agree not to judge my dislike of the season."

"The whole season?" Courtney was flabbergasted.

"I mean, basically, yes. But I'm good with New Year's—is that cool?"

"I guess I'll have to work with that," Courtney said as she adorably scratched the side of her head. "New Year's is pretty legit."

"See? I'm not so bad." Mira bumped her shoulder.

"I suppose." Courtney looked like she wanted to ask her something. "What?"

"Is this a bad time to ask if I can make a holiday playlist for you to stream over the bar's speakers during the party?"

Mira sighed. "You're killing me."

"Is that a no?" Courtney flashed a megawatt smile, and Mira caved.

"Sprinkle in some instrumentals, and you have a deal."

Courtney cheered. "Now about that garland…"

Mira gave her a look.

"Okay, I'm sorry. I just really need this party to go off without a hitch," Courtney replied.

"It'll be great, I promise," Mira reassured her. "We do this kind of thing all the time."

"I know. It's not you, it's just…" Courtney frowned. "I applied for an event planning position at my work, and I know that if the party is perfect, then it'll prove I have what it takes for the role."

Mira could see that Courtney was serious. "You really want that job, huh?"

Courtney nodded. "I need a change, and I love people and parties and—"

"Yuletide cheer," Mira supplied.

"Exactly," Courtney said. "This is *my* holiday. My family didn't nickname me the Queen of Carols because I half-ass anything Christmas related. If I can't get this party right, then I don't deserve the job."

"Don't you think you're putting a lot of pressure on yourself?" Mira asked.

"Maybe. But if I don't give it my all, then it's not worth doing."

Mira admired that. She was certainly guilty of fully immersing herself in work. But she had the bar of her dreams to show for it. There was something about tenacity that she always appreciated, and Courtney seemed to have it in spades.

"I get that," Mira replied.

She leaned back and let herself appreciate the funny, complex woman before her. Courtney looked great today. And she thoroughly enjoyed her company, even if they had a difference of opinion about the holidays. Nothing about this dinner had felt like a work meeting. It felt a lot like a first date. Mira wondered if that would be in the cards for them sometime. She found herself hoping it would be.

"Is this party for the employees only? Or will there be plus-ones around?" Mira asked.

"Everyone is allowed to bring a guest. If they have one."

"Are you bringing a guest?" Mira was dying to know.

Courtney leaned back and mirrored her position. She rested her elbow on the back of the sofa and leaned her head against her hand. "No, actually."

"Because you don't have anyone to bring? Or you don't like to mix business with pleasure?" Mira wasn't sure what had come over her, but she found herself at the edge of her seat waiting for Courtney's answer.

Courtney's lips parted, and Mira's gaze was drawn to them.

"I have no problem mixing business and pleasure," Courtney replied. As the noise in the bar around them seemed to increase, Mira leaned in to make sure she heard everything Courtney had to say. "I just haven't had the opportunity to."

"Oh, that's a shame," Mira said, meaning none of it.

Courtney shifted closer as the group to their left started warbling off-key again to some familiar tune. "Is it? Because I like to think that it just means I haven't found the right person yet. But I'm open to it. And if that happens through a work venture, then that's okay with me."

Mira didn't miss the way Courtney's eyes trailed over her face. "You mean, like a company holiday party? That kind of work venture?"

"Exactly that kind." The familiar dark look from their first interaction was back. Courtney seemingly had no problem switching from cute and innocent to hot and sexy. Because the woman looking at her right now was no meek little lamb who talked about bells and angel wings. Mira appreciated her versatility. She hoped it translated to the bedroom, too.

"Good," Mira replied, leaning in closer. She got the feeling that if she kissed Courtney in this moment, Courtney would kiss her right back.

Just as she was about to test that theory, Johnny Marks struck again, ruining her moment and catching the attention of the gleeful group nearby.

"Shit, sorry." Courtney leaned away from her to silence her phone, but it was too late. The guys had already loudly begun their rendition of the holiday standard.

It was only then that Mira noticed Teagan waving to her from the bar. She pointed to her naked wrist and tapped it. Mira checked her phone—it was later than she thought. Time seemed to speed up when Courtney was around her.

Mira sighed. Shaun's shift was ending, and Teagan needed help. "It's okay, I have to get back to work. We're down a bartender tonight."

Courtney looked up from her phone, and Mira didn't miss the look of disappointment on her face.

"I know. I feel the same way," Mira said, reaching out to take Courtney's hand. "But we're only a week out from your party, and I'll be here to make sure it's everything you want it to be and more."

"That sounds like a promise." Courtney intertwined their fingers, and Mira warmed at the touch.

"It is," she confirmed. "And to be honest, even if I wasn't covering the bar that day, I'd come in anyway."

"Just to see me?" Courtney ran her thumb over the back of Mira's hand.

"Just to make sure you don't bring a snow cannon," she said as she leaned in and placed a chaste kiss on Courtney's cheek before pulling away.

Courtney used their entwined hands to pull her back to her. She placed a soft, almost too delicate kiss on the edge of Mira's lips, as she said, "I'm bringing garland."

The table of guys next to them whooped and hollered at the all too brief kiss, and Mira laughed, both at the situation and at Courtney's decorating threat.

"Thank you for dinner," she said as Courtney stood to give her a hug good-bye.

"Next time let's try someplace that's not the back of the bar," Courtney said. And Mira loved the idea of doing this again.

"And maybe with less of an audience," Mira said as she stepped out of Courtney's embrace. She'd never leave if this kept up, and Teagan must be drowning by now. But she needed to know one last thing. "Is 'Holly Jolly Christmas' your favorite song?"

"For the holiday? No, 'White Christmas' is." Courtney didn't hesitate in her reply.

"Why's that?"

"Because there is nothing more magical than a fresh snowfall on Christmas Day. It's why I love living in Boston—there's always a chance of it," Courtney replied. "Something about it feels both nostalgic and new. Like it's a blank canvas for memories to be made, I guess."

"That's beautiful," Mira said, surprised by the depth of Courtney's response.

"There's a lot of beauty in the season. I think you just have to step back to see it sometimes." The sincerity of her reply made Mira pause to let the words sink in. She couldn't remember the last time she'd watched the snow fall on Christmas Day and not cursed it.

"You might be on to something there," she said, as she started toward the bar.

"Have a good night, Mira." Courtney gave her a wave. It was adorable.

"Thanks. You, too." If Mira could have walked to the bar watching her the whole time without tripping in the process, she would have. Because no part of her wanted Courtney Rivers out of her sight.

❖

"Is it baby time?" Mira momentarily panicked at Kelly's name on the incoming call screen.

"No, I can't sleep with Shannon Squared pummeling my bladder in any position that's not sitting," Kelly replied wearily.

"We're getting close though, huh?"

"I sure hope so. I'm not sure how much more of this I can take."

"I bet." Mira didn't envy her friend at all.

"Enough baby talk, I want the deets. Tell me all about Mom, did she love the PowerPoint presentation I sent last week? Did I save the day, and am I the best friend ever? You can tell me I am," Kelly rambled excitedly.

"You are, and she did. I just dropped them off now," Mira said into the phone with a sigh.

"Why do you sound so disappointed, then?" Kelly asked.

"No reason." Mira wiped at her eyes to relieve some of the ache from crying. Dropping her mother and her aunt off at the airport had been harder than she'd expected. Luckily, she'd managed to keep it together until she drove away, but she quickly fell apart after that.

"Mira," Kelly coaxed.

"I'm glad they're going, but I'm sad, too." She hated how much this affected her. She wanted nothing more than to send them both off on the trip of a lifetime and be happy for them the whole time. She felt selfish for wanting them around. And she felt small for wanting them to be there for her birthday and for Christmas. As much as she loathed sharing her birthday with such an overly commercialized, bloated holiday—and though she'd never admit it to anyone—there *was* something special about it. Something that Courtney had said the other day had sat with her. She'd said that there was a less obvious, hidden beauty in the season that could go overlooked if you weren't careful. Mira realized that maybe she'd overlooked some of the magic of the holiday Courtney kept going on about because she was too annoyed with it overlapping with her birthday. Or, more realistically, because it meant that with her mom and aunt being away and with no significant other in her life, she would be alone for both occasions. And that void felt endless right now.

"You know you can come spend your birthday with Sarah and the Shannon Squared bump, right?" Kelly said, and Mira knew she could. And she also knew it wasn't a sympathy invitation either, but she still couldn't do that.

"These are your last few days before you guys are moms. You need to be worrying about you, not me," Mira replied as she pulled into her driveway.

"Sarah is plenty bored of my swollen, pregnant ass, I assure you," Kelly replied. "Come by for dinner—we're having prime rib."

"I'll think about it," Mira said.

"You'll be there," Kelly commanded.

"Okay," she acquiesced.

"Are you home safe?"

"Yes, Mom."

"Don't forget to send me that video of your mom's reaction to—"

"Slide eleven, chapter three. Don't worry, I'll never be able to unsee it or forget it." Mira cringed at the memory. Kelly had linked a video of a nearly naked man strategically holding a coconut drink in front of his junk as he said, "Welcome to paradise," before the camera switched angles and showed his back and naked butt as he moved the coconut and sipped the straw with an overly sexy moan. Initially her mother seemed embarrassed, but after she'd replayed it four times, laughing and giggling with her sister, Mira had had to switch screens to keep from getting nightmares.

"Stop being a prude—it was for your mom."

"And we both love you for helping us create more embarrassing shared family moments."

"Love you, too. Go to bed—it's late."

"'Night." Mira glanced at the clock. Kelly was right. She'd spent far too much time at work lately, and late nights like this seemed to have become the norm recently. This was doing nothing to help her social life.

She climbed out of the car and walked the short distance to her front door, cursing herself for forgetting to put the timer on for her front step lights. She fumbled in the dark to get her keys in the lock. She gave up and used her cellphone flashlight app to get her through the door. Once inside, darkness met her again. The quiet emptiness of a home that felt forgotten.

She flicked on the light in the front room and blinked as her eyes adjusted to the brightness. Her place was beautifully decorated and everything she'd wanted it to be, but it was quiet, and dark, and empty at night when she forgot to leave a light on. It didn't matter that during the day this place had the best natural light she'd ever seen. The nighttime made it feel as hollow as she did right now.

"You chose a life of nights and weekends, bub," she said to herself as she shrugged off her jacket and dropped her keys on the table by the door. "And you've never minded being alone before, so what's different now?"

Mira knew what was different. Courtney had entered her life, and in the short time since they'd first met, Mira felt herself drawn to her. There was something about her that was bubbly and sweet and yet still sexy and compelling. Mira had found herself thinking of her often since their first meeting and even more so since their dinner date last week. Because for the first time in an awfully long time, Mira felt herself wanting someone's company. And not just in a sexual way— she'd had plenty of bedroom partners—but in a dating way. She found herself imagining what it would be like to date Courtney. And the playful banter about Christmas and the holidays during their dinner had certainly felt like dating conversation. And the way Courtney had nearly kissed her and held her close, well, that had certainly felt like the promise of something greater. And Mira loved that.

She walked into the kitchen and turned on the pendant light over the island. She opened the fridge and pulled out one of the premade chicken salad containers that effectively made up her entire diet most weeknights. She grabbed a fork and took a few bites out of the container as she leaned against the counter, tired and weary from another long day that slipped into night.

The small ceramic Christmas tree that she'd made as a little girl sat on the table in the corner. It was her sole Christmas decoration, and she only put it up because her mother loved it and made her. She walked over to it and switched the little black button on underneath, and the hand-painted tree lit up with brightly colored plastic ornament lights. The tree gave off a pleasant rainbow glow with the dim overhead light as its only accompaniment. Mira let herself admire it as she finished her dinner. The longer she looked at it, the more she warmed to the idea of embracing Courtney's perspective on the holiday. This little tree did look magical in the quiet darkness of her home. A home she was proud of and felt safe in, even if it was quieter than she would have liked right now. This tree felt like the heart of this room, unwavering in its colorful cheerfulness.

Mira decided to get a timer for this, too, so she'd have something to greet her when she came home late over the next few weeks. And maybe, if she played her cards right, she'd have the chance to show it to Courtney sometime, and have a dinner that was cooked and not prepackaged. She'd like the chance to cook for Courtney and to share the story of how she'd cracked that little ceramic tree the day she picked it up from the ceramics class her mother had forced her to take. And she'd hidden the crack from her mother until she had a chance to fix it. Mira would tell her how she stayed up late and used her mother's superglue and favorite tweezers to fix it but glued her fingers together in the process. Her mother never noticed the barely visible crack, nor did she know about the superglue debacle, but she did notice that Mira hadn't put the tweezers back in the right spot. She laughed at the memory. And she smiled at the desire to share that memory with someone who wasn't her family.

"Oh, girl, you got it bad," she said as she shook her head, heading out of the kitchen toward her bedroom. And she looked back at the little tree she'd left lit, and her heart felt happy. Because she liked Courtney Rivers, and something about how they'd met felt serendipitous. She was sure Courtney would tell her that was because the Christmas season was upon them. Something that Mira wouldn't argue with, for once.

CHAPTER SEVEN

Courtney held up the red dress under her chin for a moment as she checked herself out in the mirror. "Red or green?" She swapped the red for green and shook her head. "Red."

She placed the dress on the edge of the bed and put the green one back for another day. Although both were plenty festive, the red was a little sexier and had that nice slit on the thigh. Choice made. She had every intention of looking good for Mira at the party later.

Their impromptu dinner date-slash-meeting had been on her mind constantly since that night. Courtney liked the immediate chemistry she'd felt with Mira, and flirting with her came as easy as breathing. So when Mira dialed it up and kissed her cheek, Courtney knew that they were on the same page. She only wished she'd had a chance to kiss her the way she wanted to.

But this was fine, she thought. Because the anticipation of what could be was making her thrum in all the right places. Now tonight wasn't just about having a successful party, but also about seeing Mira again. And that was something she was very much looking forward to.

A buzzing sound nearby reminded her that she'd silenced her phone while at the gym earlier. She reached for it and swiped her thumb across the screen to answer.

"Hi, Mom." She put her on speaker so she could finish getting ready.

"Hi, dear," her mom replied. "Are you ready for the big party?"

"Getting there," Courtney said as she started to braid her hair to prep it for the updo she had planned for tonight. "How's Grandpa?"

"He's good. Just anxious about getting to the cabin. You know how he gets."

Courtney nodded—she knew her grandfather disliked flying these days. She wasn't a huge fan of it either, but it was the only way for her to see her extended family, so it was a necessary evil. "He'll be glad once he's all settled in."

"You're right, he will." Her mother was humming something. She must be baking. She always hummed when she baked.

"What are you making?" Courtney almost didn't want to ask because she knew whatever it was would be amazing and not for her. She missed her mom's baked goods.

"Snickerdoodle cookies to bribe Grandpa to behave on the flight and to hold everyone over once they arrive until we can get the grocery delivery sorted out." Her mother sighed. "I wish you were going to be here this weekend, too. I miss you."

"Me, too." Courtney frowned. Her family was arriving this weekend and spending the entire week of Christmas together, but she had too many end-of-year things to finish at work. So her flight wasn't leaving until Christmas Eve, and it had cost her far too much for how incredibly inconvenient the whole thing was.

"When are you getting in again?"

"Nine." Courtney had gotten one of the last seats on the last flight out of Boston for the night. She was landing *way* later than she would have liked, and she was more than a little sore about it. But Chet and the partners were giving them the two weeks after the holiday off, if they could finish their yearly audits and reach their goals. And they would if they all worked right up to Christmas. But still, she hated missing time with her family for any reason, especially a work-related one.

"We'll make do, and we'll have a blast when we're all together," her mother assured her. "And I'll make you a fresh batch of snickerdoodles, hot out of the oven. I promise."

"Thanks, Mom." That made Courtney feel a little better.

"I'll let you go. I don't want you to be late for your big night," her mother said. "Oh, did you end up finding a plus-one to bring?"

"Not exactly," Courtney replied, her thoughts returning to Mira. "I'm fine with that, though."

"Okay. I'm happy if you're happy," she said. "Good luck tonight. And make sure you call me tomorrow and let me know how it goes. I'm sure that promotion is going to be yours."

Courtney hoped she was right. "Love you."

She disconnected the call and looked at the red dress once again. She knew tonight would be a success because regardless of how the party went, she had every intention of making sure she and Mira got the chance to have that kiss they seemed to keep missing out on.

❖

The wind whipped against her face as she reached into the trunk of her car. The New England winter was upon them this evening, and Courtney pulled her jacket around her tighter to keep out the cold.

"Need a hand with that?" Mira's voice was barely audible over the next fierce gust of wind.

"Yes, please." Courtney stepped back and let Mira, in her black leather jacketed glory, reach in and easily maneuver the box that Courtney had struggled getting into her car.

She closed the trunk and shuffled to the back seat to pull out the remaining decorations while Mira watched on, looking amused.

"What?" Courtney put up the furry hood of her jacket to keep from shivering.

"Nothing, you're just cute," Mira said with a shrug, making that box look like it weighed nothing at all.

"Just cute?" Courtney was hoping for a greater reaction than that.

"I mean, like, how excited you are. Cute in that way." Mira walked with her through the loading door out back and into the bar area inside. "But the jacket and fluffy hood combo is adorable."

Courtney slipped off the hood and looked around her for the first time. "Oh, wow."

Mira placed the box on the nearest table and asked, "Do you like it?"

"I love it," Courtney said as she noted how different the bar looked. Mira and her crew had reconfigured the tall bar tops and couches to line the perimeter of the room, expanding the open floor plan farther for mingling. They had somehow even managed to get a small dance floor in the back. The catered buffet was set off in the corner, and to Courtney's delight, lit white garland framed the table, illuminating the incredible smelling covered dishes.

"Good," Mira replied as she motioned for Kevin to come over. "We'll help you get the rest of these decorations out before everyone gets here. Kevin will take your coat for you."

Courtney gave Kevin a broad grin and unzipped her jacket, handing it to him.

"Well, damn. Cute was an understatement," Mira supplied, and Courtney gave her a little twirl.

"You approve?"

"You look great wrapped in red," Mira said, making no attempt to hide her appreciation. Courtney was glad she'd chosen the sexier of the two outfits.

She motioned for Mira to come closer.

Mira glanced left and right before stepping into her personal space. Courtney rewarded her with a gentle nuzzle to her earlobe as she whispered, "When this is over, I'd love for you to unwrap me."

Courtney felt Mira's hand on her hip, holding her close. Mira kept her eyes toward the back of the bar, but the want in her voice was unmistakable. "Let's cancel the party altogether. I'll pull the fire alarm. No one will even question it. Then we can unwrap sooner rather than later."

"Here at the bar?" Courtney reached down to Mira's hand and slid it lower, along the outside of her thigh, before bringing it back up to the more respectable place by her hip.

Mira licked her lips and faced her. "On the bar, behind the bar, wherever. I can get creative."

"I bet you can," Courtney said as she lost herself in the darkness of Mira's eyes. "That's a tempting offer, and I'm not saying no, but I am saying not now, because I really need this party to be a success, and that seems less likely to happen if you have me naked somewhere on the premises when my boss gets here."

"I suppose that's true," Mira begrudgingly agreed.

"It is," Courtney said as she put some space between them since she didn't *really* trust herself. "Plus, all that food would go to waste, and we can't have that."

After a brief squeeze, Mira's hand dropped from her hip. She watched as Mira dragged a thumb over her bottom lip as she replied in a near whisper, "I'm sure we could find other things to eat, but I'll follow your lead."

"You're torturing me. This is practically criminal," Courtney whined, as her lower abdomen tightened at the implication of Mira's words. This was not the time to be getting turned on, she thought.

"I told you I was no Hallmark heroine," Mira said with a laugh.

"I'm seeing the benefit of that," Courtney replied.

"Mm, I'll give you a hands-on demonstration sometime," Mira

promised. "But in the interest of the perfect party plan you have in mind, you should probably finish setting up. It's getting late."

Courtney looked up at the clock over the coatroom entrance and cursed. "I better hustle."

"Let us know how we can help. I'm going to start getting some of the drinks prepared for your final approval. I'll see you over there when you're ready." Mira directed that same thumb that had been on her bottom lip toward the bar behind them, and Courtney was momentarily distracted by Mira's lips and the smoothness of the bar top she was motioning toward. More specifically how much she wanted to be on it and under Mira.

"Thanks." She shook her head to clear the naughty thoughts and redirected her attention to the box Mira had placed down for her. She had just enough time to spread out the final decorations and sidle up to the bar for one last quick review before people started arriving. She could do this, right?

❖

"Peppermintini, Santa Clausmopolitans, Jingle Juice, Sex on a Snowbank, and a signature margarita. Something for everyone." Mira pointed to the five incredible drinks on the bar before her. "I used your drink list as a loose guideline and made some tweaks to make them unique to Mirage. I hope you like them."

"That's five drinks, not four," Courtney pointed out.

"I felt bad about the Drunk Jack Frosties, so we crafted a margarita for you instead," Mira said.

"They look amazing." Courtney was vibrating with excitement. This was more than she could have asked for.

"Try them."

"All of them? I'll never make it through the party," Courtney warned.

Mira shook her head. "Just a taste. Here, like this." Courtney watched as Mira placed a small black stirring straw in each drink. "Where should we start?" she asked.

"Let's go left to right," Courtney suggested.

"Peppermintini—crisp, light, and with a pleasant aftertaste. This is a great sipping cocktail for appetizers but maybe not an all-night rager kinda drink." Mira pressed her finger to the top of the straw, trapping some of the drink's contents in the shaft. She cradled the now full straw with her thumb and lifted it toward Courtney's mouth. "Give it a taste."

Courtney parted her lips and leaned forward, as Mira let the contents of the straw drip down onto her tongue. She closed her eyes and let the flavors swirl in her mouth. "Mm, that's wonderful."

She opened her eyes to see Mira giving her an amused look. "What?"

"Nothing, you're just—"

"Cute?" Courtney supplied with a look.

"I was going to say *enchanting*," Mira replied, and Courtney melted. "Anyway, that's how you taste the cocktail without getting drunk—the straw technique. It's a bartender's best friend."

"Does that mean you aren't going to personally feed me each drink? Because I was thoroughly enjoying that service," Courtney teased as she played with the cocktail napkin under the peppermintini.

Mira wiped her hand on a fresh bar napkin and reached for the next straw. "I'd hate to disappoint you. Are you ready for number two?"

Courtney loved the playfulness of their exchange, and she loved each and every drink more than the last. The Santa Clausmopolitan was a souped-up cosmo with pomegranate juice and a bright green lime twist as a garnish. And the Jingle Juice was Mira's interpretation of a festive winter sangria with Grand Marnier and clementines mixed with mulled spices and cinnamon sticks.

"And this one is a personal favorite because I love coconut, and because I like the innuendo," Mira said with a mischievous smile as she held out the straw with the Sex on a Snowbank sample in it. "Maybe if you're lucky I'll tell you what we call it behind the scenes."

Courtney slid her tongue out to catch the straw this time, making a show of it for Mira's enjoyment. And if the way Mira was biting her bottom lip was any indication, she was enjoying it plenty.

"Ooh, this is nice. Sweet, refreshing, memorable." Courtney approved of Mira's choice. "I like that."

"Ready for the last one?" Mira moved toward the last straw, but Courtney stopped her.

"What about the behind-the-scenes name? Don't leave me hanging."

Mira looked pleased. "I'll warn you, it's not safe for work."

"Very little of our interaction lately seems to be," Courtney added as she licked her lips.

"That's fair." Mira motioned for her to lean in.

Courtney got both forearms on the bar and lifted herself up until Mira's lips were at her ear.

"We're calling this the Frosty Fuck out of earshot, but the truth is a few of these will heat you up, not cool you down. You know, like a good snowbank romp should." The closeness of Mira's mouth to her skin was turning her on, but what Mira said made her wetter than she expected. Mira's lips ghosted along the skin of her cheek as she pulled back, and Courtney let out a low moan of disappointment at the distance between them.

The delighted look on Mira's face indicated she'd noticed.

"Is it time for the party to be over yet?" Courtney asked as she lowered herself into her seat, slightly more uncomfortable than before.

"It's just getting started," Mira said as she reached for the final straw. "I made this especially for you—a touch of coconut milk in our signature margarita with fresh lime and floating cranberries for that extra festive kick you love so much."

This drink was a gorgeous milky white in its mason jar with brightly colored berries surfing between ice cubes at the surface. It almost looked too pretty to drink.

Courtney accepted the last taste with a happy hum. "Oh, wow. This is amazing. What are you calling this one?"

"A White Christmas margarita," Mira said, and she looked almost shy.

Courtney was touched by Mira's thoughtfulness and the attention to detail she put into each cocktail that sat before her. "I don't know what to say."

"Say you like them," Mira offered.

"I love them. All of them."

"Good." Mira held her eye contact for a long moment, and Courtney was glad she'd chosen Mirage as the site for her holiday party for this reason alone: Mira was here.

CHAPTER EIGHT

Amazing party, Courtney, really. A bang-up job. Super cool." Every word that Chet uttered sounded fake, but he did seem to genuinely enjoy himself tonight. And Stephanie, she'd noted. But that was the last thing on her mind right now because only Chet and a few other lingerers stood between her and the alone time with Mira that she so desperately wanted.

The party had gone off without a hitch. The decorations were tasteful and festive, and her colleagues were jolly and well-behaved. The food was great, and the bar service was impeccable. But the drinks stole the show—everyone oohed and aahed at the signature cocktails. And throughout the night, Mira gave the compliments to Courtney again and again, praising her suggestions and creativity. Which seemed unnecessary since Mira had been the one to bring the drinks to fruition. Courtney had the idea, but Mira and her staff made it happen.

Still, they were nothing but congratulatory, and by the middle of the night, Courtney knew she'd secured that promotion. In part because the majority of the partners had flat-out told her. And Chet seemed happy. Mission accomplished. She'd killed this party, and now she was ready to reward herself with a little Mira time.

"Looks like he had fun," Mira said from across the bar as Chet stumbled while trying to put on his coat.

"That's my boss, a Buxby himself. And I'd say so." Courtney was trying to be polite.

"Who's the shorter woman in the black skirt that he was pawing over all night? Does she work with you or is she a plus-one?" Mira asked.

"You noticed that? I thought I was the only one."

Mira raised an eyebrow in her direction. "There isn't much I miss from this side of the bar. Job hazard, I suppose. They've been mostly discreet about it, but it's clear they're carrying on in some way. Like, right now, he's drunkenly trying to convince her to kiss him under the mistletoe by the coat check."

Courtney whipped around in time to see Stephanie give a quick look around the bar before pecking Chet on the lips and scurrying away. "Gross."

"Agreed," Mira said as she stacked clean glasses into little rows.

"I assume Chet's not your type, but Stephanie isn't either?" Courtney turned back to the bar, intrigued once again by the beautiful brunette before her.

"I didn't talk with her much, but she seemed like a vapid airhead. And you don't like her, so that's enough for me," Mira replied.

"I didn't say I didn't like her," Courtney pointed out.

"You don't have to—it's all over your face. You'd be terrible at poker, Rivers," Mira teased.

"So if she's not your type—pretty, vapid, probably opportunistic— then who is?" Courtney asked as she waved to the last retreating coworkers, thanking them for coming as they passed.

Mira leaned against the back shelf of the bar and surveyed her. "Blond, bubbly, really into Christmas carols, and gorgeous in red."

"That's pretty specific." Courtney *had* been fishing, but she was pleased by the answer nonetheless.

"I'm pretty particular," Mira replied.

"What else did you notice tonight?" Courtney asked, wanting to know more.

Mira stepped forward and placed her hands on the bar between them. "I noticed you schmoozing and putting everyone at ease. And I noticed how much your coworkers genuinely seem to like you, except Stephanie, who I think might hate you, but we already know our feelings on her."

Courtney laughed. "Anything else?"

"I noticed you watching me mix drinks and talk to your guests. I seemed to have your attention tonight," Mira said, and she was right. Courtney hadn't taken her focus off Mira the whole night. She couldn't. And the multiple shared glances between them tonight told her that Mira was watching her as well.

"Did that bother you?" Courtney asked.

"No, I liked it." Mira's reply was low.

"Good, because I liked watching you," Courtney said, making no attempt to hide her leering. Mira was wearing another fitted black dress shirt tonight, the sleeves rolled up at her forearms like before, but this time, Courtney noticed she had a few extra buttons undone. Something that she greatly appreciated now as Mira leaned her forearms on the bar, exposing a little cleavage in the process.

"What happens now?" Courtney asked, her eyes directed to the soft flesh peeking out of Mira's shirt.

"At this very moment?" Mira asked, staying close. "At the bar or between us?"

"Yes, and yes. At the bar, behind it, whatever," Courtney repeated from earlier.

"Business-wise, I need you to sign off on the final total for the night." Mira licked her lips. "But pleasure-wise, once they finish tidying the bar, you and I need to find someplace to unwrap that dress."

Teagan and Shaun both passed behind Mira as they spoke, cleaning and tidying as they went. But Courtney wasn't sure how much longer she could wait. "Tell me you have an office with a door," she breathed out, her voice full of want.

"I even have a couch," Mira said.

"Take me there. Now." Courtney was out of her seat before she finished getting the words out.

Mira met her at the end of the bar and lifted the hinged portion of the counter for her, before leading her behind the bar to a short hallway.

Courtney noticed Shaun loading something into what looked like a stockroom, and a small door next to it, slightly ajar, led to a private bathroom. The last door on the right had a plaque on it that read *Office*.

Mira opened the door, and Courtney followed closely, shutting the door behind them.

Courtney reached for Mira's hand, spinning her to a stop as she stepped into her personal space.

Mira brushed an errant hair from Courtney's forehead as she gently caressed her face. "I have so many things planned for you, but I need one extra minute to make sure we aren't interrupted."

Courtney couldn't have stopped the pout if she wanted to.

"You're teasing me with that lower lip." Mira ran her thumb along it as she spoke. "Let me send the guys home and close out the account for today. Then I'm all yours."

"*Fine.*" Courtney sighed dramatically.

"I'll make it worth the wait, I promise," Mira said, and Courtney was counting on it.

Mira squeezed her hand before heading to her desk. "This is the last bit of paperwork I need your John Hancock on, and then we're good."

Courtney skimmed the sheet before signing it, probably overenthusiastically.

"So, no questions, then?" Mira laughed.

"None." Courtney dropped the pen, turning toward her.

"Okay, one sec," Mira said before she disappeared through the door, leaving Courtney alone in the office.

Courtney took in the room for the first time. The office was a good size, with a stylish but practical desk. There was a minifridge with a microwave, and a coffee maker in the corner. And across the room was an oversized leather couch that looked particularly inviting. She was examining Mira's coffee selection when she noticed Mira's handwritten notes on the whiteboard over the coffee maker. She was sure the shorthand and numbers made sense to someone, but she was clearly not that person.

"Learning all my secrets?" Mira's voice sounded from behind her.

"As if I could decipher this chicken scratch. It's a miracle I could even read the cell phone number you scribbled down for me the first time," Courtney replied, smiling at the sound of the door closing behind Mira.

"Lucky me you figured it out," Mira said, her voice closer now.

Courtney turned when she felt Mira's hands on her waist.

"Hi," she said as she wrapped her arms around Mira's shoulders.

"Hi." Mira pulled her close. "Did I mention I love you in red?"

"You didn't." Courtney nuzzled Mira's nose.

"Well, I do. You look very festive." Mira ghosted her lips across Courtney's.

Courtney felt herself heat up at the near contact. She moved her hand from Mira's back to her collarbone, tracing her fingers along the flesh just inside the lapel of her shirt. She tugged the fabric back and moaned when she saw the red silk bra strap underneath. "Talk about festive."

"You approve?" Mira echoed their banter from earlier.

"Very much so," Courtney said as she caressed the soft skin before her. "I've wanted to touch you all night."

"Just touch?" Mira asked as she dipped her head to catch Courtney's gaze. "Or taste, too?"

Courtney managed a slight nod, but words escaped her. She

reached out to cradle Mira's jaw, and soon Mira's mouth was on hers, and full lips kissed her in a breath-stealing crescendo of want and need and lust that made Courtney dizzy.

She slid her hand into Mira's hair, opening her mouth to deepen the kiss as Mira's hands moved up and down her back and along the outside of her thigh, massaging and teasing with each and every kiss and lick of her mouth. Courtney's hips bucked forward when Mira's hand found the slit in her dress, nudging the fabric up and out of the way as she kneaded Courtney's thigh before she slid inward to dance along Courtney's inner leg.

Courtney was starting to pant, the breaths coming short and fast as Mira didn't let up on her mouth or her thigh. Kissing and teasing, caressing, and rubbing—there were so many sensations at once. And yet they still didn't feel like enough.

"Couch." Courtney barely got the word out between strokes of Mira's tongue against hers.

Mira walked them backward toward the sofa, pulling Courtney onto her lap as she sat. Courtney shifted, hiking up her dress so she could rest her knees on either side of Mira's hips, and the newly exposed skin on her thighs was immediately owned by Mira's hands and fingers.

"You feel so good," Courtney exhaled between hungry kisses. She had never quite been kissed the way Mira was kissing her now. She was more than sure she could be kissed like this forever and never get tired.

"Watching you tonight was torture," Mira said against her mouth. Courtney felt her hand leave her thigh to run up over her chest, briefly palming her breast before cupping her jaw and holding her close. "You are so gorgeous, Courtney. I've been dying to kiss you."

"Just kiss me?" Courtney parroted.

"To start," Mira said in reply, and Courtney gasped when Mira's other hand pulled the stretchy fabric of her dress up over her hip, then settled on her ass.

Just then the phone on Mira's desk rang loudly, shocking Courtney out of her blissful make-out haze. Mira's mouth left her skin, and a concerned look was on her face, as her hands wrapped around Courtney in an almost protective way.

"Are you expecting a call?" Courtney asked between pants, trying to wrap her head around what was happening since she was sort of definitely just about to ask Mira to do more than kiss her. But now all flirty, sexy touching seemed to have ceased.

"No," Mira replied, her brow furrowed. "No one calls the office line this late."

The ringing stopped but started right back up.

"Courtney, I am so, so sorry, but I think I have to get that." Mira looked mortified.

"Of course," Courtney said as she scrambled off her lap, adjusting her dress so she could sit on the couch with some modicum of decency. She crossed her legs and shifted to relieve some of her built-up arousal, trying to be subtle in the process.

Courtney looked up to find Mira reaching for the phone, her eyes on Courtney and a knowing smile on her lips. "I'll fix that, I promise."

"I was hoping you'd say that." Courtney shifted again. She couldn't remember the last time she'd been this turned on only to have it all come to a screeching halt. It wasn't an unpleasant feeling—it was just one that felt like a lot of wanting and yearning. Which was making her hot all over again.

"Hello?" Mira spoke in the receiver. "Sarah, hi. Wait, slow down."

The concerned look from before was back on Mira's face. Mira nodded to no one, and though Courtney couldn't make out what was being said on the line, she could tell the words were coming fast, and they sounded frantic.

"Okay, okay, calm down. I'll meet you there. Go. Bye." Mira hung up the phone, looking two shades paler than a few minutes ago. "I'm sorry, I have to go. Something is wrong with Kelly and the baby, and Sarah needs me to—"

Courtney's hand flew over her mouth. The baby. Mira must be talking about her coworker and Courtney's previous Mirage contact, Kelly. She was off the couch in less than a second. "Of course, go. What can I do? Can I help?"

Mira shook her head, looking dazed. "No, I think I'm good."

"Let me grab my coat. And we'll walk out together, okay?"

Mira was already slipping on her leather jacket and fumbling with her keys.

Courtney followed Mira back to the front of the bar, grabbing her coat as Mira flicked off the lights and made sure the front door was locked.

"I am so sorry." Mira helped her into her coat, zipping her in with care.

"Hey, stop. It's fine." Courtney touched her face and kissed her to quiet her concerns. "There will be lots of opportunities for you and me to get into sexy trouble. I'm sure of it. Right now, it sounds like your friends need you more than I do."

Mira rested her forehead against Courtney's and exhaled shakily. Courtney could tell she was upset.

"Let's go," Courtney said as she tugged Mira's hand toward the rear exit they'd come in earlier.

Mira nodded and took the lead, holding Courtney's hand the whole way to her car. She opened Courtney's driver's side door and paused. "Shit, your box of stuff."

"I'll come by and get it later." Courtney kissed her once more. "Go be a super-friend. Text me later so I know you're okay."

"Thank you. For tonight. For understanding. For everything." Mira still looked shaken, but Courtney was less worried about her passing out now.

"Don't thank me. Go. And don't forget that text, okay?"

"Than—" Mira stopped herself. "Drive safe."

Courtney slipped into the seat, closing the door as she watched Mira race to her car and disappear out of sight. As she started her car and headed home, her thoughts were filled with Mira and how worried she was about her. Everything was going to be okay, right?

CHAPTER NINE

Mira felt like she had aged a decade the last two days. Sarah's frantic phone call had put her in a tailspin, but thankfully Courtney had helped her pull her head out of her ass long enough to get to the hospital safely. Once there she found a panicked Sarah waiting for answers and for Kelly's mother to arrive. Things were tense until the doctor filled them in on what happened.

Kelly had fainted while at home and there was an issue controlling her blood pressure. She was stable now and the baby was fine, but it had given everyone—Mira included—a scare.

"Will you stop fussing? I'm fine," Kelly said from the hospital bed, swatting at Mira's hand on her forehead.

"I'm just checking your temperature," Mira reasoned. "How's that nasty head cut?"

"I'm at the hospital—that is literally someone's job. Stop worrying. You're worse than Sarah. I can't believe she even called you."

Mira feigned offense. "Listen, when my best friend and best employee takes a nosedive into the bathroom sink and opens up her head while carrying my birthday baby twin, I am the first person on the list to call after emergency services and your mom."

"That would make you the third person on the list," Kelly pointed out.

"Rude." Mira sat back in her seat next to Kelly's bed with a huff.

"I know you're my designated babysitter while Sarah and my mother finish all the stuff at home, but I don't need you worrying over me. What I'd like is a distraction from this concussion with some juicy gossip about your Christmas angel dream girl."

Mira sighed. She felt awful about how she'd had to jet out on Courtney the other night. But if her texts were any indication, Courtney didn't share the same concern. If anything, Courtney seemed genuinely worried about Mira. Which was an unexpected but nice surprise.

"See, you're smiling just thinking about her. Don't make me work so hard for gossip—I'm bedridden here." Kelly nudged her with her foot.

"She's great," Mira said, giving in. "She's smart and funny and sarcastic—"

"That'll help with you and your occasional grumpiness. We need a girl who's got humor and shade-giving abilities," Kelly chimed in.

"I am not grumpy," Mira argued.

"Not now that you've met your Christmas loving pixie, you aren't. But you usually are this time of year. She seems to have changed that."

Mira thought about that for a moment. Kelly was right. She was a Grinch in every sense of the word, and with her family being away, she should be more like that than ever. But for some reason she wasn't as agitated by the holiday as usual. She wondered if that had to do with Courtney showing up in her life.

"So, have you two talked after the near hookup? Which, might I add, I can't believe happened at the bar when I wasn't there to listen through the door."

"That's a creepy thing to say, Kelly. Even for you," Mira replied.

"I'm joking. Mostly I wish I was there to see all the not so subtle flirtation between you two at the bar like Teagan told me about."

"Teagan?" Mira shouldn't be shocked, but she kind of was. "I'm firing her."

"I need to keep my fingers on the pulse of the workplace while I'm out. Do you think I trust you to be my source? You didn't even tell me this thing between you and Courtney was getting serious when you know I live for such information. You've been depriving me. I had to go to my other sources," Kelly replied.

Mira got hung up on something Kelly said just then. Was this thing between her and Courtney getting serious? And what did that mean?

"Hey, this talking thing only works if you also open your mouth and speak." Kelly nudged her with her foot again.

"I really like her." Mira surprised herself with her own honesty. "I feel like we have a real connection."

"Even though she's all holly jolly about your least favorite holiday?"

Mira nodded. "Yeah, maybe because of it."

Kelly looked shocked. "Wow."

"What?"

"That was pretty deep for you."

Mira frowned. "You say that like I'm shallow."

"I didn't mean it that way." Kelly sat up a little but touched her forehead and grimaced before leaning back again. "What I meant was you are loyal and loving and wonderful with your family and your friends. I mean, you are at least the third person to call in an emergency."

Mira laughed.

"But when it comes to women and dating or getting serious with anyone—I haven't seen that in a very, very long time. Maybe the entire time I've known you, honestly. You have flings and bring cute girls around for a while, and then you move on to the next. But it's been a long time for that, too. I've been worried that you were closing yourself off to the idea of finding someone. But this Mira is not the same Mira I left at the bar when I took my maternity leave. This Mira has moon eyes for a Christmas elf. And it's a freaking miracle."

"Don't start with the miracle nonsense," Mira said, putting up her hand. "I have my limits."

Kelly rolled her eyes. "Fine. I'll shelve that obvious rationale, because you are irrational. But I'm right about Courtney."

"I know," Mira admitted. "I think about her all the time. And I talk to her just about all the time, too."

As if on cue, her phone buzzed. She grinned when she saw Courtney's text, checking in on Kelly. She was so thoughtful. Add that to the list of her amazing qualities.

"Right. So what are you doing here, then? I mean, I don't want you to leave because I'm super bored and this headache makes it impossible for me to watch TV, but, like, shouldn't you be courting her or something?"

"Courting Courtney?" Mira shook her head.

"Exactly."

"She's working. A lot. I guess she has a few big end-of-year things to finish off at work before Christmas Eve. Then she's hopping on a flight to Colorado to be with her family for the holiday. So nothing is going to happen until after she gets back, I guess," Mira said.

"Oh." Kelly looked as disappointed as Mira had felt when she'd first found out that Courtney would be out of town over her birthday.

She had no intention of telling her that she was going to be alone for the first time ever over the holiday, or that it was her birthday, but she had hoped that if Courtney had family nearby that maybe she could steal her for a few hours during the day to do something nice for her since she knew how important Christmas was for her. Hell, she'd even bought lit white garland to surprise her, and that was way out of the norm for her. She knew she'd do anything if it would make Courtney happy.

Selfishly, she had been hoping to spend some time *not* alone, and the prospect of spending any time with Courtney made her feel hopeful and alive. Because spending time with Courtney was high on her priority list, and she knew that meant that Courtney was special.

"I'm trying not to dwell on it. I'm just going with the flow, and so far, the flow has brought her into my bar and into my life," Mira replied. "It's just a day like any other day. There will be more of them. Hopefully after this is all over and when Shannon Squared is here, I'll have someone to bring by to introduce her to."

"I could be having a boy," Kelly noted.

"Shannon is a boy's name, too," Mira argued.

Kelly laughed. "Okay, I'm excited to meet this Courtney again, this time as your girlfriend. Even if I have to wait a little longer."

Girlfriend. That sounded nice. She fired off a quick text to the woman in question and smiled when Courtney wrote back something cute immediately.

"Man, you are goo-goo over this woman."

Mira kept smiling because she felt like she finally had something to smile about. "Yeah, I think I am."

Courtney checked her company email again. There was still no word from Chet about his promise to fast-track her application for the transfer after the successful holiday party. She checked and rechecked the company website, and the opening remained unfilled, which seemed odd since she was under the impression they wanted that decided before the office closed for the holiday. But maybe they were just a little behind. It had been hectic around here lately, and she imagined the same was true for Philanthropic.

She looked up her flight itinerary next—boarding was delayed forty-five minutes, but the flight was still almost on schedule, which was good.

She sighed as she stretched and rolled her shoulders to get some of the tightness out. She had worked late every night since the night of the holiday party, and she was paying for it physically and mentally. But that was all about to change since she was clocking out in a few minutes and about to start her two-week vacation.

She'd had an epiphany late last night when she finally left, sometime after seven. The darkness of New England winter evenings was not something that usually bothered her because winter also brought snow and hot cocoa, which were two of her favorite things. But when she was cooped up in an office doing mindless busywork to meet a deadline, it bothered her a lot. Last night was one of those nights. The darkness outside had felt like an abyss, and she wanted nothing more than to close her eyes and find herself back at Mirage under the tiny white Christmas lights that hung from the ceiling, illuminating the room with that soft, ethereal glow that framed Mira in a sexy radiance while she mixed drinks and flirted across the bar.

That was her epiphany. When she wanted an escape from the winter and the doldrums of work, her mind didn't go to the upcoming Colorado vacation. It went to Mira. Mira was on her mind a lot. She had been since before the party, and now, after their false start of a hookup, she was practically the only thing she saw when she closed her eyes and the work computer screen filled with numbers faded away. She had realized that, over the last week, the only thing that got her through work was the promise of seeing Mira again. She was like a beacon, and Courtney knew that was because she was head over heels for the charming bartender.

She messaged Mira because she could. When Mira didn't write back right away, she wasn't worried. It was Christmas Eve, after all. Mira had mentioned she would be at the bar with a skeleton crew, so Courtney knew she would be busy. But she wanted her to find a text knowing that she was thinking about her, because she was.

She looked out the window at the end of the row of cubicles and began to worry. It wasn't quite two p.m. yet, but the sky had grown ominous and dark. The snow had been falling off and on all day, but the heaviest snow was expected in the next few hours, and it was projected to be a complete whiteout overnight and into Christmas Day. Which she normally would have rejoiced about, if she didn't have to get on a flight during an epic snowstorm.

She moved her suitcase out of the way to walk to the window and get a better look outside. It was already coming down fast. She decided to pull the trigger and head to the airport before it got any worse. But she frowned as a realization hit her hard—if she went right to the airport, she wouldn't have the chance to drop off Mira's Christmas gift. Maybe if she hustled, she could still do both and not miss her flight. All she had to do was check in with Chet, and then she was free.

She knocked on his door and waited for his reply.

"Come in," he called.

She walked in to find him mid-laugh as he looked at something on his computer screen.

"Cat videos. I mean, so funny. Right?" Chet chuckled, and Courtney restrained the eye roll she so desperately wanted to unleash. She came in early and worked late to get his projects done, and he was watching cat videos on the internet. What a jerk.

"Yeah, sure. Look, I'm heading out now. The projects are done, and I want to get to the airport before the roads become undrivable." Courtney didn't have time for small talk if she planned to swing by the bar first.

"Right. Makes sense. Happy holidays. I hope you have a nice break." Chet gave her a wave as he turned his attention back to the cat videos.

"Chet?"

"What's up?" he asked, not bothering to look at her.

"Any news on that event planning position?" Courtney had to ask. What was the holdup?

"Oh," Chet said as he turned to face her. "I thought you knew. They filled the position from within the company. We decided that Stephanie was the best person for the job. She'll be starting at the beginning of the year—an announcement should be going out soon. Thank you for your interest, though."

Courtney blinked. "What?"

"I said, Stephanie—"

She held up her hand. "I heard what you said, Chet. It was a rhetorical *what*, like, *What do you mean you gave the position to someone else after I organized the most perfect holiday party of your life?* That kind of *what*."

"Oh, I see." Chet looked embarrassed. Good.

She waited for him to expand upon that, but he just looked at her blankly.

"That *was* a great party, Courtney. Thanks."

That was it? That was all he had to say? Courtney felt like she might scream.

"Okay, well, you're welcome. Um, have a great holiday and I…"

She noticed an empty box in the corner and pointed to it. "Can I have that box?"

"Sure." Chet shrugged. "Need it for anything in particular?"

"To clean out my desk. I quit." Courtney gave him her brightest, fakest grin. "Merry Christmas, Chet."

"Thanks." A pause. "Wait, what?" she heard behind her as she closed his door with more force than was necessary.

Her phone pinged as she packed up her desk. It was a message from the airline. Her flight was just canceled. Merry fucking Christmas indeed.

Chapter Ten

Don't worry about it, I'm heading out soon. Tomorrow is fine. Thanks, Jake," Mira said, then hung up the phone directly behind the bar. Jake was her snowplow guy. He told her they were expecting more snow than was previously anticipated and that he might be late clearing the front path and parking lot but that he'd make sure it was cleared out by morning. Which was fine by Mira since she'd already sent all her employees home.

Bad weather had been predicted, but this was getting to be unsafe. So she'd thanked them all and gave them an extra Christmas bonus for covering all of Kelly's shifts with minimal complaint and sent them on their way. No reason to risk life and limb over a mostly empty bar the night before a holiday.

"Can I get another?" Tori—a regular, and her only customer at the moment—asked from across from her.

"Sure, T." She poured her another Sam Adams and handed her one of the emergency bags of potato chips they kept behind the bar to help people sober up. "We're going to close early tonight, T. So the chips and that last beer are on me, okay?"

"Ending my party early, huh? Fine." Tori cackled. She looked out the window behind her and exclaimed, "Whoa. It's really coming down."

"I know," Mira said, worrying her bottom lip. She'd texted Courtney back a little while ago, but she hadn't heard from her yet. She knew her flight would be leaving shortly, but Mira would be lying if she said she wasn't a little worried. She wasn't a huge fan of flying to begin with, but a snowstorm seemed like an extra bad time to be on a plane.

She wiped down the bottles and emptied the dishwasher as Tori finished her drink.

"Merry Christmas, Mira," Tori said as she shrugged on her puffy jacket.

"You too, Tori. Be careful getting home."

"I think I'll survive the two-block walk," Tori said with a wave. "Closed tomorrow, right?"

"Yup, but I'll see you the next day?" Mira asked, knowing the answer.

"You betcha." Tori disappeared out the front door but not before a gust of wind brought a blast of snow into the bar.

"Shit." Mira climbed under the bar and grabbed a mop. She had just finished cleaning up when the door next to her flew open again, this time bringing a larger gust with more snow drift. And someone looking to come in.

"Sorry, we're closed due to inclement weather," Mira said, shielding her eyes from the freezing pellets that accompanied the snow.

"Can you spare a drink for a weary traveler?" Courtney's voice was muffled from beneath the furry hood of her jacket.

"Courtney?" Mira barely recognized the snow-covered form in front of her. Courtney was carrying something that was caked in snow and slush. "Jesus. Come in, come in."

She took the box from her and placed it on a nearby table as Courtney reached back outside to pull in her suitcase, which looked like a snowball on wheels.

"You must be freezing," Mira said as she locked the front door. She ran back to Courtney's side to take the bag and brush the clumps of snow off her shoulders.

"I've certainly been warmer," Courtney said before shivering. The fur around her hood was saturated in icy slush, and her cheeks were bright pink from the wind outside.

"Come here, take that thing off." Mira helped her out of her jacket before draping it on a chair by the heater next to the door. "What did you do, walk here?"

"Sort of. My Uber got stuck on a side street about a block away, but I figured I could just hoof it." Courtney blew a strand of hair out of her eyes.

"With a box and a suitcase? In a snowstorm?" Mira gave her a look.

"The box wasn't planned. Nor was I expecting that to be the longest block of my life. Did you know it was also uphill? Phew. That was a doozy." Courtney wiped her brow dramatically.

"You're something else." She was glad to see her.

"Is that a compliment?" Courtney asked with another shiver.

"Yes," Mira said as she reached out to squeeze Courtney's ice-cold hand. "Go grab a seat—I'll make you some tea. I have a blanket out back, let me go get it."

"I'll be f-fine." She shivered again.

Mira ignored her. "Go sit. I'll be right back."

"Okay."

Courtney turned toward the bar, but Mira stopped her by their joined hands. "Hey, I'm really happy to see you. Did I mention that?"

"No, you were too busy being bossy. But I'm happy to see you, too," Courtney replied before she stepped into Mira's embrace.

"Baby, you're freezing," Mira said as she kissed the cool skin of Courtney's temple.

"I'm warming up by the second," Courtney said as she turned her head to catch Mira's lips.

Mira kissed her long and slow, glad to feel Courtney's lips against hers. "I missed you," she said between kisses.

"The feeling is very mutual," Courtney murmured across her lips before kissing along her neck.

It was Mira's turn to shiver when Courtney's wet hair brushed against her cheek, and her cold hands slipped under Mira's shirt.

"You're supposed to be warming up," Mira said between gasps, flinching from Courtney's still cold touch but loving the contact.

Courtney settled her hands against Mira's stomach and snuggled close. "You are so warm. I am very happy here."

"Go sit and let me take care of you. Then I promise you can have more of this." Mira coaxed her toward the bar.

Courtney stopped short and shook her head. "Kiss."

"Kiss?"

Courtney pointed up. Mistletoe.

Mira laughed. "Weren't we just kissing?"

"Yes, but I didn't know we were in such close proximity to mistletoe at the time. It's, like, bad luck to not kiss under mistletoe."

"Did you just make that up?" Mira asked, before happily connecting their lips again.

"Don't argue with me. I'm the Queen of Christmas, I know all things Christmassy. And kissing under the mistletoe is a requirement."

"No arguments he—"

Courtney silenced her with a finger to her lips. "I really needed that kiss and those lips and you today. Thank you for being here." Courtney smiled, but for the first time, Mira noticed she looked tired, too.

"You okay?" Mira brushed Courtney's wet hair off her forehead.

"I will be." Courtney squeezed her hand. "Blanket and tea, please."

"On it."

When Mira got back to the front of the bar, she found that Courtney had taken the same seat she'd sat in the first time they'd met. For some reason that made Mira exceptionally happy.

"Here," she said as she draped the blanket over Courtney's shoulders. "Let me get to work on that tea."

Courtney burrowed into the blanket, wrapping herself up like a burrito and pulling a portion of it over her head like a hood. Mira laughed so hard at the sight of her that she almost spilled the piping hot water.

"Feel free to pour some whiskey in that," Courtney murmured from under the blanket fort she'd built around herself.

"Hot toddy, coming up." Mira added lemon and honey with the whiskey and made herself one as well.

When she sat next to Courtney at the bar, Courtney sneaked a hand out to touch her leg and scoot closer. Before long Mira had some blanket on her lap, too.

"This is so good," Courtney said as she inhaled the hot beverage.

"I'm glad you like it," Mira replied, holding Courtney's free hand.

"Why is this blanket so big? It's like a blanket for a bed. Why do you have a bed blanket here?" Courtney asked, looking adorably curious.

"Because I have a bed here," Mira said between sips of her drink.

"Say what, now?"

"That couch in my office—"

"That's a very memorable couch," Courtney added.

"Agreed." Her time with Courtney on that couch was one of Mira's new favorite memories. "It pulls out to a bed. I keep sheets and stuff here out of habit. I used to use that as a bed in my early days when I was saving money to buy this bar and couldn't afford to also rent a place. But that was forever and a day ago. I have a home now, a nice one. But something in the back of my head tells me to always be prepared."

"Well, I am very grateful for this bed blanket." Courtney had a warm, pink glow on her cheeks now, not like the frostbitten rawness that was there before.

"So, what's in the box?" Mira pointed to the other end of the bar.

"My work stuff," Courtney said nonchalantly.

"You have that much work to take home?" That seemed a little crazy to Mira, considering it was Christmas and all.

"No, it's my desk contents. I quit."

Mira almost choked on her drink. "Quit?"

Courtney nodded. "Chet gave the job to Stephanie and didn't even have the decency to tell me. And I have been busting my ass to get his stupid projects done, and you know what he was doing when I went to his office today? Watching cat videos on YouTube. Cat videos."

"I never liked that Stephanie," Mira said with a frown. "Or Chet."

"Hear, hear." Courtney raised her glass in agreement before draining the contents. "The truth is that I've been unhappy there for a long time, and this was exactly the kind of outrage I needed to get the guts to quit. So I did."

"Do you think you'll regret this in the morning?" Mira asked.

"No. Maybe when my rent is due, yes. But I have a healthy savings. I can take time to figure out how to get a job doing what I want to do."

"Which is what exactly?"

"Event planning, party coordinating. Something to do with celebrations and situations of joy." Courtney seemed completely calm about the whole thing. "Basically, anything that isn't busywork and computer stuff all day long, and I'm sure I'll be happy. Or at least happier."

Mira had a thought. "Well, I know of this bar that is in desperate need of an event coordinator for the next three to six months. I can't promise that it pays much, but it might be a good stepping-stone for something else. And I'm pretty sure I could put in a good word with the owner if you were interested."

Courtney shrugged off the blanket hoodie and gave her an inquisitive look. "Would some behind the bar training be necessary for this job?"

"There would certainly be room for growth and development in the intoxicology department, yes."

"Sounds like a perfect opportunity, then," Courtney said as she pulled Mira's chair closer to hers. "Can the training start now?"

"Certainly," Mira said as Courtney and her blanket ended up on her lap.

"Then I accept."

Mira smiled against Courtney's lips and savored the warmth and weight of her. She hummed contentedly when Courtney draped some of the blanket around them both. She moaned when Courtney's hands found their way under her shirt again. This time with a seemingly different purpose than before.

"How long until you have to leave for your flight?" Mira asked as Courtney started to undo the buttons on her shirt.

Courtney paused, and Mira thought maybe she'd said something wrong.

"The flight was canceled. And as of now there are no flights with open seats going out tomorrow, so I guess I'm stranded here alone on Christmas." Courtney looked so disappointed.

"I'm so sorry, Court." Mira knew how much that trip had meant to her.

Courtney looked at her and shook her head. "You know, I was really hoping for a Christmas miracle."

Mira pulled back. "What do you mean?"

Courtney sighed. "Everything seemed to be going so well. The party was perfect. I was up for my dream promotion. I had this incredible family trip planned." She paused to place her hand over Mira's heart. "I met you. It all seemed too good to be true. And I guess deep down I was just hoping for some of that holiday magic to make it so. Like maybe all the good things could happen for once like they do in those movies I love so much. I was just sort of hoping for a Christmas miracle. And not surprisingly, it didn't happen. I just have to get over that."

Mira pressed her hand against the one over her heart. "You don't have to be alone on Christmas."

"Well, unless you have a snow-proof private jet around here that can take me to Colorado, then I will be." Courtney combed her fingers through Mira's hair as she spoke. "The rest of my family flew out there last week. I'm the last straggler."

Mira stilled Courtney's hand as it dropped away. "Spend Christmas Eve with me. I can help you get to the airport tomorrow if something opens up. I promise."

Courtney looked surprised. "I'm sure you have plans."

Mira shook her head. "I don't. My mother and aunt are on a cruise ship in the Caribbean and won't be back for days. They are my only family. I was going to spend the holiday alone, but I'd much rather spend the time with you. If you're open to it."

Courtney looked like she might cry. "Really?"

"It would certainly make my Christmas," Mira said honestly.

"Well, in that case"—Courtney grazed her thumb against Mira's bottom lip—"your place or mine?"

Mira nipped at her finger. "I'm sure you have more decorations at your place."

"You're probably right. My place it is." Courtney hesitated for a moment. "But can you drive? Or should we call a car? Because I left mine home today."

"I'll drive," Mira said.

"What are we waiting for, then?" Courtney was off her lap in a flash.

Mira cleared their cups and went about the final check on all the doors and windows before cashing out the register. She grabbed Courtney's box, and they made their way to her office to pick up her car keys and jacket.

"I'm going to head out and get the car started," Mira said. Courtney was still wrapped in the blanket, looking adorable.

"I can help," Courtney replied.

"You're barely warmed up. Stay, visit with your favorite couch. I'll be right back."

"I do love this couch," Courtney said as she draped herself across it dramatically. "Hurry back—we have many Christmas Eve activities to accomplish."

Mira raised an eyebrow in her direction. "Is one of them strip "Jingle Bells"? Because I'd like to vote for that."

"Go," Courtney said with a shooing motion.

"Be right back," Mira said as she raced out the office door toward the back exit with an extra bounce in her step. This was going to be the best Christmas Eve of her life. She just knew it.

CHAPTER ELEVEN

Courtney was so warm and content that she had almost forgotten she was jobless and not going to see her family on her favorite holiday. But was she really jobless? Mira had sort of offered her a gig here at the bar, with the chance to work behind the bar as well. That would be good money and a great experience in the interim while they waited for Kelly to come back from maternity leave. She wondered how Kelly was. When was the baby due?

Her mind went back to Mira. She was so kind and affectionate and *sexy*. Like, damn sexy. And the way she kissed made Courtney immediately wet, even when she was shivering cold. She was being honest before when she told Mira she was heating up fast under that mistletoe. And being back in this room, on this couch, was getting her turned on from the memories of last time. And the promise of a full night with Mira, which she hoped would be sleepless.

"Okay, I have bad news and worse news," Mira said as she came back into the room, snow-covered and looking dejected.

"Uh-oh." Courtney didn't like the sound of that.

"The front door is frozen shut, and though I can't see straight out, from the side window it looks like a snowdrift of five or so feet is against it. So that's a no-go."

"And the back door?" Courtney was afraid to ask.

"That one I can mostly get open, and though there's about four feet of snow in the parking lot, the real issue is that the city plow blocked the parking lot entrance with a frozen mountain of snow twice that high. And though I have all-wheel drive, I don't drive a tank."

Courtney laughed, because of course that was how this night would turn out. "We're trapped here?"

"We can check the car service apps," Mira suggested as she shook the snow out of her hair and coat.

Courtney pulled out her phone and loaded one app after another. They all had an emergency weather advisory note of some sort and warnings of delays or limited service. After several minutes of spinning, no one could offer her a pickup window.

"Well, that settles it, then," she said, tossing her phone to the side.

Mira looked confused. "That settles what?"

"We're going to have our Christmas Eve here, where it all began." This wasn't how Courtney had planned her night, but she wasn't mad about it.

"On this couch?" Mira said, her tone naughty.

"I heard a rumor it pulls out into a bed," Courtney said as she motioned for Mira to come closer.

"This is true," Mira said as she dropped to her knees in front of her.

Courtney wrapped her legs around Mira's hips, pulling her flush to her front. She lowered her head to bring their lips together as she dipped her forefinger into the hint of cleavage in front of her. "You never did get to unwrap me last time."

"I plan to do more than unwrap you tonight." Mira kissed her deeply, and she moaned at the feeling of Mira's tongue dancing against hers. That mouth was irresistible.

Mira cupped her jaw and pushed her back into a reclining position on the couch as Courtney fumbled with the buttons on Mira's shirt. Mira shrugged off the shirt and rose from her knees, revealing the lithe form that Courtney had been daydreaming about since they had first met. Mira was strong and fit. Her shoulders were well-defined, and her collarbone was delicious looking, but the swell of her breasts in the black lacy bra cups was what had Courtney's mouth watering.

She reached for them, and Mira gasped as she dragged her thumb over a pert nipple. She needed to have them in her mouth, now. She pulled Mira to her, keeping one hand tightly gripping her belt buckle as she teased along one of the cups before her. She pulled and pushed against the front of Mira's jeans, rubbing the heel of her hand against Mira's sex as she freed one breast from the offending lace and brought her lips to the impossibly soft flesh.

"Courtney," Mira sighed as she licked and sucked around the areola before latching onto her nipple and flicking her tongue against it.

Mira's hand found her shoulder to steady herself, and Courtney released her grip on Mira's pants long enough to free Mira entirely of the bra. She lavished both breasts with attention, switching back and forth as Mira's hands found their way into her hair. Mira's chest and abdomen were so, so warm, and she wanted to feel them against her own naked skin. Preferably, while under her.

"I need you," she said as she kissed down Mira's chest to her stomach. She licked around Mira's belly button down to her pants, stopping just short of her destination.

She looked up at Mira as she flicked her tongue along the soft skin before her as she undid Mira's belt and opened the top of her pants. She eased the pants off Mira's narrow hips and delighted at the matching black lace panties before her.

"I'm supposed to be unwrapping you," Mira said as she stepped out of her boots and jeans, looking fine as all hell in the process.

Courtney reached out and took Mira's hand, shifting on the couch to pull Mira down on top of her. "I was just getting warmed up. I'm ready now."

"Good," Mira said before taking her breath away with a passionate kiss. Courtney hummed in ecstasy at the feeling of Mira's hands moving under her cashmere sweater. Mira stripped her of her sweater and bra between kisses, and Courtney relished the heat and weight of Mira's body against hers.

"Yes," Courtney said as Mira palmed her breast while kissing along her neck. She bucked her hips when Mira took her nipple between her thumb and forefinger, rolling it while she sucked on her pulse point. Courtney gripped Mira's hair, bringing her mouth back to her breast when Mira slid one hand easily under the waistband of Courtney's yoga pants.

"Mm," she purred at the sensation of Mira's lips on her chest and her fingers rubbing and teasing at the front of her thong. She spread her legs, and Mira rewarded her by slipping beneath the soaked fabric to caress along her swollen lips.

She threw her head back with a moan when Mira bit down on her nipple as she gathered her wetness. Courtney thrust against Mira's hand as Mira brought their mouths together again before Mira entered her with two confident fingers.

"Yes, fuck, don't stop." Courtney rolled her hips against Mira's hand, taking her fingers deeper with each movement as Mira nuzzled her cheek and sucked on her bottom lip.

Courtney reached between them, finding her way to Mira's sex and sighing in contentment at the arousal she found there. She rubbed along Mira's swollen clit as Mira continued to slide in and out of her, winding her up tighter and tighter.

"You feel so good." Mira's breaths were short and fast against her mouth, her kisses varying from deep to tender as Courtney felt herself start to clench around Mira's fingers.

"Mira," she warned as she felt herself climbing too fast. Mira nodded against her lips, and Courtney rubbed Mira's clit faster in hopes of bringing her to climax with her.

When the heel of Mira's hand pressed against her clit on the next thrust, Courtney cried out as she came hard and fast. To her delight, Mira followed shortly after, making the sexiest noise Courtney had ever heard.

She dropped her head back against the couch with a gasp as she tried to catch her breath, while Mira placed delicate, teasing kisses along her jaw. Mira shivered, and Courtney remembered the forgotten blanket beneath her.

"Here," she said as she maneuvered the blanket to encompass them both. "Come here."

Mira settled into her arms, resting her head on Courtney's naked chest as Courtney played with her hair. She closed her eyes and let herself bask in the postcoital cuddle and the tenderness of this moment with Mira.

Until her stomach growled, ruining everything.

"Hungry?" Mira asked, looking up at her.

"So hungry," Courtney admitted. "More so, now."

Mira propped herself up on her elbows, and Courtney stole a glimpse of her chest, because she could.

"I'm not sure how you feel about ersatz Chinese food, but I ordered enough to feed an army earlier today before the weather got bad. It was supposed to be my Christmas Eve and Christmas Day feasts since I hate cooking for one. Interested?"

"Is there crab rangoon and lo mein in this feast?" Courtney was already salivating.

"And teriyaki chicken," Mira said with a quick peck to her lips.

"Sounds perfect."

Mira slid off her and pulled on her shirt as she walked toward the minifridge across the room. Courtney let herself admire Mira's ass for a moment before she slipped on her sweater and grabbed her laptop from her carry-on bag outside the office door.

"How do you feel about *Elf*?" she asked.

"Elves? Like the fictional little people that help make toys at the South Pole?"

"North Pole," Courtney corrected. "And I said *Elf*, as in singular. *Elf*, the movie."

"Never seen it," Mira said as she put a container of food into the microwave.

"I'm offended by this information." Courtney put down her laptop and helped Mira convert the couch into a bed.

"I would apologize, but something tells me we're watching it in bed with Chinese food, so this seems like a wrong about to be righted."

"You're a wise woman." Courtney put the cases on the pillows as Mira disappeared for a moment. Mira reappeared with the box Courtney had left there after the holiday party.

"If we're camping anyway, I figured we could make it festive." Courtney's heart sang when Mira held up the white garland. Courtney watched as she draped it along the window above the couch, using an extension cord to plug it in and flood the room with fairy lights. "How does it look?"

Courtney loved the ambiance, but she was more interested in the way Mira's open shirt framed her bare breasts. That and the hint of black lace panties still visible beneath the shirt's hem had her full attention.

"Incredible," she replied. Mira's smile told her she hadn't missed Courtney's leering. Tonight was going to be awesome.

❖

She felt Mira leave the bed before she recognized the scraping noise outside. A plow. She sat up and reached for her phone. It was just after seven in the morning. She stretched and snuggled back into the warmth of the bed as she let herself wake up.

Last night had been nothing short of amazing. A day that had gone so incredibly wrong had ended so wonderfully, blissfully great. After their impromptu bed picnic while watching Christmas movies on her laptop, Mira surprised her with hot cocoa and whipped cream to complete the evening. They revisited the whipped cream later on for less wholesome Christmas Eve fun, which meant Courtney would never look at whipped cream the same way again.

"What's that look all about?" Mira said from the doorway.

Courtney was smitten. "I was thinking about last night."

"About how I cried at *Miracle on 34th Street*? Because if anything I think that shows I'm complex and versatile," Mira said defensively.

"Oh, I know you're *versatile*," Courtney said as she shifted onto her side to face her. "If you must know, I was thinking about the whipped cream."

"I swear I'm still sticky." Mira shifted, and Courtney laughed.

"Good."

Mira walked to the edge of the bed and sat down. Her touch was cold but gentle on Courtney's cheek. "Jake came and cleared the mess. I'm warming the car as we speak, just so we don't get stranded here for another night with a dead battery or something."

"Would that be so bad?" Courtney teased.

"No." Mira kissed her. "But we might need more food at some point."

"Details," Courtney murmured between kisses. "I saw your whipped cream stash—there's plenty of that for another night or three."

"I could survive with only you on the menu for a lot longer than that." Mira licked across her lips and Courtney moaned. "But we should probably see about that flight for you, if you still want to head to Colorado."

Courtney had almost forgotten about that. "Valid point. But know that I am all for this other option as well."

"Good." Mira intertwined their fingers. "Oh, I got a text last night. I didn't want to wake you—"

"Because you exhausted me?"

"I regret nothing," Mira said. "Anyway, Kelly had the baby last night. A little girl."

Mira was beaming. It was adorable.

"And the name?" Courtney loved babies. And baby names.

"Eve."

Courtney cooed. "A Christmas Eve baby named Eve? Shut up. Life is perfect." She flopped back on the bed, drawing a laugh from Mira in the process.

"Come on," Mira said as she tugged at Courtney's hand. "Let's get out of here and find out about that flight for you."

Courtney didn't want to leave their little bubble, but she knew that was the responsible thing to do. "Fine. If you insist."

"I do, but only because I desperately need a shower after all the sex and whipped cream shenanigans, and as much as I love this place, I'd like to spend my free time somewhere else."

"Is there breakfast in the immediate future? Because I will get out of bed for breakfast."

"I'm sure we can find a Dunkin' open somewhere." Mira pulled her out of bed and into her arms. "I'll even get you a doughnut."

"You spoil me," Courtney said as Mira kissed her neck.

"It's Christmas," Mira said matter-of-factly.

"Yes, it is."

CHAPTER TWELVE

I can carry those myself," Courtney said, though Mira seemed more than capable.

Mira tossed her messenger bag on top of the stacked boxes before blowing her a kiss. "Just open the door and let me handle the heavy lifting. Someone has to carry the rest of the doughnuts."

Courtney held them close to her chest. "I will protect them with my life."

Courtney keyed into her apartment, and Mira placed the boxes on the floor. One held the remaining decorations from the holiday party that, apparently, she now owned forever since the second box held her work supplies to the job she no longer had. This had been a weird two days.

"Okay, I'll check back in with you in a few hours, okay?" Mira asked.

Courtney nodded. Mira was heading to the hospital to meet the baby before going home to freshen up. Courtney hadn't succeeded in getting a flight out today, but she had secured a seat for first thing tomorrow. And though she was a little disappointed, Mira had invited her over for dinner and offered her a ride to the airport the next day. So Courtney had plenty of sexy distractions to look forward to.

"Great." Mira gave her a far too brief good-bye kiss for her liking. "I can't wait for tonight."

"Say hi to Kelly and the baby for me," she said.

"Will do." Mira gave her a wave before disappearing out the front door.

Courtney flopped back on the love seat nearby, her body sated but tired. She was looking forward to taking a little nap after a long hot shower. Her gaze settled on the boxes, and she sat up.

Shit. Mira had forgotten her messenger bag.

She dragged herself off the couch and retrieved the bag before falling back onto the sofa again.

She texted Mira: *You left your bag here*

Mira texted back: *Well that's going to make buying a baby gift hard*, with a cry face emoji.

I'll bring it to dinner.

Your Christmas present is in there. Don't go snooping.

Mira had gotten her a Christmas present? Well, that was exciting news. Also, that was practically an invitation to snoop.

I won't, she lied.

Mira replied: *See you later*, with a kissing emoji.

Courtney thrummed her fingers on the bag, contemplating Mira's request. She weighed the pros and cons before ultimately deciding not to snoop because Mira had asked her not to.

She tossed the bag onto the seat next to her, dislodging Mira's wallet in the process. That was an accident. She hadn't been snooping. But now that it was out in the open…

She flipped open the wallet and found Mira's license on display in the clear window.

"I don't believe it," she said, her jaw on the floor.

This changed everything.

❖

Mira was glad she'd had a grocery delivery just the other day. And she was also glad she had enough ingredients to whip up something decent for dinner, since she had company coming over.

She looked over at her little tree and let out a contented sigh. Last night had been so wonderfully unexpected for so many reasons. Courtney showing up was a happy surprise that led to a night she would never forget. And it seemed like there might be more of those in her future, which she was more than open to.

And Kelly and the baby were healthy and happy. Eve was so freaking cute. And she'd managed to dodge the curse of a Christmas birthday, though she'd cut it pretty close. Kelly and Sarah were over the moon, and Mira couldn't wait to spoil that little kid.

So many happy, joyful things had happened that she wasn't expecting. Like having an actual dinner *date* on Christmas and her birthday. Which had never happened. Ever. And she was practically giddy over it. She couldn't believe it. On a day she was supposed to be alone, in so many ways, she wasn't. There was a new baby, a new budding relationship with Courtney, and a newfound appreciation for Christmas movies that she wasn't ready to admit out loud but had already accepted.

Courtney coming into her life seemed to have changed things for the better, and Mira was excited to see just what that meant.

Her doorbell rang. Courtney was right on time.

"Ho, ho, ho. Merry Christmas," Courtney cheered as Mira opened the door.

"What's all this?" Mira was immediately bombarded by balloons and Christmas music.

"You're making dinner, so I brought the decorations since you told me your collection was lacking," Courtney said as she breezed past her into the living room. "Which, by the looks of it was an understatement."

"Hey, I have a tree," Mira argued as she pointed to the tiny ceramic tree. Balloons kept hitting her in the face. "What's with the balloons?"

"You'll see." Courtney dismissed her as she went to work.

In a matter of minutes, Courtney had dressed her fireplace and mantel with garland, hung two small red stockings adorned with handmade paper snowflakes, and dusted some fake snow throughout the scene, which made Mira's eye twitch.

"Relax," Courtney said, seeming to have seen the face Mira tried to stifle. "It's like a handful, and I promise to clean it up."

Courtney then turned toward Mira's tree and cocked her head.

"There's nothing wrong with that tree," Mira said.

"It's perfect," Courtney replied. "It's just in the wrong spot."

Mira watched as she unplugged it and moved it to in front of the fireplace.

"Is there a plug here?" she asked.

"Over there." Mira pointed.

Courtney plugged in the tree and clapped. "I assume there's a remote for the gas fireplace?"

"Top drawer of the coffee table." Mira leaned against the wall, watching Courtney bop to the music still streaming from her phone.

The fireplace flickered to life, and Courtney danced over to her, taking the balloons, and offering her a sweet kiss.

"Hi," Mira said.

"Hi," Courtney replied as she handed the balloons back to her.

"Since when are balloons part of Christmas decorations?" Mira asked as she swatted them away from her face. These things seemed to have a mind of their own.

"Since now." Courtney took her free hand. "Happy birthday, Mira."

"Thank you." She paused. "Wait, how did you know that?"

"Your wallet fell out of your bag," Courtney said, her hands up in surrender. "I didn't snoop, I swear."

Mira laughed. "I believe you." She looked at the balloons in her hand and shook her head. "Where did you find balloons?"

Courtney scrunched her nose. "I might have bought red balloons for the holiday party, and a portable helium tank, but at the last minute I chickened out asking you if I could use them since you seemed so anti-Christmas."

"You have a helium tank?" Mira asked, astonished.

"It was a really good deal!" Courtney replied. "I needed that party to be perfect."

"And it was," Mira said. "Even without the balloons."

"It really was. Even without the balloons and even though I didn't get the job." Courtney took the balloons and tied them to a chair before stepping back into Mira's arms. "But I did get something so much better."

"Oh yeah?" Mira loved the way Courtney seemed to fit perfectly in her embrace. "And what was that?"

"You," Courtney said as she looked up at her with such genuine affection that Mira found herself speechless. She couldn't remember another time a romantic partner had looked at her that way. It was a wonderful feeling. "My Christmas Miracle."

Mira blushed, feeling embarrassed. "I told you not to snoop."

"And I told you your wallet fell out by accident," Courtney argued, playfully. "But what I don't think was an accident was you and me meeting the way we did. That was serendipity. That is the Christmas magic I've been talking about all along. And you, Miracle Anne Donahue, are the last piece of the puzzle—the Christmas miracle I was hoping for all along that I already had and didn't know it."

"This might be the first and only time in my life I haven't hated my mother for naming me that." Mira ran her hand through Courtney's hair. "She had tried multiple times to conceive before she had me, so I was always fated to be named Miracle. The Christmas Day birth was just an unlucky coincidence."

"Or just destiny," Courtney reasoned. "I, for one, am thrilled with this revelation. And I think your mom is a very smart and classy lady."

"She'll be glad to hear that," Mira said, still unbelieving that this lovely, generous, and kind woman was in her arms.

Courtney looped her arms around Mira's waist. She slipped her thumbs under the back of Mira's shirt as she asked, "How long until dinner?"

Mira checked the clock across the room. "About forty minutes. Why? What did you have in mind?"

"This." Courtney kissed her as her hands slid up Mira's back and under her shirt, gently massaging the skin of her back.

She sighed contentedly into the kiss, and Courtney walked her backward until she was against the wall behind them. She felt Courtney's hands move to her front, teasing along the sides of her breasts before stopping at her belt. Mira reached out to help her, but Courtney shook her head, swatting her hands away as she kissed her still again.

"I can do it," she breathed against Mira's lips, and Mira felt her lower abdomen tighten in anticipation.

Courtney had the belt undone and off her hips in no time, but left Mira aching for more.

"I'll be right back. Keep your eyes closed," Courtney said as she stepped out of Mira's grasp, leaving her gasping.

"You're kidding me," Mira whined, but Courtney's forefinger pressed against her lips.

"I'll make it worth your while. I promise."

Mira nodded, letting her head fall back against the wall behind her as Courtney shuffled something nearby.

"Okay, open your eyes."

Courtney was standing in front of her with her hands behind her back, looking mischievous as ever. "Do you want your birthday present first? Or your Christmas present?"

Mira thought for a moment. "Normally I would say birthday present, but since I have a Christmas present for you, let's do Christmas first so we can do a swap."

"Deal." Courtney brought her left hand forward and produced a long, thin rectangular box with a red bow on it.

Mira took the box and shook it. Whatever it was felt heavy.

"Open it. I'm dying here," Courtney pleaded.

Mira took the lid off the box and found an antique ringed metal bottle opener with a snowman sculpted on the hilt.

"He's adorable," she said. She pulled it out and cradled it in her hand. It had a nice weight to it and was smooth to the touch. This would slip easily into her back pocket. She would put it into her work rotation immediately. "I love it."

"Something practical because you're not *so* into the season, but also a nod to the first thing you noticed about me."

"Your gorgeous face and dazzling blue eyes," Mira supplied.

"*My* snowman ring," Courtney corrected. "Though flattery will get you everywhere."

"Everywhere, huh?" Mira stepped toward her, and Courtney stepped back.

"In due time." She pointed toward Mira's bag before asking, "My turn?"

"Fine. That's fair I suppose." Mira reached into the front pocket and pulled out the palm-sized silver pouch she had tied with a white ribbon. "Just something small to let you know I appreciate you and the way you've helped me see Christmas in a different light."

Courtney put down whatever she was holding behind her back to take the pouch. She loosened the ribbon and reached inside, pulling out the crystal studded snowflake brooch Mira had agonized over.

"I thought it might look nice on that jacket you look so cute in," Mira said.

"It's perfect," Courtney said as she finally stepped close enough for Mira to hold her again. "I love it. Thank you."

Courtney gave the best hugs, and this time was no different.

She pulled back, and that mischievous look from before was back. "Ready for your birthday present now?"

"Yes," Mira said but she kept her hands on Courtney's waist. "But stay close. I missed touching you."

"That can be arranged," Courtney said with a wink before handing her another box. This one was larger than the last and adorned with a gold ribbon. "I had to get creative about the birthday thing, so consider this a placeholder for something else in the future."

Mira opened the box and laughed. Inside was her belt, the one Courtney had just taken off, but tied to the buckle with a red ribbon was a small bunch of mistletoe.

"Try it on," Courtney said, taking the empty box from her and discarding it.

Mira raised an eyebrow in her direction but did as she was told. Courtney stepped back, positioning her fingers like a frame in the direction of Mira's crotch as she nodded happily.

"Perfect fit. Just like I thought." Courtney licked her lips and Mira moaned. "You know the rules around mistletoe, Mira. This is serious business."

"Come here." Mira reached for Courtney, connecting their lips just as someone knocked and opened her front door.

"Happy Birthd—Oh." The words died on her mother's lips as she whipped her head in her direction.

"Ma," she said dumbly, breaking away from Courtney's lips at the sound of Aunt Celeste's cackling.

"Happy birthday, indeed," Celeste cheered as she unceremoniously dumped their suitcases in Mira's foyer. "We came home early because we didn't want you to spend your birthday alone. Seems like we could have gotten those extra piña coladas, though." She marched right up to Courtney and extended her hand. "I'm Celeste. You must be Courtney. She's talked all about you."

"Has she?" Courtney gave Mira a look before accepting the handshake. "It's nice to meet you."

Mira felt her mother's eyes on her, and she panicked, pulling Courtney in front of her and blocking her crotch when she realized she was still wearing Courtney's gift. "Ma, this is Courtney."

Her mother greeted Courtney with open arms and immediately started chatting her up. Mira took advantage of her distraction by slipping off the belt and shoving it back in the box, narrowly escaping any further mortification.

"Something smells good. I'm starved," Celeste said as she headed toward the kitchen.

"Happy birthday, dear," her mother said as she passed, kissing her on the cheek before following her sister. She was nearly through the doorway when she paused, pointing to the box with the gold ribbon Mira had tried to kick under the sofa. "We won't stay long. You'll be able to get back to your gift exchange soon enough, I promise."

Mira groaned, dropping her head as her mother left the room.

"Well, that's not the first impression I wanted to make on your mom, but..." Courtney let out a low whistle. "Seems like I'm that girl, huh?"

Mira took Courtney's hand and brought her back into her embrace. "You're definitely *that* girl. If by *that girl* you mean the first woman to help me find joy in Christmas *and* my birthday. Then, yeah. You are my Christmas miracle."

"Well, when you put it that way." Courtney smiled and all the stress previously on her face melted away.

"Merry Christmas, Courtney."

"Happy Birthday, Mira."

About the Authors

GEORGIA BEERS is an award-winning author of nearly thirty lesbian romance novels. She resides with her pets in upstate New York on the shores of Lake Ontario. Her goal in life is to drink all the wine, eat all the cheese, and pet all the dogs. She is currently hard at work on her next book. You can visit her and find out more at georgiabeers.com.

MAGGIE CUMMINGS is the author of seven novels. She hails from Staten Island, NY where she lives with her wife and their two children. She spends the bulk of her time shuttling kids and procrastinating writing. She is a complete sucker for indulgent TV, kettle cooked potato chips, and pedestrian chocolate.

FIONA RILEY's greatest literary achievement is being crowned the Queen of Steam by her readers. She loves being by the water, eating seafood, writing confident female characters, and spending time with her family. It should be noted that she never takes herself too seriously, so you shouldn't either.

Find Fiona on Twitter: @fionarileyfic, Instagram: @fionarileyfiction, or her website: http://www.fionarileyfiction.com.

Books Available From Bold Strokes Books

16 Steps to Forever by Georgia Beers. Can Brooke Sullivan and Macy Carr find themselves by finding each other? (978-1-63555-762-6)

All I Want for Christmas by Georgia Beers, Maggie Cummings & Fiona Riley. The Christmas season sparks passion and love in these stories by award-winning authors Georgia Beers, Maggie Cummings, and Fiona Riley. (978-1-63555-764-0)

From the Woods by Charlotte Greene. When Fiona goes backpacking in a protected wilderness, the last thing she expects is to be fighting for her life. (978-1-63555-793-0)

Heart of the Storm by Nicole Stiling. For Juliet Mitchell and Sienna Bennett a forbidden attraction definitely isn't worth upending the life they've worked so hard for. Is it? (978-1-63555-789-3)

If You Dare by Sandy Lowe. For Lauren West and Emma Prescott, following their passions is easy. Following their hearts, though? That's almost impossible. (978-1-63555-654-4)

Love Changes Everything by Jaime Maddox. For Samantha Brooks and Kirby Fielding, no matter how careful their plans, love will change everything. (978-1-63555-835-7)

Not This Time by MA Binfield. Flung back into each other's lives, can former bandmates Sophia and Madison have a second chance at romance? (978-1-63555-798-5)

The Found Jar by Jaycie Morrison. Fear keeps Emily Harris trapped in her emotionally vacant life; can she find the courage to let Beck Reynolds guide her toward love? (978-1-63555-825-8)

Aurora by Emma L McGeown. After a traumatic accident, Elena Ricci is stricken with amnesia, leaving her with no recollection of the last eight years, including her wife and son. (978-1-63555-824-1)

Avenging Avery by Sheri Lewis Wohl. Revenge against a vengeful vampire unites Isa Meyer and Jeni Denton, but it's love that heals them. (978-1-63555-622-3)

Bulletproof by Maggie Cummings. For Dylan Prescott and Briana Logan, the complicated NYC criminal justice system doesn't leave room for love, but where the heart is concerned, no one is bulletproof. (978-1-63555-771-8)

Her Lady to Love by Jane Walsh. A shy wallflower joins forces with the most popular woman in Regency London on a quest to catch a husband, only to discover a wild passion for each other that far eclipses their interest for the Marriage Mart. (978-1-63555-809-8)

No Regrets by Joy Argento. For Jodi and Beth, the possibility of losing their future will force them to decide what is really important. (978-1-63555-751-0)

The Holiday Treatment by Elle Spencer. Who doesn't want a gay Christmas movie? Holly Hudson asks herself that question and discovers that happy endings aren't only for the movies. (978-1-63555-660-5)

Too Good to be True by Leigh Hays. Can the promise of love survive the realities of life for Madison and Jen, or is it too good to be true? (978-1-63555-715-2)

Treacherous Seas by Radclyffe. When the choice comes down to the lives of her officers against the promise she made to her wife, Reese Conlon puts everything she cares about on the line. (978-1-63555-778-7)

Two to Tangle by Melissa Brayden. Ryan Jacks has been a player all her life, but the new chef at Tangle Valley Vineyard changes everything. If only she wasn't off the menu. (978-1-63555-747-3)

When Sparks Fly by Annie McDonald. Will the devastating incident that first brought Dr. Daniella Waveny and hockey coach Luca McCaffrey together on frozen ice now force them apart, or will their secrets and fears thaw enough for them to create sparks? (978-1-63555-782-4)

Best Practice by Carsen Taite. When attorney Grace Maldonado agrees to mentor her best friend's little sister, she's prepared to confront Perry's rebellious nature, but she isn't prepared to fall in love. Legal

Affairs: one law firm, three best friends, three chances to fall in love. (978-1-63555-361-1)

Home by Kris Bryant. Natalie and Sarah discover that anything is possible when love takes the long way home. (978-1-63555-853-1)

Keeper by Sydney Quinne. With a new charge under her reluctant wing—feisty, highly intelligent math wizard Isabelle Templeton—Keeper Andy Bouchard has to prevent a murder or die trying. (978-1-63555-852-4)

One More Chance by Ali Vali. Harry Basantes planned a future with Desi Thompson until the day Desi disappeared without a word, only to walk back into her life sixteen years later. (978-1-63555-536-3)

Renegade's War by Gun Brooke. Freedom fighter Aurelia DeCallum regrets saving the woman called Blue. She fears it will jeopardize her mission, and secretly, Blue might end up breaking Aurelia's heart. (978-1-63555-484-7)

The Other Women by Erin Zak. What happens in Vegas should stay in Vegas, but what do you do when the love you find in Vegas changes your life forever? (978-1-63555-741-1)

The Sea Within by Missouri Vaun. Time is running out for Dr. Elle Graham to convince Captain Jackson Drake that the only thing that can save future Earth resides in the past, and rescue her broken heart in the process. (978-1-63555-568-4)

To Sleep With Reindeer Justine Saracen. In Norway under Nazi occupation, Maarit, an Indigenous woman, and Kirsten, a Norwegian resister, join forces to stop the development of an atomic weapon. (978-1-63555-735-0)

Twice Shy by Aurora Rey. Having an ex with benefits isn't all it's cracked up to be. Will Amanda Russo learn that lesson in time to take a chance on love with Quinn Sullivan? (978-1-63555-737-4)

Z-Town by Eden Darry. Forced to work together to stay alive, Meg and Lane must find the centuries-old treasure before the zombies find them first. (978-1-63555-743-5)

Bet Against Me by Fiona Riley. In the high-stakes luxury real estate market, everything has a price, and as rival Realtors Trina Lee and Kendall Yates find out, that means their hearts and souls, too. (978-1-63555-729-9)

Broken Reign by Sam Ledel. Together on an epic journey in search of a mysterious cure, a princess and a village outcast must overcome life-threatening challenges and their own prejudice if they want to survive. (978-1-63555-739-8)

Just One Taste by CJ Birch. For Lauren, it only took one taste to start trusting in love again. (978-1-63555-772-5)

Lady of Stone by Barbara Ann Wright. Sparks fly as a magical emergency forces a noble embarrassed by her ability to submit to a low-born teacher who resents everything about her. (978-1-63555-607-0)

Last Resort by Angie Williams. Katie and Rhys are about to find out what happens when you meet the girl of your dreams but you aren't looking for a happily ever after. (978-1-63555-774-9)

Longing for You by Jenny Frame. When Debrek housekeeper Katie Brekman is attacked amid a burgeoning vampire-witch war, Alexis Villiers must go against everything her clan believes in to save her. (978-1-63555-658-2)

Money Creek by Anne Laughlin. Clare Lehane is a troubled lawyer from Chicago who tries to make her way in a rural town full of secrets and deceptions. (978-1-63555-795-4)

Passion's Sweet Surrender by Ronica Black. Cam and Blake are unable to deny their passion for each other, but surrendering to love is a whole different matter. (978-1-63555-703-9)

The Holiday Detour by Jane Kolven. It will take everything going wrong to make Dana and Charlie see how right they are for each other. (978-1-63555-720-6)